CONTENTS

HER DARK REFLECTION

HAILEY JADE

MIDNIGHT TIDE PUBLISHING

Midnight Tide
PUBLISHING

For Glen Charles Nicholls, who taught me to love stories.

CHAPTER ONE

T he Winking Nymph was always crowded after the Burnings.

The atmosphere was never quite the same as it was on a busy night at a regular tavern; the dim lighting encouraged the shadows closer instead of banishing them, leaving pockets of space where patrons could lurk without being recognized. Women drifted across the floor, flirting with the light as it caught on their spangled wrists and ankles and throats, and at the front of the room a beautiful redheaded girl sang with a voice as sweet as sun-warmed strawberries.

It was going to be a big tipping night. The city was beginning to bulge with visitors attending the treaty celebrations, and a sun cycle holiday had beckoned them all to the streets, thrilled by the morning's violence and drunk on bloodlust.

I was eager to get out on the floor, but Madam had saddled me with initiation duties, so I was instead lingering in a corner by the bar, doing breathing exercises with the novice.

Aalin's perfume was a thick, ghastly confection of jasmine, violets, and something sugary that made my head ache. Everything about her screamed *new girl.* The heavy make-up, the chains and sparkles everywhere she could hang a jewel, and a gown in blood-spill red that revealed more than it concealed. Confusing *decoration* with *desirability* was usually part of the reason girls dressed like this, but it was mostly a screen for nerves. I could have told her that she'd earn more from calculated vulnerability than by dressing to look like her idea of a *maisera,* but she wasn't ready to hear that. That night, she needed to feel like she belonged, and all that perfume was a part of the uniform.

'They're just men,' I soothed as she chewed on her lip and smoothed her dress over and over again. 'And they're mostly drunk men. They want to be pleased. And they'll be excited to see a new girl.' I tucked a lock of wiry hair back into her updo.

'I don't think I know how to be sexy,' she admitted in a small voice. 'I thought I did, but now that I'm standing here...'

I ducked behind the bar and collected a bottle and two glasses. Pouring a generous helping of clear liquid into each glass, I pressed one into her hands. 'Here,' I said. 'This will help.' I knocked back my own serve, wincing as the gin scorched its way down my throat. Madam Luzel didn't like us drinking on the clock, but one drink to fortify against first time jitters was surely justified.

Aalin brought hers to her lips, and I gently pushed the bottom of the glass, forcing her to take a mouthful instead of a sip. I grinned as she coughed and spluttered. With her wide, dark eyes, smooth skin, and perky tits, she looked impossibly young. I hoped she wasn't as young as she looked, though. Madam wasn't exactly thorough when she checked things like the age of her new hires; she was an expert in plausible deniability. If the king's soldiers decided to raid her, they'd never pin her doing anything she shouldn't be. Though, with one of the king's generals currently lounging in a private booth and drinking on the house, I doubted it was a decision they'd be making anytime soon.

'See him over there? With the bushy beard?' I leaned closer to Aalin and pointed out a bear of a man seated by the stage. She nodded, taking another sip from her glass. 'He's a regular. He's friendly and he tips big. Go and ask him if he'd like you to pour his drinks for him. He'll look after you.'

'But what if he...' She trailed off and her gaze shot down to the floor.

'If he?' I pressed. When she seemed unable to continue, I finished the sentence for her. 'If he wants more than just his drinks poured?'

She nodded at the floor.

'If anyone expresses an interest in booking you privately, you have two options. Either direct them to Madam Luzel or deflect.'

She looked back at me with wide eyes. 'Deflect?'

'Playfully. In a not now, but maybe one day sort of way. This is a suvoir, not a flesh house. They know you can turn them down.'

She took a deep breath. 'Okay,' she said, swigging the last of her drink. 'I can do this.'

I watched as she edged over to the man I'd pointed out, her posture slightly stooped, like she was trying to make herself less visible. When she was greeted with a broad grin, I knew she'd be alright. As I picked up my lute and took to the floor myself, I didn't feel even a whisper of nerves. A part of me envied Aalin's anxiety and the adrenaline that would come with it. I had been just as nervous on my first night working the floor, if not more so. But at some point, the job had become routine, had lost its thrill of doing something wicked, something that would shock my prudish mother. It still paid better than I could earn doing almost anything else in Lee Helse, though. No more shivering through the winter for me; I kept the fire in my room burning as long and hot as I liked.

I began circling the room, immediately checking in with Lord Bernier, the governor of a minor estate north of the city. Balding and wrinkled, with his body bulging out of clothes that seemed to shrink tighter around him by the day, he was a regular, and I flashed him a coy smile as I picked up the bottle on his table and refilled his glass.

'Will tonight be the night?' he rasped. 'Will you let me take you away with me?'

'How you tease me, my lord, with your pretty promises. My poor little heart can't take it.' My tone was light, but I danced out of reach of a hopeful hand.

'I could arrange everything. A set of rooms on Peak Street. An allowance. All the fine clothes you could dream of.' His droopy eyes blinked up at me hopelessly, his offer spoken with all the weight of air.

'All the fine clothes I could dream of would bankrupt the king himself. Now, hush with your temptation or Madam will throw you out for trying to steal away her girls.' I blew him a kiss and moved on, resisting the urge to roll my eyes. He had a wife and five daughters to support on the income of a handful of tenants and a small, unproductive landholding. He couldn't afford to rent rooms anywhere, let alone Peak Street—evidenced by last year's jacket he'd had altered to fit this season's fashions. But he liked the fantasy of being a big man about town, and we all did our best to simper and fawn over him. I had never accepted him as a private client, though he'd requested me from Madam often enough. I was beyond the days of trysting with men who repulsed me.

I moved about the room, peddling songs and refilling tankards, taking the measure of anyone I didn't recognize. A table of three drew my attention the way an act of violence does, the way the mind recognizes and catalogues a threat. I'd never seen them before and I assessed them quickly: all three were broad and muscled, with bulging shoulders and thick necks. One caught my notice for his dirty blond ponytail, a length not common amongst men in Lee Helse, and I watched as he stared at Aalin across the room, his mouth curled with greed. One of his companions had a silvery scar running from the outer tip of his eyebrow all the way to the corner of his mouth, and the third man seemed younger than the other two, with razor nicks marring the stubble on his chin. The trio looked deep in their cups, aggression rolling off them like heat. Unease prickled down my neck as the youngest reached for his drink and I caught sight of a length of black cord wrapping his forearm. *Binders.* Men who made a living catching and selling fall spawn, which was a profession as dangerous as it was lucrative. They tended to be sinewy, brash sorts, with tempers as short as their lifespans. And if they were hot off the back of a sale, they'd have money to burn on liquor.

I kept a wary eye on them as I continued my rounds, even when I was called away to serve a private booth full of cloth merchants conducting a deal. A few rounds of drinking games later, I caught the moment the blond stood to intercept Aalin on her way to the bar. I was already on my way over before he'd laid a hand on her. I made eye contact with Cotus, one of the brawny men waiting on the fringes of the room, ready to keep order and manhandle patrons when necessary. He nodded in acknowledgement, letting me know he was watching.

Aalin smiled shyly at the hulking man in her path and ducked past him, but he snaked an arm around her waist from behind, pulling her against him. She cried out in alarm at the unexpected contact.

'Do you need someone to break you in, gorgeous?'

She protested timidly and struggled to free herself, but stilled as he said something in her ear. The girl's eyes grew round as coins and the blood drained from her face.

'Hands off her. You don't touch unless invited,' I barked as I reached them, my voice containing enough force and venom to momentarily shock him into slackening his grip, allowing Aalin to break free. His eyes met mine.

'I want to book time with her.' His voice was rough, brutal, as he shifted his gaze back to Aalin. 'What do you say? You can make more than you'll get collecting tips if you take me upstairs.'

The girl shook her head, her expression creased with anxiety. An ugly scowl cut across the man's face and he looked as though he was about to reach out and grab her again.

'If she's not available, then she's not available,' I snapped, standing my ground as he turned his attention back to me, squaring up and moving close enough that I could see the grit in the pores of his nose.

'How about you then, pretty?' he said, assailing me with the smell of sour liquor. 'How about we go to a private room?'

My anger simmered slowly, not hot enough to burn just yet, but enough to make me wrinkle my nose and reply, 'Not with that breath.'

A few patrons nearby snickered, and his eyes snapped to them, his nostrils flaring. If I'd checked to see that we had an audience, I might not have said it. Asking such a man to handle rejection and public humiliation at the same time was not a smart move. I should have known he was going to try and take back the power I had just stolen from him. With a speed I wouldn't have expected from him in his state, he reached out and snatched a handful of my hair.

'I thought the whole point of a whore was being available,' he snarled. I dropped my lute and it clattered to the floor as I grabbed his hand with both of mine, holding it to my scalp so he couldn't pull any harder, and ducked behind him, twisting his arm until he let go of me with a yelp.

I waved at Cotus, who was already crossing the room to place his burly hands on the blond's shoulders. 'I think you've had enough for tonight,' he said, and the man seemed ready to put up a fight until he took Cotus in properly, assessing his towering height, his broad shoulders, his scarred face. Clearly realizing this was an opponent he couldn't beat, he turned his attention back to me.

'You're going to wish you treated me better,' he spat.

'Unlikely,' I sang, wiggling my fingers in goodbye as he was steered firmly towards the door, his face growing puffy and red with rage.

I felt Madam Luzel's tight-lipped frown from across the room before I saw it, and I slowly lowered my hand, taking Aalin's arm instead. 'Let's take a break,' I said, leading her towards the bar.

Her big eyes were bright with unshed tears, and she kept them fixed firmly on the floor.

I suppressed a sigh as I assessed her. 'That's going to happen from time to time,' I said. 'Try not to take it personally. Men are brutes.'

'I should have taken him upstairs,' she mumbled. 'Madam Luzel will get rid of me now.'

'Not a good idea. Girls with bruises can't work. Nor can dead ones.' She stared at me, and I shrugged. 'It happens all the time. You'll learn to pick what men want from you. Some want to fuck, some want you to stroke their head while they tell you about their mother, some want to beat you within an inch of your life. Avoid the last sort.' I peered at my reflection in the mirror behind the bar, smoothing at my dark hair and ensuring the pigment around my eyes and on my lips hadn't smudged.

'Rhiandra, someone in the southern booth has asked for you.' Nataya had been working at the Winking Nymph longer than me, and my curiosity was piqued by her flushed cheeks and bright eyes. She seemed flustered.

'For a song?' I asked, and she blinked, her face going blank for a moment.

'I didn't ask.'

'I suppose I'll find out myself.'

She lurched towards me to grip my arm. 'Rhi,' she whispered breathlessly. 'He's gorgeous.'

I raised my eyebrows. 'Is he rich?'

She touched her hand to her mouth, as though trying to keep in her excitement. 'You won't care either way when you go over there.'

'I doubt that.' I looked around for my lute, catching sight of it still lying where I'd dropped it to the floor. I swooped in to rescue it before heading for the table in question, reflecting on the flicker of unease I felt as I did.

Two men sat in the booth, but one drew my immediate attention. The first thing I noticed about him was the way the shadows seemed to cling to him, bathing him in a deeper darkness than was usual, even for a dimly lit suvoir. His eyes cut through that darkness with a needle-sharp gaze, and when he pinned me with it, my step faltered before I mentally shook myself and kept walking, assessing him with more interest. He held a languid pose, his arms sprawled out over the back of the bench seat, one foot crossed over his knee, tapping out a measured rhythm in the air. Dishevelled dark hair fell about a sharp-jawed face, and he was smirking slightly as he cocked his head at me, watching my every step. I would have called him vicious before I'd called him gorgeous. I'd seen all sorts in my time working at the Winking Nymph, and I could tell a dangerous man when I saw one. I could tell an *unnatural* man when I saw one, too, though I couldn't have told you exactly what gave him away. Perhaps it was the sense of wrongness about him, like he was overlaid on the scene, not quite belonging to the same world as the rest of us.

'I hear you'd like a song from me?' I said, smiling invitingly as I neared him. He subjected me to a slow, lingering examination, his gaze dawdling from my face to my breasts, my waist, all the way down my legs, and back up again. I was used to being looked at, of course. What I wasn't used to was the hot, fluttery feeling that bloomed in my abdomen. My heart beat just a little faster and my skin suddenly felt flushed and sensitive. I was *attracted* to him. Well, that was unexpected.

'This one?' His companion's tone was incredulous, and I shot him a glare, remembering to smile just a fraction too late. He was a reedy specimen, with a flop of sandy hair and hands that seemed too big for his body.

'This one,' the dark-haired man answered as I returned my attention to him. 'What's your name?' he asked.

'Vixen,' I replied, leaning against the table and strumming my lute. I never gave my real name.

He raised an eyebrow. 'Vixen,' he purred, the sound rolling over me like the rumble of distant thunder, prickling my skin. 'What a fitting name.'

'Is it?' I asked, continuing to strum my lute, fumbling a chord as he ran a thumb along his bottom lip.

I needed to get a hold of myself. I was not the sort to fawn over a stranger, and I usually found the whole untrustworthy aesthetic a deterrent. There were girls on the premises who seemed to be drawn to thieves, mercenaries, and binders like iron filings to magnets, but I wasn't one of them.

Flicking his fingers at his companion, he said, 'That sorry lump over there is Lester,' before pulling an arm from the back of the chair to grasp at my hand, freezing my strumming. His fingers were long, cool, calloused, and my entire body seized up at the contact, my lips parting slightly. 'And I'm Draven.'

'I'm booked,' I spluttered, yanking my hand back and stumbling away from the table. When I was out of arm's reach, I paused and tried to collect myself, to smooth over how rude the reflex to escape him must have seemed. The last thing I needed was a complaint against me. Madam would be waiting to chastise me over the scene with the binder as it was. I didn't need to lose her any more money. 'I'm sorry, I'm very busy. I'll send someone else over.'

'Busy insulting patrons?' Lester asked, surprising me. I'd forgotten he was there. 'We saw your little show down by the stage.'

I narrowed my eyes at him. 'In case you didn't notice, the scumbag had me by the hair. He deserved a lot worse.'

'He did,' Draven said, shooting a look at Lester that made him slump back in his chair and scowl into his tankard. 'You handled the situation well.'

'Thank you.'

'It won't be the last you see of him, though.' There was a confidence in this comment, like he was stating an absolute fact. 'Where did you learn to break out of a hold like that?'

Chewing my lip, I considered him. I wasn't sure what his aim was, why he was talking to me, asking me these sorts of questions. Did he have a kink for violent women? It wasn't unheard of, though if he wanted to be tied up and spanked there were other girls in the room far more experienced in games of dominance. 'It's a good idea to be prepared for anything in this business,' I replied.

A hand brushed my arm, causing me to jolt with surprise. I hadn't even noticed Aalin approaching me. 'Madam wants to see you,' she whispered, and I sighed. My grace period seemed to be up.

'I have to go. Perhaps I'll see you again,' I said, my words stilted and awkward, my body tense at the idea of turning my back on him when the instinct to keep him in my sights rang through me as clear as a bell.

His mouth twitched with a smirk. 'You will.'

Madam Luzel watched me cross the room and jerked her head towards her office. Not a good sign, but I held my head high as I followed her.

Her office was furnished with all the luxury that her considerable wealth afforded her, but I always felt the sting of resentment whenever I entered. She was not a generous woman by any measure, though her terms of employment were admittedly fair, which was more than could be said for other suvoir in the city. She paid a base rate, let us keep our tips and, most importantly, never forced us to take clients to bed, though she did keep forty percent of our earnings when we did. And that forty percent was all I saw when I admired the heavy oak desk, the supple leather of her armchairs, the gleaming crystal decanter and glassware perched on a sideboard by the window. I could afford to be picky with who I took to one of the upstairs rooms now, but I hadn't always had that luxury. It would never feel right that she took a cut of the nights I endured at the hands of violent or repugnant men.

She sat in the chair behind the desk, steepled her fingers, and pursed her pale lips at me. In her heyday, Madam Luzel had been a great beauty and the memory lingered in her high cheek bones, long-legged figure, and penetrating blue eyes. 'Tell me you weren't insulting another of my patrons just now.'

'What makes you think I was?'

She tapped her fingers against each other. 'You weren't playing or dancing or serving drinks. You certainly didn't look like you were flirting. And since you've already provoked violence tonight, it fits your particular pattern.'

I clenched my fists by my sides. 'You were the one who asked me to look out for the new girl.'

'I asked you to show her the ropes, not to become her white knight. She needs to learn to manage those situations herself, and hopefully in a less antagonistic manner than you do.' She considered me for a long moment while I bit my tongue against the desire to justify myself. I knew she wouldn't care. 'I'm having this conversation with you too often, Rhiandra. Perhaps you need to take some time off to reflect on whether you wish to continue working here. No amount of popularity can make up for chasing away paying customers.'

I took a deep breath and let it out slowly. She was right—I was letting my temper get the best of me too frequently these days. I needed to show her I could be as calm and restrained as she was, because working at the Winking Nymph was all I had, and I'd pinned every plan for my future on it. I didn't want to be a maisera forever. What I wanted even more than putting a few brutes in their place was to have enough money and influence to do as I pleased. And Madam Luzel was the most direct path I could see to that goal. After all, she wouldn't live forever, and madams often selected their successors from amongst their girls.

'You're right. I'm sorry. Maybe I just need to rest for a few days.'

She relaxed as I said this, her frown softening into not quite a smile, but at least a slightly friendlier expression. 'You do that. I don't want to lose you.' She didn't need to add *but I will if I have to*. I already knew I was a commodity to her. She had plucked me from the streets when I was a scrawny teenager and let me work washing glasses and wiping tables while tutoring me in the arts of entertaining, flirting, and fucking, shaping me into one of her perfect temptresses. But she was a businesswoman, and I had long since paid out my indenture. Our history meant nothing if I turned out to be a sour investment.

'I don't need you on the floor tonight. You can go,' she said as she began shuffling papers around her desk.

I wanted to protest, to ask for another chance as I envisioned the tips I would miss out on, but I bit back my words. My dignity was worth more than a few tips. I withdrew from her office and headed straight for the bar, pouring myself my second helping of gin for the night. Another notch against me, but I needed to rinse the bitter taste out of my mouth.

'I'm heading up early,' I said to Nataya as I washed out my glass and replaced it on the shelf.

'Do you have a booking?' she asked, waggling her eyebrows at me. I smiled and gave a half nod. Better for her to think I was up with a client than that I was being sent to bed early like a naughty child. She shimmied her shoulders, her eyes bright with excitement. 'Let me know if he's as gorgeous with his clothes off.'

I frowned at her in confusion before I realized she was talking about the man in black. *Draven*. 'Yes. Sure,' I mumbled, waving goodbye and taking the stairs behind the bar that led to the rooms above.

CHAPTER TWO

The air was warm, the coals still glowing in the fireplace, when I reached my room. I threw a log in the grate and stoked the flames back to life before shoving a few discarded gowns from a chair to sit at my dressing table. A jumble of pots and bottles littered the surface of the table. One bottle had even keeled over and was oozing onto a knot of jewellery I had given up on untangling, but I paid the mess no attention as I pulled pins from my thick, dark hair, watching the firelight glinting from the ornate gold frame of the mirror above the table.

I had watched my mother do the exact same thing countless times as a girl, watched her slowly brush out her curls, gazing at herself in this same mirror. My dream-dipped, impractical mother who had sat idly waiting for the man who'd fathered me to swoop in and rescue her from poverty. Her mirror didn't fit here. It was a relic of her life before me, of a world I had been shut out of by virtue of being born. Huge, oval-shaped, with a plethora of flowers and twirling vines carved into its golden frame, it was clearly an object someone like me couldn't afford. It stood out amongst the debris of my more common possessions, not only because of its quality, but also because an enchantment that repelled grime made it the most brilliant thing in the room.

Having finished with my hair, I surveyed the mess with flared nostrils. It was ridiculous that the only people who could afford the enchantments spun by druthi, Brimordia's sanctioned magic weavers, tended to be the people who had a troop of servants who cleaned their manors for them anyway. I was the one who needed everything in my room charmed to stay clean. As it was, I stole the nips of enchantment for the mirror from Madam Luzel when it wore off, which was every few months. It was a stupid risk, but I couldn't quite bear to let the mirror fall to grime and tarnish like everything else I owned.

Thumping my hairbrush down, I realised just which bottle had spilled all over my table, and groaned as I picked it up and peered into it. Completely empty. I grabbed my favourite cloak from a pile at the foot of my bed and swung it over my shoulders. The apothecary would likely be shut, but the owner himself lived only a few doors down. It wouldn't be the first time I had banged on his door late at night because I'd run out of birth control.

'Where do you think you're going?' Cotus's gruff voice chased after me as I tripped down the stairs towards the back door.

I turned to him with narrowed eyes. 'Just because I'm a maisera doesn't mean I'm blood bound. I can go wherever I wish.'

His forehead creased as his brows drew together. 'I didn't mean... I mean, I just want...' He rubbed the back of his neck as he ducked his head, hiding his eyes behind his floppy red hair. 'It's late to be out alone. Madam Luzel won't like it. There's all sorts in town for the holiday.'

'Which you'd know best, since you've been out hocking swoon to them all afternoon.'

He frowned at the sharp reminder that I knew his secret. 'I've got no swoon.'

'After spending a whole week in the Yawn? What happened, did Baba Yaga catch you and strip you of your snatchings?'

'Rhi, please,' he urged, glancing around as he did. 'Keep your voice down.'

I rolled my eyes. 'You know I wouldn't have said anything if anyone was nearby. Now, stop being such a lick spittle and let me out.'

He scuffed at the ground with his boot. 'She'll have my balls if she finds out.'

'She won't. I'm just going to the apothecary. I won't be long.' I paused before continuing through the door, taking in his embarrassment, and feeling a little guilty for being terse with him. 'Thank you for helping me earlier. I feel safe in there knowing that you're looking out for us.'

His ears turned red as he smiled at the ground. 'I can come with you.'

'No, you're needed here. I promise I'll be back in twenty minutes. If I'm not, you can come looking for me.'

He nodded, though his face was still tense. 'I'll hold you to that.'

On a whim, I stood on tiptoes and planted a kiss on his stubbly cheek. 'Thank you,' I said, and was satisfied to see the red flush his entire face before I walked out the door.

The stagnant smell of the sluggish river behind the Winking Nymph squirmed its way up my nose. The cold night air played host to the croon of a sea shanty, the shouts of revellers and the grunts of someone enjoying the wares of one of the girls who could be bought off the street for three peythas a knock. Those who couldn't spare the coins for a bed often bunked down in the slimy undergrowth beneath the trees behind the suvoir, though I had no idea how they could sleep with that smell hanging over them.

I mused about how sweetly awkward Cotus was for such a big man as I walked the alley between the Winking Nymph and the tavern next door. I knew he liked me more than he should, which I found charming, so charming that I was too absorbed in preening my ego to notice the footsteps behind me as I rounded the building and stepped out into the street. The hand that clapped around my mouth made me jump, but the fear didn't hit until I heard the voice that hissed in my ear.

'Come quietly and we won't kill you where you stand.'

I didn't obey, beginning to struggle and squirm with everything I had in me, managing a piercing scream that was cut short when a rag was shoved into my mouth. One of my assailants cursed.

'Someone will have heard that. Move her. Quick.'

I was carried, dragged, towards the woodland by two sets of hands, one on either arm. They forced me into the trees as I fought them, pulling and kicking and trying to expel the rag from my mouth. A glow leered out of the darkness as I was hauled towards a makeshift camp, a few scraggly tents pitched around a smouldering campfire.

I was thrown to the dirt and I hit it hard, my palms cutting against the rocky ground. Scrambling to my feet, I pulled the filthy rag from my mouth and faced my assailants. Shock stole away my breath as I realised it was the three men I'd had thrown out of the suvoir.

The scarred one sneered at the sight of my expression. 'I bet you'd have been a bit friendlier if you'd realised we were your neighbours.'

Fear crawled over my skin. 'You want to teach me a lesson. Fine, consider it learned. Let me go home,' I said, my eyes flitting about my surroundings, trying to determine whether I could dart around them and make it back to the Winking Nymph.

'Not so lippy out here away from your keepers, are you, pretty?'

My heart was a thunderstorm in my ribcage as they drew closer, throwing sinister grins at one another as though checking to make sure they were all in this together.

'You don't need me as an excuse to get close to each other,' I blurted, regretting the words almost immediately. The sneers turned to scowls. The blond man shot towards me and managed to land his beefy hand on my dress, his fingers closing on the fabric, yanking me back as I tried to scurry out of his reach. The scarred man moved in, grabbing me by the shoulder as he pulled his arm back. I closed my eyes just as his hand connected with my cheek, making lights burst behind my eyelids, and sparking a sharp, hot pain in my face. The metallic taste of blood coated my tongue and I spat into the dirt at their feet, my expression an ugly contortion of hatred and wrath as I glared back at them.

'Big men, aren't you? Three against one,' I hissed, my anger taking precedence over self-preservation. The blond man caught my wrist, then tugged hard and caged me against him with an arm around my waist. I lashed out with my feet as I tried to claw at his face, but my hands and feet were quickly captured by the other two and they strung me out between them as I squirmed and screamed.

'Put her on the ground,' the blond ordered, and they lowered me down as I shrieked until my throat was burning. Surely someone would hear, would come, would help? No, what a stupid thought. No one had ever stopped to help me. As the blond straddled my waist, the fury searing through my veins was so hot it should have burned away my skin. The hands on my ankles melded to me like molten lead and no matter how hard I kicked out, I couldn't shake them. My wrists were pinned to the dirt, pressed hard beneath unrelenting knees until they throbbed. The blond pressed his face to my neck, his foul breath against my skin, his hand gripping hard at my hair. I turned my head and found flesh, sunk my teeth in until I heard a cry, then kept biting down as he struggled to pull away from me, the metallic taste of blood spilling across my tongue.

His fingers clamped down around my neck, squeezing until I let go, and he pulled away, his hand against his cheek, red trickling down his chin. When he looked at the blood on his fingers, the rage that gripped his features rivalled my own.

'Bitch,' he snarled, smacking me again so hard my ears rang with the force of it. My throat was so raw it felt as though something caustic had been poured down it, but I kept screaming and scream-ing, even as he shoved a hand over my mouth to muffle the sound, his other hand tearing at the bodice of my dress.

Cold air hit my breasts and a chorus of jeers followed as he succeeded in ripping the fabric, and he took his hand from my mouth to paw at me roughly. I took advantage of the moment to spit in his face, the globule landing right in his eye. He roared and wiped at it with disgust.

'Fine. We'll do this the hard way, then, stupid whore.' He rose from me and gestured to the others with a jerk of his head. They dragged me a few feet along the ground before I realised where we were headed.

'No, no, no, please. I'm sorry, I won't fight,' I began to babble, panic tightening my throat, making my voice high pitched. The coals of the campfire glowed a hungry orange. Smoke clogged my lungs.

'Too fucking late for that.'

The heat thudded against my skin as he gripped my head in both his dirty hands and held me above the coals, leering down as I thrashed and strained away from them. The smell of singed hair filled my nostrils. I couldn't escape, couldn't get free when there were three sets of hands shackling me, three bodies intent on my ruin, forcing me down, defeating my writhing limbs, deaf to my pleas and screams.

'Whores don't do so well without a pretty face,' the blond heckled, and my panic grew so big it felt like it would burst from my skin as I caught the flare of flames out of the corner of my eye, licking up the strands of my hair, blistering my scalp, my cheek, searing my nerves with agony, white-hot and inescapable. My shrieks ripped my throat apart to escape and I tasted blood, tasted fear, tasted death. *They're going to kill me,* I thought as I felt my very flesh shrivel away from the flames.

A roar echoed through the night, shredding the laughter and jeers of my tormentors, and suddenly the blond man was wrenched away from me and I was sent sprawling, my wrists and ankles free. I rolled in the dirt, batting frantically at my head and face, trying to smother whatever flames might have chased me from the firepit before I scampered away on my hands and knees, gasping for breath as movement exploded around me, trying to put as much space between myself and the flames as I could, thinking only of escape. A tree trunk loomed out of the gloom and I lurched for it, throwing myself onto the grass behind it and curling up into a shaking ball amongst its roots. I flinched at the cries and thuds behind me, rocking back and forth with my arms curled tightly around my knees, my face and scalp still ablaze with pain so consuming that my mind wanted to escape my body, wanted to shut down, to black out and protect me.

I hardly noticed when the sounds behind me faded, leaving only a voice calling my name. I could barely hear the voice over the chattering of my teeth. My vision faded in and out as footsteps approached me, and suddenly Cotus's face was peering down at me, though I didn't know how I had wound up lying on my back. The horror in his expression chased my consciousness into the dark as I blacked out.

The musky smell of boiled calendula. A searing, clawing thirst. The throb of pain. I peeled my eyes open, wincing as the simple movement transformed the throbbing on the left side of my face into a lancing agony. I couldn't see. The world was dim, fuzzy, and I began to thrash my arms and legs in panic, struggling against a weight on my body, fresh screams bubbling up my throat.

'Hush, Rhiandra. You're safe,' a voice crooned as a hand stroked my hair.

'I can't see! I can't see,' I cried, my voice croaky, broken.

'It's just a bandage. You're safe in bed.' It was the voice of Madam. I could smell my perfume on the sheets, spicy and comfortingly familiar, and I took a deep, shuddering breath, releasing the panic, willing it to dissolve, leaving my muscles limp and shaking.

'What happened?' I rasped, wincing again as pain crackled across my nerves.

'Not now. We won't talk now. Sleep some more first.' Something was pressed to my lips and the bitter taste of opium ran across my tongue. I sucked at it greedily, eager for the numbness that was sure to follow.

'Not too much now, that's enough,' Madam chided softly, and I felt her hand stroke my hair again. Unconsciousness beckoned once more, and I went to it gratefully.

When I awoke fully again, it was to a burst of morning sun. I cracked my eyes open, squinting against the invasion of light. The bandage was gone, and as I blinked my bedroom into focus, I realised with a shiver of relief that I could see.

Madam finished tying off the curtains and turned to face me with her hands on her hips. 'Good, you're awake. Time to eat. You can't live on opium,' she commanded as she gestured to the bowl steaming away on my bedside table. Gingerly, I pushed myself up the headboard of the bed, my stomach lurching queasily and my head spinning as I eyed her. There was a forced cheeriness to her tone that didn't match the tightness around her eyes. I didn't like it. Not one bit.

'How long have I been asleep?' I asked, my mouth chalky, my words thick. I took a sip of water from a glass by the bed, and it tasted like cold ambrosia as it tumbled down my wretched throat. Every movement sent pain careening across my face, milder than the last time I'd awoken, but still formidable.

Madam perched on the side of the bed, smoothing at her skirts, her eyes darting about the room, fixing everywhere, anywhere but on me. 'On and off for about three days. The doctor thought it best to keep sedating you, since every time you stirred you started screaming.'

I raised my hand to the left side of my face, still hidden behind thick bandages that reeked of herbs. Madam gently grasped my hand with a small shake of her head.

'Best not to touch it,' she said. She only met my eyes for a moment before glancing away. 'You've got some healing to do still.'

I steeled myself as I searched her face. 'How bad is it?'

She pressed her lips into a pale, pencil-thin line. 'It's hard to tell until the bandages come off.'

'That bad?' My voice wavered.

'Eat your soup,' she ordered, rising from the bed. 'You're lucky Cotus happened across you when he did. Best not waste his good deed by starving.' She headed for the door with quick steps, like she couldn't get away from me fast enough. 'The doctor will be by later this afternoon to check on you again. The best thing for you to do now is rest.' The door clicked behind her, and I could hear the tapping of her shoes as she fled down the hallway, the barking of her voice as she told a couple of girls off for lurking about by my door.

I sat up straighter, beating back the tears that wanted to overwhelm me, to dismantle me. I had survived, hadn't I? And they could have done much worse. I was lucky. My jaw quivered as I raised a trembling hand to the bandage and gently brushed my fingertips over it, noting how it stretched from my jaw all the way into my hairline, reaching over my ear and leaving a hollow space where once there had been handfuls of dark hair. Memories flashed through my mind: the smell of singed hair, the feel of searing heat against my skin, of dirty hands holding me down. I shuddered and collapsed back into the bed, rolling onto my uninjured side and wrapping my arms around my knees. My eyes stayed dry as I shook like a leaf in the wind.

I stayed bed bound for a week, eating soup and getting steadily more restless. The doctor saw to my dressings and each time he did I tried to read him, tried to determine how bad my injuries were, but he had one hell of a poker face. His expression didn't flicker once. He muttered frequently about infection and eyed me closely for signs that never manifested, finally—and with a hearty dose of incredulity I might add—declaring me out of the woods.

Madam visited every day. Each time she told me to buck up, focus on healing and keep my pretty little hands off my dressings, and each time she said it my stomach sank a little lower. I saw nothing of Cotus, or anyone else for that matter.

Finally, I couldn't take the suspense any longer. After one of Madam's visits, I swung my legs out of bed and strode to my mother's mirror, my spine straight as I tried to feel confident in what I was about to see. *No matter what, no matter how bad it is, I'm still lucky to be alive,* I told myself.

The dressings obscured the majority of the left side of my face. I peered into the glass at my left eye, swollen and lashless, and sent up a prayer of thanks to Aether and Madeia that I could still see. While the swelling was bad, it didn't look like there was permanent damage, and surely my lashes would grow back. A tiny spring of hope bubbled up in my chest as I reached for the dressings with trembling fingers and began to peel them away from the rest of my face.

That spring of hope dried up fast.

The dressing peeled away from blistered, weeping wounds, angry red even through the balm smothered all over me. Gone was my creamy skin, the roses in my cheeks, my eyebrow, my hair. The creature looking back at me was a stranger, a monster of puss and swelling. The burn kept going as I kept curling the dressing back and I had to force myself to stop. I clamped down on the despair that wanted to liquify my bones, to see me weeping on the floor, and swallowed gingerly as I carefully covered my face back beneath the blessed neutrality of the white dressing.

This explained why Madam had been so shifty. I was worthless to her now. There wasn't a druthi enchantment in existence that could fix this. Never again would someone pay to spend a night with me. My future, my plans, always shaky but still visible, were now a yawning abyss lying before me. My saving grace, my one source of power and autonomy, had been my looks. Those men had set fire to my entire life.

Because I had made a smart comment. Because I had made them feel small.

I slowly sank into the armchair and stared at the wall. I thought I'd known the worst of what the world could do to me, but the despair that laid claim to me was rabid and merciless. It opened its dark maw and swallowed me whole.

CHAPTER THREE

Rain misted down in a slow, constant drizzle, not quite enough to drive me from the streets but enough to make me feel miserable. I wrapped my cloak a little tighter around my shoulders, adjusting the hood to ensure my face was partially hidden by the fabric. It didn't obscure nearly enough, though. I could tell by the expressions of horror or pity frequently inspired in any gaze that landed on me long enough to take a proper look.

I had grown attached to that hood in the months following the attack. I should have exposed my scars, used the pity cast my way as a weapon against the studied apathy of passers-by. Hiding them meant that even those who noticed could pretend they hadn't seen, could soothe themselves with pleasant little lies enough to walk past without feeling guilty. But I just couldn't bring myself to do it. I didn't want their pity. After all, I wasn't *begging*. The damp, grey rug displaying the motley collection of everything I had left to sell could tell them that.

A few items of jewellery were placed carefully beside each other, robbed of their gaudy glimmer by the oppressive cloud cover. They were costume jewellery, the pieces that contained no hint of real gold or gems, otherwise I would have sold them to the jeweller with the few of my mother's trinkets—those had been the first items to go. They were almost worthless, just baubles to decorate my neck and wrists when I danced for clients, but I was hoping they might catch the eye of a shopper on the street and earn a few coins. If they thought there was any real value to them, then all the better.

A few clothing pieces were displayed alongside the jewellery. Nothing special—the silks and fine lace were already gone. As was the coin they had earned. What remained was growing wet, despite the burlap sack that I kept propping up over my wares to ward off the rain.

A bone china tea set was perched somewhat above the rest of the collection, as though scorning the possessions of a common suvoir girl. My mother's, of course. Fine lines of paint swirled around the lips and handles of the mugs, and all over the teapot. Depictions of flowers—bluebells and daisies and forget-me-nots—were wrought so exquisitely that the quality of the set was surely obvious. A chip in the handle of the teapot peered from the fine handiwork; an ugly scar. That, along with the fact that one of the mugs was missing, made this set something I couldn't sell to someone who knew the worth of such things, so here it was on my rug on the sidewalk.

Propped up against the building behind me, and looming over the rest, stood my mother's mirror. Every time I caught sight of the droplets of rain treading paths down its surface, a vice clamped around my heart. I couldn't look at it for long.

A woman and a little girl advanced down the footpath and I smiled at them hopefully. The girl slowed, her eyes wide as she looked from my face, then to my rug-come-shopfront. She tugged her mother's arm and pointed to the mirror, her voice trilling about how it would match her bedroom, but the woman pulled her past without pausing, hissing about never giving money to beggars. I scowled down the street after them, swallowing at the lump that seemed permanently lodged in my throat these days.

The woman's scorn ate away at me like acid. I *wasn't* a beggar. What I had to sell might not be much, but it was all I had left in the world. Initially, I had tried earning my keep at Madam's by cleaning, but clients had complained that the sight of me put them off their erections. A bitter comment when not so long ago they had all been clamouring to wave them in my direction.

I'd met with the same problem when I'd tried selling swoon for Cotus. He'd been unwilling to give me a chance to begin with, only agreeing after I threatened to expose him to Madam. Sometimes, when I was feeling like indulging my self-pity, I thought on the two different versions of Cotus I'd come to know. There was the man who'd bragged that he was a snatcher just to impress me, presenting the illegal plants and fungi he'd swiped from the Yawn as though it couldn't get him arrested, and then there was the one who kept his eyes fixed to the ground or the wall when he spoke to me. Whether it was because of my lack of success as a swoon dealer or just my lack of patience with his tendency to disappear when I needed more product, I'd given up trying that avenue of income.

Now, I had a little work cleaning at a boarding house a few streets away, but my earnings weren't enough to cover my rent at the suvoir. I'd had some savings, but once those were gone, I'd toured the district, selling anything of value that I owned. Now that that was all gone, here I was with what was left.

Most mornings, I woke up clouded in a fog of bitterness so thick I could hardly see through it to the pathetic scrabble for survival my life had shrunk down to. I would have been the last person to ever describe life as anything even resembling fair, but even I was blindsided by the cruel trick it had played on me. I was lower even than I had been before Madam and the suvoir. And this time, I couldn't see a way up.

I surveyed the street again as the rain grew heavier, contemplating whether I should just pack up and go home for the day. Dinner was a distant possibility with the limited peythas I had managed to pry from my few unwilling customers, so I really needed to keep trying, but people were scarce in this weather, just a few men smoking out the front of a workhouse on the other side of the street and an old woman picking through a bin further up. I watched her for a few moments, my stomach sinking as I wondered if I was looking at my future.

'Begging becomes you.'

I started as a voice found me between the sounds of the rain; a smooth, burned toffee voice that I had heard before. Casting my eyes around, I fixed on a man leaning against the wall a few steps away from me. He hadn't been there a moment ago. I would have seen him, even considering the gloom that clung to him as though what little light permeating the day was shy of falling on his dark cloak. A smile spilled slowly across his mouth when I met his cold, pewter eyes. *Draven.*

'I'm not begging,' I replied, straightening my spine even while I tugged at my hood, hoping he couldn't see my face. There was that twist to my stomach again; the fluttering heartbeat and rush of blood that was my hormonal system sitting up to pay attention.

His smile deepened. 'No, forgive me. You left the Winking Nymph to become a merchant.' With languid steps, he moved closer and cast an eye over my rug before flicking his gaze to my face. 'What? You're surprised I recognise you?'

I frowned as I assessed him. 'Perhaps you've a special lady you'd like to buy a gift for?' I said after a moment. I was sure he had money, and if he'd stopped just to peck at me then I would make sure he bought something.

'You do have an interesting collection here,' he mused, stroking his chin between his thumb and forefinger. 'Where did you come across that mirror?'

I folded my arms. 'I didn't steal it if that's what you're asking,' I snapped. 'But it's a fine piece. I could do you an excellent deal, since we're old friends.'

His humourless laugh rumbled from deep within his chest and sending a thrill of foreboding down my spine. 'I have a better idea, *friend*. A proposition.'

I licked my lips and fiddled with my cloak. It wasn't that the idea didn't excite that heady, involuntary response to him I seemed to have, and I was used to men trying to exchange money for my body, but I felt so vulnerable out here in the street, with no Cotus watching over me, no Madam negotiating a best price. And he'd be in for a rude shock when I removed my hood.

'Don't look so suspicious, it is not that kind of proposition. I see a different future for you than scratching out a paltry living in the street.' He began to circle me slowly, his steps deliberate, his arms folded, his fingers still stroking down his chin. 'The way you speak, the way you hold yourself,' he paused for a moment and cocked his head to the side. 'Almost like an aristocrat. A woman of your bearing would be wasted on such a life.'

'Speak plainly. What do you want?' I asked, my tone sharp, turning my head to keep my eyes on him as he prowled around me.

'A trade. For someone who has been ground into the dirt by this city.' His hand darted out so fast I couldn't dodge it and he yanked the hood from my head. I cringed away, scrabbling to tug the fabric back in place, to hide myself in shadow, but he stepped closer and grasped my shoulders, firmly turning me to face the rug. To face my mother's mirror.

My ruined face stared back at me from the rain-streaked glass. Shiny, puffy skin stretched over the left side of my face, mottled pink and white, pulling at the corner of my eye until it was narrowed and strange compared to the other. Scraggly patches of hair dripped along masses of scar tissue on the left of my scalp, little clumps that I hadn't had the heart to shave off, though, looking at myself now, I should have.

I flinched away from the sight, but he took my chin in his cold fingers and held my gaze in place. 'What would you do to have the power to seek revenge on those who hurt you, Rhiandra?'

What a stupid question. The men who'd hurt me had fled. I had no idea who they were, and the Lee Helse gendarmerie were not going to waste resources tracking down men who'd abused a maisera.

'How do you know my real name?' I asked quietly, looking at him in the mirror, my expression hard.

'I know a great many things,' he said softly, his voice a breeze brushing across my ear. 'I know, for instance, how to return your face to you.'

A shiver ran across my scars, like tiny hands were ghosting over my skin, and as I blinked the rain from my eyes, my reflection shifted. My skin was creamy-white once again, my dark lashes returned, my hair thick and full, the bare patches gone. It was my face from before the attack, but different. I had been pretty enough, and, paired with an ability to charm, it had ensured my success at the suvoir, but I'd never been the sort of beautiful that would turn heads in the street.

But I was now.

My skin glowed, my eyes were luminous, my lips were plump and flushed with colour. My hair was darker, lusher. The sight made my throat dry with longing.

'What is this? Magic?' I asked, my voice hushed. If he could wield magic, then I had even more reason to be wary of him. Was he a purveyor of tricks, the kind sold in dark alleyways to desperate souls, the kind that would see us both burning on a pyre before the palace gates? Was he a druthi, trained by the Guild and in the employ of the king? Or, worse still, was he fall spawn, an unnatural creature from the depths of the Yawn? Whatever he was, this was like no magic I'd ever seen before. I knew of enchanted lotions that kept age at bay a little longer, but I'd never heard of anything that could create this kind of beauty.

'You shouldn't be wary of magic, not when it can do so much for you. You can have it all. Your face, your power, your revenge. I can give you everything you crave,' he crooned.

I raised my fingers to my face and tentatively touched my skin. The bitter taste of disappointment slid down my throat as my fingertips told me what the mirror did not; I could still feel the ridges of my scars. Gently, he gripped my wrist and pulled my hand away. 'It's a simple glamour,' he said. 'But I can weave something strong enough to mask the texture of your skin as well.'

I turned away from the mirror to face him directly. 'Why would you help me? What would it cost?'

He cocked his head, his strange eyes flashing. 'All I ask in return is that you deliver something for me,' he said, his tone casual as he reached into his pocket and pulled out something round and as red as a ruby. He placed it in my hand and I studied its glossy, perfect flesh.

'An apple?' I asked, raising an eyebrow. 'You want me to deliver an apple?' Desire tingled in my mouth as I held it, curling down into my stomach until I was salivating and almost desperate to bite into it. I didn't much like apples, didn't like their unrelenting flesh against my teeth, but the sight of this one had me thinking that an apple was the most divine fruit in all the land.

'Three, actually.' He took the apple back and tossed it back and forth. 'I want you to deliver this one to the king.'

I snorted. This was ridiculous. 'I think the king can procure his own apples.'

'But this is not just any apple,' he continued, rolling the apple to the tip of his finger, where it balanced perfectly, unnaturally invulnerable to the pull of gravity. 'This one will make him fall hopelessly, desperately in love with you.' My mouth fell open slightly and he laughed that ominous laugh again. 'What do you say, Vixen? Would you like to be Brimordia's new queen?'

An answering *yes* resounded through me, gripping me in all the empty spaces where my old dreams used to live. *Queen.* But it was a deal that made no sense. 'You would restore my face to me *and* make me queen? What's in it for you?' I asked, and the laughter slipped from his face.

'You don't seem to realise what it is I'm offering you,' he drawled, his eyes narrowed.

'I know what you're offering,' I said evenly. 'And I'm not stupid. I know you aren't some fairy godmother bopping about granting wishes for the love of it. Are all three apples enchanted?'

Anger cracked across his face like a lightning strike, turning him otherworldly and strange. 'Yes,' he admitted, his voice low and harsh.

'And what of the other two apples? What will their enchantments bring?'

'That is none of your concern. You have my terms. You'll have to accept them with the knowledge I've already given you.'

I chewed on this for a few moments, studying the man before me. Druthi, fall spawn, or whatever he was, a deal bound with magic was not to be entered into lightly. I sensed a world of entanglement attached to this deal that went far beyond a few apples, but the promise to be rid of my scars, to become *queen,* was seducing me with a power I knew I couldn't resist.

'I can tell you that the enchantments of the other two apples won't be intended for you,' he prodded, edging me closer to the teetering brim of a bargain that would send me plunging down, shattering everything left of my old life.

'How would I even get the apple to the king?' I was stalling for time, delaying the inevitable moment that I hoped I wouldn't one day come to regret.

'It's a treaty renewal year. The palace is about to be flooded with dignitaries from the three kingdoms, and the royal family will be showing off Brimordia's grand hospitality. The king's chamberlain is sourcing entertainment, and you will be one of the selections.'

'What if I'm not chosen?'

'You will be. Do we have a deal?' He held out his hand, and I chewed my lip. 'There are other women who wouldn't make me wait so long.'

I took a deep breath and took his hand. The grin of a snake spread slowly across his mouth like the creep of dusk at sunset. My hand prickled, then lanced with shooting pain that made me gasp, but he held on tight. The smell of gunpowder filled the air, and a bitter taste coated my tongue. Movement in the surface of my mother's mirror attracted my gaze. The glass swam with shadow as a whirling, smoky darkness seemed to spring from the mouth of Draven's reflection to encase our hands, though I saw nothing with my naked eye.

'Wonderful,' he hissed, placing his other hand over the top of our clasped two. 'We have a deal.'

CHAPTER
FOUR

I ran my hands down the blush pink silk taffeta of my gown, marvelling at the way the fabric flowed beneath my fingertips like water in a stream. My petticoats washed around my legs in layers, bathing my skin with fine satin.

'Here, these will suit.' Draven tossed a pale blue box at me from across the room. I snatched it out of the air and opened it to reveal a pair of fat pearl-drop earrings displayed against white velvet, a perfect complement to the multi-strand pearl choker already wrapping my neck. Lace ruffles decorated my sleeve cuffs, a sheer fichu draped my shoulders in fine gauze and black silk bracelets accentuated my slim wrists. I was used to dressing up, given my profession, but the quality of these clothes was far beyond anything I'd ever laid my hands on. I was beginning to feel giddy with the luxury of it all.

'I thought the king's chamberlain was coming to select maisera,' I murmured as I secured the earrings in place and turned my head to watch them bob about my exquisite new face. Anyone looking into the room might have wondered why I favoured the small, oval mirror on my dresser—big enough only to show parts of my face at a time—over the large one in an ornate gold frame suspended above the fireplace. I hated standing before that particular mirror now.

Draven appeared behind me and the image of his dark-clothed form so close made the skin on my arms and back quiver with awareness, though I was sure to keep my expression impassive. His hand briefly touched the pearls, tracing them with his fingertips. I hoped he hadn't detected the hitch in my breathing.

'He is,' he said, addressing my comment, his breath stirring the hair around my shoulders ever so slightly.

'Then why am I dressing like this? These stays are so stiff I can hardly move.' I loathed to point it out, given how enamoured I was with the clothes, but Madam always encouraged us to shun the restrictive fashions currently in vogue in favour of more provocative styles.

He leaned in a little so that I could see his eyes, stormy and endless, considering me in the mirror. 'Eyes on the prize. If you want to be a queen, you need to dress like one.'

'Fine.' I walked towards the window, feigning an interest in the street below, when really, I needed to put some distance between us. His proximity lured sensations out of my body that I had thought long dead, slaughtered by my indifference to the hands and eyes of paying clients on my skin. When he was close to me, adrenaline raced through my veins. It was disorientating. I pulled my thoughts to heel, focusing on the window, and frowned when I fixed on the thick grime coating the glass. 'This room is filthy.'

This room was the first I'd ever occupied outside of the Trough, Lee Helse's poorest neighbourhood, named for its sunken, swampy position in the city. I'd been disappointed to find that the boarding houses higher up the hill could still be dank and grubby. I'd placed a bunch of tulips on the windowsill that I'd bought from a woman in the street, but the splash of red made the sad little room look even more washed out. At least the window looked out onto a neat, busy street. The occasional beggar wandered down it to whine at shop keepers, but they were moved on before I could sink too deeply into memories of how close I'd come to being one of them.

Across the street stood an establishment called The Snow White that was clearly a cut above the drab, seedy taverns I knew. It had been christened after a nickname given to the king's fifteen-year-old daughter, and a silhouette of a skipping girl was painted in bright ivory on the sign. It was one of the more upmarket establishments in the city, but I found it distasteful for the king's chamberlain to be selecting maisera in a place named after the princess.

Draven had taken my mirror and left me in the street after we made our deal, but a key had appeared on my windowsill only a few days later, along with forged identity papers and a note scrawled with the address of this room. Madam had accepted my departure without protest; it was clear she had been on the verge of asking me to leave. She was not a charity.

He had appeared twice since. The first time had been to take me to visit a swishy seamstress far out of the price range I usually dallied in. He had picked fabrics and styles with a discerning eye and an attitude not to be argued with, issuing instructions from his position leaning against the wall with folded arms. He had ignored most of my suggestions and preferences, and I only bore it because he was the one paying for the privilege of an opinion, and because the way his gaze sat against my skin made me feel like I was stark naked anyway.

The second time had been to deliver the mirror.

'After today, you'll be living in the palace,' he said, eating up the sensible distance I had just erected with a few steps. 'Are you ready?'

I turned to him, looking up at him from under my lashes. By the time Draven had knocked on my door an hour earlier, his arms full of boxes of clothes, I had long since made up my mind to seduce him. I had flushed as I'd pulled on the clocked stockings and white chemise that I sported beneath the gown I now wore, wondering if he'd imagined what I would look like in them.

I traded in desire, but usually not my own. I had felt it before, of course, but this was disconcertingly intense. I felt like there was too much blood in my body, keeping my skin perpetually flushed and sensitive. It was inconvenient, especially since everything about him suggested that I needed to be on my guard. Fortunately, the solution to lust was usually a tumble between the sheets, and once my curiosity was sated, the desire usually went with it. I would have him, and then my head would clear.

He held my gaze and leaned forward a little. I tilted my head, my breath coming faster. The smell of him was heady, rattling my senses like a stiff drink.

Then, he smirked. 'Get your head on straight. Enchantment or no, you're about to enter a den of vipers. Your wits need to be sharp.'

I let out my breath in a huff, flushing scarlet as I stormed away from him, heading straight for the door, mentally chastising myself as I did. Stupid little idiot. I wasn't some maiden to be played by a cunning knave.

'Rhiandra,' he called as I placed my hand on the doorknob. I looked back at him, schooling my expression into one of blasé detachment.

'Yes?'

'Have you forgotten something?' He gestured at the mirror over the fireplace, and I scowled at it for a few moments, hating it, before slowly walking over to it. I gritted my teeth and braced myself as I stepped before the glass.

The beautiful girl in the small mirror on the dressing table was not the one that greeted me now. Staring back at me was my ruined face, the one that haunted my nightmares. All I wanted to do was get away from the sight, to run from this heinous reminder of what had happened to me, but I stood waiting. The feeling of phantom fingers brushed over me, over my scars, and my skin went strangely numb, then flushed ice cold. As soon as the sensation had faded, I backed away from the fireplace, glancing at the regular mirror on the dressing table to make sure I was still whole and gleaming. It seemed a particular kind of cruelty that the enchantment now woven into my mother's mirror revealed my true face even as it hid it. I would be forced to look on my scars whenever I refreshed the glamour, and I wondered whether it was an intentional cruelty.

'You can't forget while you're in the palace.' Draven was still, his gaze sharp as he watched me. 'Don't wait until your time is almost up before you refresh the glamour.'

'My, how lucky I am to have your sage wisdom supplementing my poor feminine brain,' I snapped, my lip curled with sarcasm, begging for a rise, but he remained as impassive as a stone wall. 'What happens if I meet a druthi? Won't they see the glamour?'

'You've nothing to fear from druthi. You could crack one over the head with your mirror and he wouldn't understand what it is. A bunch of incompetent parasites.' There was something in the way he said this, a simmering anger that drew my attention.

'How can you be sure?' I said. 'They burn people every month for unsanctioned magic use. If they catch me—'

'They won't.' He sounded irritated now. '*Trust* me, Rhiandra.'

'I don't trust you.'

He tilted his head and offered a vicious smile. 'And yet, here you are.'

I sighed with frustration and turned for the door again. He was taking up too much space in this too-small room and I was ready to be out of it.

He didn't follow me into the street, and when I glanced up at the grimy window of my room, I didn't see his face, so I assumed he was trusting me to undertake the selection alone. A flutter of nerves awoke in my stomach at the realisation. Draven seemed confident that I would be among those selected for the palace. Whether he had a hand in more than just my glamour to ensure that, I didn't know.

I entered the Snow White behind a small group of young women. From their ample jewellery and lack of restrictive stays currently squeezing my curves into submission, I guessed them to be maisera. Warm air woven with the chatter of a well-attended lunch service enveloped me as soon as I set foot inside. The madam the maisera had followed into the building approached a man standing by the bar who was clad in the purple and gold livery of the palace. They spoke briefly before he gestured to a door in a shadowy corner of the room, away from the crowded tables. When the gaggle of women headed for that door, I followed them.

The room we entered was stark white, full of daylight streaming in from several large windows puncturing the wall. No kind lighting to hide any flaws. A few dozen women were milling around the room, throwing calculating looks at one another as they waited. Several of them glanced my way as I entered, their faces twisting with a mixture of loathing, awe, and dejection. I absorbed the reactions with some satisfaction; I must be beautiful to provoke such responses.

A trio of men from the palace stood at the front of the room muttering to one another, their eyes roving over the gathered women. The largest of the men stepped forward. He was dressed as a soldier and his armour gleamed in the bright room. And it should be gleaming, given that Brimordia had enjoyed a century of peace. He surely had little else to do other than polish it.

'Line up in rows, the first starting here. Wait silently while we assess you.' His voice boomed out across the room, silencing the chattering maisera, who began jostling to assemble. I crossed my arms as I watched the activity. Well, that's a fine how-do-you-do, I thought. No hello, no thank you for coming. Just shut up and line up.

I joined the end of a line and my neighbour, a slender girl with a face like that of a doll, pursed her lips at the sight of me before switching to a different spot. The trio of men began to peruse the offerings, occasionally pausing by one girl or another to request that they turn around or to ask questions, and bypassing others completely. Aside from the soldier, there was a squat man in a clerk's hat taking notes with an eagle-feather quill and a tall, bony man with sallow skin and a haughty countenance who I took to be the king's chamberlain. He wore an expression of distaste, often wrinkling his hooked nose at whichever girl he happened to be viewing and giving little more than a curt nod in response to anything said to him.

When his eyes fell on me, he skipped two girls entirely to stand before me, flicking his hand irritably at the clerk who trotted to catch up.

'Name?' the clerk asked.

'Rhiandra Beaufort.' I replied, using my new surname, picked from my favourite bottle of perfume. Discarding Tiercelin—the name my mother had insisted I use—was something I did with no regret.

He made a note on his scroll, his quill jerking about as he scribbled. 'Turn please.'

I gritted my teeth at the humiliation of it but complied, slowly turning, feeling their eyes creeping over me as I did.

'Can you sing?' The chamberlain spoke this time, his voice nasally, his words clipped.

'Yes,' I lied. 'And I can play the lute.'

'Dance?'

'Yes.'

'Hmm.' He glanced at the clerk's notes, murmuring something to him before moving on.

The clerk checked my identity papers, then reached into a satchel slung around his shoulders and withdrew a coin. 'Be waiting here for collection at dusk. Show this to gain entrance to the palace.' He gave me the coin and hurried after the chamberlain. I turned the coin in my fingers, realising it was some sort of token with an imprint of the royal crest—a three-headed serpent, each head topped with a set of horns—on a copper disk. I let out a sigh, feeling a tension leave my shoulders, like the muscles had been strung taut ever since I had crossed the street and they were only now slackening. The token was warm in my palm, and I clenched it tight. This was my ticket to a new life.

Several glares followed me as I left, my pace quick, hurrying to escape that room. I wouldn't have put it past any of those girls to knock me out and steal my token. I would have done it. Hungry people do desperate things.

My room was empty when I returned to it, and there was no sign Draven had ever been there. Was he so confident in my selection that he didn't even wait around to confirm it? A cold dose of loneliness washed over me as I realised I had been hoping he would be waiting so I would have someone to share my excitement and nerves with. With a pang of regret, I thought of the girls at the Winking Nymph.

I began to gather my meagre belongings, preparing them to pack into the small chest waiting under my bed. Spreading a soft blanket on the bed in readiness, I turned to pluck the mirror, my most treasured and most loathed possession, off the wall and noticed the glistening red apple perched on the mantlepiece below. It begged to be eaten. The mere sight of it stoked a hunger in me as I imagined the sweet smell, the crisp flesh, the cool juice against my tongue. Shaking off the feeling, I picked it up warily, almost expecting it to spark when I touched it, but it behaved like any regular apple.

Beneath it was a note scrawled in slanted, spikey lettering:

I've kept my end. Now it's your turn.

The ruined girl that hid beneath my glowing skin and gleaming hair looked back at me from the mirror, her future clutched in her hand. Dark magic clutched in her hand.

Treason clutched in her hand.

If I was caught in possession of such an object, if I was found trying to hand it to the king, if someone recognised it for what it was, the consequences would be severe.

I tucked my hand into the slit in my dress and slipped the apple into the pouch I wore strung over my petticoat. Best not to get caught, then.

CHAPTER
FIVE

I rubbed my hands together, my breath misting the air as I stomped my feet against the cold. Brimordian winters were mild compared to those weathered in Yaakendale, the mountainous kingdom to the south, but the temperature still dropped below freezing occasionally. This felt like one such night, though my judgement may have been skewed by the fact that I had already been waiting by the road for almost an hour. I watched a pair of soil smearers traipse slowly down the street, their feet sinking into each puddle without concern, their arms linked as they walked with their faces turned towards the sky. The ecstasy in their expressions and the filth coating the skirts of their white priestess robes made me clench my jaw. I hoped they wouldn't drop to their knees and begin bathing themselves in mud right there and then. I hated the sight, the way they begged for Aether's blessing with a fervour that seemed almost lascivious.

'If they were going to be this late, at least they could have let us wait somewhere warm.' There were a dozen girls waiting with me, and this comment came from the one closest to me. I looked over at her and caught her eye. She was blond-haired and green-eyed, with a round face and lips that were a little blue with cold, and I realised she was the same girl who had been next to me in the line at the selection earlier, the one who had moved away.

She smiled and stuck out a gloved hand. 'I'm Senafae,' she said.

I eyed the proffered hand for a moment, suspicious, before accepting it. 'Rhiandra.'

'Sorry if I offended you earlier. I just knew they wouldn't even look at me if I was standing by you. No one has any business being that beautiful.' There was no bitterness in her tone and her expression remained friendly.

'Thank you,' I said carefully.

'We'll probably be competing for attention in the palace, so I should hate you, especially since they hired you without putting you through the rounds of skill testing the rest of us had to suffer through. I could refuse to talk to you and try to best you, but I don't like fighting battles I'm guaranteed to lose.'

'You're very frank.' I liked her instantly.

She shrugged. 'I'm no good at plotting. Better to befriend the strongest player than to try to outdo them.' She grinned, her white teeth dazzling in the low light. 'Besides, we're all about to make a pile of money, no matter who is the most popular with His Majesty. And this won't be my first time at the palace. You go a little crazy if you spend all your time competing with everyone else.'

A handsome coach pulled by a duo of glossy black horses caught my attention as it made its way down the street towards us, and I gestured at it to Senafae. 'I think this might be our ride.'

'Finally. If they made us wait any longer, they'd have to reimburse me for all the new shoes I bought for this. My feet were moments away from falling off.'

The three coaches that pulled up before us weren't marked with the royal crest, but anyone taking an interest would be able to tell they were owned by someone with plenty of money and importance. The wood gleamed, the horses were of a thin-boned, sleek breed that were a far cry from the stocky nags usually populating the streets of Lee Helse, and the fittings were in glistening brass.

'Can you please give me a hand with these? My fingers are completely numb,' Senafae said to the driver of the coach nearest us. He was gruff-faced and had a scarf wrapped so high around his neck that his mouth was almost completely obscured. He looked like he was about to deny the request, but Senafae smiled so sweetly, blinking her big green eyes up at him, that he was on the ground and helping with the trunks within a few moments, looking for all the world like he wasn't sure how he'd wound up doing so.

'And you say you won't be able to outplay me,' I murmured to Senafae, and she flashed that bright smile again.

'I suppose that would be quite a good speech to give if I wanted to throw you off my scheme,' she said, climbing into the carriage.

Once I'd settled myself on the bench, I turned to her. 'What rounds of skills testing did they put the rest of you through?'

'Dancing, singing, conversation skills. I think they made some girls answer questions on current events and show they knew what diplomatic issues would be up for negotiation during the celebrations.' She hiked a shoulder, and I just managed to keep the disbelief from my face as the first real niggle of doubt began to whisper at me. I could flirt and strum an instrument, but of the other skills maisera were known for, I was mediocre at best. If I was put through my paces, I'd seem like an imposter.

I ruminated on this as two other girls climbed into the carriage with us. They spent most of the ride ignoring me, which suited me just fine. Senafae talked unceasingly to them both, wondering at who they'd meet at the palace, what we'd be given to eat, whether the king would be a brute in bed, until they thawed enough to allow their mouths to move and began responding to her. They hadn't stood a chance at hating her, really, though they might hate her later for how easily she broke through their animosity.

The royal palace dominated the very centre of Lee Helse, surrounded by acres of sprawling gardens that obscured it from the eyes of common street dwellers. I'd only ever seen paintings of the building itself, though I'd passed the enormous curling gates set in the middle of a towering wall often enough. When the coaches pulled up at those same gates, I poked my head out the window and watched as two armed guards began opening each one. I tried to avoid looking at the dark stains dotting the road, some overlapping each other. Soot, and other things I didn't want to think about.

When the guard reached our coach, the door was wrenched open and a ruddy-faced man with a brush moustache peered inside.

'Tokens please.'

One by one, we handed over the little copper discs we'd been given at the selection, and he eyed each one carefully before handing it back. He shut the door, knocked on the coach twice, and it began to roll on. We sat in tense silence as Senafae trained her eyes on the window and watched the shadowy gardens pass by.

'There it is,' she said after several minutes, her voice high with excitement. I peered around her just as the first spires of the palace became visible as slithers of darkness against the indigo sky. The path curved and suddenly there it was, sprawling before us like a huge, bloated dowager dressed in all her finery. A collection of looming buildings fronted with white stone façades, abundant with columns, balconies, and latticed windows; a collection of slim, straight towers, and from some central building, an enormous domed ceiling arched high above.

The coach bypassed the front of the palace, following the road around and pulling up at an inconspicuous side door where a man in the livery of a palace servant awaited us. We poured out of the coaches in a rush of hair and fabric and gathered before the servant, craning our necks as we took in the palace.

The servant was a stout man with heavy brows. He held his hands clenched before him, and I noticed they were chapped and red.

'Leave your belongings with the coaches and please follow me,' he said, his voice gruff and cold. We did as commanded, following him through a narrow hall and up a dingy flight of stairs before we were ushered into a large, cheerless room. He stood by the door as we filed past him, then yanked a white cloth from his pocket and rubbed vigorously at the door handle, muttering under his breath as he did. Without another word, he left us there.

I felt a swooping disappointment as I looked around the room, at the bare stone, the sparse furnishings. I hadn't been expecting to be ushered in the main entrance by a train of footmen all bowing a welcome, but I had expected something a bit grander than we had so far been treated to. I hoped the rest of the palace wasn't as underwhelming.

I eyed my companions. Some whispered to each other, some were shifting or fidgeting nervously, some stood stock still. A few shot wary glances at me.

'Do you think we'll get to eat whatever I smelled cooking in the kitchen?' Senafae asked.

'How can you think about eating? Aren't you nervous?'

'Nerves make me hungry. And anyway, dreaming of what they eat in this place has been my primary occupation ever since Madam Telfour told me she'd be putting my name forth. I tried oysters last time. Oysters! All the way from the ocean!'

I laughed softly, enjoying her nonchalant attitude, but also wondering whether it was an act.

The door to the room opened and a stout, dour woman with an upturned nose and hair pulled back into a tight bun entered. She stood before us until our chatter petered out. 'Welcome. I'm Mrs Corkill, the head housekeeper. I oversee the running of the palace, and nothing happens within these walls without my knowing about it.' She cast her hard gaze over us, taking each of us in. 'I am not one to mince words, so let us speak frankly. You are here to provide entertainment while dignitaries from the three kingdoms are visiting for the renewal of the Treaty of Wenderstad. While you are here, I require that you do not mingle with my staff, do not wander beyond the servant's quarters without prior approval from myself, and do not think you will be leaving without a thorough checking of your belongings and your person.'

'So, she thinks we're a bunch of thieves,' I whispered to Senafae.

'Well, she probably isn't wrong. If I can find a way to pocket something, I will. I bet even a fork from here is worth a mint,' she hissed back.

'I will provide each of you with a rough schedule of events you may be invited to, though there will likely be occasions when our visitors request your presence beyond those times,' the house-keeper continued. There was a slight wrinkling of the skin on her nose. She was hiding her distaste well, but I was experienced in picking it out. It was always a good idea to know exactly who approved of maisera and who did not. We were generally accepted as a necessity, but there were many who would prefer not to rub shoulders with us. I suspected Mrs Corkill was one of this number, though she must appreciate that we were the best way to keep the king's visitors from bothering her maids.

She cleared her throat and ran her hands down her dress, which was black, severe, and practical. 'Now, I will show you to your rooms. There are two beds in each, so please be prepared to select someone to share with.'

A low hum of muttered complaints broke out around me, sug-gesting that I wasn't the only one who hadn't suspected they'd need to share a room, but Mrs Corkill paid them no heed, leaving the room without looking back.

She led us through the servant's quarters where maids and foot-man bustled past us without so much as a second glance. Our rooms were in a corridor separated from the male staff quarters by a locked door, and Mrs Corkill was sure to let us know she possessed the only key. She began opening doors, revealing small, neat rooms furnished each with two single beds, a table and chairs, a slim wardrobe, and a single dressing table.

I stood in the doorway of one room, blinking at it incredulously. *One* dressing table? *One* wardrobe? Was she looking to start a war?

Senafae dawdled over to where I stood. 'Well, this looks as bleak at the rest. I don't suppose there's any chance you'd take a bribe for your half of the wardrobe?'

I snorted. 'You're certainly an optimist,' I said, wandering into the room, amused at her confidence in assuming we would room together.

She overtook me in a few strides and sunk onto one of the beds, patting at the mattress with a hand and wrinkling her nose 'Worth a try. Perhaps I can bribe that carriage driver to drag my trunk up here instead.'

'The footmen will bring your belongings to your room.' Mrs Corkill appeared in the doorway holding a sheaf of papers. 'And you will not speak to them when they do. The evening meal is being served in the servant's dining room as we speak, so head back down the stairs soon if you expect to eat. Here are your calendars of events.' She handed me a few sheets of paper and I scanned the list of dates. 'Those circled in blue are those you are required to attend. There is a map on the rear to help you find your way around, though you should never be wandering the palace without an escort and without an appropriate reason.'

Senafae joined me a moment later and peered over my shoulder. 'Oh,' she said, her voice an eager exhale, 'we're going to the Armistice Ball!'

My gaze quickly raced down the page, over the various balls, state dinners and 'gentlemen's evenings', many to which we were apparently not invited, until I snagged on the words 'Armistice

Ball' circled in bright blue ink and attached to a date two weeks away. My stomach twisted with excitement.

'Do not get carried away. You are attending as staff and performers, *not* as guests.' Mrs Corkill's voice was tight with disapproval. 'You'll note the rehearsal marked on your schedule, where you will be briefed on your role at the ball. And while we are on the subject of your duties, our head butler, Mr Guilcher, has asked me to inform each of you that you are required to be clean and disease-free for the duration of your stay. Make liberal use of the baths.' On that peculiar note, she left us to go and bark at another pair of girls.

'I hope she doesn't give so warm a welcome to the visitors from Oceatold and Creatia. They might never leave,' Senafae said, her tone heavy with sarcasm. She returned to the bed, laying down and spreading herself out on it, as though testing the perimeters of the narrow mattress.

'What was all that about being clean?' I asked as I sat lightly on the other bed.

'The butler, Guilcher, is batty about disease and inspects all the servants every morning to make sure they haven't got the pox.' She rolled on her side to face me, propping herself up on an elbow. 'So, what's your story?' she asked.

'My story?'

'If we're going to share a room, I should know it.' I drew my brows together, but if she noticed my resistance, she ignored it and continued. 'Come on, every maisera has a reason for winding up in a suvoir. No little girl decides she wants to fuck for money when she grows up.'

'Maybe I did.'

'And maybe the king is actually a donkey dressed as a man, but the likelihood is about the same.'

I eyed her, wondering what she would do with any information I gave her. 'How about you tell me yours first.'

'You're a suspicious one, aren't you?' She rolled onto her back in a rustling of skirts and fabric and crossed her hands behind her head, her fingers moving to fiddle with a plaited bracelet she wore on her right wrist. It caught my attention because it looked the sort of thing made by a child, not something that ornamented a high-class maisera, just a twist of worn leather tied off at the end. Perhaps it had some sort of sentimental significance for her.

'I'm one of eight,' she began. 'When I was little, my parents bought a farm bordering the Shifting Plains and you can imagine how well that worked out. My father sold me and two of my sisters to Notes of Ivory, for money to feed the others.'

Pity briefly gripped me; I knew the place she spoke of. Despite the name, there was nothing about that miserable, dingy hovel that evoked ivory. Suvoir were places of entertainment, with sex as something of a bonus transaction, often bought at a high price and at the discretion of the maisera themselves. Notes of Ivory was a brothel, and a low quality one at that. Those who worked there were usually slaves.

'How did you become a maisera?' I asked, curious now.

She tilted her head and met my eyes again with a grin. 'I'm beautiful. And I can sing. And I was young enough for a madam to take me on and train me up. I was worth more sold on to a suvoir than as a whore.'

I considered her in silence. I didn't ask about what happened to her sisters, about whether she had ever seen her family again, about the pain of being sold into such a position by someone who was meant to protect her. Life was full of pain. Wallowing in it was pointless.

'Your turn,' she pressed. 'You must have a good story. Are you a disgraced Creatish princess? Your speech is polished enough.'

How much should I reveal of myself? How much did I need to tell to keep her from suspecting me of having secrets? I thought of the dark stains by the palace gates. I couldn't have anyone looking too closely at who I was and where I'd come from. Such scrutiny might turn up the story of a girl with a ruined face, and when that story was held up against me, there would be questions that I didn't want anyone trying to answer.

'Nothing that exciting. My mother was... particular about my education. Not about feeding me, though. She mostly let me fend for myself while she wasted away regretting how unfair her life was. I was scraped off the streets when I tried to steal from a madam, and she gave me a job instead of turning me over to the gendarmerie.'

'Which suvoir were you indentured to?'

'Oh, I've drifted from one to another,' I lied. Senafae raised her eyebrows, and I expected her to question me further. If a maisera was moving between suvoir, it meant she was either the kind who made fast enemies of the other girls, or she was a cold fish in bed. But she didn't ask, and I wondered which reason she assigned to me.

She stretched out her slender arms and pushed herself into a sitting position. 'Shall we go and eat? I'll turn into something wholly unpleasant if I miss dinner.'

Together, we hunted down the small dining room by the kitchens. The servants were busy attending the royal household, so the food was left on a side table, and we were trusted to serve ourselves. I inspected the clusters of women with interest, noting how alliances had already begun to form, how some sat closer to each other, leaving wide gaps between one group and the next.

I ignored the stares pointed my way as I took a seat near the end of the long table, inhaling the scents of roasted duck, mashed parsnips, and buttered beans with relish. It was by no means the fancy fair I was sure the royal family was being treated to, but I appreciated a well-prepared meal. Senafae joined me moments later, her plate piled high, and I raised my eyebrows as she tucked into her food. She was a slender creature, all legs, with little in the way of breasts or hips. I hadn't expected such a hearty appetite.

After watching her for a few moments, fascinated as she shovelled food into her mouth, I turned back to my own plate and caught a stare from across the table that ought to have scorched a hole through me.

The woman behind the stare was stunning, with slanted, feline eyes and a face that looked like it had been carved by sculptors. She had a glorious mane of thick red curls and porcelain-pale skin, which led me to suspect that she could afford both the druthi tonics to enhance her colouring and hide the freckles that usually accompanied it. It was a shame she hadn't found herself a potion that would cure her of the sour look on her face.

'Where have you come from?' she demanded, sounding as though she was accosting a thief in the street.

'I'm Rhiandra,' I said. 'And where I come from is really none of your business.'

She placed her cutlery carefully on either side of her plate, leaned back in her chair, and folded her arms. 'Rhiandra,' she repeated slowly. 'I've never heard of any maisera of note with that name. Why would they select someone with no reputation for an occasion as important as this? You're likely to make a mockery of our king.'

The sound of Senafae chocking distracted me for a moment, and I patted her back awkwardly as she coughed. The red-haired woman looked on with revulsion.

'Back off, Vanaria,' Senafae said finally, her eyes watering and her voice croaky. 'There are dozens of suvoir in the city. Not everyone wants to work at Quality. '

The woman smiled coldly at Senafae. 'You would say that. Given that your application was rejected.' With that, she stood, picked up her plate, and moved down the table, followed by those sitting either side of her.

'That's Vanaria Rosach?' I said, my voice low as I watched the woman settle herself into her new seat.

'I'm surprised you couldn't tell the moment you saw her. She practically has *I make more money than you* scrawled across her forehead.' Vanaria's parting jab didn't appear to have done any damage to Senafae's appetite and she was happily digging into her dinner once more.

Vanaria Rosach was whispered to be the highest paid maisera in the city, charging thousands for a night of her company. She had starred in huge theatre productions, worked at Quality, the most upmarket suvoir in Lee Helse, and, if the rumours were to be believed, had a queue of lords clamouring to keep her as a mistress—and willing to pay through the nose for the privilege. She must have some big fish in her sights to be tempted to come here.

Probably the very same fish I was set on.

While Senafae was helping herself to a second plate of food, I snuck away, stealing back up the stairs and down the dingy corridor to my new room, where I found my trunk had been dumped by the door. Kneeling before it, I opened it up to reveal the mirror, still wrapped in the cloak I had used to protect it during transport. I ripped off the fabric with gritted teeth, revealing my grim, scarred reflection, staring back with hollow eyes. Spectral fingers and numbness crawled over my face, then a biting cold. As soon as warmth began to return to my cheek, I yanked the fabric over the vile thing. I chewed my lip as I looked around the room at the few furnishings, finally dropping down to peer into the narrow gap beneath the bed. After a moment's hesitation, I slid it into the gap, still wrapped in the cloak, and glanced frantically at the door. It remained shut.

Sharing a room made everything a little more complicated. As much as I liked Senafae, I would fully expect her to turn me in if she discovered an enchanted mirror under my bed. The Guild paid a handsome reward to anyone with information leading to a conviction for profane magic use, and possessing magic of that power would be enough to see me burned, no matter that I wasn't the one who wove it. It was clearly magic beyond what could be purchased from apothecaries and weave markets.

Plucking the apple from where it had been practically burning a hole in my skirts, I stuffed it into the drawer of the bedside cabinet, piling shifts and stockings on top until it was completely buried. Not the most sophisticated hiding spot, but I couldn't bear to continue carrying it around, waiting for someone to find it on me, wondering if someone would somehow know it for what it was.

If I was going to accomplish what I set out to do, I would need to keep my secrets close to my chest.

CHAPTER SIX

The pile of gowns on the slim bed was growing at an alarming rate, until it was a towering mountain of silk and fur and satin and velvet and lace. It was so large that I could barely see Senafae whenever she stepped behind it, though I could still hear her perfectly.

'This is hideous,' she moaned, flinging yet another gown onto the mountain, causing a small avalanche that deposited a petticoat and a single glove discreetly onto the floor. Taking yet another gown from the wardrobe, she held it against herself and turned before the mirror, her head tilted, her forehead creased. 'Hideous,' she repeated.

I narrowed my eyes as she snatched another from the wardrobe, reassessing exactly where 'half' began and ended. 'I don't know why you paid for so many gowns that you find hideous.' I was sitting at the vanity, already dressed and decorated, my hair coiffed, my skin perfumed.

She shot me a look. 'Did you really have no trouble choosing what to wear for something as important as this?'

I smoothed at my own gown—a burgundy velvet, trimmed in ivory lace and silk ribbons, the back falling away in loose box pleats—with a covert smile. Perhaps, before my life changed, I would have struggled just as much as Senafae. But the glowing beauty of my new face seemed to be above the influence of dress; every fabric complemented my complexion, and every style suited my features.

When I looked back at Senafae, her frown suggested she was thinking the same thing. I stood abruptly, crossed the room, plucked a gown from her pile, and thrust it at her. 'This one,' I said. 'Blue suits your hair and skin, and the cut is just daring enough without being too risqué to walk past Mrs Corkill.'

She grimaced and turned back to the mirror, holding my selection against herself. 'Are you sure?'

'It's a beautiful dress. It'll be perfect,' I said, a thread of impatience creeping into my voice. 'And if you take any longer, it won't matter what you wear as you won't be meeting the king at all.'

She took the admonishment with good humour and threw herself into her preparations, selecting the rest of her outfit with far more speed than I thought she was capable of. Despite her reluctance to make a final decision, she possessed a keen sense of style, easily selecting accessories for the gown that left her looking neither overdressed, nor slovenly. Though she didn't remove the plaited bracelet, which was an odd choice, but I didn't comment on it.

There was an ease to Senafae in evening dress that I had never possessed, little gutter rat that I was. It reminded me of my mother, who had also possessed this instinct for fashion and always seemed a different version of herself when she dressed in her finery, though there had been few occasions to do so when I was a girl. It had usually been when we were in direst need of money, when the meals had become few and far between enough to drive me to thieving from the markets. I had a handful of such memories of my mother: gaunt and hollow-eyed, dressed in moss-green satin that was several seasons out of fashion and hanging from her bony figure, she had still looked regal and rich blooded.

Sometimes, when she returned from wherever she went in her finery, we ate like royalty for days, feasting on caviar and exotic fruits and tender cuts of pork. That was my mother—all or nothing. I'm sure we could have eaten a more modest fare for months on what those feasts must have cost. Eventually, the feasts had stopped altogether, and the green dress hung as a neglected ghost in the wardrobe, a phantom of a previous life too painful for her to look upon.

'Are you ready?' Senafae's voice broke my reveries, and I shook the past from my back like a bird ridding its feathers of rain.

'I've been ready for half the day. Let's go.'

We convened in the same bare room as we had when we'd arrived the previous day and the air buzzed with an excited energy. Looking around, it was clear everyone else had taken as much pain to prepare as Senafae. Faces were painted, the gowns ranged from fashionable to scandalous, and the hairstyles were elaborate and bedecked with feathers or ribbons or jewels. The war being waged by an array of perfumes made me want to sneeze. Vanaria wore an expensive gown of midnight blue that set off her hair spectacularly, and when she caught me looking, she glowered and turned to whisper to the person next to her.

When Mrs Corkill joined us, she acted as a dampener on both the mood and the noise.

'Tonight, your role is simple: mingle, talk, and entertain. His Majesty and his council have been in trade negotiations with dignitaries from Creatia and Oceatold all day, and this dinner is designed to ease the tension of those negotiations. They are to have a good time.' Her expression communicated extreme disapproval, but whether that was disapproval of the dignitaries, the trade negotiations, or of 'good times' in general, I wasn't sure. Perhaps all three. 'Do you have any questions?'

If anyone did have any questions, I was sure they were all too afraid of her to ask them. She gave a curt nod and turned as though to leave, but changed her mind. She turned her judgemental gaze back to us, her lips pressed together so tightly they seemed to be completely swallowed by her face.

'I am not your madam,' she said firmly. 'I will make no negotiations on your behalf. Those matters are your own business to handle. Now, if you'll follow Leela, she'll take you to the Lesser Hall.'

A housemaid led us down a series of hallways, up a flight of stairs, and through a door where we stepped into a lavish, high-ceilinged hall hung with woven chandeliers. I almost gasped at the sight of them—I'd never seen glisoch before, but this was surely what it was.

The art of weaving magic was a secret jealously guarded by the druthi guild, but the enchantments that could be bought by common folk were contained in cord and woven around bottles or into knots, depending on the purpose. Glisoch was woven with real gold cord. The light emitted was cold and steady, utterly unlike candlelight. The glisoch was twisted and knotted together in decorative dips and swirls, dripping with crystals that sparkled in the glow. I'd never seen it because it was not only damn expensive, but like all druthi weaves, the enchantment was finite, so these opulent things would need to be replaced regularly. And embedding the gold with the enchantment that produced light corroded it away, so the gold itself would be completely worthless by the end, only fit for picking through by hungry street children who hoped to find a crumb of the metal untouched.

And there were *dozens* of the chandeliers. If I'd felt guilty over what I had come to the palace intending to do, I didn't feel so now.

The housemaid led us through what was clearly the part of the palace enjoyed by those who weren't servants, revealing glimpses of gilded sculptures, vaulted ceilings, paraquat flooring, frescos, marble columns, and glossy furniture. By the time she stopped, my head was spinning with the opulence of it all.

The housemaid eyed us with interest as we approached the door as a group, the hushed rustling of excited whispers swaying through us like a breeze through dry grass. I could feel Vanaria's stare burning into me from behind, but I tried to put it from my mind. I had a purpose here and I needed to focus. It didn't help that focus when a few moments later I was jostled roughly as she shoved past me to get to the front of the group.

I glared at her. I didn't blame her exactly for hating me—jealousy is a potent poison—but it made me all the more eager to deliver the apple hidden in my room. She would be furious if it did as Draven promised it would. All I had to do was fashion an opportunity to present it to the king. And somehow convince him to eat it.

The door ahead opened, and girls began filing into the room beyond. I smoothed at my dress, ran a hand over my hair, and took a deep breath and stepped over the threshold.

The room was dimly lit, richly furnished and full of men in fine clothing. The conversation paused briefly as we entered and I felt dozens of eyes running over me and the other maisera, taking our measure, categorising and appraising us. Fans fluttered, hair was tossed, gazes locked, and then the sound of talk resumed as we spread through the room like a drop of dye in water, seeking distance from one another, wanting to make ourselves distinct from the collection.

I scanned the assemblage, the men bristling with self-importance, noting the groupings, the body language, who was an aggressor and who was already conquered. The envoys of three kingdoms stood in this room, princes and ambassadors and priests and lords, all jostling for their place in the pecking order. Any would be a handsome prize, but there was only one king among them, and I picked him out within moments.

Even if I hadn't seen portraits of King Linus, I would have known him from those around him. On the king's right, a golden-haired young man in a royal sash sat turned towards him, even though he spoke with someone on his other side, and behind the king sat an old priest with a hooked nose and severe brows, watching him intently, awaiting any moment of attention to ply him with fervent talk. Every other man in the room continually glanced in the king's direction, as though they were goats checking the location of a lion, making sure the beast hadn't begun to stalk them.

The king himself was grey and weathered, but he held himself with the confidence of someone used to having all eyes on him, all open posture and relaxed gestures. He cast a passing glance over the women infiltrating the room, maintaining his conversation with the priest as he did. I watched as those eyes snagged on me and widened, interest suddenly flaring in his face. The priest took several moments to realise he had completely lost the king's attention. He made a few attempts to claw it back before turning his cold eyes on me, a sneer of distaste on his mouth. I smiled sweetly, enjoying the old codger's irritation.

I moved slowly across the room, determined to be the first to engage the king in conversation, ignoring the pointed gazes of other men eager to talk to me. Someone stepped in front of me, forcing me to pause and turn my attention away from my target. I frowned as I looked into his face.

A sallow-skinned man stood leering at me, a greedy smile on his thin-lipped mouth. He was round-faced and weak chinned, with a tall, wiry figure, and there were specks of what could have been dried blood on his white cravat. 'What's your name, darling?' he said, his words oily. Behind him, I saw Vanaria approaching the king, flicking her unbound red curls as he smiled at her.

'Rhiandra,' I replied, my voice stony, seething with resentment.

He glanced towards where my eyes were fixed, and his expression soured. 'You might think about paying more attention to what is right in front of you,' he sneered, gesturing to himself with his hands, and as he did my eyes snagged on the sigil hanging from a heavy gold chain against his chest. Three interconnected circles encased within a triangle. Fear prickled at the back of my neck.

The sigil of the Druthi Guild.

This was what I'd been afraid of. I'd been in the palace for a day and already I had encountered someone who might have the ability to oust me, to recognise the use of magic. *Might.* I offered him my sweetest smile, trying to hide my panic as I searched his face for any sign that he could tell I was glamoured, but his expression relaxed as he gained my full attention.

'And what entertainment are you offering tonight?' he asked as his gaze slithered down my body and I supressed a shudder.

I lifted my lute and shook it, trying to keep my expression playful, though he surely would have detected the mockery if his eyes hadn't been busy elsewhere.

'A songbird? Come, treat us to a tune,' he said, sweeping his arm towards a small group who sat huddled together in a corner of the room. I followed him with my heart pounding, surveying the gathered men for more sigils.

'What's this?' The words were spoken in the lilting accent of Oceatold and came from the mouth of a large, red-faced man clutching a tankard in his fist, his eyes twinkling at me. 'I will not buy your fall spawn at the price you ask, Dovegni, no matter how pretty a girl you seek to distract me with.'

I felt my face pale. I perched on an empty chair and arranged my lute with hands that now trembled. *Dovegni.* Everyone knew that name. It was signed on every Custody Notice, those dreaded red envelopes served to the nearest kin of those who would soon be chained to a pyre. Grand Weaver Dovegni. The head of the guild. Not only had I encountered a druthi, but I had managed to find myself before the most powerful one in all of Brimordia.

'I believe our negotiations are at an end for today, Perrius. You're about to discover our host's famed hospitality,' Dovegni replied as he sank into a chair.

I began plucking at the strings of my lute, sweat prickling on my forehead as I felt his eyes on me. Draven may have laughed off my concerns, but I remembered the soot stains on the road by the gate of the palace all too clearly. I was sure at any moment he would suddenly jump to his feet, declare me a witch, and call for my arrest. I could picture his face at the head of a courtroom all too clearly, the cold smile he would wear as he gave evidence before the Grand Paptich. But he simply watched me play as the other men returned to their conversations, his fingers twisting at a ring on his left hand, set with an enormous black stone that glinted with veins of blue.

Around the room, the other maisera were converting the focus of the guests, deftly smoothing over the transition from business to pleasure. Senafae moved towards me when I caught her eye and she listened to me play for a few moments before beginning to sing.

'I had once a young love,
When spring was fresh and new.
His hands could calm wild horses,
His smile was bright as dew.'

Her voice was as exquisite as she had promised: as high and as clear as a mountain stream. Eyes all across the room turned to watch her and conversation grew hushed. I glanced at Vanaria just as the king turned his attention away from her and she looked as though she might start breathing fire.

'He held me oh so tightly
Through sweltering summer nights,
But when autumn leaves were turning

Another drew his sight.'

Dovegni continued to watch me as Senafae sang, twisting obsessively at his ring. His eyes weighed on me like shackles and sweat prickled at my brow. I needed to get out from under his attention.

'Now my skin is cold as winter,
My heart a dying thing,
But the thaw is drawing closer
And love can bloom in spring.'

'What a fine song,' a deep voice thrummed, and I glanced behind me to see the king standing by and watching our performance. 'And even finer musician,' he added, his eyes settling on me. I held his gaze and let a few final chords fade away. But before I could rise from my seat, the young man in the Oceatold sash appeared by his side and drew him into conversation, leading him away from me.

As impatient as this made me, I soothed myself with the knowledge that I had already caught his eye enough for him to wander over. After all, easily won was less valuable. I could command his attention from across the room.

'Forgive me if I seem a little flustered. I've never seen so many important men in one place before. And I had no idea you would all be so handsome,' I said, widening my eyes as I looked around at the group who had congregated to hear the song. Several chuckles broke out and a few chairs were dragged closer.

A kindly-looking man with watery eyes and an embroidered waistcoat settled himself at my right and watched me with rapt attention. When he caught my gaze, he turned his surprisingly plump mouth in a tentative smile. 'High Lord Faucher at your service, madame,' he said with a nod, before adding 'of Renia,' with a slight jutting out of his chest.

'A pleasure to meet you, *High* Lord Faucher,' I simpered, offering my hand. 'I'm very fond of Renian wine.' I'd never met a High Lord before and found myself disappointed by how ordinary he looked, not that I was going to let him know that. If all the estates in Renia were beholden to him, he must be very rich.

Without waiting for further invitation, he launched into a rolling commentary on the grape crop this season, then began regaling me with stories of his latest hunting exploits, interspersed with advice on breeding good hunting horses. I was tremendously bored within a few minutes, but he didn't seem to notice, requiring no more from me than the occasional nod and murmured 'oh, really.'

'My Lord,' I finally interrupted him as I watched the blond man in the sash continue to monopolise the king. 'I feel so lost amongst all these fine people; I could use your help. Could you tell me, who is that over there?' I pointed at the man.

Lord Faucher blinked himself out of his tangent on the soft hooves of eastern horse breeds to look to where I was pointing. 'Prince Tallius of Oceatold.'

Prince Tallius. Interesting. 'Is he the prince set to marry Princess Gwinellyn?'

And when Faucher leaned a little closer and lowered his voice, I was delighted to discover that this fusty old man was a gossip. 'Theoretically,' he said. 'Poor fellow has been loitering around the court for years waiting for His Majesty to finally grant them an official engagement. I hear,' he lowered his voice to just above a whisper, 'he is a bit of bed hopper while he waits. Already has himself a sack of wild oats, so to speak.'

I touched my fingers to my mouth in mock scandal. 'No! What does he do with them?'

'I imagine he pays their mothers to take them off to the country nice and quietly.'

'What are you two whispering about over there?' the Grand Weaver interrupted suddenly, his eyes narrowed.

'Yes, stop hogging her, Faucher,' Perrius boomed, turning from his other conversation to join ours.

I straightened up, plastering a smile onto my face. 'Would any of you like to play a game?'

I spent the next portion of the evening playing a drinking game that involved throwing coins in a bowl across the room while flirting and holding court like I was already the queen. There was enough laughter and commotion to draw notice, and I caught the king looking over more than once.

I kept an eye on him, noting what he was drinking and when his glass needed refilling, picking my moment. Part way through an argument between Lord Perrius and a Creatish dignitary over southern trading tariffs, I rose to my feet.

'You are both so badly behaved that I'm just going to have to leave you here,' I chided.

'So long as you return,' Lord Perrius chuckled. 'I promise we will stop talking politics if you do.'

Dovegni snorted. 'Stop talking politics? You? You must be in love.'

I smiled sweetly and bowed my head before withdrawing with my lute in hand. Swiping a bottle of the wine I'd seen the king being served, I made a beeline for him and his now empty glass, but as I crossed the room, someone bumped into me with enough force to send me stumbling.

I felt hands on my skirts, steadying me, and I almost thanked whoever it was for keeping me from toppling over, but when I saw Vanaria standing there I shook her off with a scowl.

'So sorry,' she simpered. 'I didn't see you.'

'I'm sure you didn't.' I quickly surveyed my dress, making sure I hadn't splashed it with wine, which was undoubtedly her intention, but I hadn't spilled a drop. I smirked at her, and to my surprise she offered me a heavy-lidded smile in return, looking as pleased as a fattened pig.

'Enjoy your evening,' she said, and with a flick of her hair she sauntered away, quickly finding Elovissa, another maisera from Quality, and whispering to her while looking over at me. Whatever she was up to, I was sure it meant nothing good for me, but I dismissed all thoughts of her as I continued towards the king.

I flitted in behind him, leaned close and murmured, 'More wine, your majesty?' just by his ear. He assented without looking, but when I leaned over him with the wine bottle his gaze flicked up at me and interest lit his eyes.

'Ah, the musician,' he said. 'Sit by me. I'd like to hear you play again.'

'Of course, Your Majesty.' I curtsied low, then settled myself on a chair close to him. He turned in his seat, completely withdrawing from his previous conversation to face me, leaving the man he had been speaking to looking crestfallen.

I began to play a soft, easy tune that required just a few repeated chords, allowing my attention free to focus on the monarch now watching me so closely. For someone on the later side of fifty summers, he was still handsome, broad-shouldered and lean, with wide hands and a straight back. He had the mild expression of someone used to guarding his thoughts from onlookers and I couldn't quite tell if my playing pleased him or not.

'What game were you about over there? It seemed to be a hit,' he said after a moment.

'Just a silly amusement, Your Majesty. A coin tossing game.'

'Maybe you can teach me.'

'There isn't much to teach. I'm sure it would bore someone of your faculties.'

His mouth twitched, and I reassessed. Maybe he wanted bawdy and fun. Perhaps behind that curated expression was a gnawing boredom. Perhaps offering him more of the polite company he was surely up to his neck in every day was the wrong idea.

'But I do have a deck of cards. Do you fancy a game of Pack the Priest?' The offer was tentative as I tried this new angle, but I was rewarded when the king grinned.

'With our own Grand Paptich in this very room? You live dangerously.'

Taboo and titillation. Madam Luzel's teachings served me well yet again. I winked at him. 'We'll just have to be sneaky. It can be our little secret.'

The priest, none other than the Grand Paptich himself I now knew, seemed to sense that we were talking about him and glanced over. When he saw His Majesty was looking his way, he brightened and began towards us. The king waved a hand as though to shoo him away, and his expression drooped into a frown.

'He won't be happy with me now. You'd better let me win.'

'That depends entirely on the stakes,' I teased as I began to deal the cards, feeling pleased with myself. The king was smiling, and he'd glanced at my cleavage more than once. This was going very well.

'Forgive me, Your Majesty, Mrs Corkill requires Miss Beaufort's immediate attendance.' The words came from the butler with the rough, red hands who I'd seen the day before. He bowed low enough that he must have missed the flash of temper that tore across my face. The king raised his eyebrows at me.

'Far be it for me to keep Mrs Corkill waiting. We might have to postpone terrorising priests.'

I kept my frustration at bay just long enough to rise from my seat, flash a coy smile, and bob a curtsey. 'As you wish, Your Majesty.'

The servant led me from the room, and I clenched my fists tightly as I followed him. Of course, Mrs Corkill would send for me the moment I was where I needed to be, the moment I had the king's attention. And what did the old fuddy duddy want, anyway? Why would she want to see me?

We moved away from the lavish hallways and stairwells of the entertaining part of the palace and back to the nether regions of the household, into the unadorned servant's quarters, where Mrs Corkill was waiting in a small office. As soon as I saw the deep frown scoring her face, I knew I was in trouble.

'Thank you, Mr Guilcher,' she said as she stood from the arm-chair she had been seated in. 'Please stay, if you will. I may have need of you.'

Mr Guilcher inclined his head and lingered by the doorway.

Mrs Corkill then turned to me. 'Miss Beaufort,' she said stiffly. 'Thank you for being so prompt. I am going to give you this chance now to be honest. Is there something you would like to confess?'

Immediately, my pulse took off, rushing in my ears like an overfed river until I could barely hear her. Someone had found me out. Someone had gone through my things and found the mirror or the apple, perhaps both. Someone had somehow realised the items were more than they appeared. I was going to be arrested. I would be tried. I would be sentenced to public execution and burned on a pyre by the gates of the palace.

'Miss Beaufort?' Mrs Corkill repeated. 'I'm waiting.'

'I don't know what you're talking about,' I managed to choke out.

Her frown deepened, drawing her whole face into the expression, carving valleys into her forehead and around her mouth. 'Very well. Please hold out your arms. I am going to search you.'

Search me? Did she suspect me of having other magical paraphernalia on my person? I did as she bid, feeling light-headed with panic as she began to pat at my skirts, my ears straining for the pounding of boots on the floor of the halls. Could I push her aside, dodge the butler, and make it out of the palace before the gendarmerie arrived? It was my only chance. If I stood trial, I would be convicted. People were convicted on far less evidence than the objects I possessed.

I felt her grope around in the pocket of my skirt before she pulled back and held something out between us.

I blinked.

'This is not yours.' She was holding a heavy, ornate silver fork.

'No, it is not,' I said slowly, my mind whirling.

'I'm disappointed that you did not confess to stealing when I gave you the chance to do so. I will be reporting this incident to His Majesty, and I would not be surprised if you are to be dismissed from the palace immediately.'

'I am... I don't...' I stuttered as took stock of this new situation, reeling back from the arrest and execution I had been sure I was about to face. There had been a fork in my pocket. She thought I had stolen it. A memory flashed through my mind: a stumble, hands on my skirt. *Vanaria.*

'I hope you are not about to feed me an excuse when you have been caught in the very act.'

'I am... deeply ashamed of myself,' I said finally. 'I just wanted some token of my time here, meeting the *king*. I didn't think anyone would miss one tiny piece of cutlery.' If I told her I'd been framed, she would never believe me. Better to own up to the act, display remorse, try and wrangle a tiny drop of sympathy out of this old dish rag of a woman. If I could convince her I hadn't pocketed the piece to sell, I might be able to convince her I wasn't desperate enough to steal again.

'Each tiny piece of this cutlery is worth more than your dress and is my personal responsibility. And not to mention stealing from this household is stealing from your king,' she barked, and I turned my eyes to the ground, trying to cloak my seething rage with a demeanour of regret. *I would kill that red-haired wretch.*

'It was a stupid decision made in a moment of weakness. I'm so very sorry.'

She nodded curtly. 'You're at His Majesty's mercy now. I suggest you return to your room and pack your belongings. I expect you will be permitted to remain the night, but you should be ready to leave in the morning.'

My face was hot with embarrassment and rage as I stormed back to my room. What now? I was about to be turned out of the palace over *a fork*. I wouldn't be able to deliver on my end of my bargain. What would Draven do? Would he rescind the deal, take back the glamour, go and find himself another girl to turn into a queen? No. I wouldn't let that happen. I couldn't just sit and wait to be thrown out onto the street. My future was not to scrounge through bins and beg for coins. Flashes of memory clawed at me, of the vulnerability of sleeping in an alleyway with the wet ground soaking into my skin, of the humiliation of being spat on, of a stomach hollow with hunger while I was fondled and kicked. It would be so much worse if I wound up there again, now that my face was ruined. I would have nothing left to sell that anyone would think worth paying for.

I was lying beneath the covers, waiting on Senafae when she returned to the room hours later.

'Rhiandra,' she called softly. 'Are you awake?'

'Has everyone gone to bed?' I asked, sitting up slightly.

She bounded in and threw herself onto her bed. 'I thought you'd gone off with some lord! I had no idea you'd come back here. Why did you leave so early?'

'I wasn't feeling well.'

She deflated a little. 'Oh. That's too bad.'

'Was the king there much longer after I left?'

'Hours!' She sat up and began plucking pins from her hair. 'Vanaria had her claws in him for half the night, of course. Here, will you help unlace me?' She turned and bent her slender neck

and I sat fully upright to reach for her. 'Did you see the prince of
Oceatold?' She shot me a look out of the corner of her eye. 'Don't
you think he's handsome?'

'Very,' I murmured as I worked at her bodice.

'And Lord Boccius already has his sights on Carina. He invited
her to a picnic tomorrow, and she agreed. He'll be a fine catch for
her, though he is married and quite fat, but he is a councillor and
nephew to the king, and I hear he is rich. He must be to sit on
the king's council, and—why are you still fully dressed?' She had
glanced over her shoulder at me and now she turned fully round,
her hair loose, her dress gaping open at the back.

'I think I might go and find the infirmary.' I stood as I said this,
arranging my skirts and checking myself in the mirror.

'I'm sorry, here I am babbling when you're unwell. I'll come with
you.'

'No!' I said, a little too forcefully, and her face pinched with
suspicion. I quickly amended my tone. 'Sleep. You'll need to be
fresh tomorrow. I won't be long.'

I didn't give her time to ask questions, leaving the room quickly and shutting the door definitively behind me before skulking
through the servant's quarters, unfolding the schedule of events
Mrs Corkill had given me upon arrival, and squinting at the map
on the back. Most of the rooms weren't labelled, no doubt as
a precaution against the 'unapproved wandering' we had been
warned about, but a suite of rooms butting onto the large, central
courtyard caught my attention. The suite of rooms was not ex-
plicitly spelled out as belonging to the king, but it was enormous,
comprised of what looked like eighteen different rooms across two

floors of the palace. No other apartment was anywhere near that size. Who else could it belong to?

I moved through the palace like a cat, ducking out of sight when I heard drunk voices in the halls ahead, along with the feminine laughter that suggested there were still those continuing the night's festivities. Silly girls. They should know better than to give of themselves so quickly. The high status of the clientele must have thrown off their better sense. Any maisera worth her salt knew that the longer she kept a man from her bed, the more he would be willing to pay for the pleasure.

The palace was a labyrinth, and I was left standing at a dead end where I thought there should be a hall more than once, muttering curses as I tried to place myself on the map, but eventually I entered a sweeping hall of gold-panelled walls and a polished floor cloaked in embroidered rugs the colour of ripe plums. A young, spotty guard was posted by a door halfway down the hall, and I allowed myself a small smile of satisfaction. Who else's room would be guarded?

The guard eyed me as I approached, and I bowed my head demurely, trying not to look threatening. 'Is His Majesty in?'

'He's turned in for the night and won't take visitors,' the guard replied.

I smiled sweetly. 'It will only take a moment. It's very important.'

He seemed to physically thaw, his stiff stance slackening as he stared at me with a slightly open mouth. 'Sorry, ma'am. No visitors.'

'Maybe you could ask him? Or even take a peek inside and see if he's still awake? Please? I'd be ever so grateful.'

'I'm sorry ma'am, I really can't—'

The door behind him opened, and the guard jumped to attention.

'It's alright, I'm awake. Miss Beaufort, what a surprise to see you. Would you like to step inside?' King Linus gestured with a sweep of his hand, and I curtsied low.

'If it please you, Your Majesty,' I said, before sweeping past the young guard without a second glance. The king closed the door behind me. We were standing in a dark antechamber, lit only by what firelight was escaping from a door to an adjoining room.

'I apologise for disturbing you so late,' I began, but he waved my words away.

'I'm a night owl. But when I said we could continue our game another time, I didn't mean tonight. I already have someone here.'

I wondered who he had in the apartment with him. Vanaria? He can't have been too smitten with whoever it was since he had come to the door for me. 'I've come to beg your forgiveness,' I said, looking up at him from beneath my lashes.

His silver eyebrows climbed higher up his forehead. 'My forgiveness? What for?'

'I did a foolish thing. After meeting you earlier, I was so overcome. I thought to myself that there would never be another night like tonight, and I desperately wanted something to remember it by, some small token. So, I... stole from you.' I turned my gaze to the ground.

'What did you steal from me?'

'A piece of cutlery,' I said softly. 'A fork.'

'A fork,' he repeated.

'And Mrs Corkill found it. She made me realise that it really was a shocking thing to do, and I understand that you will send me away from the palace in the morning. But I just wanted to see you once more, so that I could tell you how sorry I am, and how I didn't mean to offend you.'

'I don't know about all that.' His voice was thick with warmth and amusement. 'It seems a harsh punishment, to send you away for the sake of a fork. Perhaps if you had pocketed the entire cutlery set, but if you promise not to do that, then I think we should be able to let this little incident slide.'

I beamed up at him. 'Thank you. I appreciate your mercy.'

'I expect you'll make me glad of it,' he said, his gaze slipping away from my face and down my body.

I curtsied low, feeling pleased. He was flirting with me. 'I should leave you to your evening and your companion. Goodnight, Your Majesty.'

He seemed for a moment as though he was going to say something else but didn't stop me as I withdrew from the room and back past the young guard, who gave me a hopeful smile. I flicked my hair and blew him a kiss, then twiddled my fingers in a wave as I walked back down the hallway.

That had been easier than I had anticipated. If only I had brought the blasted apple along with me. I hadn't wanted to be caught wandering the palace with it, especially when I wasn't sure whether the apartment I was looking for was even the king's. And if Mrs Corkill had discovered me out of my room, she would have gone through my pockets again, thinking I was stealing a few last-minute items before I was thrown out in the morning.

Now I just had to hope that the king wouldn't change his mind.

Senafae was snoring softly when I slipped back into our room, and I watched her for a few moments, marking the slow rise and fall of her chest until I was convinced she really was asleep. Then, I opened the side table drawer and rooted around in my underclothes until my fingers met with smooth, cold skin. I pulled the apple out for a moment, feeling the pull of sudden hunger, the craving to bite. It still looked perfect. How long would it stay that way? Would it begin to rot, or was it immune to Taveum's influence?

How would I get the king to eat it?

Sitting here, I realised how absurd it was. I had seen the delicacies being served that night. A humble apple was hardly going to fit in on his table.

I stuffed the apple back in the drawer, undressed, and slithered into bed. Apple dilemma or no, I was looking forward to seeing the look on Mrs Corkill's face in the morning.

CHAPTER SEVEN

The next day dawned without an escort waiting to stuff me into a carriage and wave me off, so I went about dressing and breakfasting as I usually would. Mrs Corkill found me in the dining room and beckoned me into the hall. I wore my best approximation of someone meek and sad and solemnly accepting of her punishment. The housekeeper, on the other hand, looked as though someone had served her a plate of earwax for breakfast.

'His Majesty and I have decided to offer you a second chance,' she began, and I resisted the urge to laugh. *His Majesty and I* indeed, as though the two were bosom buddies, partners in making a decision, when I knew very well that he would have pronounced his verdict and she would have swallowed it without a word of protest.

'You will be permitted to remain in the palace for the duration of the treaty celebrations, as originally agreed in your contract, provided there are no further incidents that call into question your trustworthiness,' she finished.

'Thank you, Mrs Corkill. You've no idea how grateful I am,' I said, my tone syrupy.

She stared at me with eyes as cold and hard as river rocks. 'I will be watching you. Do not think you will be excused twice.'

'Of course. It won't happen again.' I clasped my hands together and tried for sincerity, and it must have been at least halfway convincing for she nodded curtly.

'Good. You may resume your breakfast.' When she turned her back, I couldn't help but stick my tongue out at her.

When I returned to the dining table, I caught Vanaria watching me with a feline interest, before she turned to Elovissa and said in a loud whisper, 'I wonder what's wrong with her? If she's poor enough to steal cutlery, she mustn't make very good money as a maisera.' Elovissa shot me a glance, caught me looking, and quickly turned back to Vanaria to murmur something behind her hand. They both collapsed in a fit of giggles.

'I should thank you, Vanaria,' I said. 'Your little ploy was actually very helpful.'

She tossed her hair. 'How pathetic, to try blaming *me* for your weakness. I almost feel sorry for you.'

'As much as I appreciate your pity, it would be wasted on me. After all, I had an excellent excuse to seek out the king last night. He was *very* understanding.'

The smirk slipped from Vanaria's face like melting butter. 'Beauty will only get you so far. It takes charm and talent to be a true maisera. He'll quickly lose interest.'

I offered her an icy smile. 'You'd better hope so. Because if he doesn't, you may have made yourself a powerful enemy.'

She only rolled her eyes. 'You think a lot of yourself for such a nobody. Where have you come from again? Probably some flesh house in the Trough.' Her expression suddenly perked with interest, and she leaned forward on the table. 'Maybe I should find out.'

I chewed on a reply for a moment before swallowing it and turning away from her to find my seat at the end of the table. The last thing I needed was for that viper to go poking about in my history.

Senafae was fixing me with a strange look when I sat back down. 'What's wrong?' I asked.

Her brows were drawn, her mouth rigid, and she sat with her cutlery dangling from her hands, her meal forgotten. 'You told me you went to the infirmary last night,' she said. 'I thought you weren't feeling well.'

'What are you, my madam?' I snapped. Her face twitched, hurt spilling over her expression, and regret stung me in the chest.

She stared at her plate for a moment, before dropping her cutlery to the table. 'You don't owe me your secrets. But I don't want to be fed your lies, either.'

'I never—' I began, but she stood, pushing her chair back with a scrape of legs against the floorboards. 'Where are you going? You haven't finished eating.'

'To the infirmary. I don't feel well,' she said. And with that, she stormed from the room. Vanaria looked as though she was ready to start cackling as she threw a look in my direction.

I was determined not to chase after Senafae, instead lingering to finish my breakfast and then deciding on a stroll in the gardens. A long stroll. But winter had well and truly set in, and the weather was bitter and cold as I marched past withered shrubs and skeletal trees, clutching my cloak tightly around me. Nursing any kind of friendship in this place was stupid. I had too much to hide. But the look on Senafae's face kept returning to me, and each time my stomach squirmed with guilt.

Perhaps I couldn't have friends, but Senafae had clearly thought me hers.

With the weather bullying me back indoors, and my recent run in with Mrs Corkill still fresh enough to keep me from wandering where she would be unhappy to find me, I decided I had little choice but to return to my room.

Senafae was sitting on her bed reading a letter when I opened the door. She didn't acknowledge me, only held the letter a little closer to her chest. With a sigh, I sat at the dressing table and began fiddling with my hair, readying myself for that afternoon's Armistice Ball rehearsal as the silence grew thicker and heavier, settling over us like a cloud of noxious gas.

Finally, I turned in my seat to stare at her, but she still didn't look up.

'Who wrote you?' I asked.

She glanced up. 'My family.'

'Any news from home?'

'Nothing much.' She carefully folded the letter and slipped it into her bedside drawer. I was disturbed to learn she was still corresponding with her family if they sold her into slavery. If they were destitute enough to sell their daughters to a flesh house, it seemed odd that they'd spend the money it would cost to send a letter from a border town all the way to Lee Helse just to communicate with one of those daughters. Surely the moment you sold your child to a place like Notes of Ivory, you were consigning her to death or misery so great that you'd never expect to hear from her again.

'I'm sorry I lied to you,' I said finally, unable to handle the discomfort any longer. 'I was embarrassed about the stealing situation, and I honestly didn't even know if I'd be able to find the king to beg for forgiveness.'

She played with her plaited bracelet for a few moments before finally speaking. 'At least now I know what you're here for.'

'What do you mean?'

She met my eyes, and her expression was grim. I hadn't known her lively, cheerful face could look so grave. 'You want the king.'

'Don't be ridiculous. I went to beg him not to throw me out of the palace.'

'What, because you risked your time here to steal a fork? You don't think I'd actually believe you'd be that stupid, do you?'

Should I tell her of Vanaria's involvement? Would she believe the truth any more than the lie? I began to speak again, but she held up her hand. 'That's enough,' she said. 'I don't want to talk about it anymore. Let's just put it behind us and move on.'

'Of course,' I readily agreed, surprised that she was willing to drop the issue. 'Thank you.'

'I'm going to change. Have you seen what we have to wear for this rehearsal? I thought we were supposed to dress more conservative while we're here, not less.'

And just like that, it was as if nothing had happened. She flittered around the room with an energy as effervescent as champagne, sharing bits of gossip she'd gleaned about the noblemen she'd met and wondering what was planned for the Armistice Ball. I mostly let her talk, chiming in only occasionally as I puzzled over her ability to switch moods with such speed, but by the time we were ready to follow the other maisera to the empty parlour that would serve as the rehearsal space, I had pushed it out of my mind to focus on my growing excitement.

The Armistice Ball was legendary, and opportunities to attend were scarce. The Treaty of Wenderstad was signed every eight years in homage to the length of the war that spawned it, and each of the three kingdoms took turns playing host for the celebrations, which meant Brimordia only hosted every twenty-four years. The Armistice Ball was the most opulent event on the celebration itinerary and noble families from all over the three kingdoms attended. People begged, bribed, and stole their way into the Armistice Ball. My mother had attended one once, before she'd been ostracised from her family by the scandal that ended in me.

The idea of attending, even as 'staff', as Mrs Corkill had put it, made me giddy with anticipation.

We filtered into the parlour as a rippling sea of beige due to colour of the tight, stretchy fabric we'd all been given to rehearse in. Scandalously indecent, the gowns clung to every plane and curve of the girls around me, looking dangerously close to skin, with a gauzy skirt the only nod to modesty.

To my surprise, the man I'd met the night before, *High* Lord Faucher, sat in an armchair at the front of the room. Surely, he wasn't going to be instructing us?

I could feel the chorus of raised eyebrows behind me as I quickly crossed the floor and bobbed a curtsey before him. 'My lord, how fine it is to see you here. I had no idea you were a choreographer.'

'Oh no.' He chuckled and shook his head rigorously. 'No, I'm here strictly to observe and report. Boccius has put so much work into organising this ruddy ball. He wants eyes on everything.'

'Of course,' I said, pretending I knew who Boccius was. 'Then who—'

The door sprang open again and all eyes in the room turned on a man strolling in, sweeping his arms wide as he went. 'Ladies, welcome. I am Master Perunicus, your choreographer. We are going to make exquisite art together,' he announced

A battle of colours fought for territory over his body, and I spent several seconds trying to make sense of it all. Greens, blues, purples, reds; all were represented. As he surveyed the women arrayed before him, he blinked hard, as though he'd just caught the sun in his eyes.

'Why are we dressed like this?' The question came from Elovissa who stood at the front of the group with her arms crossed.

Master Perunicus flicked his hands at her. 'I need to see you as you will be in the Great Hall without ruining your costumes.'

'Costumes?'

But he only clucked his tongue and began prowling through us, sizing us up, fluttering his hands to shoo some of the girls to different positions in the room. When he reached me, he took a hold of my hands and tugged.

'This way, please,' he said as he walked backwards to lead me to my own section of the floor, right next to where Vanaria was now standing. She crossed her arms and turned so she was facing the other direction and I rolled my eyes.

When Master Perunicus seemed satisfied with our positions, he walked to the centre of the room so that we were all fanned out around him.

'Now,' he said with a clap of his hands, 'we will begin.'

My excitement quickly faded when the dance I thought we were to be taught turned out to be just a series of poses, each held for a few minutes before cycling to the next. He demonstrated each pose before checking to ensure we were copying to his satisfaction, directing us to slightly lift a hand, turn a little more to the left or just hold *still*, would you?

Of the tools in the arsenal of a maisera, dance was one I had long neglected, so my strength and flexibility were not the most impressive in the room. By the time we had cycled through a dozen poses, I was ready to clobber Master Perunicus.

'You are the marble sculptures of the palace come to life,' he urged as he moved around us, poking at limbs and torsos when he wanted to correct a stance. 'When you are still, you are solid, immovable, frozen. When you move, you are swift, graceful until ah! You are still once more. And did we see you move?' He hid his face behind his hands, then peeked out from between his fingers. 'We can't be sure. Now, watch carefully, this one will challenge you.'

He raised himself up on one leg, tilted forward with his arms outstretched, then gripped his floating leg by the ankle and extended it above his head in a display of flexibility I'd never seen in a man before. I huffed a breath and tried to mimic him, my muscles now shaking slightly. He drifted over to me and frowned as I tried to hold myself still.

'Higher,' he pressed. 'Stretch your head towards the roof and pull your leg higher. You should be a sleek curve, pleasing to the eye. None of these angles.'

Gritting my teeth and stringing together colourful chains of curse words in my head, I pulled at my ankle and curved my spine as the leg I balanced on wobbled dangerously.

'Higher!'

I could barely breathe as I stretched, my face turning red with the exertion of trying to keep my balance, until a pain lanced through my thigh as my muscle spasmed. I gasped and lost my position, tumbling forward in an effort to escape the cramp, knocking right into Vanaria. My hands shot out and grabbed at her shoulder and hair to try to right myself. She shrieked as she lost her balance and we both went sprawling to the floor. I lay atop her, dazed, before she began to squirm.

'You clumsy idiot!' She shoved me off her.

'It was an accident,' I muttered as I climbed to my feet, massaging at the throbbing rope of pain in my thigh.

'*You* are an accident.' She made to rise, but as she put weight on her ankle she hissed in pain. I caught sight of Lord Faucher pushing his way past Master Perunicus to bend down and help Vanaria to her feet.

'Easy does it,' he said as he hitched an arm around her waist to steady her. She kept her eyes on me, her face twisted and red with fury.

'You shouldn't even be here,' she seethed. 'If they'd put you through the rest of the rounds like everyone else, they would have realised you are nothing more than a pretty face and you would have been eliminated. Someone who can't even hold a pose has *no business* calling herself a maisera.'

Lord Faucher stood awkwardly staring at the ground, muttering 'now, now' while Vanaria spilled her vitriol, but once she'd had her say he sprang into action, ushering her away from me. She resisted him for a moment and seemed ready to say more, but then she turned from me and let herself be led, limping, over to his chair against the wall. It seemed as though she spent the next hour trying to glare a hole through me while Lord Faucher brought her drinks and sweets and cushions, but when she eventually joined the rehearsal once more she seemed steady enough on her feet.

By the time the rehearsal was finished, the endless twisting and holding of my body had effectively wrung every drop of enthusiasm for the Armistice Ball out of me. No dancing, no performing, just holding poses, like we were to be nothing more than decoration in the room. What a waste of talent.

Luckily, I had no talent for dancing, so the waste wasn't mine.

'Is the theme of the ball lunacy? Because it feels like it might be,' I grumbled to Senafae as we made our way to the servant's dining room for dinner.

Senafae rolled her neck, wincing. 'Likely. I can't possibly hold that last pose for more than half a breath. What did he call it?'

'The weeping swan, which seems fitting. Any swan would weep if it was forced to stand like that.'

She sighed as we reached the base of a flight of stairs, looking up as though hoping it might take pity on her and turn into a level hallway. 'They aren't going to tell us anything about what to expect on the night, are they?'

'I doubt Mrs Corkill would trust us not to spill any secret they let us in on.'

'You don't think she's had anything to do with the planning, do you? I hope she hasn't.'

I snorted. 'I doubt it. Not unless the theme this year is sobriety and respectability.'

'I don't know,' Senafae giggled, 'she might be hiding a wild party girl coiled up in that tight bun. With the right amount of—' she shut her mouth as we summited the staircase and found the lady herself pacing towards us, her heavy keys jingling with every step. We bobbed our heads demurely at her as we crept past. Her eyes bulged as she took us in, clearly dismayed by our scanty clothes.

'At least she knows I'm definitely not hiding any cutlery,' I whispered, but rather than eliciting the laugh I'd hoped for, Senafae sobered.

'Let's hurry. I'm starving,' she mumbled, lengthening her stride until she was a pace ahead of me and I was scurrying to catch up.

We were forced to attend a handful of rehearsal sessions over the next few days, though how anyone thought we were thick enough to forget how to stand still and look pretty was beyond me. Our evenings were often our own, with the occasional event thrown in. We attended a wine tasting and a card night, but the king wasn't at either of those, and I spent the time trying to charm while simultaneously dodging all advances. I contemplated trying to fashion an opportunity to encounter him, but it was a terrible idea. It would reek of desperation. But in the meantime, the apple and the mirror featured always at the back of my mind, like a pair of lit fuses burning towards an explosion.

It didn't help that every morning Mrs Corkill inspected our rooms when she checked us over for signs of bad health. I worked to be tidier than I'd ever been in my life, keeping my clothes orderly and every surface wiped and neat, trying my best not to give her a reason to look any closer. After all, she already thought me a thief. She hardly needed an excuse to go through my belongings. Every day that she didn't felt like an unlikely stroke of luck, and every day I didn't make any headway in my purpose for being there it felt like I'd wasted that luck.

But the Armistice Ball shone ahead of me, promising a distinct opportunity. There was no way the king would miss it.

CHAPTER EIGHT

A frown tugged at my mouth as I scrutinised my face in the mirror of the dressing table. When I had imagined myself at the Armistice Ball, it had not been dressed like this. Every inch of visible skin was painted white, from the neck of my gown all the way to the top of my forehead. My hair had been drenched in a druthi potion that turned it stark ivory, which I vehemently refused at first. But Senafae had managed to convince me to allow it by promising the potion would only strip the lustre from my hair for a few days after.

'It's like swoon,' she'd said. 'A little every now and again isn't a problem. It's when you reapply it too often that you run into trouble.'

I'd heard too many stories about regular users who'd had to cut out enchantments suddenly for one reason or another to be anything other than wary. I also had other reasons for my reluctance. I'd screwed my eyes up tight when they had applied the hair potion, my heart pounding as I feared what might happen when the magic of my glamour met the magic in the bottle, but when I'd opened them it was to find my hair stark white but otherwise unharmed.

Now, it was piled atop my head in a twist that exactly mimicked Senafae's, Vanaria's, and the hair of every other girl in eyesight. We were a sea of white paint and white fabric, a tide of women rendered almost identical by the team of maids who had spent the better part of the day painting and arranging us.

My face felt tight and itchy with the paint, and I was already anticipating the moment I could scrape it off me, a fact that aggravated me to no end. I had been eagerly dreaming of dancing and flirting at the ball, of ogling the assembled nobility and trussing myself up as though I was one of them.

But this? I would never be mistaken for a member of the nobility like this. Perhaps that was the point.

At least our gowns were beautiful. The fabric shimmered and flowed and clung to *everything*, accentuating curves in a way that was sure to scandalise any guest that hadn't known what to expect. They'd have to be incredibly sheltered or stupid not to have expected to be scandalised, though. This was, after all, why tickets to the Armistice Ball were so coveted.

I eyed Senafae as she stretched her willowy limbs. I hated being reduced to just another maisera, almost identical to every other in the room, but I could see how the white rendered us otherworldly and exotically beautiful, the paint possessing a subtle iridescence that caught the light, leaving us glittering like a field of fresh snow.

She caught me looking and flashed me a grin. 'Winter?'

'Maybe. I can't imagine the Great Hall decorated in paper snowflakes.' I eyed myself in the mirror again, contemplating the whirling silver pattern that climbed the white paint of my hands, wrists, and forearms, then the tiny horns poking out from my hair. 'I think we might be snow sprites.' A legend of Yaakandale, snow sprites were said to inhabit the soaring mountain ranges. Some stories said they lived in the deep crevasses in the ice and tricked their prey close enough to fall, others said they convinced travellers to lie with them and sucked the heat from their body as they did, until all that was left was a frozen corpse.

'I hope not,' Senafae replied, screwing up her nose. 'That will attract a certain type.'

'Your attention please,' Mrs Corkill's voice called, and the room fell quiet. 'I would like to remind you of your role tonight. You are performers first and foremost. Keep to your podiums for the early portion of the evening. Once the fire-eaters have entered, you can move about the crowd, but there will be ladies present. Please limit any bawdy behaviour to the private rooms.' As usual, her face was pinched with distaste, and I wondered what had made her such a prude.

'Fire-eaters?' I whispered to Senafae. She waggled her eyebrows.

'Please gather yourselves and follow me,' the housekeeper finished, and without waiting for us to 'gather ourselves,' she turned and left the room at a sharp pace. There was a bustle about me as other girls clamoured to give final, harried looks at the mirror, swiping at stray hairs and fiddling with low necklines before falling into Mrs Corkill's wake.

Senafae grabbed my hand. 'Come on,' she said in a voice hushed with excitement as she tugged me along.

We must have been quite the sight as we streamed through the palace like a giggling avalanche, sweeping gazes along with us as we passed servants in the halls, leaving some frozen in place and staring after us. There were people everywhere. Footmen and maids and hall boys raced around in a chaos of preparation while valets and coachmen tried in vain to garner help for some errand or other, their foreign liveries heralding the arrival of the first guests.

Mrs Corkill turned abruptly before we entered the Great Hall, causing Elovissa to walk directly into her. Mrs Corkill shook the girl off.

'*Please* try and remember that you are representing your king and your country tonight.' She stared directly at Elovissa as she said this, and the girl seemed to shrivel and shrink. 'The Great Hall is not a suvoir, and these guests are not tavern dwellers. Remember where you are at all times. Comport yourselves with dignity.'

I wanted to roll my eyes. Dignity, indeed. I imagined she had been kept far, far away from planning the Armistice Ball. It felt like everything within a hundred-yard radius of her lost all its energy and lustre.

With a final scour of her hard gaze, she opened a small service door and allowed us to pass by.

The scene in the Great Hall was dazzling. Hundreds of enormous mirrors had been stationed around the room, strung from walls, or propped up on stands. Crystal chandeliers dripped from the ceiling like elaborate icicles, and the light from hundreds of slender candles bounced from the surfaces of the mirrors below. The effect was of a huge, sparkling space of unfixed limits, where masked guests drenched in furs and silks and finery stepped in and out of sight as they moved, as though they were blinking in and out of existence.

The sight of so many mirrors sent unease tiptoeing down my spine. So far, I'd seen nothing to suggest there was a single flaw in the glamour but staring into my enchanted mirror every night and seeing my real face was beginning to result in an instant of fear every time I caught sight of a regular mirror, as though one might someday betray me.

Senafae squeezed my hand. 'Good luck,' she whispered, her face aglow.

I squeezed back. 'I suppose I'll see you after the fire-eaters.'

A footman led me to a podium in the corner of the room, staying only to help me climb onto it before disappearing. This part of the night was sure to be the dullest; we were to stand almost as statues while guests ogled us, changing position whenever the orchestra housed in one of the galleries above changed songs. I interpreted my role of 'statue' loosely as I looked around, watching footmen dart from guest to guest, balancing silver trays loaded with glasses of champagne. The far wall was lined with glass doors, which were thrown open to the courtyard beyond, where flickering torches hinted there might be more to see. How were they keeping the room warm with the doors open like that?

The music shifted, and I obediently swept an arm above my head and arched my neck, feeling gazes crawling over me as I did so. Two women approached, their masks mere strips of lace about their eyes. I watched them in my peripheral vision as they regarded me, fluttering their fans and cocking their heads.

'How peculiar,' one said in the sharp, hissing accent of Creatia as she looked me up and down. 'To dress these creatures up in such a fashion and display them like this. I really don't see the appeal.'

'Perhaps their theme promises too much. Would this girl be considered a marvel, or a monster?' her companion replied, leaning closer to me as though she was inspecting the pores of my skin, as though I really was a statue.

The music changed and I took the opportunity to swing my arms suddenly, causing the woman to jump back in fright.

'Well,' she sniffed, 'I hope there are more impressive displays than a few harlots in face paint.' The two returned to their group, which contained a few young men who obviously thought I was an impressive enough display as they gaped at me.

I endured similar treatment from other guests as they poured into the Great Hall, filling it with chatter and laughter as they promenaded around, preening themselves before the mirrors and eyeing each other up. Fortunately, no one had been so uncouth as to actually poke me, but several seemed to be contemplating it. My limbs grew stiff from holding poses and my feet ached in their white slippers.

Finally, a set of trumpets piped a vibrant refrain, silencing the orchestra. A hush fell over the room as the king appeared in a gallery above and people shuffled around to stand where he was visible. Though he was far away, I could see that he was dressed impressively: A cloak of thick white fur hung around his shoulders, and the gold of a crown glinted on his head.

A servant hurried forward to clip a woven circlet around his neck so that when he spoke his voice rumbled off the walls and reached every corner of the hall.

'Welcome,' he boomed, spreading his arms wide, 'to a night of monsters and marvels.'

There was a scattering of applause, and he waited for it to die out before continuing.

'When the Creatish king, Thorgil the Sly, held the first Armistice Ball, I doubt he knew we would be continuing the tradition centuries later. After all, he used it as a ploy to gather information on his new allies. What better way to ensure peace than ply everyone with drink, entice them to act their worst selves, then flood the celebration with spies.'

Laughter greeted this statement, and a young couple nearby turned to each other to share a few whispers.

'So, in the spirit of those ancestors who were badly behaved enough to ensure a hundred years of peace, I implore you to drink, dance, be merry, and rest assured that there will be no spies to make you regret yourself in the morning.'

A wave of cheering and applause rose around me, then the shrieking began.

Several streams of blue fire roared from different corners of the room, sending heat and the rushing of air arcing high over the heads of those assembled, eliciting a more enthusiastic round of applause and cheering. From my position, I could see two dancers now moving through the room, producing bursts of flame as they whirled across the floor. They had the olive skin and dark hair of the northern tribes who wandered the Shifting Plains, and I was surprised to see one was a woman. Her hair was shorn close to her head, and she wore the same dark breeches and shirt threaded with gold as the man a little further along. With a torch in each hand, she moved her arms in great arcs of fire, and as I watched she touched one of her torches to her back and was entirely engulfed in flame.

A fresh burst of screams sounded around the room as the other dancers erupted into cerulean fireballs, the flames flaring high until the hall was filled with a blue glow. I watched with my mouth slightly agape. It was magic. The blue of the flames, the way they were completely engulfed and yet continued to dance, it had to be magic.

The dancing flames were reflected in the surfaces of the dozens of mirrors until the whole hall seemed to be on fire, and then just as suddenly as they'd begun, the flames died out. The dancers bowed, and a deafening applause rattled the room. As it died away, the dancers disappeared, stepping out of sight easily behind the many pillars and mirrors.

The orchestra struck up a cheerful tune as the crowd seemed to recover and chatter filled the air once more. With a sigh of relief, I climbed down from the podium and stretched, seeing glimpses of rippling white around the room as the other maisera within eyesight did the same. I moved away from the podium immediately, darting around the mirrors and servers and clusters of guests as I looked for Senafae. I snatched a glass of champagne from an unattended tray and sipped at it as I went; I may have a job to do, my official one as well as my secret one, but I was determined to enjoy myself while I was here.

Unfortunately, the sight of Vanaria fawning over the king soured the taste of the champagne in my mouth. Tucked into one of the pockets partitioned around the central dance floor, it looked as though she had somehow managed to sequester him away for herself already, though I doubted that would last long. I was never going to have a shot at him with her constantly vying for his attention. I may have matched her in the beauty department, but she was clearly the highest-paid maisera in the city for a reason. As I watched, the music changed to something low and rhythmic and she began to dance, raising her arms above her head and shifting her hips so gracefully that she seemed more liquid than solid.

But the king wasn't the only one watching her dance. A few paces away, Lord Faucher had his watery eyes fixed on her, his mouth hanging slightly agape. I sidled up to him with a smile.

'My lord,' I simpered with a curtsey. 'How pleased I am to see a familiar face.'

'Yes, yes, good to see you,' he said, ripping his eyes away from Vanaria and kissing my offered hand. 'What a spectacle all this is, eh?'

'It is at that. I find it's getting a little too much for me, though.' I fanned at myself, then took his hand and pressed it to my forehead. 'Do I feel hot to you?'

'Mm, yes,' he mumbled, his gaze immediately fixing on my mouth. 'Perhaps you should rest.'

'I should. Won't you help me find somewhere to sit?'

He jumped to attention, slipping my hand into the crook of his elbow, and leading me away from the pillars and to a shadowy alcove furnished with a settee and draped in gauzy curtains. He settled me down, then waved over a footman with a tray and swapped my empty champagne glass for some water.

'It's so nice to be taken care of,' I said, smiling at him from beneath my lashes.

He sat beside me and patted my knee. 'You girls must spend a lot of time on your feet. And all that paint looks hot. Have they painted... everything?'

I smacked him playfully. 'Restrain your wandering mind. You mustn't flirt with me like that.'

He flushed pink and fumbled his reply, turning it into a garbled string of sounds I couldn't make head nor tail of. I wanted to sigh, but I refrained from doing so as I waited a few more moments for him to attempt to mumble something coherent before I jumped in and talked over the top of him.

'Because we have a code amongst maisera,' I said, and he fell quiet, 'we don't covet shared beds.'

His eyebrows shot up towards his receding hairline. 'I'm sorry? You don't what?'

'If a gentleman is a patron of another maisera, we don't try and take him for ourselves.'

'I think I am misunderstanding you. I don't... I haven't...'

'There's no need to be so coy, my lord.' I leaned forward and lowered my voice. 'Vanaria has talked about you so often over the past few days. We all know she's got her sights set on you.'

His eyes flicked back towards the centre of the hall, his eyebrows climbing even higher. 'She has?'

'Oh, yes. Ever since you helped her from her tumble, she's been fixated on having you for herself. You were just so caring, checking on her so often to make sure she was alright. I think you quite won her over.'

A puzzled look stole over his face and a frown doused the light of hope that had sparked in his eyes. 'Are you sure? She seems occupied with someone else most of the time.'

'Oh, she's just toying with you,' I said, waving him off. 'She knows how fond of hunting you are. She's waiting for you to give chase.'

The reference to hunting seemed to bolster him and he puffed out his chest. 'If she wants to play at hunting, I'll show her a thing of two. I always catch my prize.'

'I only hope you haven't kept her waiting too long. She might think you've lost interest, the poor thing.'

'You're right. No time to waste.' He rose to his feet, then seemed to remember that he was supposed to be helping me. 'You're alright now?' he asked half-heartedly.

'*So* much better. Go and win your prize. I *adore* a good love story.'

He grinned and marched back into the fray, nodding to himself and looking every bit a puffed-up fool. I snorted as I watched him go, imagining Vanaria's face when he cornered her somewhere. All that rubbish about hunting ought to make him persistent enough to buy me some time without her lurking around.

As I was looking around for another tray of champagne, I caught sight of Senafae. She was standing between two mirrors, intently engaged in conversation with a blond man in a beaked mask and dark blue cloak. He had a hold of her hand and was playing with her bracelet. I started to move towards her, but as I drew closer her companion laughed and I realised she was with the Oceatold prince. Well, good for her then. I wouldn't interrupt her. Faucher surely had to have his paws on Vanaria by now in any case, so I had no time to waste.

The noise in the hall crowded my ears after the relative quiet of the alcove, but I plunged into the din of voices and music with a confidence renewed by the warm kiss of the champagne. Darting through the crowd, I made my way back through the encircling walls of mirrors to where I'd last seen the king, but he wasn't there any longer. Cursing under my breath, I looked around the hall, over the couples twirling their way around the floor and the hopefuls clustered around the edges, whispering of scandals and eying potential partners. The mirrors reflected the room back from dozens of different angles, duplicating each guest a hundred times over into the infinite distance. Marvels and monsters, indeed.

I'd never find him in here.

Chewing on my lip as my gaze roamed the galleries and across the fresco above, where the fall of Aether was rendered in a stunning display of colour, I considered where a king would spend a ball. If not dancing, then where? What did I know of kings and how they spent their time?

I wandered aimlessly for a few songs and was rewarded by a glimpse of Vanaria standing with her back against a wall, her eyes darting about as Lord Faucher spoke to her with obvious passion, gesturing wildly with his hands and leaning close to her. Hopefully he was as dogged and oblivious as I suspected him to be and would keep her cornered for a while yet.

As I watched them, I caught a whiff of something that incited a hollow protest in my stomach, which sparked an idea. I'd wait in the dinner room. Even kings had to eat.

I jolted in shock as a hand clasped around my upper arm.

'I've finally found you, pet,' a voice rasped into my ear. 'Whose idea was it to dress you all the same?'

The shock held me frozen, but only for a moment, and as I realised who the voice belonged to, I jerked away from him. 'Please don't sneak up on me, Grand Weaver,' I said as I scowled at my arm. The paint was smeared slightly where his fingers had been.

'I want you to play me a song. Somewhere private.'

'I'm not available for private performances at the moment.' My irritation slipped the bonds of my control and leaked into my voice. I'd fended him off at every event I'd attended, and I was getting tired of his persistence.

'You'd do well to treat me with a little more care, you know. I'm one of the most powerful men in the kingdom. There is much I could do for you.' His words ran into each other on the way out of his mouth, and I realised he'd been drinking. It made me wary. After all, I knew better than most how volatile an intoxicated man could be. Was he the type to weep into his cup, or the type to want to watch others do the weeping?

As much as it irked me to waste any time, I forced a smile and touched his arm. 'Of course, Grand Weaver. You honour me with your attention. But I must remain in the hall until midnight,' I said, improvising. 'Perhaps I can find you afterwards?'

He wound a hand around my waist and pulled me against him. 'Or I'll come find you.'

'If you'd prefer,' I said as I peeled myself away from him. 'How about you have a seat and I'll go and fetch you a plate of supper?'

The suggestion seemed to soothe him, and he released his hold on me.

'I'll be right back. Just wait here,' I said, for a moment not caring how furious he'd be when I never returned. Fortunately, I was heading for the dinner room in any case, so he wouldn't realise I'd given him the slip for at least a little while.

Following the smell of food and the streams of guests, I found my destination quickly. Long tables groaning with the weight of the feast that had been laid out lined the walls. Whole suckling pigs rested beside stuffed geese with skin crispy and speckled with spices. Cheeses and fruits were displayed on towers surrounded by jellies, trifles, and knotted pastries dusted with powdered sugar. I'd never seen so much food in my life. Footmen hurried around the room, serving plates and drinks, and replenishing the tables, darting through the press of bodies. This was a popular room. As I watched, a woman threw back her head in a laugh and stumbled back a step, sending a footman swerving around and over her in an impressive display of agility.

It was as I was watching this feat of dexterity that my attention was caught by the sight of Vanaria crossing the room, and I cursed. Faucher, the tepid chump, how had his confidence burned out so quickly? She must have skewered him to escape. And there was the king, standing in a knot of activity, and she was making a beeline straight for him. I huffed an angry breath and looked around. Mr Guilcher, the butler, lurked at the edge of the room, overseeing the staff with his hawk-eyed sneer, and I had an idea. I sidled up to him.

'What a sensational party, Mr Guilcher. You've truly outdone yourself,' I said.

He didn't take his eyes off a gravy boat making its way across the room in the hands of a nervous young man as he grunted in reply.

'I do wonder at Vanaria Rosach being here tonight, though,' I continued. 'She seemed so ill this morning.'

His eyes widened and his gaze flashed to my face. 'Ill?'

'Oh, she wouldn't want anyone worrying about her. She's a professional, after all. I'm sure she'll make it through the night on her feet, but it looked a mighty painful rash.'

'What rash? I see no rash.' He looked over at Vanaria now, his brow pinched.

'You wouldn't. It was only on her back. I saw it coming out of the baths. A cluster of tiny little spots, about this big.' I held up my thumb and forefinger to indicate the size, and the colour drained from his face. He pushed past me and stumbled towards Vanaria, his movements erratic. Within a few moments, he had accosted her and hurried her towards the exit despite her obvious protests. As they reached the door, she caught sight of me.

I raised my hand and waved.

The look she gave me should have set me alight, but a few moments later she was out of sight. I allowed myself a snort of amusement before I straightened up and licked my lips, drawing on that slightly boozy confidence still humming at the edges of my perception. I didn't even bother looking at my reflection in a window or a platter; of all the things I had to be worried about, beauty wasn't one of them while the glamour still heated my skin.

The throng around the king eddied and flowed as those seeking his attention won a position by his side, and were quickly displaced by others. I felt a little sorry for him for a moment. He looked tired, his eyes glazed and turned towards the wall. Even at a ball, he was managing petitioners. And I saw exactly what Vanaria had been able to exploit—even in this, the most salacious of affairs, he wasn't allowed to simply enjoy himself. When she'd danced for him, she'd been offering him an escape that he felt he couldn't take.

I had to be more compelling.

I swiped two glasses from a footman, because temptation should come bearing alcohol, and slipped around a red-faced man who spoke with such conviction that spittle periodically sprayed everyone around him. I took a deep breath and leaned close to His Majesty's ear.

'I thought the Armistice Ball was supposed to be fun?'

He turned his face towards me slightly.

'Has it not met your expectations?'

'Oh, I'm having a marvellous time. But it doesn't look like you are.'

He turned far enough around to look me full in the face, and I watched as he took me in before I backed away with a smile. He spoke a few words to the spittle man before clapping him on the shoulder and excusing himself.

He came towards me with all the confidence and rippling expectation of a man used to his every need being met, and I felt a sudden pang of insecurity. Even with my glamour, what could I say and do that would captivate a king? How would I ever convince him to *marry* me?

But I quickly numbed that pang with the thought of the apple in my drawer. I didn't need him to fall in love with me tonight—I just needed him to want to spend enough time with me that I'd have a chance to feed it to him. Surely, I was a skilled enough maisera that I could manage that.

'Does your idea of fun involve pocketing cutlery?' he asked, then he smirked, as though he was quite pleased with his own wit.

I touched a hand to my chest. 'Your Majesty, how could you suggest such a thing? I couldn't possibly fit any more forks in my trunk.'

Disapproval flashed across his face. He smothered it quickly enough with a genial smile, but I was well-versed in reading what people wanted. Perhaps he preferred when his women simply laughed at his wit instead of matching it.

I changed tact. 'I hear there are some wonders to see in the gardens, but I find I'm a little too nervous to go out there alone.' Widening my eyes, I lowered my voice. 'I hear there are *fall spawn* on display.'

His smile broadened and he offered me his arm. 'There is nothing to be afraid of. The creatures on display are well contained. But I can walk with you if you'd wish.'

'Would you? I'd be so grateful. Thank you.' I placed my hand on his arm and he began to lead me back into the Grand Hall and out through the closest doors. As we went, I caught sight of Senafae standing by a pillar, scanning the room as though she was looking for someone. Her eyes fell on the king first and she looked as though she might begin towards him, then she caught sight of me. An odd expression crossed her face. I smiled at her, and she frowned.

I thought on it as we passed into the gardens. Was she jealous?

'It's impressive, isn't it?'

'Oh yes, *so* impressive,' I murmured as I scrambled to abandon my thoughts and figure out what the king was talking about. The gardens were alive with the yellow flickers of torches interwoven with a steady, cold glow.

'The guild has been weaving it for months.'

I craned my neck. Glisoch orbs were hung from a net that stretched high above our heads, pulsing faintly with light. 'What is it?'

'It's keeping out the cold. The committee were set on making use of the gardens for the ball.'

And there again, just as I'd felt when I'd first seen the glisoch in a hallway, was a cold stab of fury that seemed wielded with the memory of cold fireplaces, gnawing hunger, a hollow-eyed girl pressed by a thrusting man against the wall of an alley for a crust of bread.

'Incredible,' I murmured, numbing the fury with reason. It was none of my business how much money the king wanted to spend on a ball. If he wanted a net of gold woven with enchantment and strung across the sky, he could very well do as he pleased. The last thing I wanted him to suspect when he looked at me was the street creature I'd been. Poverty is hardly a titillating subject.

'I'll show you some of the monsters on display,' he said as he led me deeper into the gardens, a labyrinth of hedges and maples and stone walls wreathed in moon lilies that hung their heavy perfume on the unnaturally humid air. Every shadow hinted at figures of courtiers, hiding away from prying eyes while they indulged in the debauchery the king had promised them. Their whispers and giggles twined with the rustling of leaves and the thud of footsteps as we moved towards a huge marble fountain surrounded by weeping willow trees.

A crowd was clustered around the fountain, murmuring and pointing at something behind the slim gold bars that encased the whole thing, making it look like a giant bird cage.

'Quite something, isn't he? I've always admired the Morwar Toth, even though they cause so much damage to the coastal settlements.'

As we drew closer, I saw what he was referring to. A figure sat bowed over in the fountain. He was bare-chested, his rippling torso decorated with whirls of ink that spread to entwine his biceps and down his arms, but what drew my attention even more than the tattoos was the bottle-green fins that flared from his forearms and from either side of his spine. His chest heaved, as though breathing was an effort, and I picked out the flicker of gills on his neck.

'He was captured during a raid half a moon ago. All that, the gills, the fins, isn't even visible when they're not in contact with salt water,' the king continued, turning his eyes on me. I quickly plastered a smile onto my face.

'What a marvel. What will happen to him after the ball?'

'Now, why ask such a question, my sweet? You don't need to think about such brutal things. How about you go and take a closer look. You're unlikely to see another, unless one is charging in, ready to skewer you on one of their tridents.' He laughed and nudged me closer. 'Nothing to be afraid of. He's well contained.'

The idea of drawing closer to the heaving creature made me queasy, especially as I watched a young man scoop a pebble from the ground and lob it through the bars, where it bounced off the Morwar Toth's shoulders and he flinched away.

'Come on, fish breath. Do something entertaining,' the young man called as he bent for another stone.

'Would you care for a drink, Your Majesty?' I fixed my gaze determinedly on a small table manned by a page boy.

'Yes. Why not?' the king replied, and I headed for the table with relief.

'Mulled wine, ma'am?' the boy offered.

'Two please. Big ones,' I replied, and he scooped his ladle into a great silver urn.

As I waited for him to pour the wine into the cups, I was violently shoved and Vanaria bore down on me, all teeth and fury.

'What in the *fall* is wrong with you?' she hissed, her fingers gripping tight enough to bruise. '*Why* would you tell Guilcher that I had the pox?'

I wrenched away from her, straightening the creases in my sleeves. 'I have no idea what you're talking about.'

'You're a snake,' she spat, her eyes twin pools of pit fire. 'I know what you're after. You think you can tear me down so easily? I've worked *years* to get to where I am. Do you *really* think that you have what it takes to be the king's mistress just because you're beautiful? And do you really think I'd *let* you?'

'I don't think you have much control over that,' I said carelessly.

Her answering smile was humourless. 'Maybe I have more control than you think. Tell me, was the Winking Nymph sad to lose you?'

The smile slid from my face. My heart began to beat faster. She must have seen my reaction because her expression grew gleeful.

'I find it *so* interesting that some rundown suvoir in the Trough wouldn't make more of a fuss over having someone so beautiful working there. And why would someone so beautiful choose to work there when you'd make much better money elsewhere?' She tapped her finger against her chin. 'Something about it all doesn't make sense. Perhaps you'd like to shed some light for me?'

'My past is none of your concern.'

'And then there were the whispers of some terrible *accident*.'

I don't know what made me angrier: The fact that she was poking around into my history, or that what had happened to me was thought of by anyone as an *accident*. 'Stay out of my business,' I hissed.

She shot a glance over at the king, who was now in conversation with someone else. 'Your business is everyone's business if you want to be around His Majesty. What will I find if I keep digging? Because I know there is something not right about you.'

'Lucky for me, what you think of me doesn't really matter.'

'Maybe. Perhaps we should leave that for His Majesty to decide.'

'Stop this, Vanaria. It's pitiful.' Tilting my chin, I brushed past her.

A gush of warmth spilled over my back, and the shock of it seized my body, hunching my shoulders over as red rivulets poured down the white of my dress and made tracks through the paint on my arms.

The page boy watched me in open-mouthed horror. Vanaria stood with an empty cup dangling from her hand.

'Whoops,' she said, touching her fingers to her lips. 'I'm so clumsy.'

I wanted to scream. I wanted to claw her eyes out with my fingernails. I wanted to wrap my hands around her slender neck and squeeze until her tongue lolled from her mouth. But I stood frozen as tittering laugher broke out from a nearby cluster of courtiers. I was almost glad of the white paint. At least it would hide the humiliation heating my cheeks.

Without another word, I strode away from her. If I spent another moment with her within arm's reach, I'd do something I wouldn't want all these witnesses to see.

'Your Majesty,' I said when I reached the king, prompting him to turn away from the man he had been speaking with.

His eyebrows hiked up his forehead when he caught sight of me. 'What happened to you?'

I didn't trust myself to answer the question. Everything was ruined, there was no way I could beguile him while covered in mulled wine, and I just wanted to scrub the itchy paint from my skin and go to bed. 'By your leave, I'll retire from the ball.'

He looked on the verge of laughing and the humiliation began to burn at my eyes as I blinked away tears. I bobbed an angry curtsey, but he stopped me on the verge of walking away.

'I don't mean to offend you. Go and clean yourself up, but I'd be pleased if you'd wait for me in my suite afterwards. I'll send word for you to be let in.' He smiled conspiratorially. 'After all, you still owe me a game.'

I readily agreed, and the triumph was sweet enough that I completely ignored the gasps and laughter that followed me as I left the ball.

I was waiting when His Majesty returned to his rooms, the wine and the paint gone from my body. My hair was soft and perfumed, my skin pink, my glamour reapplied for another day, and I was dressed in something loose and easy to remove, with Draven's apple tucked securely away in a pouch sewn into the lining of the skirt.

'Why are you sitting so far away from the fire, sweet one? The maids would have stoked it for you if you'd asked,' he said as he shut the door behind him.

'I'm not cold,' I lied, shooting a glance at the glowing coals across the room. Enduring the sight of flames while I was already so nervous was not something I wanted to test.

I must have appeared serene as he removed his cloak and the circlet of gold on his head, but inside I was crawling with anxiety.

I shouldn't have worried, though. He took one look at me and swept me up into a hungry kiss. So much for our card game.

My nerves quickly faded away. Beneath his finery, his body was pale, his flesh moving towards softness, his stomach rounded, the skin around his torso beginning to loosen. He was still an imposing presence, but these imperfections, when paired with the urgent way he moved his hands over me, showed me that for all the pomp and bluster surrounding his position as ruler of the country, he was just a man. And I knew men.

I quickly sank into the routine I had perfected over my years as a maisera, a carefully choreographed succession of moans and sighs, of a hand here and a kiss there, of a swish of the hips and an entwining of legs. I took him in my mouth, because I knew how men liked such things, and while he gasped and panted, I wondered how the Winking Nymph's new girl, Aalin, was getting along. This part of the job was not something that came naturally to everyone, after all. It used to be something I dreaded, but since I had realised the power in making a grand man squirm and shudder to my bidding, I had found ways to enjoy myself. No matter how mighty the man, they were all as vulnerable to pleasure and teeth when they had their cock in your mouth.

When he finally crawled on top of me, he didn't last long enough for me to grow bored. After a few minutes of enthusiastic thrusting, followed by the spasmodic groan of release, he heaved himself off and settled onto his back with a contented sigh. I stroked the silver hair of his chest and tried to look satisfied.

'I'm famished,' I said, sitting up and eying a platter on a low side table. He couldn't sleep yet. Not until I had achieved what I came for. He made a low grunt. I climbed off the bed, deliberately rocking the mattress as I did, and thumped across the floor, casting a quick glance in his direction as I patted at my discarded petticoat. His eyes were already closed, the fragile skin of his eyelids slightly purple.

I cobbled together a plate of meats and cheeses from the platter, trying to pick the pieces that looked least appetising and dumping them together, so it looked more mess than smorgasbord, before placing the apple slightly off to the side, separate and perfect and gleaming, still as ripe and fresh as the day Draven had left it on the mantlepiece.

The king was snoring quietly when I plonked down next to him, jostling him enough that he woke with a start.

'Oh, I'm sorry,' I said, blinking at him in exaggerated surprise. 'Were you asleep?'

He rubbed a hand over his face, clearly ready to doze off again, but perked up when I held out a glass.

'Are you hungry?' I asked as he sat up and sipped at the wine.

'What a sweet thing you are,' he said, and I held out the plate, watching as his eyes immediately caught on the apple.

I plucked a piece of cheese and offered it to him, smiling wickedly. 'Sweet, perhaps, or selfish enough to know that replenishing your energy might prolong this night.'

He ate the cheese directly from my fingertips, grinning like he was my accomplice in a crime. 'I see you are a woman who knows what she wants, and how to ask for it.'

So predictably blinded by ego. I selected a slice of salted pork and popped it into his mouth.

'I find myself craving something sweeter,' he said. Before I could pick something else, his eyes slid back to the apple. Placing the plate on the bed, I picked up the apple and ran my hands over it, my mind darting back to the way Draven had spun it on his fingertips in the street, his movements deft and sure.

'Do you know of the apple trees in Myrshda?' I asked, pushing the memory away. 'I've heard tell there are groves of them north of the capital that bear fruit of burnished bronze, and that they gift waking dreams to any who eat them.'

'Waking dreams?' the king smiled indulgently. 'And where would you have heard such a tale? It's rare for anyone to cross the Shifting Planes.'

'Rare, but not impossible. I've also heard that lovers eat them together, to strengthen their love beyond the material realm. Isn't it romantic?'

His eyes were fixed on my hands. 'In the dealings I've had with Myrshda, I've never thought of them as a romantic people.'

I smacked him lightly. 'How you crush a girl, Your Majesty, with all your worldly knowledge. Leave your rationality in the throne room. Tonight, anything is possible, and every fanciful tale is true if we want it to be.' I held the apple up to his mouth, locking onto his gaze. 'Will you dream with me?'

When he bit into the fruit, his eyelids drooped in pleasure. I had thought that I would have to cajole him into finishing it, since

Draven hadn't mentioned exactly how much would need to be eaten for the enchantment to take hold, but I needn't have worried. After the first bite, a crazed hunger seemed to possess him, and he took the fruit from my hand to better be able to tear at it, quickly ripping the flesh apart and crushing it between his teeth, consuming the whole thing in a few bites, core and all.

Then, as he licked juice from his fingers, he looked at me and froze. His pupils dilated to swallow the blue of his irises, his jaw slackened, and he stared at me like he had suddenly realised I was a goddess. Reaching out, he touched his sticky fingers to my cheek, then cupped my face in both hands.

'I feel as though I've been aching for you all my life and I didn't even realise it.' His voice was hushed with wonder. I had known what the apple was supposed to do, but seeing the effect now was startling. He was looking at me with *hunger*. It was almost frightening.

He had me again, and again, and seemed still unsated.

The hunger remained.

CHAPTER NINE

I snuck from his bed when the dawn was still grey and slipped back to the servant's quarters. Perhaps it might have been a gamble to leave like that, but it's never a good idea to be too available. And I wanted a bath.

The early hour at least meant the shared bathroom was unoccupied, and I stayed in the water for a long time while I soaked away the night's activities. Had I really spent the night with the king? It seemed such a far-fetched idea. The memory of holding the apple to his lips was already taking on a hazy quality and I could almost have convinced myself that I'd dreamed the whole thing.

The day had well and truly set in by the time I entered the servant's dining room, and I found the other maisera already eating and Mrs Corkill milling about, chastising a girl for the state of her room. The sounds of the bustling kitchen filled the halls, and maids ran back and forth just beyond the door as they set about their morning tasks. They often looked in at us as they passed, slowing down just long enough for their gazes to rove over the gathered maisera, their expression reflecting whatever judgement they were casting, whether they thought us evil harlots or poor wretches suffering from unfortunate circumstances. One glare from Mrs Corkill sent them scurrying away to their chores.

Senafae was frowning at another letter when I entered the room, but she grabbed at my arm and pulled me into the seat beside her when she saw me. 'Where were you last night?' she asked, her voice tense.

I'd promised not to lie to her again. What harm would the truth do? 'I was with the king,' I admitted, and she gasped loud enough to draw the attention of everyone nearby, then clapped a hand over her mouth. Mrs Corkill sent a stern frown in our direction.

'Sorry,' she said, glancing to where Vanaria was watching us with her eyes narrowed.

'I don't care if she knows. It isn't a secret.'

She seemed to recover from her shock enough to stop gaping at me in a way that bordered on horrified. 'What was it like?'

I screwed up my nose. 'I know you want me to tell you it was the best night of my life and he's a lover like no other, but he was just another client.'

'Is he... physically gifted?'

I laughed. 'No more than average.'

'At least tell me his room was impressive.'

'Oh, you wouldn't *believe* how soft his sheets were. I've never felt silk so fine.'

She snorted and began fiddling with her plaited bracelet, fixing her gaze on it as she asked, 'Do you think he'll call for you again?'

'I'm counting on it.'

By the afternoon, news of how I'd spent my night had spread. Servants whispered behind their hands as I walked past, and I was treated to lingering examinations by anyone I encountered, as though the whole palace was sizing me up and picking out what had drawn His Majesty to me over any other. I relished the attention but didn't appreciate the murmured conjecture on whether the night was a once off, since that aligned too closely with my own supressed anxiety. I kept picturing the expression on his face after he'd eaten the apple to reassure myself. Surely, he would seek me out after looking at me like that?

But the day wore on with no word from the king. No secret letters were pressed into my hands by servants, no unexpected gifts were left for me, no clandestine meetings were arranged. With most of the guests in the palace still suffering for their indulgences the night before, there were no events to distract me from the insufferable tension of waiting.

By the time the evening rolled around, I was in a poor temper, and I ate my dinner in silence beside an equally silent Senafae. If that damn apple hadn't worked, where did that leave me? I'd given up my body for nothing, and when the treaty celebrations were over, I'd be back on the street where Draven had found me. A shadow of that yawning despair fell over me, the one that had darkened the days after the attack had disfigured my face, before Draven had found me and offered a different path. I would *never* be that hopeless again. Never.

I thought that perhaps I could convince Draven to let me keep the glamour. It was only right, given that I had done exactly as we'd agreed, and it was his magic that had failed, but I didn't imagine he was the sort to do something just because it was right. He didn't seem inclined towards either honour or sympathy, and I doubted I could seduce him into compliance.

I left Senafae lingering over her plate, picking apathetically at her food, when I was ready to retire for the night. My mood wasn't improved when I found Vanaria skulking by the door to my room.

'Do you have anything *special* planned tonight, Rhiandra?' she called as I approached.

'A good night's sleep is always special,' I replied.

A cunning smile curled at her mouth. 'So, no *friends* to see? Just off to bed?'

I paused with my hand resting on the doorknob. 'Aether's teeth, Vanaria. First you poke around my life outside the palace, now you want to know about my night-time habits. Do you think I'm a spy?'

'I just know how disappointing it is when *friends* spend one night with you and never want to see you again.' She tilted her head, pursing her lips in an expression of exaggerated contemplation. 'Actually, I don't know. No one ever spends a night with me without clamouring to see me again.'

'Goodnight, Vanaria,' I called, rolling my eyes as I entered the cold, empty room.

'Oh, I'm sure it will be,' she called after me as I closed the door.

Someone was sitting at the foot of my bed, staring at me.

'Who are you?' I asked.

The figure leaned forward and I caught a flash of blond hair as he passed through a shaft of moonlight.

'What a pretty face,' he sneered, reaching his dirty hands out. I wanted to leap out of bed and run, but I couldn't move. He grabbed a hold of my leg through the blanket and dug his fingers in hard.

'Let go!' I screamed, but he only laughed as the blanket burst into flames. My right calf seared with pain as the flames rose and the smell of singed hair filled the air.

'Rhiandra, you're dreaming.'

I opened my eyes to Senafae peering down at me. I sat bolt upright, gasping for breath, my eyes darting about the room. No flames, no blond-haired man, but I still felt the fire and I batted at my blanket in a panic, trying to extinguish an invisible blaze as agony seared up my calf and spread through my thigh.

'My leg!' I shrieked, and Senafae took a handful of my blanket and ripped it off me as she jumped back. I kicked out and leapt from the bed, cringing away from the creature now menacing us with two wicked-looking pincers.

It was long, with a segmented body that was almost translucent and tapered into a stinger at one end. I could see its guts through its exoskeleton, pink and blue and pulsing. Several bulging black eyes swivelled to fix on us as it opened its maw to reveal rows of tiny, pointed teeth.

Hissing and clicking, it arched its body, coiling up before launching itself almost off the bed in a single jump. We screamed and ran for the door, reaching it just as Mrs Corkill appeared, her hair dishevelled beneath her night cap.

'By the fall, what's going on?'

Her eyes caught on the creature, and she stumbled back, clutching her chest. I tried to speak, but my mouth wouldn't respond and all I could get out was a groan. She slipped in and out of focus, jumping around in my vision until she seemed to be dividing into two Mrs Corkills, then morphing back into one. I felt hands around my arms, and I thought for a second that I was being pulled to the ground, but it was gravity overcoming me as my own legs gave way. I was lowered down as a wave of nausea washed over me, nudging up my throat. Senafae bobbed down before me, shaking me gently as she blurred almost beyond recognition. The pain in my leg flared brighter and my vision darkened.

A collection of impressions eased in and out of my focus. Echoing footsteps on stone. My body being shifted and laid out straight as I tossed and struggled against the pain. A torrent of words babbled in Senafae's voice, high-pitched and urgent. The acidic burn of bile in my throat as I choked on my own vomit. A rush of activity around me, people moving and touching me and talking to each other in voices that whipped and snapped past my ears. King Linus's grim face floating above me, clear for only a moment before my vision blurred, my eyelids crashed down, and my consciousness darted away like a frightened sparrow.

My awareness crept back to a sense of stillness, to a quiet room and a body that was curiously numb and heavy. Cool hands brushed over my face, down my body, and then there was a prickling sensation throughout my leg. The pain reignited with a vengeance, and I screamed. The pain crushed me beneath a leaden oblivion, and I slipped away with the bitter scent of gunpowder in my lungs.

I was woken by pale sunlight and the smell of bread. My eyes felt dry and gritty when I pushed them open and my head pounded like I'd been dwelling at the bottom of a bottle, but when I stretched my limbs the pain in my leg was gone.

'Oh! You're awake!'

I swivelled my gaze in the direction of the voice.

'Everyone will be thrilled!' The voice was soft, feminine, putting me in mind of the cooing of a dove. It was matched with a pair of huge eyes the colour of rich soil. A woman. A girl, really, with the softness of youth still rounding her face and an innocence about her that was so strong it practically emitted a scent. I knew who she was immediately, though I would never have expected to meet her in such a way, with me lying in a bed in what looked like an infirmary. But surely the pitch-black hair, lily-pale skin, and exquisite beauty could belong to no one else.

'How are you feeling?' she asked as she moved closer to my bed with her small hands clenched before her.

'Quite well... your Royal Highness?' I replied, my voice raised in question.

Her cheeks flushed a beguiling shade of pink and she glanced down. 'No one calls me that in here,' she said quietly. 'You can call me Gwin. Or Snow, I suppose. That's what my father calls me... I mean, only if you'd like... I think my father would like it if you did. He must think very much of you. I've never seen him visit the infirmary before, and I'm in here all the time...'

Her brow puckered and she touched her fingers to her lips. 'Oh, that must sound very ungrateful of me. I'm never very ill when I'm here, I'm sure he would visit me if I was... And everyone was so sure you were going to die. Even the Grand Weaver said the nagwis venom was going to kill you.' She chewed her lip as she watched me with those big eyes, and there was something in her face that reminded me of the stray dogs I'd seen roaming the streets of the city, of the hunger in their eyes. But this was *the* Snow White, Princess Gwinellyn, living in a palace surrounded by a team of servants who catered to her every whim. What did she have to hunger for?

Then my groggy mind finished digesting her words and I forgot her hungry eyes.

'A nagwis?' I repeated incredulously. 'That's what was in my bed?'

'A hall boy managed to catch it. I'm so glad he did. I don't think I could sleep knowing it was wandering around.'

I slowly pushed myself into a sitting position, and a crawling feeling crept down the back of my neck as I remembered the creature launching itself across the mattress, waving its pincers in the air, its dozens of legs rippling. I had never seen one, but I'd heard of the aggressive insects that swarmed travellers who dared to brave the Shifting Plains to the north-east of Brimordia's border, land so treacherous that the kingdom beyond was all but isolated, both protected from the expansionist efforts of its neighbours and cut off from all trade. What one of those hellish creatures was doing this far south, and in my bed no less, was beyond me.

'Rhi! You're awake!' I turned just as Senafae barrelled into the room in a burst of frantic energy. 'You almost died!'

'So I've heard.' I glanced back to where Princess Gwinellyn had been standing only to find her gone.

Senafae followed my eyes. 'Oh yes, I saw her talking to you. I'm surprised she was. Funny little thing.' She lowered her voice. 'One of the nurses told me she's mad. Has fits where she falls to the floor, frothing at the mouth. She was milling around a bit last night, but she always seems to duck out of sight. I think she has a private room to hide away in.' Senafae sat in a chair by my bedside and lifted the cover from a tray that rested on the side table, revealing a meal of soup and soft white bread. 'Lucky she's the heir to the throne,' she continued, inhaling appreciatively, 'or she'd be locked in a temple somewhere. Are you going to eat this?'

'Indeed, she is,' a new voice snapped, and Mrs Corkill entered the room, straight-backed and severe as ever. Senafae dropped the tray cover and snatched her hands into her lap. Mrs Corkill harrumphed before casting an eye over me.

'Since you are decidedly alive, you'd best eat. And thank Taveum for whatever whim led him to let you from his grip. I was certain the sand in your glass had emptied.' She took up the tray and placed it on my lap before thrusting a spoon at me. Beneath her bullying stare, I swallowed a spoonful of soup, though my stomach lurched queasily. She gave a curt nod.

'I suspect the creature that stung you entered the palace with some of the entertainers who were staying for the Armistice Ball. Have you been keeping... intimate company with any of them?' Her mouth shrivelled like she had sucked on something sour.

I glanced around to make sure no one else was close enough to hear what she'd said. This was how rumours started. 'No, I have not,' I snipped, scowling at her.

She sniffed. 'Good. I suggest you use your recovery time to thank the gods for your life. I'll inform the physicians that you're awake. You've had half the palace hovering over you, though why so many would take such interest in a maisera is beyond me to understand, nagwis or no.' Pursing her lips, she shot a final glare at Senafae and marched away.

Senafae watched the housekeeper leave with an expression curling with dislike, before leaning towards me. 'It's true. Even the *king* was here.' Her tone was intense. 'When you started vomiting blood and his physicians told him you weren't going to live, he sent for the Grand Weaver himself.' She sat back in her chair and folded her arms. 'What exactly happened between you that he would come racing to your sick bed?'

'He must think I'm a good knock,' I said blithely, and her brows pinched in a frown. My blasé attitude was just a front; a shudder of unease was rolling through my bones. The king taking such an interest was welcome news, but I didn't like her description of the state I'd been in. I mentally checked over my body again, probing for any lingering signs that I might still be in danger, but my headache was fading already. I felt strangely well for someone who had been through what she had described. 'Dovegni did something to me then?'

'He flapped about for a while, then said he could do no more. Actually, it was the strangest thing. He arrived in all his glory, billowing robes and all that business, and sent everyone out of the room to work his great and mysterious magic.' She widened her eyes and waggled her fingers in the air. 'Then he came out and explained to the king in minute detail what he'd tried to do and why you couldn't be saved, but by the time we returned to your bedside you'd stopped thrashing around and gasping like you couldn't breathe and were fast asleep. I don't know if he told us he couldn't cure you because he has a penchant for drama, but it made for quite the moment.'

I took another spoonful of soup and was relieved to find that my stomach seemed to have settled. In fact, it had roared to life and demanded to be filled. 'I'm not thrilled to owe my life to Dovegni,' I muttered between mouthfuls.

Senafae watched me take a few bites. 'People don't usually die from just one sting, you know. City folk don't understand that. It'd make you monstrously ill, yes, but it usually takes a swarm of them to kill a fully-grown adult. You had a reaction to the venom.'

'If you say so.' I poked at something grey and unrecognisable in my soup, wondering if I could go and eat my evening meal with the other maisera. 'All I care about now is that I'm indebted to the slimiest creature at court, and I'm sure he won't let me forget it.'

'You should be worried about how hard it has been on your body. You might want to think about going home.'

I froze with a dripping piece of bread suspended above my bowl. 'What?'

She rose from the chair. 'Just think about it. Would you like me to bring you anything?'

I shook my head, and she leaned in and gave me a kiss on the cheek before taking her leave. I couldn't believe she would suggest that I needed to leave the palace because of some bug bite. It was absurd. And I felt *fine*.

But it did leave me wondering. How *had* the creature wound up in my bed?

Despite my insistence that my health was perfect, I remained in the infirmary under observation, as though everyone was waiting for the miracle that was my survival to be revealed as a trick. I would have liked to enjoy my time being waited on and cared for, especially when King Linus visited with his entourage and bid

I ask for anything my heart desired. I asked for a specific pastry from Mrs Mylner's Patisserie on Peak Street and when the king commanded his valet go and fetch me what I asked for, the valet's skin turned a delightful shade of puce. But as the day wore on, I was painfully aware of the time ticking away until my glamour would need refreshing. I would need to sneak back to my room in the evening.

Aside from Princess Gwinellyn, who occupied a private room just off the main infirmary, there were two other patients sharing the space with me: an older woman whose dreadful cough rattled the air throughout the day, and a woman a little younger than me who sported a broken nose and two black eyes, apparently from falling down a flight of stairs. There seemed to be a trio of nurses who rotated through caring for us, and of those three, one was lovely, one spoke overly loud and slow, like we were simpletons, and one was prime evil.

It was the lovely one who served the evening meal, and she offered me a warm smile as she placed a tray across my knees.

I screwed up my nose at the watery soup. 'I see my teeth are not to be trusted.'

'You were vomiting blood several hours ago. It's your stomach I'm worried about, not your teeth.' She tucked a small, white box onto the side table, which drew my interest immediately. 'Finish your soup first, or I'll not let him send you any more little boxes,' she said when she caught me looking.

After she had served the other patients—beef stew for them, from the smell of it—she left us to eat, returning sometime later to collect the trays and bid us all goodnight. I felt a sense of relief as she dimmed the lanterns, knowing that now I could sneak away to my room. Senafae would be startled to see me, but I would tell her I'd come to retrieve some face cream.

I listened to the sounds of the other two patients shifting in their beds, and when the sound of deep, even breaths replaced the rustle of sheets, I pushed myself up and readied to leave.

A shifting shadow caught my eye, and I froze. Someone was coming through the door, someone stealthy, almost completely silent. My breath caught. Where had the nagwis come from? Surely, it hadn't wandered all the way from the Shifting Plains into my bed by its own volition. Had someone slipped it into my bed? Had they thought it would kill me? Would they want to finish what the creature's venom had failed to do?

Had they come to find me now?

The shadow moved across the long room, passing the beds of the other sleeping woman. I lay still as I frantically ran through all the items available within an arm's reach, settling on the water jug on the side table. I inched my hand towards it as the figure stepped through a shaft of moonlight and a shock of recognition jolted me.

'For the love of Madeia,' I blurted through the erratic thumping of my heart, 'as if I didn't come close enough to death today without you scaring me halfway back there. What are you *doing* here?'

'If that is how you thank me for saving your life, I might hesitate next time.' Draven finished crossing the room in moments with his long-legged stride and leaned over the bed to peer at me. The night rendered his face strange, all sharp angles and unflinching gaze, and I shrank away from the unexpected closeness, suddenly wondering at the state of my appearance.

'The Grand Weaver saved me,' I said, smoothing at my hair.

'That leech couldn't heal a papercut. You look well enough for someone who should be dead. Though you seem to be playing a risky game with your glamour.' He straightened up, and I released a pent-up breath before glancing around the room.

'I still have an hour. I was about to sneak down to my room right before you showed up. You'd better not wake the other patients.'

'They won't wake.' He spoke with utter assurance, which irritated me, but I refused to ask him how he could be so sure.

'If you've come to check whether I've delivered on my promise, I have.' If my tone was a little smug, I couldn't help myself. 'The king is besotted with me. Look.' I reached for the cream-coloured box on my bedside, grateful to have something to focus on other than Draven's looming presence over my bed.

Draven watched closely as I set the box on my lap and opened the lid. 'What is that?'

I picked up the knotted pastry and admired the glossy glaze, the scent of rose. 'King Linus sent for it especially for me. He said I could have anything my heart desired and sent someone all the way to Peak Street to get these.' I bit into the flaky pastry, moaning as the pomegranate jam hit my taste buds. I had salivated over the pastries in the window at Mrs Mylner's Patisserie many times, but could rarely justify the exorbitant expense, nor the censure of the lords and ladies who were the regular clientele.

'That does not look like food fit for recovery.'

'Well, at least he thought to get me something.' I smiled sweetly as I licked syrup from my hands.

He pinched a flake of pastry between his fingers and held it up to his face. 'Butter and sugar,' he scoffed. 'I thought your life was gift enough. Forgive me for not plying you with sweets.'

'I don't see how *you* had anything to do with keeping me alive.'

His eyes hunted mine, capturing me, holding me in place. 'Don't you?'

A memory shivered over me, of cool fingers on my skin, and realisation lifted my brows. 'You were here last night? Why?'

'You were dying. I could feel it. So, I came.' He didn't seem as though he would deign to give more explanation than that, but when I just stared at him blankly, he continued. 'Our deal. If you die, there is no chance of it being fulfilled.'

I frowned. 'Our deal let you know I was dying?'

He flicked a finger beneath my chin and smiled. 'You charming little thing. You really don't know anything, do you?'

'Have you just come to mock me, or do you have some other reason for visiting?'

'What's wrong, Rhiandra? Aren't you pleased to see me?' He rolled my name around his mouth, pronouncing it slowly, like he was caressing each syllable, as he spied the chair Senafae had occupied earlier and pulled it close to the side of my bed. As he leaned forward to sit, my gaze followed the shadow of stubble along his jaw, ran down his neck, and caught on the hollow between his collar bones.

'No,' I said, but the word came out with the husky need of a fervent *yes*.

A smile flickered at the edge of his lips. 'You should be. It seems that you're not managing well on your own. Tell me how a nagwis found its way into your bed.'

'What, you mean you haven't asked the beast already? I thought it might be a relative of yours.'

'I hope you don't expect to charm the king with that mouth.' He leaned back in the chair, appearing utterly at ease. 'I'm here to help. We both want the same thing, after all. And there is clearly someone around who has an opposing interest.'

'I don't need your help.'

'Don't be a fool. You almost died.'

I wanted to deny it, but my body still remembered the raging fever, the taste of blood and bile in my mouth, and the screaming pain that had eaten up my leg. Whatever Senafae had said about it taking several stings to kill someone, it certainly didn't look like that was the case for me. With a flash of realisation, I remembered Vanaria lurking by my door. 'There's another maisera who hates me,' I admitted slowly. 'She tried to have me thrown out of the palace by framing me for stealing.'

'What's her name?'

'Why do you need her name? What will you do?' He didn't answer, but as he held my gaze, I felt a grogginess creep into me, making my thoughts wandering and sloshy. He'd asked me something. What had he asked me? A name. I wasn't going to tell him. Aether's teeth, I wanted to run my fingers through his hair. But she deserved whatever happened to her. Whoever she was. Vera-something. Rosach? She'd put a crazy beetle in my bed. One with teeth. And venom. Not Vera, Vanaria. Vanaria Rosach.

I didn't realise I'd said the name aloud until he broke eye contact with me and the grogginess drained away, leaving me feeling a little woozy and nauseated. He rose to his feet and looked as though he was about to leave as my mind caught up.

'What the fuck was that?!' I demanded in a voice that sounded like it was being squeezed out of me. I swung my legs out of bed and stood shakily in the flimsy linen gown I'd been given by a nurse. He reached out to steady me and I smacked his hand away, squaring up to him. 'Did you use magic on me?' I was no longer worried about someone finding him here. The knowledge that he could do something like that, could toy with my head without so much as fluttering an eyelid, shook me to the core. 'How dare you, you... you brute! How dare you manipulate me and force me to speak against my will!'

He simply snorted, looking not the least bit intimidated. 'I don't have time to beg for your confidence. I needed a name, and I took it. Next time, be more forthcoming with your information and I won't have to do it again.'

'You had no right! Don't *ever* do that again, do you hear me? *Don't just stand there and smirk at me.*'

'Forgive me, anger is ravishing on you.'

Fury cracked through me. Before I could think better of it, I raised my arm and swung at him with an open hand, aiming for his cheek, but he caught my wrist mid-air. I tried to yank it away, but his grip was as hard and unforgiving as stone.

Rage rolled across his face. A cold rush of fear doused my anger as he yanked me against him, leaning down.

'You don't like my smirk? How about I treat you to my wrath in all its glory?' he growled.

'Let go of me,' I demanded as I squirmed in his grip. For a few dangerous moments I was aware of what I toyed with, of the strength of his body, of the strange energy that clung to him, making my hair stand on end like static. Then he released me, and I stumbled a few steps backwards.

'Learn to mind your wishes. You wanted me angry and then were unhappy when you got what you asked for,' he said, the picture of calm once again.

But he was wrong. Seeing the slip in his endlessly unruffled façade was thrilling. His temper was a damn sight better than his indifference, and the satisfaction of having provoked some sort of reaction quenched my anger and instead sparked a different kind of heat that burned like an ember low in my pelvis. I wanted to know if I could wring more of that fire from him. I composed myself, plucked a strand of my hair from his shirt, and patted him on the chest.

'Do that again, and our deal is off. You can take your damn glamour and I'll turn you in for unsanctioned magic use.' My voice was quiet, but for once he looked as though he was taking me seriously. As he should, because I meant it. Whatever he offered me, the beauty, the path to becoming queen, wasn't worth the sanctity of my own mind.

After a moment, his mouth twitched in the hint of a smile. 'Reasonable terms, I suppose. I'll not touch your mind again,' he said, inclining his head.

I relaxed a little and perched on the bed to look up at him from beneath my lashes. I was wearing a hideous gown and I was dishevelled from spending the day in bed, but surely, I had the skills to convince him to touch me and feed that delicious excitement that was thrumming through my veins. 'You should want to keep me on your side, given how quickly I delivered your apple for you. Are you going to give me the next one?'

'You're a long way from being ready for the next one. A box of pastries is not a marriage proposal.' He was looking towards the door instead of at me. So much for fire. Was he a eunuch? Were men more to his taste than women? He knew what I looked like beneath the glamour, but surely that memory wasn't strong enough to leech all the power from my beauty now.

He flicked his eyes back to me and if he'd noticed the look I was giving him, he didn't show it. 'You've got some work to do. Don't think the enchantment will do your job for you. Love is not enough to make you queen.'

I crossed my arms. 'It isn't as though I've been resting on my laurels. You could congratulate me on what I've already achieved instead of just telling me I have more to do.'

'You're fishing in the wrong place for compliments. Achieving what you promised is the least I expect of you. I'll congratulate you when you're queen.' He touched a hand briefly to my cheek. 'Your little rival won't bother you again. Now, go find your mirror.'

I wanted to say more. I cast around for something, anything, to throw at him, to keep him here a little longer even though all he did was rile me, but he didn't give me a chance to form more than half a syllable. In a few steps, he was a silhouette, a shadow darting across the room, and then he wasn't even that. I blew a lock of hair from my eyes. I felt jittery. I hated that he left me feeling like that. I hated that I couldn't quite pin down our relationship. I turned over the memory of his anger in my mind, feeling smug all over again when I thought of the way his expression had cracked. He may be all smooth lines and apparent indifference, but I had the sense of things beneath the surface that tantalised me. I would burrow beneath that exterior and see what I could find, see if there was anything there that I could leverage.

And when I did, he would regret taunting me.

CHAPTER
TEN

The following day, I was given permission from the head physician to leave the infirmary and return to my room. She had eyed me like she was waiting for me to collapse at any moment, but I was restless from two days of being confined to a bed and anxious to make sure no one had swept in and turned the king's attention, so I insisted.

A huge bouquet of red tulips had been delivered to me by a hall boy that morning. They didn't have a note attached, but I was sure the king had sent them. I was readying to take them back to my room with me when a short, dimpled housemaid with an impeccably styled updo bobbed before me.

'I'm perfectly capable of carrying a bunch of flowers. I don't need help to my room,' I said dismissively.

'You won't be returning to the room in the servant's quarters, miss. You're to follow me. A footman will pack your belongings for you.'

I wrapped my arms around myself as I tried to retain my composure as my heart sank. 'I don't want a footman touching my things. If I'm to be sent away, I'll pack my own belongings, thank you.' Vanaria must have done as she had threatened. How much did they suspect based on her information? Had they searched my room, found the mirror? Was I to be dragged to the dungeons to await trial? I wouldn't let it happen like that. I would find a way out of this. And I would make Vanaria pay.

The maid blinked rapidly, then bobbed down. 'As you please. If you'll follow me, I'll escort you to your new rooms.'

'My new rooms?'

'Yes, ma'am. The king has requested you be transferred from the servant's quarters at once.'

The relief that washed through me was bright and sweet and I just about floated after this wonderful, wonderful maid. *My new rooms.*

I followed her from the infirmary and into the labyrinth of halls that was the rest of the palace, trying to keep track of specific marble busts and tapestries and courtyards so I could find the way myself, but they quickly became tangled in my mind. She led me up several flights of stairs and down a narrow corridor on one of the upper levels of the palace, where she began to sort through her keys as we walked.

'Here we are,' she said finally as she stopped to open a door. She stood aside to allow me to enter, and I stared at the finery around me in delight. I was standing in a light, airy receiving room with a huge window overlooking a central courtyard. The furnishings were all in a pale green fabric patterned with foxes and phoenixes, trimmed with gold tassels and filigree. I breezed through the room, wandering through the connecting rooms with my mouth slightly open. There was a dining room, a wardrobe, a room housing an enormous tub and dressing table, a water closet, and a bedchamber dominated by a mahogany four-poster bed. Every room embraced the view of the courtyard with large windows welcoming in a flood of sunlight.

'Through here are the apartments of your personal maid,' the housemaid said, opening a door in a small antechamber leading from the bedchamber. She took a deep breath and seemed to steel herself. 'Ma'am, if I may be so bold as to ask, do you have your own maid?'

'You certainly are bold. What is your name?' I asked, contemplating her. She had so far been respectful, polite, and she didn't look as though she was setting out to disparage me with the question. If she was disturbed by my occupation, she wasn't making it obvious. Her eyes were bright and intelligent.

'Leela, ma'am. Leela Ogerton. And I would like to apply for the position.'

I laughed, charmed by her daring. 'Have you ever worked as a lady's maid, Leela?'

'No, ma'am. But I have been training in the arts of hair and beauty, and I am a skilled seamstress. And if you don't mind me saying so, ma'am,' she lowered her voice, and her expression took on an eagerness, 'I can help you. I could do much with that beauty. I could make you intimidating. You'll need that to survive the court.'

The servants in the employ of the aristocracy were expected to be demure, obedient, subservient. Leela's brazen words would be enough to deter any noble lady from employing her. But whatever my father's origins, I was no noble lady.

'Let's be frank then, Leela. I'm moving into this apartment at the king's request. Do you know why?'

She nodded solemnly.

'And you think you could work for such a mistress?' I watched her carefully.

She seemed to consider her words for a moment. 'A mistress who's found a way to climb to such standing would be one I'd be proud to serve, ma'am,' she said. 'I've a drive to make my way in the world. I think it not much different.'

Satisfied with the answer, I offered her a smile. 'Bring me your references and I'll see about giving you a trial.'

'Thank you, ma'am,' she said with a bob of a curtsey before leaving me to explore the rooms alone.

My own lady's maid. What a strange idea. But I was certain that these rooms would come with an allowance that would permit me to hire on staff, and my own maid would be vital as I began to establish myself at court. A grin began to bloom in my stomach and then to climb across my face. With a squeal of glee, I ran across the room and launched myself onto the bed. It caught me with arms of downy-soft coverings, and I stretched out, pleased to find that my fingers didn't reach the edge no matter how I arched my back.

I had done it. The king was mine.

Draven's words came unbidden to douse my joy. *Love won't make you queen.* I dismissed them. He wasn't going to ruin this moment for me, especially while he wasn't even in the room to frown at me. I'd climbed higher than I had ever expected I would, even before the attack.

Even just thinking the word *attack* brought a cluster of fractured memories charging into the room, and I sat up with a scowl. I wanted to celebrate, not to think about all things miserable. I'd swipe a bottle of something cheerful from somewhere and show my new rooms to Senafae.

'Quick, gather yourself and get ready to come with me. I have the most remarkable thing to show you.' I flew into the room, feeling as weightless and luminous as sunlight.

Senafae didn't turn to look at me as she sat on her bed, staring at the wall.

'You're going to shriek when you see what His Majesty has given me. It seems that almost dying has its advantages.' I yanked the trunk from beneath my bed, opened it and began sweeping my belongings into it with little care for arrangement. I pulled the drawers from the side table and upended them, sending debris clattering into the bottom of the trunk, before flinging open the doors on the wardrobe and wrapping my arms around several gowns, lifting them from the hanging rod and dumping them on the bed, where I easily slipped them over the top of the mirror as I pulled it out from its hiding place, and carried the whole lot into the trunk without Senafae seeing anything out of the ordinary. If the gowns were creased or damaged from my careless handling, it hardly mattered. I would have new clothes made by the finest dressmakers in the city. Clothes fit for the king's official mistress.

Clothes fit for a future queen.

My efforts at concealment seemed to have been pointless, however; Senafae hadn't reacted at all to my excited chatter, or even to my sudden decision to pack up my belongings. She sat exactly as I'd found her, staring at the wall as though she hadn't even noticed that I'd entered the room.

'I'm moving into my own suite, Sen. Here, in the palace.'

Still no response. I stood, dusted off my skirt and approached her. 'Senafae?' I touched her shoulder. 'Is something wrong?'

'I'm pregnant.' The words fell out of her mouth like stones, hard and cold and weighted, reverberating in the stillness as they clattered to the floor.

'Oh.' I sat heavily on her bed and stared at the curls of woodgrain in the floorboards as my excitement fled. 'To who?'

'Does it matter?' she snapped.

'That depends.'

'On how rich he is? Rich enough to insist on paying for me to see a surgeon.'

'You've told him?'

She was silent for so long a time that I thought she wouldn't answer. 'He knows.'

There was so much in those two words. I could hear the resignation, the disappointment. Whoever he was, what had she been expecting of him? Every suvoir had its legends of maisera being swept into marriage by a wealthy client, but they were legends for a reason. It rarely happened. She was a fool if she thought a child would make it any more likely.

A small voice in my head sniggered at the irony of *me* calling Senafae a fool for thinking she could convince a nobleman to marry her.

'Don't go to one of those butchers in the Trough,' I said, my stomach curling with the memory of a girl at the Winking Nymph who'd sought that solution. Madame Luzel had been unsympathetic when any of her girls found themselves 'in the family way'. Her policies were straight forward and indifferent: every maisera must manage their birth control. There was no place for babies in her establishment. I had been fifteen when I saw exactly what that looked like in practice. I had still been a maid at that point, cleaning the suvoir to earn my keep until I completed my training. I hadn't known the girl in person, only her laundry. She seemed to love all things shiny, even sequined her underclothes. Her sheets had been so bloody that I'd vomited when I pulled them out of the laundry bag. Madame had insisted I couldn't throw them away, that I had to remove the stains.

After that, there'd been no more spangled underclothes.

'Don't see that I have much of a choice.' She glanced at me, and her eyes were as hard as her voice.

I touched a hand to her shoulder again. 'Why don't you go to Baba Yaga?'

She jerked away from me with a cynical laugh. 'I'd have better luck in the Trough.'

'I know someone who's been to see her, Sen. She came back whole, unharmed. Which is more than I can say for those who've gone to a surgeon.'

Senafae stood abruptly. 'I don't need your fairy stories. I'll sort this out myself, thank you. Go back to your fancy new apartment and leave me alone.' Her tone was so bitter I could almost taste it.

'Why are you getting angry with me? I'm trying to help you.'

'By telling me to go into the Yawn? I don't need that kind of help.' She made for the door but paused on the threshold. 'I wish I'd never told you.'

'I'm not going to tell anyone else.'

'How would I know that? It's not like you've ever trusted me with your secrets. I know nothing about you. I certainly know nothing weighty enough to ensure your silence.'

'Senafae—'

'Enjoy your new life.' With that, she stormed out and slammed the door behind her.

I continued to sit on her bed, dumbstruck. Her anger had been so strange, so out of nowhere. There seemed to be so much resentment in it. Though why she resented me, I couldn't fathom. I wasn't the one who'd landed her in such a mess. And how had she wound up pregnant in the first place? The tonics we took were almost failsafe. Had she forgotten a dose?

With a sigh, I stood up and returned to my packing with less gusto than before. When a footman arrived to lug my trunk up to my new apartment, I was ready and waiting. I took one last look at the tiny room, the two single beds, the rickety wardrobe still hanging with Senafae's clothes, and felt a strange, sinking feeling, like I was losing something I hadn't realised I'd wanted to keep. I shook the feeling off and followed the footman through the servant's quarters, pausing at the dining room where the other maisera were gathered for lunch. I scanned them, attracting a few glances as I did, but Senafae wasn't there. It wasn't until I'd moved on that I realised Vanaria wasn't either.

And it wasn't until the footman was heaving my trunk through the doorway of my new rooms that I began to wonder at Senafae's timeline. We had been in the palace for less than a month.

When had Senafae fallen pregnant?

And how long had she known?

CHAPTER ELEVEN

There was a door in the suite that was locked. I had rattled the latch, stuck pins in the keyhole, and peered into the crack of darkness beneath it, but I couldn't fathom where it led. Was it a storage closet? Another room? It was in a small antechamber attached to my bedroom whose purpose I had assumed was as a sort of gallery displaying landscape paintings, a marble bust and a few fusty old portraits that I was going to have moved at the first opportunity. But then I found the door, tucked away behind a heavy curtain.

I decided it was probably a storage room and resigned myself to asking for a key to it in the morning. But it was that door I thought of when I heard scuffling noises coming from the antechamber later that night, when I was sitting at my new dressing table brushing my hair for bed. I stood and went to the entrance of the antechamber and peered into the gloom, lit faintly by a small light weave dangling from a bracket on the wall.

There was a low thump, then the click of a latch, and suddenly that hidden door swung open. The room echoed with my shriek as someone stepped through, batting at the curtain to clear it from his path.

I'd hardly registered that it was the king and not some creature living in a forgotten corner of the dark when he rushed at me, his arms reaching. I jumped back, my heart hammering too fast and hard in my chest, instinct ruling my head as I held out my hands to keep him back. I saw the confusion and disappointment on his face, but I still couldn't quite wrench back the control of my hands from the fear that seemed to have stolen the helm.

'You startled me,' I managed to gasp out.

He came at me again and I managed to force myself to at least be still, to allow him to put his arms around me, though I was still as stiff as a board. He either didn't notice or didn't care, because his hands were roaming over me, his mouth seeking skin.

'I've thought of nothing but you for days,' he rasped. It almost felt accusatory. 'I'm sitting through some of the most important diplomacy discussions of the decade, and I can't focus.'

'Please, Your Majesty, just... one minute...' I managed to extricate myself from him and take a deep, shuddering breath.

His face was flushed as he frowned at me. 'What's the matter? Don't you like your new rooms?'

'They are beautiful. I didn't expect... where does that door lead?' I focused on relaxing the tension in my body, trying to tether myself to the moment, to keep my mind from darting back to the smell of smoke and the taste of a dirty rag in my mouth. I was safe. He was not going to hurt me. He had just surprised me, that was all.

'There's a staircase that leads to my own apartments above, so I can visit you here without anyone knowing.'

'That's... how wonderful. Thank you for your favour.' My voice was steadier now, and I managed a smile that must have been at least half convincing, as he began to reach for me again. 'I was just enjoying a glass of wine. Can I offer you one?' I said quickly, darting into the other room without waiting for a confirmation. What was wrong with me? I needed a moment to collect my senses.

He sat himself on the fourposter bed and by the time I handed him his glass, I was composed and ready to perform my part. I pulled my lute from the wall and sat at the end of the bed, tuning it as he sipped his wine and watched me hungrily.

'How are you, Your Majesty? I've missed you,' I crooned. 'I hope these meetings that have kept you away have been worth it.'

'Call me Linus, please. I would have visited sooner, but I've been locked in negotiations with Creatia.' He ran a hand over his face. 'They've not gone well. They want us to overcommit to a defence of the Yaakandale border when I have to prioritise the coastal regions.'

My interest was sparked, but I kept my attention on the tuning peg, turning with tiny movements as I listened for the low, clear sound of the note I wanted. 'Aren't we at peace?' I asked casually.

'A country is only ever at peace until it isn't,' he said, sounding tired. 'But I've not come to talk politics with you, sweet one. I don't intend to bore you.'

'I love listening to you talk. You're fascinating.' I hoped he might keep talking his politics. If I was going to be his queen, I needed to show him that I could keep up with him. But he only smiled.

'I'd rather you distract me. Why don't you play me a song?'

'Your wish is my command.' My hair fell in curtains around me as I ran my fingers down the strings, plucking them gently into a melody, something sweet and sad. Linus watched me for a moment before stretching his arms out to me. I swayed out of his reach.

'You're so beautiful,' he murmured, and I smiled, all the while thinking of that face I saw in the mirror every night as I reapplied my glamour. If he saw me as that girl, he would never long to touch me like this.

He reached for me again and I let him catch me and pull me close.

'I need you.' He said the words against my hair and greedily pressed his lips to my skin, his hands running over me like they were searching for some kind antidote to this fever I had kindled. If he wanted a reply, he didn't wait for it.

It was simple enough to retreat into my mind, to sift through images in my head that would suit me better than the one that met my eyes. It was a trick I'd long perfected, one that had served me well many a time. I didn't see the king as he loomed above me. I simply gave in to the sensations rolling through my body, becoming a creature that didn't think or judge or analyse. I was just a bundle of nerve endings.

And it was in this vulnerable state that my mind went places it shouldn't. Warm breath stirring the hair at the back of my neck; a hand gripping my wrist; the smell of clay, of smoke, and a pair of eyes as colourless as a moonlit night. A murky rush of lust and shame washed through me, and my imagination picked up where my memories left off. What would it be like, to see Draven come undone? To see the control slip from him as desire overcame him, to have him between my thighs and own him?

The images flickered behind my eyelids as I gave a very convincing performance of a woman overwhelmed by the passion of her lover, but when it was done, I chastised myself for such a fantasy. I already had a king in my bed. Let that sate my yearning for dominion over powerful men.

Much to my displeasure, Linus demonstrated no desire for returning to his own chambers, quickly sinking into sleep. I pressed a pillow over my head to try and block out his gasping snores, my body prickling with a craving to be alone, to dance my fingers down between my legs and see to my own pleasure, which he had largely neglected. Perhaps, if he was as besotted with me as he seemed to be, I could teach him. With a weighty, sinking feeling in my stomach cooling my need at the thought of how many nights I would have to spend like this, I finally drifted off to sleep.

The morning light was coarse as it peered through the curtains, and I pulled the covers up as I blinked away the night. I was alone in my bed.

Linus was dressing himself with a brisk efficiency. 'I told your maid to wait outside,' he said as he peered at himself in the mirror and straightened his waistcoat.

I rolled onto my side, assessing his purposeful movements. He looked as though he had somewhere to be. It should be safe to flirt a little without it resulting in him crawling back into bed. 'Won't you breakfast with me?' I purred and was rewarded with a rueful smile.

'I'm meeting with council this morning to finalise the last of the treaty agreements, so I'm in a hurry.'

I sighed dramatically. 'That sounds dull. Couldn't you skip it?'

'I wish I could, my beauty, but not when we are discussing my daughter's future.'

That caught my attention. 'I met her when I was in the infirmary. She seems a sweet thing.'

His reflection frowned and he turned away from the mirror. 'She is very sweet.'

'What does her future have to do with the treaty?'

He searched the room until he found his shoes and picked them up. 'Oceatold have been pressing for an engagement to their prince for years, so they've decided to tie that up with the trade agreements we've been negotiating.'

The Oceatold prince. The one I'd seen at the ball with Senafae. 'Don't you like the prince?'

'Tallius? I like him. He'll be a strong king and he's willing to overlook some of Gwinellyn's... eccentricities. But it's not easy to promise my kingdom to another man.' He stood still for a moment and gazed out the window. Then he seemed to shake himself and leaned over the bed to kiss me. His breath was sour, and I supressed a shudder at the rubbery feel of his lips.

'Be ready for me later tonight. I'll send for you.' With that promise, he left my bedchamber to sneak back through the hidden door in the room with the paintings.

I rose slowly and wrapped myself in a satin robe, wondering at the king's relationship with the timid little princess. I had gathered bits and pieces of royal gossip over the years, despite my complete lack of interest in the affairs of anyone I thought myself unlikely to ever meet. I knew Gwinellyn's mother had been a princess from Yaakandale and that the match was supposed to lead to the building of a trade route through the mountains. But the people of Yaakandale overthrew their monarchy in a revolution shortly after the wedding, rendering their former princess's dowry worthless. Some rumours said King Linus had been deeply in love with his bride, and after birthing Gwinellyn had almost killed her, he had refused to lie with her out of a desire to protect her. Others said he had despised her.

I was no romantic. I doubted a king would choose to protect his wife over the possibility of a male heir. Whatever the truth, there'd been a gap of almost ten years between her first pregnancy and the one that had eventually claimed her life. Her child, a boy, hadn't survived either.

From the emphasis on giving away his *kingdom* instead of his daughter, I assumed the relationship with his only legitimate heir was not a close one.

'Are you ready to eat, ma'am?' Leela entered the room bearing a tray that smelled enticingly of coffee.

I sat at the small table by the window and raised an eyebrow at her. 'I don't remember hiring you.'

A faint smile turned up the corners of her mouth and she set the tray down before me. 'I hadn't heard you'd hired anyone else since we spoke. And you did say I could have a trial.'

'Luckily for you, I'm starving.' I added cream and sugar to my coffee as she began making the bed. 'I'll still want those references, though.'

'Of course, ma'am. I'll bring them to you after you've had a chance to wash. I expect you'll be wanting to, after the night you've had.' The knowing comment was delivered so mildly I almost missed it.

I sipped my coffee as I watched her go about her business. 'Are you married, Leela?'

'No, ma'am,' she said as she thumped at a pillow.

'You seem very worldly for an unmarried woman.'

She straightened and looked me dead in the eye. 'I'm unmarried, not a priestess.'

Ah. That explained a lot. Surely no maiden could make such an off-hand reference to fucking, no matter how politely veiled. Thank Aether. Perhaps she was exactly the kind of person I needed around. 'I need you to do something for me. Can you fetch me something to write with?'

She did as I bid, and I spent several minutes sketching and scribbling before handing her the page. 'Find a cabinet maker and commission that from him. I'll pay extra if he works fast.'

She scanned the page, but if she was surprised by what she saw, she kept that to herself. 'Of course, ma'am.'

'And while we are on the subject of extra payment, I know how servants like to gossip.'

She bristled and looked as though she was about to deny the observation, but I held up a hand to stop her.

'I'm merely stating a fact. Gossip is natural. Sometimes, it's even very useful. If you ever happen to hear any stories that you think I might find interesting, rumours about me, say, or perhaps news of noteworthy scandals, I'll pay you to bring them to me.' I watched her, measuring her response. Her face remained composed, but I thought she seemed to straighten a little, and a gleam of conspiracy entered her eyes. 'And don't spare my feelings,' I added. 'I want to know what is being said about me.'

She nodded and offered me a flicker of a smile. 'I understand.'

I dismissed her offer to help me dress and she dipped in a curtsey. 'Enjoy your breakfast, ma'am. I'll return for the tray.'

When she'd left, I pulled the mirror from where I'd hidden it under the bed and frowned down at it. I'd be glad to have the damned thing safely sequestered away at the back of a cabinet. No doubt the cabinet maker would wonder what the partition at the back was intended for, but surely, I wasn't the only one at court who'd wanted furniture with secret compartments. And if I filled the cabinet with bottles of liquor, anyone who opened it would think I was hiding alcoholism and that would excite them enough to keep them from looking further. But for now, under the bed would have to do.

Straightening up, I looked around my new room, a satisfied grin broadening my mouth. What a way to begin the day. A feathered bed. Breakfast on a tray. A luxurious suite of rooms all to myself. There was the minor inconvenience of the man I'd woken up next to, but I'd endured far worse. He seemed a fairly decent man, in all, and I would need to find something to love, or at least desire, in him if I was to play my part convincingly. As Draven had so helpfully reminded me, I still wasn't queen.

But I would be.

It was incredible how quickly my status at court had changed. All it took was the shift of my belongings into another part of the palace, and rather than being ignored as I moved through the servant's quarters, I was accosted by everyone I passed as they stopped to ask me if they could help me find something. I knew that summoning Senafae to me via a servant wasn't going to endear me to her, but it didn't seem that I had much choice.

I was deposited in a parlour while a maid raced to fetch her to me, and when Senafae entered the room, she eyed me warily.

'Have a seat,' I said, gesturing to the chair by me with perhaps a little too much eagerness. She did as I bid but remained perched on the edge of the chair, as though she was ready to flee at any moment.

I folded my hands in my lap. 'I have a proposition for you.'

Her eyes narrowed. 'I see. You've risen so high that you can be offering *propositions* now.'

'Stop it. It's not my fault you're in the position you're in,' I snapped, and she flinched like I'd slapped her. Well, it was true. 'Just hear me out, please.'

She looked tired. Terribly tired, her eyes shadowed and dull. It chilled me to see her so lifeless. She didn't respond, but she also didn't walk out, so I launched ahead. 'I want you to stay on at the palace as my companion.'

Her eyes widened just a fraction. 'Why? We hardly know each other.'

'I know you better than I know anyone else here.' I looked down and fiddled with the fringe of a cushion, feeling like I wanted to squirm in my seat. 'And I need someone around that I can trust.'

The silence that fell was like an echoing cavern between us. I almost took the words back, almost laughed and said something mean to cover the vulnerable flash of underbelly I'd exposed before she could stab me in it.

'A paid companion?' she asked slowly.

Miserly creature, but I smiled. I would have asked the same. 'Yes. And your own rooms here in the palace.' I hoped I wasn't vastly overestimating the privileges that came with my new position.

She twisted at her plaited bracelet, and I eyed it as she did. It was such a grubby thing.

'Alright,' she finally agreed, and she offered me a tentative smile.

Relief washed through me. I could only guess at the sort of hostility I would face from the ladies of the court, so having any form of ally would be a welcome support. And I could help keep her from one of the worse fates that awaited unmarried pregnant women in Brimordia. The memory of the red sheets flashed through my mind unbidden and I shoved it away. Senafae wouldn't want to think that had anything to do with the reason I was offering her the position.

'As my employee, I will insist on having some say in how you choose to handle your situation.' I drew myself up and tried to sound like a grand lady when I said it, but Senafae scowled.

'It's none of your business,' she snapped. 'If sending me hunting down some mad old witch in the Yawn is a condition of employment, then you can find someone else.'

'Baba Yaga could help you, Sen. I mean it. She's not just a story.' I reached out and squeezed her hand. 'She helped my mother.'

That seemed to give her pause. 'She did?'

'More than once.'

She seemed... a little too interested in this fact. 'Who was your mother?'

My skin prickled with uneasiness, and I pulled my hand form hers. 'My point is that it's a real possibility. I can help you.'

Movement drew my attention, and I turned my head just in time to catch sight of Elovissa and one of the other maisera shuffling slowly past the door, their eyes fixed forward but their shoulders turned slightly towards us, and I wondered if this was their first pass of the doorway.

'I should really be grateful for the incident with the nagwis. It has made the king *so* protective of me,' I said loudly, and Elovissa shot me a sour look. 'My apartment is so lavish, you'll just die when you see it.'

'Vanaria is gone,' Senafae said as they passed out of sight. Her tone was blunt. 'What did you do to her?'

'Me?' I touched a hand to my chest. 'Why would I do something to her? She was hardly worth my notice, let alone the energy of a scheme.'

It was a flimsy lie, and it hung in the air over us as we continued our conversation, sticking to our words like spun sugar. We traded gossip and small talk, but it felt stiff and superficial, and by the time I left Senafae to go and see about arranging a room for her use, I was second guessing my decision to invite her to stay. Whatever intimacy had been between us seemed to have dried up, like spring dew beneath a morning sun. But I couldn't help that. I couldn't very well trust her with my secrets. I had too much to lose.

CHAPTER TWELVE

Hiring Senafae as my companion didn't provide the easy company I had hoped for. She often kept to her rooms, already sick with the child in her belly and refusing to decide what she would do about it. She was bitter and angry and wouldn't listen to any more of my entreaties to seek out the witch in the Yawn. I eyed her figure constantly, waiting to see a thickening that might hint at her secret, and despaired at what I would do with an unmarried pregnant woman under my care. Though, as the king's whore, I was hardly winning any prizes for unblemished morality. Surely, my companion bearing a bastard was less of a scandal than my own indiscretions.

Senafae wrote and received a constant stream of letters. I often saw her scribbling away at the small desk in the corner of her room when I stopped by to check in on her, though she would quickly sweep the paper away into a drawer when I arrived, and I wondered if she was enquiring to places she could take herself away to have her baby in secret. When I asked who she was writing to, she continued to insist it was her family, which I continued to suspect was a lie. Why would she write so many letters to the people who had abused and abandoned her?

My new handmaid Leela, on the other hand, was quickly becoming indispensable. She had a keen sense of style and was impeccable in pairing gowns and accessories and hairstyles, seeming to always know exactly how far I could push the bounds of fashion and propriety. I knew the other women of the court were noticing. I caught their appraising glances as I moved through the palace.

Leela also had a sharp ear for gossip and quickly earned herself a tidy sum by bringing me all sorts of stories, including whatever she heard about me. And just as I requested, she spared me nothing.

'You're the talk of the court, ma'am,' she said one morning as she was arranging my hair. 'It seems all the ladies are sizing you up. Their maids are always whispering about you.'

'And what assessments have they made? I assume they all hate me.'

'Oh, they loathe you.' There was no inflection in her tone. This was how she delivered all her gossip, like a report on rainfall. 'They say you're slime from the bottom of the Trough. That you're uncouth and the king will be done with you in a month, though they admit that you've a talented seamstress.'

I arched an eyebrow in the mirror. 'They admit that, do they?'

A faint smile tugged at the corners of her mouth. 'Does my lack of modesty displease you, ma'am?'

I laughed. 'Honesty over modesty, always. Besides, the praise is well earned. So, they think I'm scum and no great threat to them.'

The eyes of her reflection met mine. 'Won't it be grand to prove them wrong?'

Aside from my worries about Senafae, I rather enjoyed being the king's mistress. The days swam past in a haze of late mornings, sumptuous meals, dress fittings, and visits from Linus. I was granted a title along with my new suite, and suddenly I was being referred to as *Lady* Rhiandra Beaufort. It was a title without lands attached, which was likely how Linus was able to grant it to me based on the forged papers bearing my false name, but it was a title, nonetheless. He was eager to give me *everything* I asked for and plied me with a hoard of exotic and expensive gifts. Sugared fruits from Creatia, perfume and fine silks from the across the Capricious Sea, enchanted face creams that promised eternal youth, though of course I didn't touch the creams.

With the new title came *invitations*. Hawking, high tea, art reveals, musical soirees—the ladies of the court invited me to all sorts of events, but they hardly spoke to me beyond superficial pleasantries and the polite inquiries into my health. Once they'd completed this duty, they would retreat behind their fans to whisper and shoot narrow-eyed glares. But I could wear their scorn. After all, I'd been invited. It was enough to know I was in so powerful a position that they couldn't afford to snub me.

There was one invitation I dreaded above all others and as the moon cycle ended, I tried to fathom a reason to be excused from attending. But it was no good. As the king's mistress, I was suddenly visible. People would notice if I didn't appear at the Burnings, and it would raise some uncomfortable questions that I couldn't afford to have anyone asking.

The whole court had been dumped in the square by a procession of carriages ferrying courtiers from the palace to the gates. The only person I knew of who wasn't in attendance was Senafae. I had pleaded with her to come with me, and she had responded with cynical laughter.

You wanted to be mistress. Wear your consequences.

I seethed about that as I waited in the square with the rest of the courtiers. I knew what she was going through was affecting her in a way I couldn't truly understand, but there was no need to take it out on me. After all, I'd done the best I could for her. She was comfortable and cared for, living in the palace with a reasonable wage for doing very little. She had a lot to be thankful for. And privileges could be taken away as easily as they'd been given.

The wind tore at me with an energy fierce and bitter. All around me, cheeks were wind-bitten and hair flew loose and tangled as it escaped from beneath hats and wigs. I rubbed my hands together, cold even in my kidskin gloves, and eyed the pyres with trepidation. There were six of them spread across the square, each standing stark and sombre in the shifting grey light, spectres of death looming before us. The anonymity of each pyre taunted me. Though I knew I hadn't been discovered, hadn't been tried before a court and sentenced, I couldn't rid myself of the squirming fear that one of them was meant for me.

The thought made me queasy with terror.

I tried to focus on my surroundings instead of picturing the heat and fury of the flames that were to come, craning my neck to peer beyond the soldiers that ringed the courtiers to separate the jostling crowds of city folk beyond. Even here there was an obvious split between commoners and courtiers. We stood palace-side, before the walls and the gates, facing the crowds who fought for standing space on the city side of the square. And between us, space, soldiers, pyres, and the heads of the three great institutions of Brimordia's governance on a raised wooden platform: the Grand Paptich, the Grand Weaver, and King Linus.

Perhaps I should have been most interested in watching my lover so that any eyes on me would see a girl besotted and report as much back to Linus and anyone else with an interest in my intentions at court. But I kept being drawn by the crowd. I'd been separated from the rabble of Lee Helse for more than a month now, had been swathed in the luxury of the palace, in three hearty meals a day, a warm room, and a soft bed. Here I stood in furs and layers of fine cloth to keep out the cold, but being outside now reminded me what it was like to be on the other side of that line of soldiers.

Directly opposite me, a gaunt, dirty boy clutched the hands of his bony mother, whose clothes were grey and thin with wear. A man with a back so stooped he was bent almost double held out a pleading palm, and a youth with skin still stained from coal dust frowned at the gathered courtiers with an expression that I might have read as hatred if I'd been standing any closer. A cluster of street children shivered together as they whined at a soldier for food or coin, but the soldier looked on impassively. With the merchant class citizens watching from nearby balconies and the gentry huddled together around me, the sight of Lee Helse's poor undiluted by its rich was unsettling. As I watched the crowd, I picked out a line of thick, twisted rope just behind the feet of the soldiers, and the sight unnerved me. Surely, for the king to have ordered a barrier woven, he must be expecting trouble. But he hadn't said as much to me. What else was he keeping from me?

If the Grand Paptich hadn't raised his arms, I wouldn't have known the proceedings had begun. The wind whipped his words away, even with a circlet of enchanted weave amplifying his voice. The crowd began to stir as a wagon entered the square and the soldiers closed the ring behind it. From the wagon, six figures were led forth in heavy chains to stand before the platform for their sentencing. As was the case every moon cycle, the sentencing was only a formality. Once convicted of unsanctioned magic use, there was only one outcome. The waiting pyres could attest to that.

I scanned the bowed heads of the prisoners, hoping I wouldn't see anyone I recognised. I'd been lucky so far in that no one I knew had wound up on a pyre, but with Cotus dealing swoon and snatching enchanted plant life from the Yawn, it was only a matter of time before someone from the Winking Nymph found their way into this square.

There were four women and two men, and none of them seemed familiar, but my attention was caught by the tattered robes of the youngest man. He looked maybe fourteen or fifteen, and the robes, while dirty and torn now from what might have been months of imprisonment, were clearly the robes of a druthi initiate. Stupid boy. What had he been doing, spilling the secrets of the guild when he had such a comfortable future laid out for him? He could have completed his training and worked at weaving enchantment for sale, or he could have gone into the employ of some rich estate. Either way, he would have been well paid, well fed, respected, and feared. Now, his life would end in flames. It was an uncomfortable reminder: If they would do that to one of their own, what would they do to me if I was ever caught?

The Grand Paptich must have finished his sentencing, for the prisoners were led or dragged towards their pyres. I felt as though the air had grown thin, as though there wasn't enough of it to feed my body as I rolled my shoulders back and tried to suck in a big lungful. The boy was weeping. I could see his shoulders shaking as his knees buckled, and the soldiers had to drag him across the cobblestones. They carried and dragged him up the steps of the pyre, where he was held firm against the central post as an executioner chained his shackles in place.

The smell of smoke undid me. I couldn't stay and watch it.

I pushed through the crowd of courtiers, gasping for air, and trying to find a place to breathe. Expressions of shock and disapproval blurred past me as my elbows and hands met the bodies of strangers, but I ignored them all as I barrelled through. The square was empty of anything except damn people, and with the crowd and the soldiers cutting off entry to the shadowy alleys beyond, there was nowhere to go.

I caught sight of a row of shapes slumbering against the palace wall and scampered towards them. Darting around a snorting and stomping horse, I threw myself to the ground behind one of the carriages that had carried members of the court to the square. Secure from the eyes of the crowd, I pressed my back against the cold stone of the palace wall and hugged my knees to my chest as I tried to suck air into my lungs.

Wind rushed around me, rattling the carriage and ripping any unendurable sounds and smells away to the east. It was a wonder I heard the quiet voice that said, 'I hate the Burnings, too. But Father always insists I come. He wants me to be seen being supportive.'

I blinked away the spots of darkness that had been consuming my vision until I could see that I wasn't the only one hiding here. Princess Gwinellyn mirrored my posture with her arms around her legs, and her pale skin looked grey.

'Funny,' I said, 'that's exactly what he said to me.'

She smiled faintly. 'I know it's important and keeps everyone safe from bad magic, but I just wish...' Her voice trailed off as the wind slackened and wisps of screams reached us. Her face shut down, her eyes glazed over, and I thought she might be sick. On instinct, I grabbed her hand.

'Look at me,' I urged. 'Focus on my face.'

She blinked rapidly and fixed on me. Her hand was limp in my grasp.

'Sometimes I have fits.' The admission was low, wavering. Scared.

Squeezing her cold fingers, I scooted a little closer. 'Tell me something good. Something happy.'

She shook her head, her lips pressed tightly together. 'I can't think of anything.'

'Surely, there must be something. A childhood memory. Something that you treasure.' If she would speak, I could focus on her and suffocate the scream struggling to claw its way out of me. I could see her face instead of the flashes of memory threatening to drag me somewhere I didn't want to go. I hoped she hadn't noticed how much my hands were trembling.

Her face lit up. 'My mother.'

'What was she like?' I asked as a whiff of smoke made my stomach lurch.

A ghost of a smile shivered at the corners of her mouth. 'She knew the name of every species of bird in the gardens.'

'That's it. How did she know them all?'

'She just loved birds. She couldn't abide seeing them in cages, though. She completely dismantled the royal aviaries and had all the birds released.'

'The king let her do that?' I asked, raising my eyebrows. Linus was infatuated with me and gave in to most of my whims, but not without significant manipulation on my part. It would take far more handling than it was worth to convince him to let me do something like that, especially when he was so fond of his caged beasts.

'Yes. He couldn't say no to her. Well, that's what Danya says.' Her eyes fell to the cobblestones.

'Who is Danya?'

'My governess.'

'You're a bit old for a governess, aren't you?'

The wind slammed back into us, stealing away her reply. It tore at my hair as I clutched my hat to my head, but at least I could no longer hear the screaming. We hunched lower, huddling down against the wall until the gust let up.

'This is ridiculous,' I grumbled, swatting at the snarls of hair now falling around my face. 'Surely, we don't have to stay here much longer.'

'I'm supposed to stay until the Grand Paptich leaves,' she said. She was hopelessly timid, this princess. Hiding away here with her eyes permanently fixed to the floor.

With me, I reminded myself with disgust. *Hiding here with me. I'm no better.*

'Right, come on then.' I climbed to my feet and dusted myself off.

'Where are you going?'

'To convince a carriage driver to take us back to the palace.' Linus would be angry, but right now I didn't give a whit. If he gave into his late wife so easily, then I'd be damned if I'd let him force me to stay in this forsaken square any longer.

This comment seemed to deflate rather than buoy her. 'They won't leave the square until the king does.'

'Hogwash. There'll be one who is open to persuasion. And if there isn't, we'll walk.'

She rose from the ground and smiled at me. 'Thank you.'

Her earnestness was almost painful as she blinked at me, so hopeful with those big blue eyes. Again, I thought of the street dogs begging for food or a touch of kindness. How could such a creature have grown up at court and kept such an open expression? No wonder Linus wanted her married off. She could never rule. She'd be eaten alive.

It became obvious that the crowd was growing restless as we slipped around the wagon. The ring of soldiers was squeezing tighter, and courtiers nearby were shifting uncomfortably, their eyes fixed on the commoners instead of the pyres.

People were jeering, I realised. As I watched, a woman taunted a soldier, drawing up close to him and spitting in his face while the man behind her scratched at the dirt like a rooster sizing up an opponent. There was a flurry of movement, and the woman was pinned to the ground. The strutting cockerel launched himself at the soldier pinning her down and received a sharp jab to the face with the hilt of a sword. His head snapped back, and red sprayed the air. The jeering grew louder.

'We need to leave,' I yelled at the princess as a stone flew over the heads of the soldiers, before rebounding in mid-air as the magic of the weave caught it. It was followed by another, and then several more in quick succession, and I wondered how long the magic would hold. The energy of the crowd was buzzing and angry. I'd never seen anything like it before.

I ducked my head at the crack of a gunshot, wildly casting about to see if anyone had been hit. As unreliable as pistols were, more likely to backfire and harm the shooter than anything else, they were still deadly. The woman on the ground started flailing wildly, drawing my attention back to her, and I saw that she was looking at us between the legs of her captor, her gaze locked on Gwinellyn as she shrieked and pointed.

Out of nowhere, Prince Tallius was before us. I'd never seen him up close before. His golden hair was thrashing around in the wind and a scowl marred his handsome face.

'Where have you been?' he demanded, grabbing Gwinellyn's hand. 'You know you aren't meant to wander on your own.'

She seemed to close in on herself, growing smaller beneath his gaze. 'I'm not alone.' The sight made me want to grind my teeth. Who was he to speak to her like that? Just some foreign prince, a spare son several steps out of line for his own throne, sponging off Brimordia's hospitality. And why was she *letting* him speak to her like that?

He tugged her away without another word, leaving me to fend for myself. Gwinellyn sent me an apologetic glance but didn't resist him. He clearly put the charm in prince charming, that one. I didn't need him, anyway. I was perfectly capable of stuffing myself into a carriage. Though as I had this thought, the one behind me suddenly lurched forward as the carriage driver whipped at the flanks of the horse. Clearly not that one, then. All around me, the courtiers were beginning to surge and scurry, grappling to get themselves into the few carriages available.

I craned my neck, searching for another to fight my way into, and something caught my attention. A point of stillness in the melee of the crowd nearby. A figure in black, untouched by the chaos, as though he existed in a void that drained away all movement and noise before it reached him. We locked eyes.

A feeble, ridiculous part of me felt better knowing Draven was here. It eroded the sharp edges from the fear that had been swelling inside me. He'd saved my life once and I was sure he'd do so again if it came down to it. He'd invested too much into me to let me die.

I didn't question my absolute faith that he would be able to save me.

A thunderous boom shook the air, sending everyone around me staggering. The weave had broken. The crowd surged forward, and chaos erupted as the soldiers struggled to keep them back, brandishing their broadswords as stones and vegetable matter began sailing into the mess of courtiers, eliciting shrieks of pain and horror all around me. The red-robed figures of druthi were now joining the soldiers to snatch at the broken weave being trampled against the cobblestones. Could they repair it? If they could, they would never do so fast enough. Already, the crowd was beginning to break through the line of soldiers.

I jumped as a hand grabbed my elbow.

'Why are you just standing there? Get out of here,' Draven's voice urged in my ear. 'This is about to turn bloody.'

I glanced behind me, beyond the pillars of flame that had consumed the pyres, to see the palace gates were open and the line of carriages was thundering through. The platform where the king had stood was empty and courtiers were streaming after the carriages on foot, shoving to get through the gates.

'They'll close the gates on anyone left out here,' he yelled as he pulled me along. 'And you're too conspicuous in that dress. The crowd will rip you apart.'

As though the gates were responding to his prediction, they began to move before our eyes and the courtiers trying to get through grew frenzied. With angry commoners now flooding into the square, there was a sea of people between us and safety. Draven cursed and looked around. 'Can't you just zap us somewhere else?' I shouted.

He levelled me an incredulous look. 'Of course not, you little fool. This way.'

We pushed through the people around us as refuse and rocks continued to rain down. Someone slammed into me and I stumbled, crying out. My knee jarred painfully against the stone and all that kept me from sprawling beneath the crush of the crowd was Draven yanking me back to my feet. We reached a lonely lantern post rising above the rolling mass of people. He wrapped my hand around it with his own.

'Wait here,' he yelled over the din. He released me, and panic gripped me, as if he had been the only thing keeping it at bay.

'Wait!' I cried, trying to grab at him, but I quickly lost him in the crowd. People jostled me on all sides and the wind was rising again to steal the breath from my mouth and send grit pelting at my face. A stray ribbon caught at my arm, straining and twisting around me for a few moments before it slipped away and upwards in a violent gust. Was I an idiot, standing still in the middle of what was quickly turning into a riot, trusting Draven to come back for me?

There was a hand suddenly at my neck, tearing at my necklace until it was cutting into my skin. I clawed at my throat, blood pounding in my head, gasping for breath, until finally it snapped. I whipped around to find a large woman with frizzy hair and huge forearms trying to pull my hat from my head. I gripped her shoulders, pulled her off balance and kneed her square in the stomach. She doubled over, winded, and with a sharp shove I pushed her onto her ass.

My gaze flashed to the gates. I had to get out of here. I had just decided to make a run for it when Draven reappeared with a palace soldier at his side. Judging from the hackle on his helmet, I guessed a captain.

'There's another way in. Lester will show us where to go,' Draven yelled, taking my arm again. He almost yanked me off my feet as he towed me through the crowd. More soldiers seemed to have joined the melee. I flinched as a young man wielding a fire poker was cut down before me and didn't look down as his blood washed the cobblestones beneath my shoes. My heart raced. Another gunshot split the air and I flinched, expecting pain. The clash of metal on metal rang in my ears as swords met poles and hammers and whatever paltry weapons the rioters had managed to get their hands on.

Through the chaos of bodies, I saw a building, then a gate hanging on its hinges. We pushed through it until we were in a narrow alleyway lined with crates. The soldier kicked over a few stacks of crates to reveal a door set low in the stone, which he crouched to unbolt with a key on a ring fished from his pocket. The door swung open.

Draven clasped his hand and nodded, and I peered closer at the face beneath a mop of sandy hair. Recognition flickered. Then I was tugged down a flight of crumbling stone stairs. When we had cleared the doorway, the door swung closed behind us and we were plunged into darkness.

CHAPTER THIRTEEN

I t was quiet. I would hardly have guessed at the chaos beyond the door if I hadn't just been dragged through it, and the dark was so thick I couldn't see the stairs, the walls, or the man leading me down into Aether knew where.

I stopped short, and when he tugged on me, I wrenched my hand from his grip and folded my arms. 'I can't see.'

The darkness sighed. A moment later, a spark of light flickered and grew until I could see that we were in a tunnel sloping down into the earth. Our shadows loomed large on the dirt walls around us.

I gaped at Draven, my eyebrows climbing my forehead as I realised he hadn't lit a torch, but was holding a handful of flames. Now, I knew very little about magic. The Druthi Guild were merciless in guarding their secrets—the young initiate burning in the square was a testament to that—but some facets of magic working were common knowledge. I knew it was somehow woven into objects. It required preparation and materials and time.

Druthi didn't summon flames from nowhere and then hold them in their hand.

'Let's go.' He was already moving, his feet quickly traversing the stairs and taking his palmful of flame with him.

'I'm coming. Just wait a moment.' I tripped after him, not wanting to be left behind. Wherever he was going, at least he had light. I didn't want to be left here in the dark. 'What is this place?'

'Evacuation tunnel. There are several of them leftover from the Great War.'

The stairs ended in a level floor of compounded dirt. The air was damp and thick, and the tunnel slithered away into the dark beyond the circle of light cast by Draven's flame. It felt like we were in the belly of some ancient, sleeping serpent.

Without warning, the light cut out and the darkness crashed down onto me. I shrieked.

'Calm down, you don't need to see. Here, keep your hand on the wall and follow it.' I felt him take my fingers and place them on the damp wall.

'Why can't we have the light?' The last word came out a squeak. I wasn't afraid of the dark, but the sense of the earth all around me made me feel like I was being buried alive.

'Because we can't. Walk behind me. I'll let you know if there's anything you'll trip over.'

Keeping one hand on the wall, I waved my other hand blindly before me until I touched fabric. I sensed him stiffen as my fingers pressed against his back, but he didn't say anything, and I didn't remove my hand.

'Come on.'

He started moving, and I hurried to keep up, one hand pressed to him and one trailing against the dirt. It felt strangely intimate, walking through the dark with my hand on him, resisting the urge to explore this new territory with my fingers. And with no sight to distract me, my mind darted about, imagining things I shouldn't, like what his skin was like beneath his shirt. Was he smooth? Hairy? He felt firm. I imagined him before me, shirtless, his back a broad expanse of smooth skin, muscles rising and falling like sand dunes. Then I shoved the image away, reminding myself that he was a scoundrel, and I didn't care what he looked like under his clothes.

'How long is this tunnel?' I asked.

'It emerges in the hedge maze.'

'But that's miles away!' Did he really expect me to—I collided with him and cursed loudly in surprise.

'Do you have a better idea?' he demanded.

I muttered under my breath about the dark and the cold and pig-headed men as we started moving again, and he ignored me. The ground occasionally squelched underfoot, and I was reminded of the thick, sticky blood on my shoes. 'Why did that guard captain help you?' I asked to keep my mind away from such unpleasant thoughts.

'Just be glad that he did.'

'I remember him. He was at the Winking Nymph the night I first met you. How do you know each other?'

Silence.

'Fine,' I continued after it became clear he wasn't going to answer. 'Don't tell me.' Still nothing. 'What were you doing at the Burnings, anyway?'

'Are you going to spend the whole walk picking me over? You should—'

'—just be glad you were?' I finished for him, rolling my eyes.

'Yes.' The edges of the word were softened, as if he was smiling. I curled my fingers slightly in his shirt.

We continued walking in silence for a time, which was strange in and of itself. I had no sense of how far we'd gone, of how deep beneath the ground we were, and there was no difference between the darkness of my closed and open eyes. It should have been terrifying, but the further we went, the calmer I felt. The rhythm of our footsteps, the feel of the shirt beneath my hand, and the light drag of my fingertips against the wall all left me feeling strangely peaceful, like I was out of place and time.

'What happened back there? I've never seen the city like that before,' I asked after a while, my voice hushed so as not to disturb the calm.

'Taxes. Rising wheat prices. Crop failure. Job scarcity. What else makes people unhappy with their monarch?'

I frowned. 'That seems a lot of motives. It wouldn't be easy to incite a riot without a common reason.'

'You're a politician now, aren't you, little Vixen?'

'I grew up on the streets of Lee Helse. I know this city,' I insisted, my mind ticking. 'Taxes have always been high, and people have always been poor. The blights on the farmlands around the Yawn have always pushed up food prices, and there has never been anything anyone can do about it. What's different now?'

'It doesn't take much for simmering resentment to boil over.'

I chewed on his response in silence. I didn't buy it. A few centuries of peace had made the people of Brimordia conflict-averse, and the possession of weapons was strictly outlawed. I couldn't see the riot being something the city's poor decided on beforehand, not with both the gendarmerie and the palace soldiers keeping the peace at the Burnings. The odds were too far out of favour. But I had seen the crowd, had seen how angry and unsettled people were before the rioting had broken out. There had to have been some sort of forethought. Unless the Burnings had provoked the crowd response, but it was such a regular, commonplace event. The pyres were lit every month without fail.

'What are you mulling over back there?'

I snorted. 'Now who's picking who over?

'I wouldn't ask, only it's making me feel like you're plotting to attack me.'

Unlikely. Not when he could conjure flames with his bare hands. 'How about I trade you an answer to your question for an answer to one of mine?'

I expected him to dismiss the suggestion, so when he said, 'Fine. One question,' I stopped dead as my mind whizzed over all the things I wanted to ask him. I lost contact with his shirt. The sudden air beneath my fingers sparked the thought that I could be left down here in the dark, shattering the peace that had settled over me. I lurched forward with my hands outstretched, leaving the wall in my panic, and I stumbled several steps into nothing.

'Draven?' I squeaked. I felt a hand fumbling for me, and I clutched onto it with both of my own. 'Don't you dare leave me down here!'

We stood still, his hand clasped in mine. My heart pounded.

'I won't.' His voice was quiet, and he gently moved my hands until I felt the fabric beneath my fingers. 'One question,' he reminded me as we began to walk again.

What would I ask him? How did his magic work? What would the next apple do? How did the king marrying me fit into whatever plan he was nursing? Who *was* he? *What* was he?

But when I opened my mouth, the question that fell out was none of these.

'What did you do to Vanaria?'

'Ah,' he replied, 'your sour-faced rival. Are you sure that's what you want to waste your question on?'

No. But a part of me wanted to know that she was at least alive. 'Yes.'

'Very well. She woke to find her hair had fallen out, and she fled the palace in shame.' His tone was indifferent, as though it meant nothing.

'Oh.' I felt a spiteful twist of pleasure at the idea, but after that faded out it left behind a heavy discomfort. 'Will it grow back?'

'Does it matter?'

'She'll never work again if it doesn't. Not as a maisera.'

'I know.'

The thump of our footsteps against the dirt was the only sound for a while as I tried to digest how I felt about this.

'My turn,' he said, interrupting my thoughts. 'What do you think of the king?'

If I'd had any idea what he was going to ask, I certainly hadn't thought it would be that. I snorted in surprise and answered without thinking. 'He's pleased with himself and easily manipulated. Much like any other man.'

Draven actually laughed at that, the sound echoing strangely against the walls. 'I take it you've found no worthy adversaries in the court. I hope that bias isn't blinding you to who your enemies are.'

'You assume that I have enemies. I'll have you know that I am a delight, and everyone adores me.'

'No doubt. If you're making so many friends, you'll be glad to know I'm about to return you to them. We are approaching our exit.'

If I hadn't been immersed in absolute darkness for so long, I wouldn't have seen it, but my eyes were hungry for something to fix on, so when I squinted ahead I could pick out what he meant: a faint slither of light on the roof of the tunnel.

'How are we supposed to get up there?' I asked as we drew beneath it.

'I'm going to lift you.' With no further warning than that, his hands were around my waist. I sucked in a breath of shock at his proximity, at the sense of him, so close yet still completely out of sight. And before I had time to collect myself, he was lifting me, his fingers splayed wide across the small of my back, my stomach and thighs brushing past his torso as he raised me towards the roof. I placed my hands on his shoulders to steady myself.

'Push up against it. It's a trap door. It should lift.'

Yes. Door. Right.

Raising my hands, I patted and rattled at the door, feeling for hinges and sending loose dirt showering down over us.

'What if it's bolted?' I asked as I heard Draven spit out the dirt that must have caught him in the mouth.

'Lester said the bolt on this one was damaged and never replaced.'

'That seems careless,' I grunted as I pushed. More dirt came raining down, but the door didn't budge. 'Are you sure?'

'A kingdom at peace thinks it can afford to be careless. Push harder.'

He lifted me a little higher as I strained with all my might. This time, I felt the tiniest shift right before my strength gave out. I shook my arms out, took a deep breath, gritted my teeth, and tried again. My muscles were starting to burn with the strain and all I managed was another tiny shift.

With a groan of frustration, I shook out my hands again. 'If I die down here, it will be your fault.'

'Try one more time.'

Once again, I braced my hands against the door and pushed, and as I did, I felt a strange spark at the base of my spine, like I'd been zapped by a hit of static. The feeling shot up my back, through my shoulders and down my arms, leaving a flush of warmth and a zinging energy behind. I surged upwards, and the door shifted, then groaned and began to rise. Dirt poured down, but I kept pushing, and something snapped, then another something did, and each snap released the door a little more until finally I flung it open with a crow of triumph, revealing a hole lined in dangling plant roots and filled with a grey patch of sky.

Something thumped to the ground, and I looked down to see a ladder had dropped from the door to touch the dirt below. Draven lowered me slowly back to the floor, and the pale daylight dusting his face was a shock as he looked down at me for a breath too long, his hands still lingering at my waist. Then he stepped away and gestured to the ladder, and the simple intimacy of the darkness was gone.

'Ladies first.'

The ladder was slender and rickety, the metal rusted so badly in places that I was sure it would snap, but it held long enough for the both of us to clamber out of the earth and into the palace gardens, at a dead end in the hedge maze. We eyed each other and I felt oddly embarrassed.

'It seems ridiculous that there are tunnels emptying out this close to the palace. Imagine if we were an army or assassins. A hedge maze is hardly a hardy security measure.' My words were too fast, too light, as I spoke to fill the silence.

'Ridiculous, but lucky for us. Try not to get yourself into any more life-threatening situations. I have my limits.' He frowned down into the hole, and I realised that he looked weary. It was odd, to think of him being afflicted by something as ordinary as fatigue.

I wondered, not for the first time, what those limits were. Naked flame conjuring, yes. Magicking us into the palace, no. Enchanted apples, magic mirrors, stealing thoughts right out of my head, all yes. And he must have some ability to manipulate flesh if he had saved me from the nagwis venom. Maybe it wasn't necessary to venture into the Yawn to seek a medical marvel.

I chewed my lip as I worried over whether or not I should ask him. Finally, I blurted out my request. 'Someone I know is in some trouble. I was wondering if you might be able to help her.'

He fixed his eyes on me, his expression guarded. 'You think me a trained monkey who doles out magic tricks for all your friends?'

Not an auspicious response. 'I would pay you for whatever help you can offer, of course.'

'You are still tangled in your last debt to me.' He folded his arms. 'What kind of trouble?'

'Women's trouble.'

His gaze cut down my body, suddenly sharp, as though he was slicing me apart, looking for evidence.

I ruffled my skirts irritably. 'I said someone I know is in trouble, not me.'

'Good. Birthing bastards won't help your cause and I hope you aren't fool enough to think it would.'

I pressed my teeth together. I wanted to snarl at him like some sort of animal, but I inhaled deeply, releasing the breath in an angry sigh. Snapping at him wouldn't get me what I wanted. 'Can you help my friend or not?'

'I don't work that sort of magic, my dear.'

I didn't know if he was telling the truth or not. He looked as he always did—detached, slightly smug, a pinch of mocking. If he had some sort of a tell, a hand to the face, a glance to the left, a twitchy bunching of fingers, then I had never noticed it. 'Can't or won't?'

'It doesn't matter which. The result is the same. And do I need to remind you that you are here to do a job? This isn't a time to be making bosom friends. Your situation is still precarious. You still aren't queen.'

'I'm working on it.'

He smiled grimly and shook his head. 'Not good enough.'

Throwing my hands up, I turned away and eyed the fork in the path before me, wondering how long it would take me to find my way out of the maze. I stiffened when I felt his hand on my upper arm.

'Don't keep me waiting much longer, Rhiandra. I know how attached you've grown to your pretty face. I'd hate to take it from you.'

'If I said I will be queen, then I will be queen. Climb back down into your hole and let me mind my own affairs.' I shrugged him off, and his hand slid away.

'Good. I'll return with the new moon. Make sure we aren't having this same conversation when I do.'

I watched him climb back down into the dark, and he stood looking up at me as I bent to lift the trap door, heavy with an inch of earth and lawn that had settled onto it over the years. When I dropped the door back over the hole, he was already gone.

CHAPTER FOURTEEN

'And that's my game again,' I crowed, slapping my cards down on the table. 'You're losing your touch, Sen.'

She sat back in her chair, folding her arms. 'I'm sure you cheat.'

'I do no such thing. You are just a poor loser. Shall we have another game?'

It was one of those rare afternoons of sunshine that occasionally graced the tail end of winter, and while we were both rugged up against the chill air, I hadn't been able to resist dragging Senafae down to the gardens for an hour. Unfortunately, there seemed to be plenty of others in the palace who'd had the same idea, and they cast us speculative glances as they promenaded past.

'No. No more cards. I've had enough. In any case, you're due to meet His Majesty soon. Shouldn't you be getting ready?' Senafae gathered the cards and arranged them in a neat stack between us. This was one of her better days, when she wasn't so ill that she couldn't keep down food, but still that bright humour I'd once valued in her rarely showed itself.

I waved a hand through the air. 'I'll just go straight to him after we're done here. I hardly need to worry about putting in any special effort. He is besotted with me. I'm sure I could make him perform naked handstands if I told him it would please me.' I had hoped it would make her laugh, but it seemed to have the opposite effect.

'That seems a dangerous power to have over a king,' she muttered, and I would have pressed her to elaborate on that statement, except the sound of a throat being cleared interrupted me. Turning, I found a man standing behind me, dressed in the long, green habit trimmed with gold that marked him as a priest. But it wasn't just any priest. I recognised that hooked nose from the very first night of the treaty celebrations.

'Miss Beaufort, I believe?' he began.

'Paptich Milton, you honour me.' I bowed my head while wondering what on earth the Grand Paptich wanted with me.

'I wonder if you would take a stroll with me? It's a fine afternoon and there's a garden of grevilleas a short distance away that are just beginning to flower.'

I shot a look at Senafae, and she was already packing up the cards, so I offered him a saccharine smile and rose to my feet. 'I do *love* flowers.'

I followed him through the flower beds as he pointed out various plants and described when they would bloom or what their origins were and waited for him to get to his point. Finally, after I had just about decided he had no point, he said, 'I have not seen you at worship.'

Ah. 'I attend worship regularly in the city. Besides, I did not think the palace sanctum would welcome the presence of someone like me.' It was a lie; I had attended worship when I was a little girl, but it had been a long time since I had set foot in a sanctum. I had seen what good a lifetime of worship had done my mother. It seemed a colossal waste of time.

'All are welcome at worship. It would be pertinent to attend, especially now that you are keeping such illustrious company.'

We were getting to the crux of his intention now as we rounded an avenue of beech trees and came within sight of a towering hedge maze. 'If His Majesty wishes me to accompany him, then of course I will.'

'Sometimes great men can require help to see their way to the glory of the celestial kingdom. When Taveum cast Aether from the sky, it was the assistance of some of the humblest of animals that helped set the world to rights and restore him. The seemingly insignificant mantis, for instance, lied to Taveum and sent him on a wild goose chase to allow Aether time to heal.'

In my experience, priests tended to be long-winded, but this felt deliberate. Like he was trying to confound me with a barrage of words to obscure his meaning. 'I know the story, paptich,' I said, trying to keep the frustration from my voice.

'Without the help of the seven, Aether would never have found his way back into the sky. His Majesty may need similar help.' He stopped beneath one of the beech trees and stared up into its rusty winter foliage with his hands clasped behind his back. 'A devout woman would be of great service to our celestial lord if she could help the king stay the path.'

'And what path is that exactly?'

He dropped his gaze back to me and his genial condescension thinned. 'If you had been attending worship, you would have heard me speak of the rise in the threat of profane magic.'

I swallowed against the sudden feeling of tightness in my throat. 'Hasn't that always been a threat?'

'There has been an increase over the past several months.' He was frowning at me, apparently displeased that I had the nerve to ask questions. 'You understand that the regulation of magic protects the populace from falling prey to all manner of wicked enchantment. It is the natural place of the sanctum to lead the battle against its influence.'

All his talk was making my head ache, but I was beginning to understand what he was getting at. 'But the guild is responsible for hunting down profane magic users.' The sanctum headed Brimordia's courts, but when it came to magic use, the guild decided who the courts would try.

'A historical mistake I have long campaigned to correct.' As he spoke, one of the burnished leaves lost its grip on the tree's branch and swayed to the earth between us. 'But His Majesty needs a little persuasion. You seem the sort of woman who can be very persuasive.'

I fluttered my eyelashes at him and tried to look flattered. 'Persuasive and devout. The prefect woman, would you say?'

His brow folded into an expression of displeasure. He could tell when he was being mocked, I'd give him that. 'Think on your worship attendance, Miss Beaufort. Women in your line of work often need powerful friends.' On that note, he inclined his head and strode away from me with fast, purposeful steps that saw him halfway back to the palace in what seemed like moments.

I was surprised that the Grand Paptich had wanted to strike up some sort of alliance with me, but his talk of the rise of profane magic use did make me uneasy enough to want to go and refresh my glamour before I met the king for dinner. So far, I had always managed to stand before the mirror with plenty of time to spare before the prickling, warming sensation on my skin let me know the magic was wearing thin, but there was no need to push my luck.

When I returned to my apartment, Leela was not there to greet me, though she had said she was planning on spending the afternoon sorting through my spring wardrobe. I moved through the rooms with some innate sense prickling at me, slowing my movements and quietening my breaths as I looked around, finding nothing amiss, nothing to explain the sense that something wasn't right. I opened the door of my bedchamber to a sight I did not expect. Mrs Corkill was on her hands and knees by the bed, peering under it. A sharp spike of alarm shot through me.

'Mrs Corkill, to what do I owe the pleasure?' I served her a cold smile with the question.

She climbed to her feet and dusted at her skirts. 'I am the head housekeeper, Miss Beaufort. It is my responsibility to ensure all rooms are maintained to a high standard.'

'Oh, so you peek under the bed of every room in the palace? That must keep you busy.' I flung back my shoulders as I stepped through the door, drawing on all my height as I approached her. 'I imagine your knees don't appreciate it.'

For all my bluster, my heart was pounding, blood rushing in my ears as my stomach tried to squirm its way up my oesophagus. 'Where is Leela?' I asked, hoping that she was here somewhere, keeping an eye on the old crone.

'I do not keep track of every maid in the palace,' Mrs Corkill replied, her expression giving nothing away.

'So, hidden dust is your responsibility, but maids are not? What an interesting role you perform.' My eyes darted to the cabinet in the corner as I tried to keep control of my panic. It would be locked. I knew it was locked. It was always locked. But I wanted to check.

'It's not dust I'm interested in, Miss Beaufort. I am here on information that you are harbouring secrets.'

I restrained the panic that wanted to crawl all over my face. Information? From who? And what did they suspect me of? 'That seems a vague accusation. Doesn't everyone at court harbour secrets?'

'Given our previous encounters, you'll understand that it's one I must give some credit.' She was, as always, no nonsense, and I begrudgingly admired her for being so straight with me. And if she was referencing the incident with the fork, I had to hope that she suspected me of something more mundane than possessing an enchanted mirror. If she thought I was involved in any kind of profane magic, she would surely be in the ear of the Grand Paptich by now, not lingering in my room, probing me for guilt.

'Mrs Corkill,' I said, drawing closer, 'surely you do not think I still harbour a desire to steal silverware?'

Her eyes widened a fraction, and I relaxed slightly as she muttered that there was plenty aside from silverware that could be stolen.

'I am in a highly influential position and have access to more money than I've ever had in my life,' I continued. 'Can you really see me jeopardising all that just for the chance to steal a few jewels?' She opened her mouth, but shut it again without answering the question, pressing her lips into a thin line as I walked to my armoire and slid open a drawer, revealing a row of neatly arranged undergarments.

'I admire your commitment to upholding the security of this household,' I said as I slid open the rest of the drawers, exposing my collection of gloves, fans, stockings, and hair pins for her perusal before I straightened and levelled her with a stare. 'You are welcome to search my room, but if you ask me, it sounds like someone is using you to act out a grudge for them.' It was no more than a guess, but I was rewarded for it when a hint of colour flushed her neck. She dropped her gaze to her hands for a moment before looking back at me with a decidedly less superior expression.

'You seem a smart girl, Miss Beaufort,' she said. 'I hope you'll take some advice. You may think I hate your kind, but that is not the case. I feel nothing but pity for you.'

My eyebrows hiked up my forehead and I folded my arms as I bit down against the response that wanted to break past my teeth. *She* pitied *me*? She was lucky I had somewhere to be, or I might just push her from that moral high ground she seemed to be so comfortable on.

'Do not continue down this path of turpitude. Corrupting a king is to corrupt a country, and you would do well to renounce your wicked ways before we all see the consequences.'

I tapped a finger against my forearm. She was going to try and convert me? *Now?*

She seemed to take my silence as acquiescence instead of self-control and she offered me a thin smile. 'Only piety will save you. Beauty is finite, and when Taveum takes the bloom from yours, you will be left with nothing but the knowledge of the damage you have wrought.'

Slit-eyed and seething, I leaned closer to her. 'Let's wait and see, shall we?'

The door clicked open and Leela stumbled in, her face flushed, her hair frayed, utterly unlike the perfectly groomed woman I had come to know. Her gaze darted between me and Mrs Corkill, a frown cutting deeper across her mouth the longer she looked.

Mrs Corkill discharged an indignant huff. 'I have a dinner to oversee. I hope you'll think on my words, Miss Beaufort. A life devoted to celibacy and service might just save you from the fate that awaits young women who sell their bodies and their souls.'

Leela stood aside as Mrs Corkill strode past her. She raised her eyebrows at me as the older woman shut the door.

I released a breath and ran my hands over my face as the tension drained out of me. 'Bloody soil smearers,' I muttered. 'Of course, the batty old hag is a fanatic.'

'I could have told you that,' Leela said, crossing the room to the armoire and sliding the drawers closed. 'She visits the Temple of the Seven every few days.'

Fitting that she was drawn to worship a bunch of glorified service animals. I strode to my cabinet and tried the latch, relieved to find it locked.

'Are you not a believer then, ma'am?'

I turned on Leela's question with a snort. 'Do I believe the fall of some god split the earth and released evil into the world? No,' I said, waving my hands about before pulling the key for the cabinet from the chain around my neck. 'But the world seems like it must be *someone's* cruel joke, so why not Aether's? Where were you, by the way? I never want her in here alone again.'

'A boy told me you wanted me downstairs, ma'am, but I wound up locked in the room he led me to.'

I blinked at her as my mind turned this information over. 'What boy?'

'Just a hall boy.'

This painted an entirely different colour over my conversation with the Grand Paptich. I needed to think it over properly before I met with the king. 'Draw me a bath, please,' I said, turning back to the cabinet and unlocking it as I heard her footsteps leave the room. Only when the door slicked shut did I raise the partition and reveal the mirror lurking behind the false backing. The sight of my reflection made me shudder, but I stood still and let the magic do its work, turning my face icy and numb before I slid the panel back into place with a sigh of relief.

The whole episode reeked of conspiracy. Someone had put Mrs Corkill up to searching my room and someone had made sure Leela was out of the way to do it. I couldn't see the housekeeper locking a maid in a room, or even of seeing a reason to make sure Leela was out of the way before she searched the place. So, who held such a grudge against me that they would orchestrate such a plot? Surely, it was no coincidence that Mrs Corkill had treated me to an echo of some of what the Grand Paptich had said to me.

I was rattled. But at least I now knew one thing. There was someone who was willing to act on their grudge against me, and that was a dangerous thing. I needed to make myself difficult to be rid of.

And I had the perfect solution to that.

CHAPTER FIFTEEN

I f you want a man to marry you, of course you cannot ask him directly.

First, I made sure Linus saw me as a restricted commodity. When he sent for me, I took my time to arrive. Once, I didn't show up at all. When he questioned me on where I'd been, I told him I had other obligations outside of him. When he raged, I said, 'I'm not your wife!' and started to cry. Though it rankled, I knew the power of well-timed tears. But I was careful to only say this once. I'd planted the seed. He wouldn't forget it.

Bit by bit, I fed him a sad story of bad luck and woe, little breadcrumbs for him to follow to the inevitable conclusion that I was some sort of fallen angel, a victim of terrible circumstances, too good for the life I led. I told him how much I appreciated him rescuing me from that life, made him feel omnipotent.

I paid careful attention to his worries and the things he shared with me, ensuring I asked after those worries periodically to make him see how good it felt to be the centre of my attention. When he stressed about an upcoming political engagement, I talked about how much I wished I could support him in person instead of being forced to watch helplessly from the sidelines. I wished aloud that we could have met in another life, where he wasn't so above my station, where there weren't such powerful forces keeping us from belonging to one another, sounding like a smitten lover who wished to spend every moment with him while subtly implying his impotence. I wanted to suggest that there was something keeping him from making decisions about his happiness. Powerful men hate to feel that there are things beyond their control. They especially don't want their lovers feeling it.

Once, when I was lying in the wet patch of his crumpled sheets and he hadn't taken off snoring yet, I admitted to dreams of having a family, a handful of *adorable* children. When he said he'd love for me to bear him children, I pulled away, turning cold enough that he roused, kept me from leaving, begged to know what troubled me.

'Any children I bore would be bastards,' I whispered. 'I couldn't inflict that on a child.' I refused to stay the night, begging for some space. Again, maintaining his view of me as a restricted commodity was paramount. He needed to think there were parts of me he could not access, not without giving me what I wanted.

Finally, one morning I visited him to say goodbye. When he was shocked that I would even consider leaving, I began to cry. I told him our time together had made me realise I couldn't be just a maisera anymore. That I wanted a family, a husband, and that I couldn't stand to be just his mistress, no matter how much I loved him. I told him that, even though I didn't think I could love another man the way I loved him, to love someone even half as much would be better than the life I led before. Mentioning a husband was important—the spectre of another man would rile him in a way my tears couldn't.

A king is used to getting what he wants, is used to the women in his bed simply pleasuring him and doing exactly what he wants of them. And thanks to my enchanted apple, he was still so intensely in love with me that the idea of me being out of his reach drove him mad.

He raged. I weathered it, refusing to give in to his demands, refusing to react. He couldn't win the argument, and he knew it; I had the moral high ground. When his temper drained away, when his pleading still wouldn't sway me, I took his hands. I kissed them. I repeated my wish that things were different.

When he said, 'there must be a way,' I let him think, let the silence lay. And when he said, 'if only I could marry you,' I looked at him with wide-eyed wonder, as though the thought had only just occurred to me.

'Why can't you?' I asked, my voice hushed, my face full of hope, my cheeks still wet with tears.

'The council, the sanctum, they'd never allow it,' he said.

I stared at him with the slightest challenge, just a trace. I didn't want him to feel threatened by me in that moment. I wanted him to feel that I was helpless without him, and that he wanted to protect me. I wanted him to want to give me everything. But there needed to be just a hint that maybe I didn't believe he would.

I took a deep breath and said, 'Aren't you the king?'

CHAPTER SIXTEEN

L inus was tense. News of our wedding had been swallowed by the council like a bowl full of barbs. The ceremony had been small, rushed, and with no prior application to the council for approval. If it weren't for the fact that Linus had reigned for thirty years already, steering his council with a firm hand, and backed by their good faith, there might have been dire consequences.

Or so he told me. Now, the sanctum and the guild were taking their time in blessing the union, which meant for a delay in my elevation to Queen Consort. Linus had spent days locked in meetings, licking the boots of the Grand Weaver and Grand Paptich and the high lords of his council as they deliberated over whether his decision to marry me would lead to a civil war. He looked haggard and his face settled into a scowl whenever he was lost in thought.

We were in my new apartment, a *royal* apartment, and I was fluttering from room to room, calling instructions to Leela on what was to be ordered and changed and kept. A handful of attendants trailed her as she followed me, a bevy of daughters and wives and sisters of council members that Linus had foisted upon me in hopes of smoothing some ruffled feathers.

'Bankrupting the Crown in order to redecorate is not likely to endear you to the court,' Linus grumbled as he watched me.

I waved him off. 'I'm only making a few small changes. Besides, I highly doubt Milton and Dovegni are interested in what I am doing with my rooms.' I ran my hand over a wall, frowning at the wallpaper, and flicked my wrist at Leela. She raised her eyebrows at the wallpaper and scribbled a quick note.

'I don't understand why you need their approval in any case. You're the king. Why don't you just bring them to heel?' I continued as I moved on to the curtains, inspecting them closely.

He ran his hand over his face. 'It is not that simple. The sanctum and the guild are not beholden to me. They wield their own independent power and half of my council is aligned with one or the other. I doubt they'd take up arms against me over something like this, but it strains our relationship, and that isn't good for the country.'

I spun around and placed my hands on my hips. 'It seems ridiculous that they have that kind of power.'

'The Crown, the guild, and the sanctum are the three pillars of Brimordia, my love. The independence of each keeps the others in check. One man holding absolute power is only a good idea until it isn't.' He shook his head as I continued to frown at him, then slowed down his words, like he was speaking to a child. 'It would take only one mad king to destroy the peace and prosperity that has taken generations to build if the Crown ruled completely. With the guild and sanctum retaining a voice in major decisions, it would take three mad men. And they'd have to be mad all at the same time.'

'Well, you're not mad. Surely, you could do away with all that,' I said, waving a hand as though flicking at an insect. 'Letting men like Milton and Dovegni act as a law unto themselves seems foolhardy. Especially Dovegni.'

'You just don't like him. That doesn't mean he is a bad man.'

I frowned at the placating note of his voice. 'I don't trust him.' I shot a look at the mob of attendants milling around Leela and lowered my voice to just above a whisper. 'He and his underlings, all holed away in the anthill with their magic and their scheming. He could be doing anything in there.'

Linus laughed. 'I haven't heard Misarnee Keep called the anthill in years. Do the common folk really still call it that?'

'It *is* an anthill. A big, dark mound full of nasty, biting insects. One day, they'll swarm,' I said, and the humour slid from his face, leaving traces of disapproval in its wake.

'I appreciate that you would like to help me, but you should focus on hosting Gwinellyn's birthday ball and leave me to rule the kingdom. I've been wearing this crown for longer than you've been alive.'

'But—'

'If you really want to help, endearing yourself to the Grand Weaver and Grand Paptich would be an idea.'

Of course, he would want me to act as his lick spittle. Much easier to ask me to do the grovelling for him than for him to need to degrade himself. 'So, you want me to attend worship?'

'It would do you some good.'

I didn't like what he implied by that comment, but I let it slide. 'Fine. But I'm not going to be a soil smearer.'

He drew in a deep breath and let it out slowly. 'I'm not asking you to become devout, only to be seen being as supportive. After the riots at the Burnings, it is more important than ever to stand united.'

Leela had told me the city had been volatile since the riot, but no matter how deep she dug, she couldn't find any suggestion that there was any kind of organisation to the unrest. It seemed everyone had woken up that morning and collectively decided they'd had enough. Linus wouldn't speak about it, other than to say the common folk had 'worn their consequences', but there had been whispers of further violence, of soldiers patrolling the streets, of groups of people rotting in dungeons.

'And for Dovegni?' I asked, my tone petulant. 'Do you want me to become the first female druthi?'

Linus's silver brows drew together across his forehead, leaving shadowed gullies in their wake. 'I don't appreciate your tone. I'm sure a visit to Misarnee Keep would suffice.'

I frowned, wondering if he was teasing me. 'Only initiated druthi are allowed inside.'

'And royalty.' He rose from his seat, rolling his neck and stretching his back. 'The guild is independent, not inaccessible. I can visit whenever I wish, and now, as my wife, so can you. So go, show that you have an interest in the guild. Perhaps you can find yourself a cause to champion.'

He took me by the shoulders and placed a kiss on my forehead before leaving me to my redecorating.

I mulled over his words, my curiosity and suspicion egging me on. The chance to see inside the anthill, to know the secrets of the guild, perhaps to understand magic better... My thoughts flashed to Draven. It was too tempting a prospect to resist, even if it would put me in the company of the Grand Weaver, and with him the ever-present fear of my glamour being discovered. Even if Dovegni himself had not yet suggested he knew, could there be some other druthi at the keep who would? Was it a risk I was willing to take?

'How about the settee?' Leela asked, pulling a face at the stiff, dated piece of furniture by the window.

I stood next to her and considered it, then flicked my fingers. 'Gone.'

She nodded in approval and scribbled on her notepad. One of my new attendants gasped, and I shot her a narrow-eyed glare. 'Is there a problem?'

She was a doughy-faced, colourless woman, the daughter of Lord Sherman, a prominent high lord of the council, and she bobbed quickly beneath my attention. 'That settee... it is a piece designed by the late dowager queen. Our own king's mother, Your Grace.'

I offered her a threadbare smile, a slight stretching of lips and a flash of teeth, before turning back to Leela and repeating, 'Gone.'

I wasn't sure what it was about these ladies-in-waiting that I found so abrasive. Their constant attendance was certainly tiresome, as was their insistence on modesty and propriety. I knew I should try and charm them, so they would in turn carry tales of my virtues to their fathers and husbands, but I just couldn't bring myself to do so.

'I'll need my cabinet brought from my old bedchamber,' I said to Leela as I contemplated the room. 'It can stand against that wall there.'

She eyed me steadily. 'You have access to the entire royal collection now, ma'am. I'm sure there are many exquisite cabinets to choose from. There is one, for instance, in the Queen Cecily Parlour inlaid with the scales of a snathimor.'

'My cabinet, Leela. I want it brought here today.' My tone brokered no argument, and she inclined her head. I could tell she wanted to ask me why. She knew that I kept it locked at all times, that I wore the key on a chain around my neck. She must have wondered why I would be so protective of a liquor cabinet. And she surely must have wondered at the design when I commissioned it, at the hidden compartment at the back. But she knew better than to pry into my secrets.

I left Leela with the list of alterations and the gaggle of attendants as 'helpers' and sidled out of my new apartment, glad for a few minutes where no one was trailing after me. The excess of people who dogged my every waking moment was not only getting on my nerves but was also making it increasingly difficult to snatch moments alone to refresh the glamour. I tried to stand before the mirror whenever the opportunity presented itself instead of each night before I slept, and it was making me feel like I was always frantically grabbing at time.

Perhaps Draven was not as clever as he believed himself to be. He had desired me to be queen, but he had given me such a large, conspicuous thing to hold his magic in. The threat of discovery was growing and with it my anxiety to be done with his deal. But even after the final apple was delivered, the daily routine of refreshing my glamour would not change if I wanted to keep my beauty. Would this be the way of it for the rest of my life?

With a sigh of resignation, my feet carried me down the hall and to a staircase that would lead me to the third floor, where I would find the modest, inconveniently placed room that I had managed to procure for Senafae. When I reached her hall, I paused at the sight of someone else closing her door as they passed out of the room. It was a man, a large one, with the red face of a heavy drinker, and I had seen him before. The memory swam to me, a little hazy for the number of new faces and information I had been trying to absorb at the time, but decipherable. A song about spring love, coins tossed to a bowl, Dovegni twisting his ring round and round, and the man with the booming voice. *Lord Perrius.*

I watched him retreat down the hall before approaching the door myself, turning over the question I would ask Senafae and how I thought she might respond as I gripped the handle and stepped inside. The air had the muggy, stale smell of a sick room, and the light that managed to find its way past the drawn curtains was watery and grey. Worry squirmed in my chest at the sight of Senafae still in bed, her skin shiny and her blond hair slick with grease.

'Good morning,' I chirped as I swept to her bedside. 'How are you feeling? You're looking much better.' The lie turned my stomach. I was acting like Madam Luzel the morning after I'd been attacked.

Senafae blinked at me blearily. 'I'm fine.'

'Would you like to come for a walk in the gardens? The weather is starting to warm again.'

'Not today. Thank you.'

I pursed my lips as she blinked up at me with those hollow eyes. She had done exactly what I had feared she would do. A week ago, she had disappeared for two days, and when she had returned, she was no longer pregnant. I had been furious; furious that she had ignored me, furious that she'd gone to see some dirty quack of a surgeon in the Trough, furious that *she hadn't told me*. And now she would hardly stir to leave her room, and I couldn't tell if there was something wrong with her body or her heart.

I perched on the edge of her bed and smoothed at my skirts. 'What was Lord Perrius visiting you for?' I asked, trying to sound nonchalant.

'To check on me.' The answer was in monotone, as though this was not something strange and demanding of an explanation. But I was not an idiot. I could fill in the blanks myself.

'Has he been concerned about your welfare... for very long?'

She was silent for a long moment, before she said, 'we're friends,' in a tone so full of bitterness that I decided to change the subject. After all, if he was the father, it hardly mattered now. He was probably only checking to make sure she had gone through with the procedure. Nevertheless, I made a mental note to ask Leela to dig for gossip and secrets concerning Lord Perrius. If I could find a way to make him pay for how drawn and miserable Senafae looked, I would gladly do it. Maybe it would bring some colour into her cheeks to hear of the man who had done this to her being humiliated or disgraced.

I chatted to her of the problems I was facing with having my marriage recognised, complained about how Prince Tallius becoming engaged to Princess Gwinellyn would mean being forced to endure frequent dinners with the entitled lobcock, then I speculated on what I should wear to Misarnee Keep to ensure I rattled Dovegni. All the while, the silences between her responses grew longer and heavier.

When I left her, she seemed in lower spirits than ever, and I deployed some of my excess of attendants in picking her some flowers from the gardens and ensuring she had something special for lunch. It was clear that she was suffering, but I was confident that she would be herself again soon. She just needed more time.

CHAPTER
SEVENTEEN

I stepped out of the carriage in a great rustle of fabric that my attendants quickly set about arranging around me. I was dressed in a stiff taffeta the colour of dried blood and the entire ensemble was a tad more ostentatious than the occasion warranted. But when I looked up at the soaring spires of the keep, like blades set to slice the slate grey sky to ribbons, I was glad of my choice. I wanted everyone who looked upon me here to be reminded of my power and position. I wanted no one to be able to see me without remembering that I was about to become their queen.

Several men in druthi robes waited to greet me, Grand Weaver Dovegni at their head. He stepped forward with a wide sweep of his hands, his heavy gold chain of office thumping against his chest.

'Welcome, my lady,' he boomed as he bowed, but I caught the faintest twitch of a sneer at the corners of his mouth. 'You honour us with a visit so soon after your wedding.'

I smiled tightly. 'Your Grace, please, Grand Weaver. The council may be dithering over crowning me consort, but my elevation to duchess in the meantime has been approved.'

His eyes narrowed. 'Forgive me, *Your Grace*.'

I let the sarcasm slide. 'The Druthi Guild plays such an important role in decisions made about Brimordia's governance that I made it my top priority to visit. I wish to be fully across what goes on here so I can best support my husband.'

The mocking smile vanished. 'I hope you don't mean to be too thorough. It is not custom for the Crown to monitor the guild. I would hate to take up too much of your valuable time.'

I curled back my lips in a smile. 'I can think of nothing I would rather spend my time on. Come now, there's no reason we can't be friends. Perhaps we can start with a tour.' I advanced towards the entrance of the keep without waiting for Dovegni to join me. My attendants fell into formation behind me.

'Your Grace, your attendants,' he called, and I paused to look back at him.

'What about them?'

'I'm afraid I'll have to insist on their remaining outside,' he said as he drew level with me. I raised my eyebrows in question; I'd gladly be rid of them, but there was no reason he should believe I would do anything simply because he *insisted*. 'Only ordained druthi may pass through those doors,' he continued. 'While the royal family are exceptions to that law, no such concession exists for your attendants. Perhaps Your Grace would like to postpone your visit until such a time as you are better prepared to be without them?' He cast a pointed glance at my gown, with its flounces and petticoats and train.

'That won't be necessary. If it is important to you that they remain here, then they will.' With a flick of my hand, I motioned for my attendants to stay put, one small submission that made me grit my teeth, no matter that I'd be glad to be rid of the gaggle of women. Submitting to him on *any* matter felt like a bitter defeat, but I wanted him to believe I was malleable.

Dovegni's smile returned. 'You'll come to learn the customs and laws associated with your position in time, Your Grace.' He swept up the path ahead of me as I glared holes through the back of his head.

Passing through the cavernous doorway, curiosity overcame my irritation. The entrance hall was dominated by a wide stone staircase lined with elaborate candelabras in the form of gruesome gargoyles perched on the polished onyx balustrade, their arms outstretched to hold out handfuls of light in their claws. The steady, white illumination of magic lit enormous marble columns flanking the staircase that stretched up to the domed ceiling and braced a series of galleries above.

'The entrance hall has been remodelled twice throughout the last several hundred years, with the balustrade and gargoyles being added in the time of Grand Weaver Erenagh...'

I quickly tuned out Dovegni's droning commentary when it became obvious that his aim was to bore me to tears. Each step up the staircase sent a thrill of excitement through me as I craned my neck to take in the room and see where the staircase would lead. The galleries above were stacked on top of each other, floor after floor after floor of them, and robed figures darted in and out of sight as they moved through the upper floors, some stopping to peer down at us.

He led me down a corridor lined with portraits of all the previous Grand Weavers and treated me to a recitation of who each was
and what their major contributions had been to the building as I
tried to peer into doors and down corridors. Madeia help me if my
whole visit was just going to be trailing along after him while he
showed me the least interesting parts of the keep. Maybe I could
club him over the head with a shoe and stuff him in a cupboard so
I could explore where I wanted.

A door opened ahead, and a crowd of boys poured into the
hallway, their voices filling the air as they jostled one another. They
quickly settled down when they caught sight of us, and Dovegni
surveyed them as they passed us, greeting them by name and nodding in approval as they shot furtive glances at me.

Dovegni led me into an utterly ordinary office, with utterly ordinary bookshelves and an utterly ordinary desk piled with utterly
ordinary papers, and offered me a seat in an utterly ordinary chair.
He sat opposite me and began fiddling with his ring, the one I'd
noticed the first night I met him. A black stone shot with blue.

'I fear I haven't yet *congratulated* you on your wedding,' he
said. 'How caught up His Majesty must have been, to wed you so
suddenly.' His thin lips stretched into a leer. 'How *eager*.'

'It's lucky he did, or I wouldn't be allowed to call on you here,' I
said, smiling sweetly as I imagined what it would be like to punch
him in the nose. 'I admit, I do have an ulterior motive for visiting.'
I let the thought dangle, let his imagination race to fill in the blanks
as I leaned forward.

'Which is?' he pressed after a glance at my cleavage.

'Oh, I'm *fascinated* by magic. The thought of being given a tour of Misarnee Keep by the Grand Weaver himself was just too enticing to resist. There must be *so* much to see here.'

He sat back in his chair and frowned. 'You understand there are secrets that even now, in your position, you cannot access.'

'I did fear that might be the case,' I said with a dramatic sigh. 'Silly me, expecting to see something exciting. I could hardly sleep last night for anticipation. I shouldn't have set so much in store for this visit. My disappointment is my own fault.'

'I didn't say I couldn't show you anything. Just not everything.'

The door opened, and a boy entered carrying a silver tray with a single goblet, which he offered to the Grand Weaver. Without a word, Dovegni twisted his ring over the goblet until rusty-coloured powder fell into the liquid, before picking up it up. He swirled its contents around then drank the whole lot in a few mouthfuls. I resented not being offered a drink myself, but watching him slurp at his own made me feel vaguely revolted and I decided I wouldn't have accepted one anyway. As he placed the goblet back on the tray, a shudder ran through him, and with a sigh he straightened up, his face flushed and his eyes bright. Whatever had been in that powder seemed to have reinvigorated him.

As the boy left, Dovegni rose to his feet and offered me his hand. 'I'm sure we can find something to... excite you.'

The act of taking his hand made me want to shudder, but I beamed at him as though I was delighted. 'I can hardly wait.'

There were no more tours of portrait galleries now, nor lectures on architecture. Perhaps he had initially wanted to bore me, but his pride seemed to have shuffled that plan off to the side. How pre-dictable. A few well-timed strokes to his ego and he was dancing to my tune. He showed me a laboratory full of clicking and whirling instruments, jars of powders, and vials of a viscous red liquid that glinted in the sun, the sight of which made me feel vaguely queasy. We toured a cavernous room that echoed our words back to us and hung with the smell of smoke.

'Weapons and defence testing,' he explained as I peered at a series of shadowy silhouettes lined against a wall. 'Not a terribly lucrative business at present, but we continue to advance our research in any case. His Majesty has shown an interest in an enchantment that renders armour impenetrable, chiefly because it also staves off other kinds of wear.'

'What other kinds of weapons have you developed?' I asked, my words reverberating off the walls.

But he refused to tell me, citing 'security,' and ushering me onwards to visit a greenhouse full of magically enhanced plants. It was a grotesque place, full of plants that were bloated and strange, bearing fruits and vegetables that were off-colour and malformed.

'You know of the corrosive nature of magic?' he asked as he peered at what might have been a broad bean, but it was the size of my forearm and riddled with bulging veins of glistening black, like streams of oil. I nodded, and he ran his fingers down the vegetable. 'We know that a little magic will enhance plant growth, but without more the plant quickly withers and dies. On the other hand, to continue treating plants with enchantment has unpredictable consequences. You can imagine the impact if we are able to solve this conundrum.'

He plucked the bean and handed it to me, and I ran my own fingers over it. The texture was wrong, slightly slimy, like the skin of a frog. 'That's why it's so important that we are able to expand our recruitment capabilities. Who knows which young man will be the one with the solution?'

'If long term magic treatment does this to plants, what does it do to, say, those that use it on their faces or their hair?'

He snatched the bean away and tossed it to the soil. 'It's only an effect we've witnessed in plant life.' His tone was offhand, his eyes directed away from me, and I was tempted to keep him from brushing the question away. What was he not saying? And could I interrogate him without it resulting in a return to the mind-numbingly dull tour he'd planned on treating me to? Unlikely. Perhaps it wasn't a question for now.

'Your Grace,' Dovegni called from the door, yanking me out of my thoughts. 'If you'd like to follow me, we can look in on a class of initiates.'

It was becoming clear that the Grand Weaver had an agenda of his own as he led me through a series of hallways, elaborating the whole way on how new members brought fresh ideas, and how greater numbers of initiates accelerated their research outcomes. We passed through a low door that emerged onto a balcony overlooking a room full of adolescents.

I peered down over the rows of desks and bent heads, watching an older druthi with wild silver hair wander between them.

'Do you know much of our selection process?'

Of course not, and he knew I didn't. 'No. I thought that was the point of the secrecy.'

He inclined his head in acknowledgement. 'Many think we look for inherent traits and abilities to work with magic, but they misunderstand how magic works. It is a learned art, a science. We seek out boys with vast intellects, as well as evident commitment to entering the profession, as these make the best students and the most effective druthi. Some come from noble families, but many are also commoners, and when a student demonstrates these traits but lacks financial support, we provide scholarships.' He placed his hands on the banister and leaned forward slightly, his expression pensive. 'It is a cause I take a particular interest in. Training as a druthi is a path out of poverty for some of our students.'

As he spoke, the teacher called attention to the front of the room, where he held up a length of cord and began to wind it in a series of knots. Periodically, he dipped the cord into a large ceramic jar, and it came out slick and dark and dripping.

'What is he doing?' I asked, straining my ears to hear what he was telling the class but only catching a few words.

Dovegni pressed his mouth together and leaned further forward. 'I believe they are weaving incendiary coils.'

I raised my eyebrows. Like all other druthi enchantments, they were too expensive for common folk to possess, but I'd seen the maids in the palace use incendiary coils to light the fire in my room. There was none of the cursing and rearranging of wood and blowing on sparks I associated with fire starting when they did. They simply tugged on their knotted cords and flames sprang forth to greedily eat up the offered tinder.

'They're weaving magic right now? Just like that?'

'Did you believe it would be a more nefarious process?'

I ignored his comment, squinting down with even greater interest now. 'But he's just dipping cord into liquid. Where does the magic come from?'

Dovegni straightened up and eyed me with an expression full of anticipation. 'To answer that question, it might be best to first show you the dungeons.'

I didn't see what the dungeons had to do with weaving magic, and his decision not to simply answer my question then and there riled my irritation, but I followed him, nonetheless. He led me down a tangle of corridors and staircases that grew steadily more austere, until we entered a small, bare stone room set with a thick iron door. A trio of padlocks held three bolts in place, and Dovegni withdrew a ring of keys to unlock them, popping each open with a click. He swung the door out with an ease that surprised me, given that it was so large, and behind the door was yet another staircase.

He took a torch from a sconce and gestured to the staircase with a sweep of his arm. 'This way, Your Grace.'

As we descended, the air grew noticeably colder, biting at my exposed skin and causing me to cross my arms tightly across my chest. Paired with the smell of mould and damp stone, it made for a clear signal that no one descended these steps for any pleasant reasons.

'Will you give me a hint as to what you're about to show me, or do you insist on the suspense?' I asked peevishly.

'We're almost there,' was the only reply I received, and I huffed a sigh as I hitched my skirt a little higher to avoid a puddle of slime on the next step down.

After what seemed like a climb into the belly of the earth, the staircase levelled out into a grubby stone floor, and I ducked my head under a low doorway to come out into the dungeon of the keep. A series of interconnecting tunnels were lined with tiny cells, complete with iron bars. It was so dark there were pits of thick shadow between territories of flickering torchlight. Water dribbled down the walls to pool in oily puddles on the floor. The sound of it dripping from above was a dreary reprise.

'I hope you don't mean to lock me up down here,' I said, only half joking as I peered into the darkness.

He gave a thin smile. 'Not unless you possess magic.'

My eyes flashed to him, wide with sudden panic, but fortunately he was walking to the nearest cell, his gaze fixed on something inside. I sucked in a breath to calm my racing heart, glad he hadn't seen the shock that had splashed across my face, but still wary at the reminder that I was in the dungeon of Misarnee Keep with my face cloaked in profane magic. But if he suspected me, he surely would have watched to see how I reacted to his comment, wouldn't he? Nevertheless, I would need to be on my guard. I followed him slowly, looking to where his eyes were fixed.

In the rear of the cell a figure was slumped on the floor. It looked like a woman with long hair knotted into matted ropes obscuring her face. She was painfully thin and smeared with filth. Dovegni held his torch aloft, shedding more light onto her, and I gasped.

'Have you ever seen fall spawn in the flesh before?' he asked, his tone smug. The additional light revealed that she had an extra set of arms sprouting from her ribcage to fall loosely across her knees. She flinched at the sound of Dovegni's voice, lifting her head to reveal a pointed face with severe cheekbones and an inhumanly long nose. Her eyes were huge, round, and luminous, catching the light like a cat's as she blinked at us. She opened her small mouth and made a trilling noise, somewhere between a gurgle and a purr.

'Why is she in here?' I asked, my throat tight. I thought fall spawn would be horrifying. They were described as ugly, terrifying, unnatural. But as she leaned forward a pair of translucent wings flitted into the space behind her and it was clear to me that, despite the grime and the strangeness of her features, she was beautiful in the same way as an exotic orchid or a colourful insect was. Inhuman, certainly, but not horrifying.

'*It* is here for blood harvest,' he said, as though the revelation was as mundane as a comment about the weather.

'For *what*?'

'You wanted to know how we weave magic. Here is your answer. The fall spawn generate the magic and we collect it, working it into enchantments or consuming it directly, depending on what we are hoping to achieve.'

Horror and revulsion oozed down my spine. 'Their blood?'

'Think of it as a raw material, like flour to a baker. We collect the flour, so to speak, and what we add to it and how we bake it leads to countless creations.' This explanation had the quality of something repeated, like he used this analogy often, perhaps with new initiates.

'So, you have no magic of your own?' I wanted to tear my eyes away from the creature on the floor, to crawl away from the knowledge that she was chained up down here in the dark, having the blood drained from her veins to make *cleaning enchantments*, but I couldn't seem to break her gaze. A small whisper of a thought flitted through my mind, just the faint echo of words, and I felt a queasy sense of an alien presence, as though the thought didn't belong to me.

Help me.

Dovegni snorted. 'Would you expect the body of a blacksmith to produce iron, or a dressmaker to shed cloth? We are craftsmen,

Your Grace. To be a druthi is to study the arts of weaving magic and to master techniques for achieving different effects, with varying degrees of finesse.' Without warning, he rapped his torch against the iron bars, causing the creature to break her stare and turn to hiss at him. 'Forgive me for startling you,' he said to me as he glared at the creature. 'It is blood bound so unable to access its magic, but some dregs of mesmerism seem to cling to this species. I wouldn't expect you to be able to resist, given your lack of experience with such a thing.'

A realisation gripped me suddenly, and I glanced down the tunnel at the flames of torches guttering and swaying on the walls stretching out for a few hundred meters before curving away and hiding the end from sight. 'How many of them do you have down here?'

'Currently? I wouldn't know. They tend to last several months before they expire, so the numbers are constantly in flux. Would you like to look at some of the others?'

I shook my head, keeping my mouth closed tight.

He smiled coldly, his eyes hard. 'Very well. If you've seen enough, I believe lunch will be served shortly. The cold down here always leaves me ravenous.'

I followed him back up the stone stairs, grappling with a thick, sticky form of sorrow. *The fall spawn are monsters,* I kept telling myself. They were so monstrous they were said to have been unleashed when Aether fell from the sky and split the earth. Binders would often pass through the Winking Nymph, regaling us with their tales of fearsome creatures who could paralyse a human with a look before devouring them while still alive and able to feel the teeth ripping through them, incapable of struggling or even opening their mouth to scream their agony. There were fall spawn who hid beneath the surface of bogs and pounced on the unwary, dragging any they captured to a murky grave, and those who could swoop down from the sky and pluck a human up in their talons to carry away and consume.

I kept seeing the luminous eyes of the creature in the cell, the way she had slumped against the wall, those iridescent, fragile wings. I knew any of the creatures the binders managed to capture were sold, but I suppose I had never given much thought to why anyone would want to buy them. Until now.

Dovegni and I were served lunch in a courtyard fragrant with jasmine, and he spoke a great deal about his plans for the guild, but I hardly listened to him, even though I was supposed to be charming him. When it came time to leave, I found I was eager to flee the incessant sound of his voice and the smug look of satisfaction he wore as he looked around at his little empire.

He walked me to the carriages awaiting to ferry me back to the palace. My attendants all scrambled to rise from where they had been waiting beneath a shaded glade of trees, no doubt grumbling to each other about having been left there so long.

'I'm sure I don't need to remind you that what you have seen today is a precious secret,' Dovegni said when we were a few paces away from the carriage. 'We wouldn't want just anyone having access to the knowledge of how magic is woven.'

'I won't be selling your secrets,' I said, annoyed at his slowed pace when I was eager to be gone.

He halted altogether, forcing me to stop and frown at him. 'In an effort to protect the populace against unsanctioned magic use, we are very serious about those who spread such secrets. *No one* is above these laws.'

We eyed each other steadily. 'I grew up in this city, Grand Weaver,' I said, my voice quiet and even. 'I don't need reminding about the lengths you'll go to protect your magic.'

That seemed to satisfy him, and he handed me into the carriage. 'I am glad we understand each other.'

As I settled onto the bench, I had an idea. 'I expect your desire to increase your recruitment capacity will require significant funding,' I said casually, pretending to focus on arranging my skirts.

'Of course.'

I looked up at him from beneath my lashes. 'I'm sure you can understand that providing a better life for the less fortunate is a cause that I'm drawn to.'

I hated needing to reference my low birth, but he surprised me with a genuine smile. 'I can understand that more than you'd think.'

Well, that was something to unpack later. 'I'm interested in your scholarships. My current situation leaves me with little ability to help,' I continued, 'but if I happen to find myself a situation where funding scholarships is within my power, you can expect me to do so.'

He considered me for a few moments. 'I appreciate your interest, Your Grace. I will have to hope you will one day find yourself in such a position.'

'If your hope is as powerful as your magic, I'll be grateful for it,' I purred, before flicking my hand to indicate that I was ready to leave. The driver closed the door of the carriage as Dovegni stepped back, his expression pensive.

As the carriage pulled away, I plucked the gloves from my hands and threw them onto the floor before folding my arms tight across my chest and glaring out the window. The whole visit had left me feeling slimy. Having to seek favour from Dovegni was revolting, but if I was honest with myself, it wasn't just the company I'd kept that was unsettling me.

When I returned to the palace, I was surprised to find the king waiting for me, pacing the hall by my door.

'Linus? Is everything alright?' I asked warily. There was something off, something in his posture and his expression that I didn't like one bit.

He scanned me from head to toe as a scowl sunk into his face. 'I know where you've been.'

The tone immediately set me on edge, but I tried not to react. 'I've been touring Misarnee Keep.'

'I was told all about it, how you were dressed like you're going to a ball, and now I can see it was true.'

I almost asked him to repeat himself. Surely, that deranged look in his eyes, the twitching jaw, and clenched fists, couldn't be *jealousy*? Over *Dovegni*?

'I don't know what to say to that,' I replied, trying to keep my voice even. 'You suggested I tour the keep, so I did. I dressed like this because I wanted to appear worthy to be your queen.'

With a jab of his hand, he reached out and seized a hold of my necklace, pulling the chain tight against my skin. I gasped in shock and grabbed his wrist, but he held on tight.

'No number of fine jewels will ever hide what you are,' he snarled.

Shock struck me dumb. Then the rage set in. 'Unhand me,' I hissed.

For a moment, it seemed as though he wouldn't. Then that feverish energy left his eyes and the anger parted to reveal confusion. He released me and I jerked away from him. He stood before me and stared as though he suddenly didn't know who I was, his hands flexing open and shut. Then the anger slammed back down over his face again.

He jabbed a finger at me. 'You're not going to leave the palace again. You stay here. I want to know where you are at all times.'

'You can't do that to me! You can't trap me here. I'm not your prisoner.'

'No. You're my wife. That gives me even more right.'

He spoke with undeniable authority, and I realised that he absolutely could do that to me. He was the king. 'You repugnant old fool,' I spat. 'Just try and keep me locked up. I'll go where I want to, and if I want to spend an entire week at Misarnee Keep, I will.'

He raised his hand and I flinched away, bracing myself for a blow. But it didn't come. He slowly lowered his hand and rubbed at his forehead.

'You'll stay in the palace,' he repeated, his voice a notch calmer, but still as firm and cold as the stone beneath our feet. 'You'll not be passing off any bastards as children of mine.'

What a fine note to leave on. I was so taken aback that I didn't even scream abuse as he strode down the hall away from me, still opening and closing his hands. I felt shaken, unsteady. The encounter was like nothing I'd seen of him before. He'd always been full of pride, and he liked me best when I was simpering and obedient, but I'd never clocked him as the sort of man who would hit a woman. Had my judgement been so off?

A hissing caught my attention, and I realised my attendants were clustered down the corridor, whispering to each other.

'Get out of my sight!' I snapped, my anger at Linus whipping out at them, and they scurried away, shooting glances at me over their shoulders that ranged from offended to smug. I watched them go, my mind whirling. Who had told Linus I'd dressed myself up for my visit to the keep? Was it one of them? Would any of those silly young girls really be bold enough to whisper such nonsense to the king about his wife?

And if not one of them, who?

CHAPTER EIGHTEEN

My fingers dragged over the spines of dozens of books, occasionally snagging on one and pulling it from the shelf before continuing on. I had an armful of heavy tomes already, all sporting such riveting titles as *Custom, Law, and Monarchy* and *The Three-Pronged Governance of Brimordia*. Essentially, if it was sure to be dreadfully boring, it wound up on my pile.

I had taken to sitting in the library to read, since sitting in bed usually led to me dozing off with the book I was meant to be studying splayed beneath my head. There was a particular hard-backed chair in the library that served me best, as it offered little comfort and no path to sleepiness, and the room itself was prone to drafts.

After adding *The Lawful Crown* to my thrilling pile of prospects, I crossed the room, dumped the books on a table and sat before a page of notes. They covered an array of subjects, from succession laws to ballroom etiquette to the political history of Cabrilla the Fair, Brimordia's only ever reigning queen. It was difficult to narrow down my study, since I wasn't sure what would be useful to me. All I knew was that I didn't want Dovegni ever making a jab at how little I knew about my new role again.

After my visit to Misarnee Keep, the guild had thrown in their support for my elevation to queen consort, so at least he'd given me what I needed. And after a few demure and beseeching visits to the sanctum, the Grand Paptich had finally relented as well. But my position still felt shaky to me, like everyone was scheming to be rid of me, so I was studying anything and everything that might help me sink my claws in and hold on tight. They would have a hard time getting rid of me.

Well, that was the reason I gave myself for spending so much time reading anyway. It had nothing to do with the incendiary arguments that had begun to plague my marriage, ignited whenever I so much as took a step out of doors. After all, what need had I to go anywhere? I was living in the lap of luxury.

'Hello,' a small voice said, and I looked up, pleased to have an excuse to leave off reading a dense passage on the Yaakandale rebellion. Gwinellyn was standing at the end of the aisle, her hands twisting in front of her.

I'd seen her occasionally since Linus had married me, at dinners usually, where she would sit silently with her eyes fixed on her plate while her father completely ignored her, but we hadn't spoken more than a few words since the strange interval we'd spent hiding behind the wagon at the Burnings.

'Hello, Gwin.' The short name she'd given me when I first met her in the infirmary slipped out of my mouth before I could think better of it, but she smiled.

'I haven't seen you here before. It's nice, isn't it, being surrounded by all these books?' She drifted along the shelf and ran her hand across the spines like I had been doing only moments ago, but whereas I was resentful, she seemed almost reverent. 'It's my favourite place in the palace.'

'I would have guessed the gardens.' I'd glimpsed her in the flower beds often enough.

'Oh, I do like the gardens as well. So long as my speaking tutor isn't there.' She let out a quick laugh, then fixed her eyes on the ground. 'I'm hiding from him now.'

'If this is your favourite place, won't he think to look here?'

She pulled a book from the shelf and ran her hand over the leather cover. 'I don't think he knows. All he knows about me is how hopeless and useless I am and how I'll never make a good queen if I can't even address a room of people.'

Was that sympathy turning at my mouth? Surely not sympathy for a royal princess who was so privileged that she had a special tutor teaching her to speak, and so beautiful that songs had been written about her snow-white skin. How could I feel sympathy for a girl who was going to marry the handsome Prince Tallius and have her life unfold before her without ever knowing true hardship, like hunger or cold or some vile old man's prick poking around between her legs.

'He sounds awful. Why can't you get a different one?

She clutched the book to her chest and said in a small voice, 'Father says it's good when my tutors are hard on me.'

A realisation settled over me, one I'd known in theory but hadn't truly felt until this moment. I was her stepmother. I was hardly old enough to be her stepmother. And if I'd been asked to hazard a guess at how she would receive having a stepmother, I would have bet money that she'd hate me. But looking at her now, at the way she kept glancing hopefully up at me, I had the sense that she didn't hate me at all.

'Well, I won't snitch on you. You can sit with me if you'd like.'

She beamed, and the expression lit her face in a way that almost made me jealous. She was definitely far too beautiful for *sympathy*. Taking a seat, she glanced over the books splayed all about the table.

'Are you looking forward to your birthday ball?' I asked as I shuffled my notes together and turned the pile face down.

'I'm so grateful to all the people who are putting so much time into planning it.'

Not what I asked. 'But?'

She fiddled with a book, curling a page headed *Revolutionary Tensions* between her thumb and forefinger. 'Everyone will be looking at me.'

I leaned back in my chair and considered her. 'Isn't that half the fun?'

She shrank a little, like a flower touched by frost. 'Yes, it will be. So much fun.'

'You'll wear a beautiful gown and dance the night away with your golden prince. And the whole kingdom will be aflutter with how lovely you are.' There was an edge of bitterness to my tone. 'The bards are already singing your praises and you haven't even had an official public appearance. Imagine what they'll say once you're sixteen and out in the world for all to admire.'

'That I'm awkward and clumsy,' she said, her voice so quiet I almost didn't catch it. 'Or that the whole court watched me fall twitching on the floor.'

At that moment, a man in a black scholar's cap turned around the corner to the nook we were occupying, his nose almost pressed against the page of his book. Looking up, he stopped in his tracks when he saw the two of us staring at him. He blinked owlishly behind his spectacles, before snapping his book shut and storming back in the other direction, muttering that women had no place in a library.

'Maybe he wants this table,' Gwinellyn said, rising to her feet.

I stared at her in disbelief. 'Gwinellyn,' I said slowly, 'you are heir to the throne of this country, and I am queen consort. Why in the name of the seven are you giving up your seat?'

She slowly sat back down and clasped her hands together in her lap. I continued to stare at her, baffled by her slumped shoulders, her downturned eyes, the time-damned *timidity* of her. I remembered what Senafae had said that day in the infirmary. *She's mad... Falls to the floor, frothing at the mouth.* 'So,' I began after a short silence, 'you have fits.'

Her cheeks coloured. 'Sometimes.'

'You're worried you'll have one in front of everyone.'

She didn't reply and instead curled more rigorously at the page, until she seemed to catch herself and suddenly started trying to smooth the curl out.

'I tell you what,' I said as I watched her, 'I'll make you a promise.'

Her hand stilled and she looked up at me with her wide blue eyes. 'A promise?'

'If you have a fit, I will do something so scandalous that everyone will be looking at me instead of you.'

A spectre of a smile pulled at her mouth. 'Like what?'

'Dance on a table?' I suggested. 'Kiss the Grand Paptich?'

Now she really was smiling. 'I can't imagine anyone kissing the Grand Paptich.'

'I *know*. Imagine how the court would gossip about *that*. But if he isn't nearby, I'll think of something else outrageous, and no one will give a fig for your fit.' The humour in her face dimmed. Aether's teeth, couldn't the girl lighten up for more than a few moments?

'Father wouldn't like that,' she said. 'He hates bad attention being drawn to the crown.'

'Gwinellyn.' The voice cut harshly into our little pocket of privacy. At the end of the aisle of books a squat, red-faced man was hurrying towards us. He was dressed fashionably, in an embroidered gilet trimmed with glass stones and blue sequins, and his gaze was fixed on the princess. He pulled up before us and offered me a stiff bow festooned with a scowl of disapproval, before returning his attention to Gwinellyn. He flung his hands theatrically into the air. 'You cannot keep avoiding your rehearsals.'

I studied the man as he began admonishing the ever-shrinking girl before him, dredging what I knew about him from my memory. He'd been presented to me, but he was one of many, and I couldn't possibly be expected to keep them all straight in my head. Croccus? Bronnius? Some high lord of the southern vales. He was listing tasks off on his fingers, and I began to gather that he was involved in organising the very ball we had just been speaking off.

'I'm sorry,' the princess mumbled, looking as though she had halved in size as she cowered in her seat. 'I know I have disappointed you.'

'Ten minutes,' he said in a tone that suggested he was talking to a scullery maid. 'Your tutor is already waiting for you, so that's all the time I'm giving you before I go to the king.'

'No!' Gwinellyn cried, suddenly animated. 'Oh, please, don't go to my father. I'll go to the hall now.'

He replied with a grunt, before repeating 'ten minutes,' offering me a curt nod, then storming back the way he'd come. I should have pulled him up on his lack of curtesy towards me, but I wanted to know who I was fighting before I picked a battle.

'Why did you let him speak to you like that?' I asked as I watched him round the end of the aisle, still muttering to himself.

'He's Lord Boccius.' She was staring at her hands, the colour high in her cheeks. 'My cousin.'

'Really?' I raised my eyebrows as I sought any family resemblance. 'That's no excuse. You should have him punished for his insolence.'

'He isn't always like that. He is... unhappy right now.' She glanced up from beneath her lashes.

'Why?'

'I shouldn't...'

I smiled warmly. 'But we are friends. I won't tell anyone.'

She returned my smile hesitantly. 'Well... he is married.'

'A blight on all humanity.'

She laughed and seemed to recover a little more from the berating she'd just received. 'His wife is quite young. And pretty.'

'And he is not.'

She leaned forward, her face suddenly alight with conspiracy. 'But Lord Terame is. They are *always* together.'

'If that's the case, I'm surprised your cousin hasn't challenged him to a duel.' Although, by the look of the man in his puffed-up clothes, I doubted he could successfully challenge anyone.

'He can't. Lord Terame is the Grand Paptich's nephew,' she explained, shaking her head.

Interesting. I filed that little morsel of information away. You never knew when a piece of gossip might be useful.

The princess rose to her feet and pushed her chair in under the table. She twisted at the fabric of her skirt for a few moments. 'You've made me feel a little better about the ball,' she said finally. 'Thank you.'

I watched her as she departed, envious of her light, graceful movements, like she was made of something other than flesh and bone. How could someone so beautiful be so painfully awkward? And how could someone so timid be born of Linus? I couldn't see any of her father in her at all. Perhaps she took after her mother.

But fire and brimstone, did she ever inspire a foreign desire to protect and nurture. What a daft promise I'd made. I just had to hope her speaking tutor's harsh methods reaped results, or I might be kissing the Grand Paptich before the week was out.

CHAPTER NINETEEN

The ballroom was hung with garlands of purple flowers, and their perfume practically choked the air. I was grateful for the fan Leela had paired with my gown, which was a whirl of glistening violet satin and lilac lace. Gwinellyn's birthday ball was my first real public appearance as queen consort, so it seemed fitting to wear the colour of the royal family. As I looked out over the room, I was satisfied to see that I was the only one who'd dressed in purples, and that while the floor was teeming with women in fine gowns the full spectrum of the rainbow, mine was a standout. I was surely the most glorious woman in the kingdom.

Though it wasn't clear whether Linus would agree. We were seated side-by-side on a raised dais at the front of the room, and the sidelong glances he kept firing at me were not affectionate. We had quarrelled before the ball; I wanted to attend meetings of his council, but he thought I was involving myself in things that were none of my business, and that I should focus my energy on befriending some of the court women I had slighted over the past few weeks. Some of the things he said, some of his knowledge of little run-ins I'd had with various people, made me suspicious that he had spies watching me. And the worst of it was, the whole argument had taken place in front of the still fragile-looking Senafae. It had been humiliating.

But what was even more disturbing was to see Linus show even veiled hostility towards me in such a public setting. He, who had been so skilful at masking his feelings, couldn't hide his resentment when he looked at me now. It undermined the feeling of victory I had been anticipating, the triumph of finally being seated at his side as queen, looking down on all those who had gossiped about me and despised me.

As I contemplated this, Linus stood and surveyed the room, and the chattering of guests seeped away like an ebbing tide as he readied himself to speak. When the last murmurs had died, he swept his hands wide.

'Welcome,' he boomed. 'You honour us with your presence here tonight as we gather to celebrate a very special birthday. Now, where is my lovely daughter?' He scanned the room below when Gwinellyn didn't immediately make herself known, as though expecting that she was having such a wonderful time that she hadn't noticed he was giving a speech. But I picked her out immediately; she was standing at the edge of the room, half-hidden by a stone column, staring up at her father with wide eyes, clearly gathering the courage to step forward. She caught my gaze and I raised my eyebrows.

She seemed to take a breath and roll her shoulders back before crossing the room to join us on the dais. I shot a look at Linus as she mounted the steps, and he was wearing his blandest expression, all polite distance, and I wondered what he was thinking behind the mask. He had to have been at least a little proud when he looked on Gwinellyn. She was radiant in a gown of powder blue, her dark hair coiled around her head in a braided crown.

'My Snow White,' he said, still addressing the crowd. The words made me unaccountably angry. It was a stupid nickname, so tied up in the colour of her skin, in her beauty. I knew only too well how beauty and respect were uncomfortable bedfellows, and respect was what she needed if she was ever to rule over this court. He was reducing her before she had even begun to speak.

'For so long you have been a little girl,' he continued, 'and now I present you to Brimordia as a woman, fully-grown and ready for her future.'

There was a spattering of applause, and Gwinellyn stepped forward to address the room. 'Thank you,' she tried to say, but her voice cracked and the *you* came out as a croak. She cleared her throat and tried again. 'I have...' She choked again, the words becoming strangled, and I watched as she swallowed a few times, her eyes scrambling over the hundreds of faces turned towards her. A few murmurs broke out and her gaze fell to her feet, the colour draining from her face, leaving her ashen and grey as her hand went to her stomach. With a jolt, I realised she was about to be sick, or to have the fit she had predicted. And *I* had promised her a scandal.

I began fluttering at my face vigorously. If I fainted, perhaps I could draw enough attention from her that she could slip away and hide out of sight. I was trying to decide where on the floor I would drop to when Linus stepped forward and placed his hands on Gwinellyn's upper arms.

'We are honoured to have with us tonight a delegation from our strongest allies and neighbours. Prince Tallius, I'd like to invite you to address the room.'

I picked out Tallius in the crowd as he immediately began pushing his way to the dais, his face glowing with triumph, though why he thought this a victory I couldn't tell. As he mounted the steps, Gwinellyn was shuffled down them by one of her attendants, all while Linus stood smiling pleasantly.

Tallius clipped a weave around his throat and began speaking on the value of the close relationship between Brimordia and Oceatold and the benefits that would flow from a closer one. Doing anything other than standing and nodding and smiling would draw the wrong kind of attention, but I couldn't steer my mind away from the sixteen-year-old girl who had no one chasing after her to make sure she was alright. I knew what it felt like to have my suffering met with indifference, the way it made the world seem cavernous and empty and cruel. It was not an experience I would have expected to have in common with Brimordia's princess.

It felt like a small thing to quietly descend the steps and follow the girl, leaving Linus and Tallius behind, but I could feel the eyes of the room picking me over, measuring my movements and cataloguing the moment for later dissection. I'd likely pay for the decision at some point, but in the moment, I couldn't seem to stop myself.

Judging from the commotion coming from a chamber just beyond the ball room, Gwinellyn hadn't made it far. A handful of attendants bobbed curtsies as I pushed my way through and the sight of the princess on the floor made me freeze, my hand flying to my mouth. Her body was twitching and spasming, her head lurched from side to side and only the whites of her eyes were visible through her slitted eyelids.

'Why isn't anyone doing anything?' I demanded, dropping to my knees by her side and helplessly holding out my hands. Should I try to hold her? To keep her from moving?

'A physician will be here shortly,' one of the attendants muttered. 'We can do nothing else but wait, ma'am.'

'We are not just going to let her lie here on the floor!' I reached out and tried to touch a hand to her forehead, but she jerked away. I tried again and managed to sweep her hair away from her face. Her skin was clammy.

A man in the blue robes of a palace physician was suddenly kneeling next to me. 'Please move away, Your Royal Highness.'

I considered defying the request, but I didn't see what good it would do, so I rose to my feet and backed away a few steps, watching closely, clasping my hands together to keep them from shaking. Gwinellyn had stopped twitching and was blinking blearily at her surroundings as the physician held a vial to her lips. She shook her head and whimpered.

'What are you giving her?' I demanded.

The physician shot me a disparaging look. I could read the expression well: *Who are you to be questioning me?* 'A sedative, ma'am. To keep her calm.'

Gwinellyn turned her head away and the physician took a hold of her.

'She doesn't want—' I began, but a hand clamped down on my shoulder, causing me to jump.

'Forgive my wife. She hasn't witnessed such a thing before. She is overwhelmed.' Linus's voice at my back made my skin cold. 'Continue with your care.'

The physician inclined his head before reaching over and clamping a hand over Gwinellyn's nose.

'Linus—'

He tugged me away just as Gwinellyn opened her mouth to gasp a breath and the vial was emptied into her throat. The sound of her coughing and spluttering filled the room as I was forced away, horror squirming low in my stomach. Linus pulled me to the side of the room and turned me to face him.

'This is not your concern,' he said, his voice low and unquestionable.

I swallowed whatever objection I was about to make. His expression brokered no argument. And he was right, it wasn't my concern. Behind him, the watching women were winding into motion, moving forward to scoop up the now limp princess from the ground, holding her between several pairs of hands.

'Where will they take her?' I asked.

'To the infirmary. It's the best place for her.'

I continued to peer past him, ignoring the glower on his face, but his grip on my arm only tightened. 'Maybe I should follow her.'

'No,' he said, with all the finality of a gunshot. 'You will return to the hall with me. My daughter will already be absent from her own ball. How would it look for my wife to be missing too?'

Our gazes locked. I was the first to look away, turning to scowl at the ground.

'As you wish, my lord,' I muttered through gritted teeth. He steered me back into the ball with a firm hand and I went with little resistance, smiling benignly as courtiers clustered around us and began vying for attention, all seeming to have forgotten the young woman currently being hauled away into obscurity, just a minor inconvenience that could be solved with a concoction of sedatives and a well-chosen husband. I pushed her from my mind as I settled into the role I had worked so hard to play. When a tray of champagne passed within reach I swiped a glass and knocked it back.

The evening passed in the endless tedium of petitions for favour. Most looked to massage Linus towards their causes, but some were sidelined long enough to seek me out in hopes that I might hold some sway with my husband. I was pestered by grand matrons seeking positions of influence for their protegees, mothers pursuing favourable matches for their daughters, Dovegni demanding I deliver on my promise of funding for his guild scholarship program and fashionable ladies extending invitations to soirees in hopes of garnering social status. Even as they were currying favour, disdain licked at the expression of every single one of them. The respect and awe obvious when they approached Linus was not extended to me. I may have been queen, but it was clear that it was a position no one wanted me in.

When the musicians began to play, I was relieved to escape the endless hounding when a grizzled old bachelor invited me to dance.

I drained my third, or perhaps my fourth, glass of champagne and we took up our positions on the dance floor as I caught sight of Lord Boccius across the room. He only drew my attention because his red face was contorted in so sour an expression that I wondered if someone had told him how he resembled a pig with his bulging belly and tight pink waistcoat. But a quick glance in the direction of his glower told me all I needed to understand. In a shadowy corner, so out of the way that I wouldn't have noticed if I wasn't looking for it, Lord Terame, the Grand Paptich's nephew, was leaning with his hand propped against a wall, talking intently to the very young and very pretty Lady Boccius.

I couldn't help but smirk as the dance begun. Gwinellyn had a better nose for gossip than I would have credited her with.

I was twirled from one hand to the next, slightly giddy with drink, trying to guzzle enough to numb the effect of the whispers that followed me wherever I went in the room, but not enough to give them all something more to talk about. The musicians slipped seamlessly from one tune to the next without my notice as I was twirled about by a procession of faces: sober men, kindly men, disapproving men, and those who looked on with lechery in their eyes, they all made as much of an impression on me as feathers falling against stone.

I was taking a break to nurse yet another glass of champagne when my hand was captured. I turned to see a head of dark hair bending to kiss it and felt a chill steal over me when my eyes caught on the long fingers gripping me.

'May I have this next dance?' asked a voice, deep and dark, burnt toffee and whiskey. A pair of pewter eyes met mine.

Draven didn't wait for my answer, tugging me after him onto the crowded dance floor. He stopped and drew me up as the song changed, placing one hand lightly on my waist, where it smouldered like an ember as he positioned me.

'What are you doing here?' I hissed, my blood rushing so loudly in my ears I could barely hear the music. He had donned the formal tailcoat-waistcoat-trouser ensemble that the courtiers favoured, but he was still dressed entirely in shades of black and charcoal grey. Surprisingly, he didn't look out of place here in this lavish ballroom, surrounded by people trussed up in the finest jewels and silks and furs that money could buy. I think it had less to do with the actual clothes and more to do with the way he wore them; his belief in his right to be there radiated so strongly from him that anyone looking on simply accepted it.

'What a greeting for the man who made you queen,' he said as he began to dance, steering me along as I tried to recover from the shock of seeing him. This past month had dulled my memories, had allowed me to convince myself that I was exaggerating the effect he had on me. With the shadow of a smirk coiling at the corners of his mouth and the slightly smoky scent of him beckoning, his presence was shattering every one of those fragile pretensions.

'You are currently jeopardising that achievement.' I stumbled as we spun and began to wish I'd drunk less champagne. It certainly wasn't helping the feeling of disorientation that was whirling through my head.

He steadied me without missing a beat, his hand slipping lower, his grip a little tighter. 'You had to have been expecting me. After all, you still have your end of our bargain to uphold, *Your Royal Highness.*' The last words were thick with sarcasm, and I scowled at him.

'I could have you arrested.' I lashed him with the words, wishing rather than expecting him to respect my new-found power.

His eyes narrowed. 'Really,' he drawled, and before I knew what was happening he was spinning me away from the centre of the dancefloor.

I tried pulling myself free as he began to tug me by the hand towards a doorway. 'Someone will see us!'

'Not if you cooperate.'

I glanced around uneasily, noting the way the eyes of those around us were conveniently turned in another direction as I caught the sharp, charcoal whiff of gunpowder in the air. Licking my lips, I allowed myself to be dragged along behind him.

The shadows of a dim hallway swallowed us up as soon as we left the light of the ballroom. Our footsteps against the stone engulfed the silence of the hall and I pulled my hand from his grip, my fingers thrumming where he'd touched me.

He stopped by a door and tried the handle, peering inside when it clicked open, then ushering me in and closing it behind us. I found myself standing in a parlour lined with dark wood panelling. The fireplace was unlit, the enormous mirror hanging above the mantel dark, and the far end of the room housed a spiral staircase that led to a small gallery overlooking the room.

The gloom only added to the sinister look on Draven's face.

'Are you thinking of breaking our bargain?' he asked, his voice containing the quiet menace of a viper.

I thrust up my chin and donned my most regal expression. 'I think you owe me an explanation before I deliver your next apple for you. I want to know what it will do.'

He gripped my defiant chin and held my head in that position as he glowered at me. 'I owe you nothing. Don't forget who gave you this life, this face.' He took a hold of my upper arm and dragged me towards the fireplace, fixing me in front of the mirror. Our reflections blinked back at us; a beautiful woman dressed as a queen, a dark man clutching her shoulders from behind. And then suddenly, that beautiful woman was gone. Mottled skin, shiny scar tissue, missing hair. I cringed away from the sight. 'I can withhold my end just as easily. And then what will happen to you, Vixen? How will you explain this to your new husband?'

'You've made your point,' I said, dropping my eyes away from my reflection and trying to shrug him off me.

'Have I?' he hissed, his breath chasing the loose hair at the nape of my neck, sending a thrill shivering down my spine. 'I hope so. Don't cross me, Rhiandra.' He released me and I jerked away from him, smoothing at my hair and clothes as my reflection shifted back, hiding the scars again. I saw him watching me in the mirror, his expression strange.

'For what it's worth,' he said after a moment of tense silence, 'being queen suits you.' He took a lock of hair that had fallen from my coiffure and carefully pinned it back in place, his hands lingering.

My heartbeat felt too light, too fast as I turned away from the mirror to look up at him. 'Are you surprised?'

'Not that you could do it. But perhaps by how well you wear it.'

I wanted to say something sharp, something clever, but there was too little space between us to leave room for wit, and for once he wasn't smirking.

'The king is starting to frighten me.' The admission fell out of my mouth, barely a whisper.

Something flickered in his expression. 'Not for much longer.'

The murmur of voices sounded at the door, and panic jolted through me.

'We can't be caught in here together,' I whispered, my gaze darting around the room for an escape. I fixed on the gallery and pushed Draven towards the spiral staircase. 'Get moving!'

His mouth quirked, but he gave in to my urging and we climbed the staircase just as the latch clicked and the door swung open. The gallery was furnished with little in the way of places to hide. There was a row of hard benches for viewing the room below and little else, but it was full of deep shadow so I pressed myself against the wall, praying whoever was down there wouldn't look up. Draven followed, though I had the distinct impression he was humouring me.

'...for dragging me in here. The king is relying on me tonight.' I recognised the voice of Prince Tallius; he sounded irritated.

'Forgive us, Your Royal Highness, we wouldn't accost you such if it were not of vital importance.' Those slow, wheezy words sounded like they came from Lord Sherman, one of the members of the council, and my ears immediately pricked. He was the one who paid household accounts, which was why I knew him at all. He'd muttered curses at Leela upon receiving the bills for my remodelling. What could that old codger want with the prince of Oceatold in an empty saloon?

I might have been able to guess if Draven had not distracted me by whispering 'oh my, vital importance' into my ear while he grazed his fingertips up my arm, rendering my brain completely incapable of rational thought.

'Come out with it then. It's bad enough that Linus is making a mockery of his court by parading his whore around the ballroom. The last thing this kingdom needs is for their future king to be absent.'

Draven stilled beside me. 'Maybe I should curse him,' he growled.

'Quiet,' I urged, 'I want to hear this.' It was interesting Tallius was already referring to himself as the future king when no engagement to the princess had been formalised.

'The whore is precisely why we have asked you here.' The cold, clipped tone of the third voice made me grit my teeth. Dovegni. 'Her influence over his majesty is troubling. His decision to marry her was out of character.'

The prince barked a laugh. 'I've had reports that she is meddlesome. But come, Dovegni, don't tell me some gutter snipe is resisting your influence. You've had Linus in your pocket for as long as I can remember.'

There was a beat of silence. 'She is shrewder than one would expect of a woman of her... character.'

'He called you shrewd, my dear. Where would he get that idea?' Draven took my hand and brought it to his lips, his voice barely louder than a breath. In the gloom, I could make out little more than his silhouette, his broad shoulders, the glint of his eyes. 'Look at you, confounding the kingdom's most powerful men. You were wasted in the streets.' He turned my hand over and kissed my palm, then my wrist.

'So, what do you want of me?' The prince's words were prickly, and I could imagine the expression of disdain on that handsome face.

'To confirm your allegiances.'

I shuddered as I felt Draven's lips leave my wrist to brush my shoulder. 'What are you doing?' I hissed.

'Imagine what they'd do if they caught you here with me.' His words ghosted over my skin and I drew in a sharp breath as I felt his teeth against the curve of my neck.

'To Gwinellyn first and foremost, and to Linus of course. If your interests align with theirs, I could see how we might support each other.' The prince's voice was more difficult to hear now. Had he lowered it, or was it just hard to focus?

'They'd kill me,' I gasped, pushing my hands against his chest with little conviction as he pressed me against the wall. 'I'd be beheaded for treason.'

'And if our king has lost sight of his own best interests...'

'Try to be quiet then,' Draven whispered, and with that he kissed me.

He *kissed* me.

Finally.

I lost all sense of where I was as I drowned in him, in his lips against mine, in the way he kissed me like he was slowly destroying me, like he was a crushing force annihilating every shred of resistance one millimetre at a time. His hands ran down my back, leaving lines of prickling fire in his wake, and I gripped his shirt and pulled him closer as something rabid and unfamiliar woke beneath my skin, something that relished in the feeling of his body against mine, something that disregarded every threat, every insult, that saw the trade of vulnerability for satisfaction and said *yes*. There was a rustling of fabric as he gathered my skirt and petticoat to skim his fingertips over my stocking and down my leg, pulling at my thigh, raising it around his waist, perching my foot on the back of one of the benches.

'...support of the guild over the sanctum...'

The words of the men below us became garbled, my mind failing to assign meaning to them and then failing to collect them at all as my focus shrank down to my body, to the way it was responding, to the way it quivered at attention as it anticipated his next move. I thrummed with wanting him, like I was the string on a lute being plucked just so. His cool fingers were a screaming presence against my hot skin as he slowly danced them higher, tantalising the molten heat that had roared to life between my legs, as though all the blood in my body had drawn to a single throbbing point.

'You don't confound me, Vixen,' he whispered. 'I know what you want.'

You. The answer tore through me with a gut-wrenching certainty, coaxed out of this newly primal part of me that only wanted to be filled, that wanted him closer, that did not care how he could ruin me.

'Touch me.' A demand, albeit a trembling one, and he obeyed, winding his other hand in my hair as he reached the part of me that ached, hissing against my mouth as he found me wet and wanting.

I dropped my head back against the wall as he traced circles against me, my breath coming faster, louder, until he took his hand from my hair, pressed it against my mouth and ordered me to hush, the command a wash of scorching breath against my ear. I gripped his neck with both hands and sunk my teeth into my bottom lip to keep from crying out as he slipped into me, his fingers slow, his pace measured, refusing to respond to the way I was beginning to tremble, the way my back arched against him, the way I pulled him closer.

The tension of months of wanting him shook me like an opium addiction, like I could scent the release I so fiercely craved. When he curled his fingers and broke the building tension, the relief that tore through me left no satiation in its wake. I was a quivering wreck of euphoria, all limp-limbed but still ravenous, still wanting more, and I gripped his hips with the intention to have it.

But he pulled away, withdrawing his hand, inviting a space between us that shocked with its detachment. He brought his fingers back up my body and held my gaze as he dipped them in his mouth, before grasping my chin between a slick thumb and forefinger.

'In case you forgot who you belong to.'

The room below was quiet and still, and I realised Dovegni, Sherman and the prince were no longer there. Perhaps it was a blessing; the fact that they'd left meant they hadn't discovered us. But that they were plotting in the very room I stood, and I hadn't been present enough to follow their conversation, left me feeling shaken. I pulled at my gown, straightening up as I kept my eyes on the wall, grateful for the dark that would hide my face. The silence was heavy.

Draven leaned in and placed a light kiss against my unresponsive mouth, then slipped something smooth and round into my hand.

'For your husband,' he said, each word landing like a stone dropped from a height.

My heart thumped.

Once. Twice. Three times.

'What will it do to him?'

There was the feather-light brush of fingertips against my cheek. 'Don't ask.'

I felt him leave, felt the shifting darkness like it was as thick as oil, felt the residue of him lingering on my lips, my thighs. I should have followed him, should have reached out and taken hold of him, demanded to renegotiate, to be told more, but my body felt alien to me, and my thoughts moved through syrup. His footsteps were loud and crisp below me, the door opening and closing like the final word in an argument we had never even began, and I was still standing in the gallery staring at the wall.

I had wanted him from the first moment I saw him lounging in the Winking Nymph, but what had just happened felt like it had nothing to do with desire. No one knew better than me how lust could be a game of dominance, and it felt like I had been played. I had been lured into a compromising position in the very room where enemies were conspiring, and if they had realised I was there, had realised I was with a man... If Draven had been looking to show me just how strongly he held me in his power, it had been an effective display.

Don't cross me, Rhiandra.

I flushed with shame as I wondered how I had allowed it to happen. I'd been attracted to men before, but this was a different beast entirely, one that seemed almost beyond my ability to resist, let alone to control. It scared me.

Gathering my skirts, my thoughts, and my composure, I packed the whole encounter into a little box in my head and shoved it to the side. I slipped the apple into the pouch in my skirts, and it sat heavily against my leg as I made my way back down the stairs. I stopped by the fireplace as I left the room, checking my hair and contorting my face until I wore a convincing expression of serenity and self-assurance. By the time I entered the ballroom, I had smothered the tumult of the feelings Draven had left me to battle and banished him from my mind completely. It was as though the whole incident had happened months ago.

I picked out the positions of Sherman, Dovegni, and Prince Tallius as I made my way across the room, noting the shifty glances they threw in my direction. They would require careful monitoring. What were their agendas? Dovegni, with all his harping on about expanding recruitment, wanted more power, I supposed. Perhaps I needed to honour my promise of funding in order to show Dovegni that I wasn't his enemy. Though the thought filled me with disgust, it could be easily achieved and would perhaps placate him for a while.

Sherman, on the other hand, was likely just the sort of leech who attached himself to people of influence, given that he had saddled me with his daughter as one of my ladies-in-waiting. I suspected he had simply thrown in his lot with Dovegni because he was a nice fat host to gorge on. And then there was Tallius, the golden prince who clearly believed he would be the next king of this country. My womb was surely the biggest threat to him, though little did he know that the idea of giving my huband a child made me curl up inside with revulsion.

I jolted when a hand clamped onto my forearm and tugged me to a halt.

'Where have you been?' Linus growled into my ear from behind.

I tried to shrug him off, but his grip was tight. 'Are you mad? People are looking at us,' I hissed back, and after a moment he let me pull away and turn to face him.

'You are supposed to be my hostess.' His nostrils flared as he spoke and I could see his temper in the red flush on his neck and the tops of his ears. 'You don't vanish when we have guests. You stay where I can see you.'

I eyed him coldly as I grappled with the desire to rebuke him for giving me orders like that, like I was one of his dogs. 'I was feeling faint after so much dancing and needed some air,' I said finally, when I was sure I could keep my tone mild.

'Then you've done enough dancing for the night.' His hand was back on my arm, and he began steering me across the room, apparently oblivious to the covert glances we were attracting. 'It's time for you to retire.'

'I thought you wanted me to play hostess?' I allowed him to pull me along towards the entrance to the hall, where a waiting Leela curtsied, eyes downcast.

He didn't respond, thrusting me towards her with a small shove. 'I will be up to visit you later.'

My gaze darted to his face, to the strange mixture of rage and desire in his expression. 'I'm exhausted. I think I'll be asleep.'

He leaned in a little closer and dropped his voice to a low snarl. *'I will be up to visit you later.'*

He turned and stormed back into the ball, his composure not quite slipping back into place, and I stood frozen, watching him go as shock and indignation and a little dread curdled inside me.

'Come along, ma'am,' Leela coaxed softly, shooting a hostile look at the retreating king. 'You can always lock the door.'

CHAPTER TWENTY

I stood before the mirror and let the magic do its work. There was that face, the one that felt unfamiliar now, that no longer seemed my own, and for once I stayed to look at it a little longer. I raised my hand and brushed my fingertips over my skin until the memories of feral heat and dirty hands overwhelmed me, until my heart began to race, my chest tightened, and my throat felt raw with bygone screams, then I turned away with a shudder and closed the door of the cupboard. It was a reminder I needed, a reminder to stay the course and not let my temper or my sympathies get the better of me. I may have climbed to the position I had wanted, had managed to marry a king and wrangle a crown, but I couldn't take it for granted. My marriage could be brought to heel if I could just swallow my distaste long enough to charm Linus back into his better self.

Later that night, the sound of heavy footsteps approaching roused me from my doze. The footsteps paused by the door, and the latch rattled.

'Let me in,' Linus demanded.

I rose from my bed, donned a robe, and wrapped it round myself.

'Now.' The latch jangled again.

I placed my palm against the wood of the door. 'I think you should go to your own bed.'

The sound of his fist thumping rattled the quiet of the night. 'Open the door.'

I swallowed, remembering my resolve to charm him, and turned the key, taking several steps back as Linus swung the door open and stormed in. He fixed on me and rushed towards me with his hands outstretched, enveloping me and pressing his greedy mouth to mine. He stank of liquor, and I turned my face away.

'You're drunk,' I gasped, pushing against him.

'Then you'll take me drunk. Have I not paid for your services in advance? Have I not married you and made myself the laughing stock of the three kingdoms?' he snarled. 'If I want you, then I will have you.'

I shuddered as his hands fumbled with my robe, and I struggled free of him. 'Get away from me,' I snapped, holding out my hands to keep him at bay.

His face twisted, his lip curling, and he continued his advance, backing me towards the bed. My heart began to pound, and I thought I caught a phantom whiff of singed hair, heard a ghostly echo of jeering voices. I struggled to keep my breathing even, trying to keep control of myself, to not let myself become overwhelmed by the panic I could feel stirring deep inside, by the scream that was beginning to bubble in my chest.

I curled in on myself, making myself small, letting my fear paint my face as I gazed up at him and gently laid a trembling hand against his cheek.

The gesture did as it was intended to; he blinked at the soft touch, the anger clearing from his eyes for a moment.

'Let me tend to you first,' I pleaded. 'Sit by the fire. You must be exhausted. You should drink some water and have something to eat.' I took his hand, and he didn't resist as I led him to an armchair and sat him down, smoothing at his hair as I did.

He caught my wrist and held it in a grip that was a stark contrast to my tender caresses. 'I'll have what I came for.'

I resisted the urge to slap him. 'You will, my king,' I soothed, managing to tug my wrist from him. He watched me with eyes like a feral dog, mistrustful and vicious, likely to lash out at any moment. The thought of letting him lay his grasping, brutal hands on me made my insides cringe. If I took him to bed like this, what would happen would be a far cry from love.

I poured him a glass of water as his heavy panting filled my room, choking any sense of refuge and peace I'd come to connect with the serene space. All I wanted was to be as far away from him as possible, and the knowledge that escaping him tonight would only mean that he'd come for me the next night, or the night after, filled me with bitterness.

As I moved to return to him with the glass, my eyes landed on the apple, glossy and enticing, perched on my bedside table. Without pausing to think twice, I picked it up and plastered a smile on my face.

'Do you remember our first night together?' I cooed, smoothing my thumb over the red skin. 'I saw this in the orchard today and it reminded me.'

His expression softened slightly as I swayed towards him. 'Waking dreams,' he mumbled.

'I was an awestruck girl already completely infatuated,' I lied in honeyed tones, supressing my instinctive revulsion as I perched on the arm of the chair and let his arm snake around my waist.

I held the apple aloft for a moment, letting the faint glow of the coals catch on it, feeling the way it seemed to reach out and beg to be consumed, dripping with enchantment that stoked longing and appetite and desire. I sensed when his gaze followed mine, locking onto the apple, his body becoming still and tense, his breathing turning shallow. I imagined how he had begun to salivate at the sight of it, how he longed to taste its crisp sweetness, to rip into its perfect flesh.

Slowly, I lowered my hand and offered it to him, meeting his gaze with an expression of wide-eyed sincerity. 'Let me take care of you.'

He snatched it from me and immediately raised it to his mouth. A coal spilt and spat up a shower of sparks as he sank his teeth into the fruit, the flaring light catching the juice that dripped down his chin, making it glisten. He consumed the apple in a few greedy bites, his lips smacking, raking his teeth along the core to capture every morsel of flesh, pausing at the end to suck every drop of nectar from the centre. Then, he reached for me, and I surrendered.

When I woke, I moved my limbs gingerly, gently stretching the tender places where I had been pushed too hard, gripped too tight. I was so absorbed in taking inventory of my body that it took me several moments to notice the cold, stiff form beside me.

A scream tore from my throat as realisation crashed down on me. When the first guard came rushing through the door, I was curled in the corner of the room, my arms wrapped around my legs, still screaming. It felt as though all the pressure and fear and revulsion and paranoia of the past few months had rushed forth like a breaking dam, drowning all reason and leaving me a trembling mess.

Leela dashed to me when she arrived in the room several moments after the guard, who was shouting orders and trying to rouse the king. She threw a blanket over me and wrapped an arm around my shoulders, her wide eyes fixed on the bed, muttering prayers to Aether in a tense and relentless burble. People began to pour into the room, servants and more guards and physicians. They crowded the bed, yelling over one another, and I could just make out the sheets being stripped back.

Dovegni was suddenly in the doorway, his eyes darting over the scene. Our gazes clashed for a moment, then he stormed in and parted the crowd, revealing Linus lying with his eyes open and unseeing, the skin on his face slightly blue, red-tinged froth gathered at his nostrils and the corners of his mouth. Then the crowd converged again, and I could no longer see him.

'Come, Your Royal Highness,' Leela said in a tremulous voice. 'Come away.'

I rose on unsteady legs and let her usher me from the room, the blanket clutched tightly around my shoulders. I began to calm as soon as we were in the hallway and away from the commotion of my room, my senseless panic replaced with a numbness that made my legs and arms feel like they didn't belong to me and were moving without my command. The image of the froth around the corners of Linus's mouth seemed burned into my retinas, scorching to life every time I blinked.

I was led to a room and placed in a chair, before a mug of hot, sweet tea was pressed on me. I barely registered the fussing going on around me as maids exchanged frantic whispers at the edges of the room. When a guard entered and loomed over me, I had a moment of panic that jolted me out of my shock. I tensed in readiness to dart out of his grasp and run, but he only stationed himself a few feet away and turned to watch the door, his posture defensive. I stared at him for several long moments before I realised that he was indeed there for me, but to protect me, perhaps from any possible assassins that might be stalking the halls. Little did he know that he should have been facing the other way, guarding everyone else from me.

The shock of his appearance seemed to have kicked the cogs in my head back into gear and my mind began to race. I had killed the king. It was too great a coincidence for there to be any other explanation. I hadn't known what the apple would do, had done exactly as Draven bade me when he had given it.

Don't ask.

I hadn't asked. I hadn't considered Draven's plans, hadn't speculated on what he would want the king to do next. I'd been too consumed with my anger at the man who had treated me worse as his wife than as his whore.

But that didn't mean I hadn't known.

Deep down, I had known what would happen when I watched Linus bite into that apple. Deep down, I had known what Draven had offered by keeping the knowledge from me.

Ignorance.

Blissful, wilful ignorance.

CHAPTER
TWENTY-ONE

B lack was a terrible colour on me. That was my main concern as I stood over Linus's coffin and tried to conjure up some tears. It was no good; I felt hollowed out, and the only disturbing waft of emotion that seemed to be lurking around my cavernous interior felt a lot more like relief than grief. I was lucky that veils of black gauze were commonly worn by mourners at funerals because my dry eyes were sure to draw comment if they could be seen.

I didn't turn when I heard footsteps against the marble floor of the hall, even though I knew who it was. The footsteps stopped at the base of the stairs leading up the dais that was Linus's temporary resting place.

'How do you keep sneaking in here?' I asked without looking around. 'If everyone could access the palace the way you seem to be able to, we would have a serious security risk on our hands.'

'Luckily, I am exceptional.'

I drew in a deep, slow breath and turned to face Draven, who stood staring up at me with a strange expression. There was a tightness to his mouth and eyes, and he ran his gaze over me like he was searching for something.

'You made me a widow,' I said without inflection.

He cocked his head to the side. 'You have made your own choices.'

'You should have told me what that apple would do.' I picked my way down the steps one at a time until I was standing just above him, and he was still tilting his head to look up at me.

'Would you have done anything differently if I had?'

'Maybe, maybe not. But it should have been my decision to make myself a murderer.'

He took a step, placing himself level with me, so that I was my usual head shorter. 'His death was a foregone conclusion,' he said. 'It was his life or yours. Enchanted love is ravenous, Vixen. It seeks to consume without ever being sated. He would have wanted more and more of you until, eventually, there was nothing left.'

An icy quiver skated down my spine. 'Yet another detail you should never have kept from me.'

'I don't remember you refusing my deal for lack of information. Don't play the victim, Rhiandra. It doesn't suit you. And you have more important things than self-pity to occupy your mind.'

With a sigh, I glanced around the hall, checking that we were still alone. It was a stark, brightly lit place to play host to a body, with white light streaming in from the tall, narrow windows lining the walls on either side, and I imagined how harsh I must look in contrast, all cloaked in black as I was. 'I have a funeral to attend, so you'd better get to your point.'

Something flickered across his face, like darkness shredding at a candle flame, making it gutter and spit. His lips twitched, his jaw ticked, and his nostrils flared. 'You weren't so desperate to be rid of me last time I visited. Unless you miss your husband?'

I snorted and descended the dais to walk the floor, and I heard as Draven fell into step behind me. The memory of our last encounter stirred from its caged slumber, but I quickly smothered it, putting it back to rest, but not before it sent a smirk slithering over my mouth. 'If I didn't know better, I'd say you sound jealous,' I shot over my shoulder.

'You have become too used to being desired. Don't conflate me with the other sops you have panting after you.'

I stopped and spun on my heel to face him, my pride smarting. 'Draven,' I said, my voice low, 'what do you want?'

He stopped with me. A shaft of sunlight caught the top of his head, bringing out warm hues of bronze in his dark hair. 'To ensure you understand your next move. You can keep the throne in your grasp now, but you'll need to act fast and smart. Princess Gwinellyn can't rule until she comes of age. As her stepmother, you're an obvious regent, but there will be others jostling for the position.'

Chewing my lip, I considered this. 'I'll need someone to back my claim,' I said slowly.

'Several someones.'

The metallic clang of the bells in Taveum's spire rang the hour, the sound dissolving into the quiet of the sanctum. I cast my eyes around the room, across the frescos decorating the walls, depicting the fall of Aether and his resurrection into the sky. The god's flaming eyes blazed down at me from above the door, and while

I'd never been devout, I felt as though he was watching me, taking my measure, issuing judgement from his holy perch. The doors themselves remained shut, but they wouldn't be for much longer.

'Right,' I said, my gaze flicking back to Draven. 'I know what to do.'

His mouth twitched. 'You always do.'

I studied him, looking for some hint in his expression of what had passed between us at the ball, a trace of possibility that he had come for more than to steer me onwards. It felt strange, to stand with him in sunlight, with no shadows to hide behind. Had he thought about it? Did the memory of his hands on me steal upon him in vulnerable moments, no matter how he tried to push it away? Was there something between us that I could leverage after all? I had always relied upon my ability to predict what those around me wanted, to scent weaknesses and massage them to my advantage. But for all the sunlight highlighting the sharp angles of his face, he was so inscrutable to me that we may as well have been standing in the dark.

Perhaps it had meant nothing to him after all.

'Of course, you'll just swan in with your third apple and ruin everything,' I said, trying to disperse the tension of our silence.

'*Ruin* everything?' he repeated, narrowing his eyes. 'I didn't realise you were enjoying playing happy families so much. Particularly when you told me you were afraid of your husband.'

'My point is that you ought to tell me who your third apple is for so I can plan for it.' I looked up at him from beneath my lashes, letting a smile shimmer at the corners of my mouth. 'We could be partners, you and I. You don't have to keep all these secrets from me.'

He was silent for a long, long moment, as he held my gaze. He reached for me. My heart stuttered, but he only tapped his fingers beneath my chin. 'Don't wear black for too long. It's doesn't flatter your complexion.'

I scowled, spinning away from him and striding the rest of the way through the sanctum and out the door without a backwards glance. Arrogant, callous, manipulative *prick*. I hoped someone found him in there and arrested him on suspicion of tampering with a corpse.

My attendants flocked to me, fluttering about offering water and fans and sweetmeats, and for once I welcomed their incessant chatter. I didn't want silence when my thoughts were altogether too inflamed right now, throbbing away inside my head. If I was honest with myself, I had never expected this deal to lead me here. Murder was not what I had bargained for. And if I was given the silence I so wanted to avoid, I might speculate on whether what I'd gained was worth the price. I might speculate on whether I would do the same again, given what I knew now.

Such banal reflections were, of course, completely pointless. What was done was done. And as I was led into a powder room for a final fixing of my appearance and saw that exquisite face, the one that had seduced a king, I suspected that I knew the answer.

King Linus the Third was to be paraded through the streets of Lee Helse. People had been pouring into the city in the days prior and the winding lanes and carriageways were choked with folk hoping to catch a glimpse of the funeral procession. The people wore purple, or waved it from their windows, or clutched bouquets of the colour, to show their respect for the crown.

At least, some people did.

His body was drawn in an open cart, purpose-built for the funeral. It was a dark mahogany, with wheel spokes of bright yellow gold, and garlands of monkshood, azaleas and lilacs filled the space around his cold corpse, obscuring the smell of death and rot. I walked behind the cart, as it was the custom for all mourners to walk with the deceased. The trampling of so many feet were thought to warn Madeia that another of her children was returning to her, with the greater number of mourners meaning a greater welcome by the goddess. Two glossy black horses with purple ribbons braided into their manes and tails pulled the carriage along and they shook their heads and snorted as they towed their burden.

The crowd lining the road within the palace grounds was so quiet as we passed them. They were palace servants and members of the court mostly, and I scanned them briefly, fixing on a pair of little girls holding hands, purple ribbons in their hair, tear tracks cutting down their faces, then a white-haired old man clutching his cap to his chest. A woman holding the hand of a little boy caught me looking in her direction and she scowled at me before bending to whisper into the ear of her friend. I was glad for the veil.

Princess Gwinellyn walked alongside me, her head bowed, grief rippling the skin of her pale face. I didn't know why she had foregone the veil, but I supposed she didn't really need to hide away for lack of emotion. She also didn't need to obscure the mess sorrow usually made of a face; she was pretty even with her red-rimmed eyes and pinched brow. There had been much muttering about her health in the immediate aftermath of the king's death. I'd heard she had been holed up in the infirmary and fed a steady diet of sedatives to keep her calm. The general consensus seemed to have been that she wouldn't attend the funeral.

But here she was, looking a little shrivelled, but otherwise surprisingly well. The spectators often pointed to her and whispered, and I realised belatedly that she'd never been officially presented to the public before this moment. Her birthday ball was supposed to mark her transition into public life, and it had ended in... well, it had ended here.

Guilt clogged my throat, and I had a harder time swallowing it down than I did when I was standing over Linus's corpse, which was ridiculous, given that *he* was the one I had murdered. I slowed my pace slightly, allowing the cart to draw ahead until I could no longer glimpse the still form of the dead king. It was making my skin crawl.

The palace gates loomed before the procession, and I wanted to sigh at the thought of how far we would need to walk. All the way to the Great Cathedral in the heart of the city. The Grand Paptich would plead with Taveum to relinquish his grip on humanity and return us to the days before time ravished the world and stole our everlasting youth, Aether would be thanked for the sun, sky, and water that fed our king's life, and then his body would be imparted to Madeia's care in the ground. The same rites no matter the man or woman, an homage to the fact that all were equal in death.

This particular man was dressed in cloth woven with real gold thread, and would be buried with enough wealth to build himself a palace in the shadow realm, but, nevertheless. I eyed the soldiers carrying the chests of said wealth as we approached the gates, wondering at exactly how much gold and jewels would be buried with my dead husband.

We passed through the gates, out of the quiet respect of the palace grounds, and into the square beyond, and the sight of the crowd made me nervous. The memory of the last time I'd been in this square was as sticky as the blood had been on my shoes that day, though I tried to scrub it from my mind. This would be different. This was a funeral.

Or at least it *should* be different.

The air beyond the palace walls was thick and heavy, laden with the heat that the greenery of the gardens had lifted from the day. The back of my neck was damp with perspiration within minutes, and I longed for a breeze or the shadow of a cloud to pass over the sun. The crowd lining the square looked wilted and aggravated, all limp hair and shiny skin as they shifted and muttered to each other, gazes flicking to the full retinue of soldiers who had fallen into formation around the procession as the cart lumbered into the square.

The sight of the crowd somewhat loosened the guilt that was hanging from me, refusing to be discarded. There was little grief to be seen here. I thought back to that flippant comment Linus had made, about the city wearing the consequences for the riot. If the mood here now was anything to go by, they'd worn those consequences with little grace. I hoped it wasn't retribution I saw in the faces of some of those I passed.

The city streets narrowed as the procession moved out of the square, pressing the crowd closer. I was forced nearer to the cart, and I kept my eyes resolutely fixed off to the side, trying my best to keep the corpse out of my eyeline, but I caught the stink of rot beneath the perfume of the flowers, which was unsurprising, given the heat.

An image flashed through my mind, of Linus sitting up in the cart and reaching for me, his eyes still vacant and the red-tinged froth still clinging to the corners of his mouth. I pushed the image away, but my stomach roiled. How undignified it would be to be sick with all these people watching. And their muttering seemed to be so much louder with the buildings funnelling us down the street. People peered down at us from the floors above, sometimes entire families complete with small children craned their necks over balconies and window ledges to get an eyeful of the decaying king.

There was a *splat* a few paces ahead of the first soldiers, and I caught sight of a little boy above being tugged back out of sight by woman with an expression of horror. He'd only thrown a cabbage, but it was enough to rile the soldiers. Already tense with the expectation of trouble, several of them began bellowing at the crowd to get back and the flash of steel caught the sun as swords were scraped from scabbards.

But the threat of the swords did nothing to quell the crowd. They began to push closer, shoving and shouting, faces twisting with anger. I flinched as something sailed over my head and met the wheel of the cart with a squelch, and the noise around me surged. My heart was a hummingbird in my chest as my gaze darted all around me, seeking some kind of escape. But I was in the centre of the road, surrounded on all sides by what was beginning to look like a mob.

A jolt of movement caught my attention and I snapped around in time to watch Gwinellyn clamber aboard the cart. What was she doing? Was she going to hide behind her father's corpse? She rose to her feet and made herself an even more obvious target, before throwing her hands out, as though she was pleading with the crowd, and crying out 'stop!'

I don't know what she thought would happen, but the jeering and shoving carried on unabated.

'Are you mad? Get down!' I called, but she ignored me as she fumbled with something in her hands. 'Gwinellyn!' I tried again as I dropped into a crouch by the wheel of the cart, my fear of projectiles overcoming my aversion to its cargo.

'Enough!' It was Gwinellyn's voice again, but this time it was much louder, projecting above the cacophony of angry commoners and threatening soldiers. 'This is a funeral!' Her voice cracked, and I looked up at her to see she was clasping a dark, knotted cord to her throat. The foolish girl had an ampliweave. Well, much good it would do her, given that she couldn't speak before a polite and listening ball room, let alone an angry mob.

But to my astonishment, the buzz of voices settled a little. People were ceasing their jeering and shoving to look at this little wisp of a girl balancing on the edge of a death cart like a crow with her black gown and black hair, her face lily pale. Perhaps they were turning to look because she was so ridiculous a sight.

'You... you might not know me,' she stammered. Which just went to show how little she knew of this kingdom she would inherit. Of course, they knew her.

'I'm prin... your princess.' She licked her lips as more of the crowd's attention zeroed in on her. A few people booed. Wonderful. Now she'd marked herself out as someone worthy of lynching and Brimordia's monarchy would end just as Yaakandale's had.

'And maybe I'm the reason you're so unhappy. Or if not me, then people like me,' she continued. The noise died right down now. They were listening.

'I know that there are problems in this... my... country that have been ignored. I have heard that you are suffering.' Her voice was growing steadier, and there was something about the way she spoke—with such sincerity—that I had to admit was captivating. 'But the man in this cart is... was my father. Not just your king. No matter his faults and mistakes, all deserve a dignified burial, at the very least for the sake of those of us who loved them. This is not the day for retribution. This is a day for grief.'

She took a deep breath, her eyes combing the faces turned towards her, and I could hardly believe the sight, but the soldiers were lowering their weapons. 'Taveum marks us all with time,' she continued, 'and this unites us, because no matter our differences, death is universal. So please, I beg you, hold your disquiet for this one day. Let me grieve for my father.'

By the time she was finished, there was complete stillness around us. Gwinellyn almost seemed to come out of a trance after the final syllable left her mouth, blinking her eyes rapidly as she shrank down and slipped quietly from the cart. She returned to her place in the procession, nodded curtly at the driver, and the next thing I knew the cart was rolling away and leaving me exposed.

I rose to my feet and eyed the crowd warily as I slunk back to my place beside Gwinellyn, and the rest of the procession began taking a few hesitant steps. The crowd drew back to allow the cart through, and before long we were marching on as though nothing had happened. Except now, heads were bowed as we passed. It was so peculiar, the way the people of the city just piped down like that, the way they whispered to one another, the strange, fevered expressions some of them wore as they stared at the princess.

I watched Gwinellyn carefully as we continued, my eyes narrowed. 'Where did that come from?' I asked when I drew close enough to speak to her, my voice carefully inflectionless.

She jolted as though I'd startled her, then flashed me a hesitant smile. 'They gave it to me, so I could speak at the funeral. I don't think anyone actually thought—'

'For fall's sake, not the ampliweave. You had a *fit* at the ball when you tried to give a speech.'

'Oh. I don't know.' She glanced at the cart ahead, her expression tight, as though she was trying to keep something in. 'This day is the last I'll have with father. I couldn't let it be swallowed up with violence.'

A cloud passed overhead, gifting a few moments of blessed relief from the sun as we walked along in silence behind the opulent cart and its motionless occupant.

'Life is happiest when you're a child, isn't it?' Gwinellyn said, her voice so quiet I almost didn't catch it. 'I didn't know it at the time. It didn't feel happy. But there was this tiny window when no one was missing yet. I wish I'd known that every other problem was so little compared to that day when someone would be gone.'

'I think you and I had different childhoods.' I was suddenly furious with her. What made her think I had *any* idea what she was talking about, princess of the realm, protected by a father and money and a palace safe from the world's rot.

She shot me a look, and... was that pity I saw? *She* was the one grieving. How dare she pity *me*. 'I expect we did,' she said, and without warning, she took my hand and gave it a squeeze. 'I'm sorry. You were so recently married. I'm sure your whole future seems like it has just been ripped from you. I'm grateful for how happy you made him these past few months.'

There was that nausea again. Surely, this time I really would vomit. I slipped my hand from hers and dropped back in the procession, letting other members of the court overtake me, ignoring the confusion on Gwinellyn's face when she flashed a glance back. I just needed to get this cursed day over with, and then I could focus on what I was here for. Before I'd merely been a consort. Now, if I played my cards right, I would reign alone.

The cart rolled slowly on ahead, each step of the horses bringing the dead king closer to his final resting place, his only daughter trailing along in his wake as she had done while he lived. He'd been distant and cold, perhaps, but was still the one person that girl could have trusted to want what was best for her, even if his interpretation of what was best was not one I would have agreed with. Now, she sailed on without that protection, so vulnerable, facing the vast world alone, her future leering at her from behind the hidden agendas of those around her.

I may never have known that window of happiness she spoke of, or the feeling of knowing that there was someone who would always fish you out of the drink in the worst of storms, but I had to wonder at who was better off. Me, for having always had to watch out for myself and knowing no different, or Gwinellyn, pining for a time long gone.

I supposed it hardly mattered. We would both be pieces in the power grab to follow. We were adrift on the same sea now.

CHAPTER
TWENTY-TWO

I sucked in a deep breath, squared my shoulders, and pushed through the door, strolling into the warm, stuffy air of the room beyond like I had every right to be there. The chatter quickly died away as the council turned their eyes on me.

'Your Royal Highness, I'm so pleased to see you out and about.' Paptich Milton spoke first, offering me a thin smile that I would not have described as 'pleased.'

I inclined my head. 'My grief will keep while I attend to the kingdom. That is what Linus would have wanted of me.'

Glances were exchanged as the councillors shifted in their seats.

'You are not expected to attend council meetings, my lady.' Lord Sherman sniffed, then offered me a placating smile to go with his wheedling words. He was a grizzled old man, with entirely colourless hair and a long nose that seemed perpetually drippy. 'Rest easy in the knowledge that we can handle necessary decisions. Your role as regent may be only a temporary encumbrance to you while we deliberate on a suitable alternative.'

I strode to the high-backed chair at the head of the table reserved for the monarch—and so still vacant—and dragged it across the floor. It was heavy and made a scraping sound so loud it seemed to echo through the chamber. There was a collective intake of breath as I sat down and curled my hands over the ends of the armrests.

'Temporary?' I leaned back and arched an eyebrow at Sherman, who looked like he was attempting to swallow a live fish. 'I am Gwinellyn's stepmother. Who could possibly be more suitable?'

From the corner of my eye, I saw Lord Boccius draw himself up.

'Forgive me for being blunt, my lady—' he began.

'Your Royal Highness,' I corrected him as I drew my gaze from Sherman.

He spluttered for a moment but managed to cough out 'Your Royal Highness,' before continuing on. 'You have not long been a member of the royal family. I hardly think there has been enough time to know all you need to fill the role of regent, or to establish yourself as the stepmother of our princess.'

'I'm a fast learner. From what I gather, I gained the right to hold the regency the minute I married the king. Or am I wrong in my interpretation of the law?' I felt the other members of the council shifting in their seats, and a few whispers broke out. At least now they knew they weren't playing cards with a fool. I had shown them I knew more of the game than they thought. I tilted my head as I examined Boccius. 'Who else could you possibly have in mind?'

'As Gwinellyn's cousin, and something of an uncle to her, I humbly submit myself as a possibility.' He bowed his head in false humility.

I cast my eyes around the table, noting the expressions which ranged from relief to indignation. With some satisfaction, I saw Dovegni's nostrils were flaring and there was a frown cutting between his brows. 'Hmm, yes, well a *third* cousin doesn't outrank a stepmother,' I said.

'The law on this matter is more of a guide than an absolute ruling, Your Royal Highness,' Sherman said. 'A regent cannot assume the position without the support of the council.'

'And the support of the heir,' I added. 'Has anyone actually asked the princess who she would like to act in her stead?'

'We would not wish to trouble the young woman.' Dovegni oozed forward in his chair, interlocking his hands on the table. 'Not with her... illness.'

There was a chorus of nods around the table.

I offered him a thin smile. 'If you won't trouble her for her vote on who should act as regent, I don't see how you can trust her to rule.'

Dovegni held my icy stare. 'Which is why I have been arguing to solidify an engagement to Prince Tallius of Oceatold. The late king always intended the union. The only reason it wasn't contracted before now was because he was waiting to use it as an enticement in the treaty negotiations. Now, securing Brimordia's rule is of greater importance.'

'We shouldn't be too hasty to broker an engagement without considering all options,' Boccius interjected.

I drummed my fingers against the tabletop. 'I would support an engagement, since I know it's what Linus wanted, but she still has the right to a vote. She ought to be offered that right. It is, after all, the law.'

A wave of grumbling broke around the table, but I could see some were nodding their heads, and Dovegni was casting speculative glances at me while he muttered into the ear of the man to his left. The public declaration of my support for the marriage was a risky play. With Leela's help, I had been carefully collecting information on every man on the Council, and I had some idea of the agendas at the table and who would vote with who. Thanks to the stroke of luck that let me overhear Dovegni speaking with Tallius, I knew the Grand Weaver was already courting the idea of the prince becoming king, so this declaration might help bring Dovegni on side, but I chanced alienating other members. I wasn't sure where Paptich Milton sat on the issue, and he had the hefty stake of the sanctum in his vote. I needed them both, and I would find a way to have them both.

'An official vote,' Sherman said with a nod, settling the room into silence again. 'A week should be time to prepare the princess.'

Prepare, indeed. Influence more likely, but I could play that game just as well as the rest of them.

'If we are to include the princess in this decision, I move to hold all other business and reschedule, so that we can invite her to attend. She should have some idea of the pressing issues facing the kingdom so she knows the effect of her choice.' This was Boccius's suggestion, and I narrowed my eyes. What was he expecting that would achieve?

Several murmured their agreement, but most seemed hardly interested in whether the princess was in attendance or not, then Sherman closed the meeting.

I rose, and they all rose with me. 'Until our next meeting, then,' I declared, before leaving the room. As soon as I had passed into the hall I massaged my temples, trying to stave off the fierce headache that was beginning to grip my skull. It felt as though there hadn't been enough air in that room. Tension cramped my shoulders and neck, but I refrained from rubbing them as the lords of the Council began to pour out of the room behind me.

Leela eyed me with concern as she joined me. 'Shall I send for tea in your rooms, ma'am?'

'Not yet. To the infirmary first,' I said with a sigh. 'Could you get me a copy of the agenda for that council meeting.'

She darted off to do as I asked, and I began the long walk to the infirmary.

Gwinellyn looked as ashen and gaunt as she had when I visited her the day before. The physicians had informed me that she rarely slept, taking to pacing her room or the halls in the night, no matter how often they ordered her to bed, and she'd had several fits in the days following her father's death. I pursed my lips in a frown at the sight of her and perched on the chair by the bed, my spine ramrod straight, my eyes already flicking to the door.

'How are you?' I asked, but the words came out stiff and mechanical. I cleared my throat, trying to summon some of the charm I'd always been able to call on freely. 'I brought you something to read.' I thrust the book onto her bedside.

Her eyes were far away when she turned them on me, but as she took me in, they tightened with something that looked like... pity. What did *she* have to pity *me* for?

I clenched my hands together, cursing that I couldn't seem to shake this damnable tension when I was in her presence now. My mouth was dry as I tried to decide how to word what I'd come to ask her, but she saved me the trouble by speaking first.

'You don't need to visit me so often,' she said quietly. 'I know you must have a lot taking up your time.'

'I do.' The words came out louder and more forceful than I'd intended, but I ploughed on. 'Not only am I acting as regent, but I have to fight to keep doing so. Lord Boccius is trying to oust me and take the position himself.'

She seemed, if possible, to blanch paler. 'Oh,' she exhaled softly. 'Well, I guess if that is what the council believes is for the best—'

'It's the best for Boccius and no one else,' I snapped. 'Aether's teeth, don't you have an opinion? This is your kingdom I'm speaking of.'

She shrank into herself, her shoulders curling forward, and that twisting feeling I felt in my stomach whenever I was around her intensified.

'I'm useless,' she whispered. 'I should be stronger. I don't know how to be.'

'The first thing you can do is help me. You're the heir, so you do get a vote, and your vote is worth more than any councillor's.'

'You can have my vote.' She seemed to be drawing deeper into her bed, sinking into her pillows as though she was hoping they might swallow her up. 'Tell them I want you as my regent.'

I sighed in frustration. 'I can't just tell them that's what you want, Gwinellyn. You'll need to attend the vote. And they want you at the next meeting so you're informed on the decisions your regent will be managing.'

Her eyes widened. 'I can't attend a council meeting.'

'Why the *fall* not?'

She chewed her bottom lip, which was already red and peeling. 'I just can't.'

I leaned forward. 'Can't or won't? Are you just going to let this pack of idiots make all the decisions for you? If it's up to them, they'll have you married off within the year and they'll put some fat husband on the throne to rule for you. You are Brimordia's heir! Does that mean nothing to you? Has all that privilege come so easily that you don't even worry to see it go?'

She wasn't meeting my eyes anymore, her face blotchy as she stared down at her sheets. 'I have... fits when I attend council meetings.'

Ah. So that was why Boccius wanted her there. He was hoping she'd fall in a twitching heap on the floor and the council would deem her unfit to cast her vote, unsound of mind. I grabbed her hand and she looked back up at me.

'Don't let them shut you out just because you aren't their perfect version of a princess. You have to fight to make them take you as you are, and if *you* believe your fits make you unworthy of your birthright, then you've already lost the battle.'

She blinked up at me, her wide eyes painfully guileless. 'But... I don't know about any birthright. Father always told me that my duty is to marry and support the next king. No one wants me making decisions. The council don't want me involved in decisions. I... I don't think I'm any good at that sort of thing.'

I dropped her hand and stood. 'If you don't stop eating up the lines you're fed without question then you'll spend the rest of your life trapped in a drawing room practising embroidery while some man rules your kingdom and your life.' In a few strides I'd crossed the room, but I paused on the threshold, my hand resting against the door frame as I looked back at little Snow White, so pale and delicate, every bit the fragile flower the nickname referred to. She had so much within her grasp, a world of power and influence just waiting for her to reach out and take it, and she was too afraid to even try.

'I'll have the details of the meeting delivered to you once I've confirmed them, just in case you decide you do care a whit about your crown and want to try and keep it out of your slimy cousin's hands.' With that, I left the infirmary, fuming at the princess's cowardice.

It didn't matter. I could win the vote without her.

I was looking forward to a nice, hot soak in a tub and a few hours of peace as I approached my suite. My shoulders were stiff and my head was quietly throbbing, partly from the day's tensions and partly, I suspected, from the wine I'd had to drink the night before. So the sight of Senafae sitting in my receiving room was more unwelcome than I would have liked to admit.

She stood as I entered, her hands balled in her skirts, her brows tilted in that particular way I had come to recognise in the dozens of petitioners that begged my ear every day. I almost groaned. She was here to ask me a favour.

'It's good to see you,' I said as I slid the gloves from my hands and handed them to Leela. I asked her to bring us some tea. She bobbed a curtsey and shot Senafae a sour look as she withdrew. 'How are you?'

'I should be asking you that. After all, you did just become a widow.' The words came out too fast.

I gestured for her to sit, and we both perched on settees as we waited for Leela to bring the tea.

'I will never understand why you insist on placing all your seating so far away from the fireplace,' Senafae said with a small smile, perhaps trying to tease. 'Though maybe it's a fine way to arrange a sitting room and you'll start a new trend,' she added quickly, after I shot a dark look at the fireplace.

'It's been a long day, and I predict tomorrow will be even longer,' I said after a moment of silence. 'It's not that I don't want to spend time with you, but—'

'I'm worried about you,' she blurted out, cutting me off.

I smiled. 'There's no need. I'm in a better place now than I've ever been before. I'm at the top of the heap, Sen. A queen. A queen *without a king.*'

'That's what worries me.' She leaned forward in her chair. 'Are you sure you know what you're doing?'

I waved a hand. 'The council is going to try and shunt me off to the side, but I have a plan.'

'Maybe you should let them.'

The words just about whacked the breath out of me. I stared at Senafae in utter disbelief, until she seemed to realise she had said the wrong thing. 'I just think,' she clarified, 'that this is a long way from being the king's favourite knock.'

I didn't speak, couldn't. I just continued to stare at her as though seeing her for the first time while my temperature slowly rose, flushing the back of my neck and creeping out towards my face.

Silence will often provoke people to speak when they should keep their traitorous mouths shut. Words began tumbling out of her. 'Frankly, it was mad enough when he decided to marry you. The whole country was a few wrong moves away from civil war, and all you seemed concerned about was *decorating*. And now you want to reign as regent? I just don't think it's a good idea. What do you know about ruling a country?'

She tempted me to speak with another short silence, before leaning even closer and placing a hand on my knee. 'Wouldn't it be better to leave ruling to those who know how? Give the princess permission to marry before she becomes of age. Marry her to Prince Tallius as has always been the plan, and then someone who knows what they're doing can take the throne. You'll still be rich, and a dowager queen, and you won't have to worry about all this political nonsense you've been involving yourself in.' She sat back and offered me a sympathetic smile.

'Get out.'

She frowned. 'There's no need to be rude. I'm just speaking the truth.'

'Get out.' My voice was louder this time.

'Rhiandra—'

'And when did you have time to formulate such well-formed opinions when you've been so absorbed in your own mistakes? You have the nerve to give *me* advice? To warn me off doing the very thing I've been working *so long* for? To *deny* my abilities, my *rights*, after everything I've done to get here?' I boiled over. My eyes burned. I shot to my feet, flung my arms about, began to scream the words. 'Get out! Get out! Get out before I have you thrown out!'

Senafae scrambled out of the chair and backed towards the door, her hands held up as though to fend me off. Leela came barrelling into the room and looked from me to Senafae. She placed the tea tray on a side table.

'I think it's time to go, miss,' she said firmly, ushering the woman I had once thought my friend and ally towards the door as I stood with my chest heaving, a finger still jabbed in the direction of the exit.

'If you spent one moment looking beyond your own self-interest, you'd know I'm right,' Senafae shot around my handmaid.

Leela managed to steer her out of the room, leaving me alone with my fury.

Everyone else. I could take it from *everyone else*. I could take the insinuations of incompetence, the schemes to unseat me, the disrespect, the sweet lies and double-edged truths from *everyone else*. But not her. Not from someone who was supposed to support me. Not from someone I'd *done so much for*.

'Run me a bath,' I sighed, massaging the bridge of my nose as Leela returned. 'I want to soak this miserable day away.'

'Of course, ma'am.' She bobbed her head in assent.

'No, wait.' My eyes snapped open. 'Have one of those useless creatures out there do it.' I flicked my hand in the direction of the door, where my mob of attendants waited. 'Did you find a copy of the meeting agenda?'

She brought me the sheet of paper, which I poured over eagerly, noting where different items sat in the schedule. 'I need you to send a missive for me.'

'Who is the missive for?' Leela sent me a sidelong glance as she arranged a cup and saucer before me.

'Lord Boccius. Inform him that I'd like the next council meeting rescheduled. It needs to be held in the early morning instead of the afternoon. That's very important. Don't leave until he has agreed to a morning time.'

Her expression was curious, but when I didn't elaborate, she simply inclined her head and slipped out of the room to do as I bid. I didn't have the energy to pick apart my next move with her tonight. That could wait until tomorrow.

After adding sugar and cream to my tea, I slumped back against the settee and stared at the wall. I didn't want to examine what had just happened, but I couldn't quite drag myself away from it. Senafae didn't think I should fight for my right to reign, that much was clear. And she had begun the visit with such an expression of neediness. How could she have thought that I'd grant her any sort of favour if that was the road she wanted to drive the conversation down? Had she just come to undermine my confidence? But what possible good would that do her?

Later, I lay awake in the stiff embrace of an indifferent night, thoughts caterwauling through my head. The moment the curtains around my bed had shut, I'd found the automated self-assurance that had been driving my every move since Linus's death drained away. I felt tired and lonely. I didn't know who my friends and allies were, or even if I had any. And what was I doing here, anyway? I was a street girl and a maisera, not an aristocrat. I had no business playing these games of politics where the stakes were the reign of a country.

The memory of Draven's voice whispered through my mind. *You were wasted on the streets.* Was he right? Could I really scheme my way into a regency? The memory of those words unlocked that little box I kept buried at the bottom of my subconscious, and suddenly I was remembering his lips on mine, his hands on my skin, and heat surged through me. My hand wandered down beneath my covers and dipped between my legs as I remembered the cold of the wall against my back, the prickle of his stubble against the curve of my shoulder. He would never need to know I'd thought about that moment again, so what harm would it do?

A moan escaped me, and the still room was filled with the rustling of skirts.

'Is everything alright, Your Royal Highness?' one of my attendants asked. 'Would you like a hot posset or another blanket?'

'No,' I said through gritted teeth. 'I'm fine.'

No one spoke, but I could feel them listening and waiting, ready to jump to attention. With an angry sigh, I yanked my hand back out from beneath the covers.

'Perhaps a—'

'Absolutely fine!' I snapped and I rolled onto my side, now tense with frustration. It seemed I'd be afforded no relief of any kind tonight.

CHAPTER
TWENTY-THREE

T he footsteps of my attendants was driving me to distraction. I had taken to walking at a pace close to a gallop in
an effort to put some distance between me and them, but they
were apparently as capable of walking fast as I was. Snapping at
them to give me space worked sometimes, but I was wary of overly
offending them, since they were all daughters, wives, or sisters of
the councillors.

Their presence meant I needed to be mindful of how I communicated with Leela, but she already knew her task. She positioned
herself by the door and she would stay there now until she had
what I needed. She nodded at me as I passed through into the office
within. The air was stuffy and overly warm. The Grand Paptich
was pouring over a ledger as I entered, almost as though no one had
announced my arrival, even though they had. Slowly, he closed the
ledger and stood.

'Your Royal Highness,' he said, giving a stiff bow. 'To what do I owe this surprise?'

I surveyed him with the attitude of an ice sculpture before I remembered that I was there for reconciliation and managed to inject a degree of warmth into my expression. 'Please be seated, Grand Paptich. I would like a few moments of your time.'

His eyebrows shot up his forehead but he returned to his seat as one of my attendants rushed a seat to the opposite side of his desk just in time for me to claim it. I flicked my hand and my attendants withdrew, closing the door behind them.

We watched each other across the desk, two opponents sizing each other up, awaiting the first move that would commence the battle.

'My condolences again on the loss of your husband,' he said finally, his words as slick as oil. 'You appear to be coping with your grief commendably.'

Of the jabs he could have taken, this one hardly bothered me. It didn't much matter if anyone thought I was madly in love with Linus anymore and phony grief wasn't going to get me what I wanted. 'Focusing on safeguarding his kingdom helps keep my mind from my grief. Which is why I wanted to speak with you.'

He leaned forward a little. 'I'm listening.'

'I think we could help each other.'

Milton stretched his lips into a poor imitation of a smile. 'You've made it quite clear that helping me is not something you prioritise.'

'But do you think I prioritise it more than Lord Boccius? Or the Grand Weaver?'

He grew still, watching me with more interest now. 'I don't see why either would not hold the interests of the sanctum in a place of high priority.'

'Do not talk nonsense to me, paptich, you know I do not buy your honeyed barbs. The tension between the sanctum and the guild is obvious.'

There was a moment of silence as he eyed me, perhaps trying to guess at my intentions.

'And why are you so interested in potential rivalries between the sanctum and the guild?' he asked slowly.

I placed my hands on his desk, spreading my fingers wide over the cold, polished wood, then leaned forward. 'If the council votes against granting me my rightful position as regent, Boccius will be the one who reigns instead. Princess Gwinellyn will be of age in only a few years, so perhaps it doesn't matter terribly to you who is regent, but I suspect he could wreak plenty of damage in that time.'

'And you believe you would do less damage?' he sneered.

'Surely, having someone who is, if not favourable, then at least neutral to your cause would be your preference. I have information that Boccius is aligned with Dovegni and his intention would be to diminish your role in the unsanctioned magic trials.'

His nostrils flared like a horse scenting a predator and I could almost imagine his eyes rolling back in fury. 'Where would you have come across such interesting information?' He attempted to keep his tone even, but I could hear the tension simmering beneath his words.

'I have my sources.'

He leaned back in his chair and steepled his fingers. 'Without knowing the source of your information, I do not see how I can trust it.'

'You'll just have to take my word for it. Or don't, but you can't say I didn't warn you.'

We regarded each other in silence. I watched him chew over my words, tasting them for flavours of deception, for motive.

Finally, he said, 'And I suppose you're promising to further my cause? To grant the sanctum the power to curb unsanctioned magic use without the guild's involvement? Dovegni has been able to use the Burnings for his own gain for years, with the guild deciding who is brought forward to be charged.'

The soot stains before the palace gates flashed through my mind and I felt a little sick at the idea that burning someone alive could ever be anyone's gain. 'I can certainly promise you a regent far more open to persuasion than Boccius. I have no secret alliance with Dovegni.'

He tapped the tips of his fingers against his lips, then dropped his hands, stood up, and bowed. 'Thank you for this elucidating conversation, Your Royal Highness. I will take some time to consider your argument and perhaps try to verify the validity of your claims myself.'

'You're a smart man, paptich. I believe if you start to look closely, you will not fail to see the collusion between Boccius and Dovegni,' I said as I rose to my feet. 'Thank you for your time.'

I mulled over the conversation as I left Milton's office. The sceptical old man would need some prodding to believe what I wanted, but I had expected that. When I returned to my rooms, Leela was waiting for me.

'Did you intercept the messenger?'

'Of course, ma'am.' She handed me a missive, which I quickly scanned before throwing it into the fireplace.

'Good. Any word from Princess Gwinellyn?'

'No, ma'am.'

I sighed angrily. If she would only pull herself together and cast her vote, the outcome would be all but ensured. But if I couldn't have her, then I would just have to proceed without her.

As requested, the meeting the following day was held early in the morning. And the Grand Paptich was conspicuously absent. I caught Dovegni glancing at the empty chair as a vote was called on a budget alteration that would have granted the sanctum funds for renovations of the Grand Cathedral, and when the council voted to deny the request, he smirked.

We were several agenda items further along when the door clashed open, cutting Sherman short, and the Grand Paptich entered with a flick of his robe, his attendant hurrying before him to pull out his chair.

'Paptich Milton, we were wondering where you were,' I said mildly as he sat down.

'You're lucky I am here at all. I was not aware our meeting had been moved.' His voice was tight with displeasure.

'Oh? Lord Boccius, didn't you inform everyone of our schedule change?'

'I sent a missive yesterday,' Boccius replied. 'Perhaps it became lost amongst the papers on your desk, Milton.' He was all ease, lounging back in his chair, unresponsive to the glare being cast in his direction by the cantankerous priest. He might have been less relaxed if he'd known that his missive was a pile of ashes in my fireplace.

'Perhaps,' Milton said, his eyes slitted. 'But now that I'm here, might we move on the budget alteration I proposed last meeting?'

'Unfortunately, we have already voted on that matter. The alteration has been denied. We have moved on to matters of trade.' Boccius nodded at Sherman, who once again launched into his droning lecture on the importance of the lentil trade with Creatia while Milton turned blotchy and red.

Trade matters were voted on, and Boccius finally called for any other business before closing the meeting.

'I have a matter I wish to bring before the council,' I said, my voice steady and clear, my spine straight as all eyes in the room turned on me.

Lord Boccius offered me a patronising smile. 'A matter, Your Royal Highness? What sort of matter?'

'A decision needs to be made on a vacancy for Grand Cofferer of the Wardrobe. Several candidates have been proposed to me and I would like advice on who to choose.'

'The reigning monarch—or temporary regent, as it were—usually makes such appointments at their own discretion to allow more pressing matters to occupy the council.' Boccius paused and glanced at Lord Kewin across the table, and the two exchanged a smirk before he turned back to me. 'But please, if you believe this requires our attention, by all means, proceed.'

'The two candidates that I believe are most suitable are the High Lord of Terame and the High Lord of Welkin. Both come highly recommended, and I believe both are deserving of an office at court.' I folded my hands in my lap and kept my face carefully blank as Milton sat up straighter.

Dovegni leaned forward, ready to seize the chance to further his influence, as I knew he would. Welkin was the brother of a druthi high in the ranks of the guild. 'The High Lord of Welkin is a strong candidate. He is young, eager, and his family has shown unwavering loyalty to the crown for generations.'

'A family that has been reclusive,' Milton cut in, a heavy frown marking his face. 'Welkin is barely out of boyhood, and I have never known his late father to attend court. You can hardly support his right to office over that of my own nephew.'

Milton may not have been watching Boccius, but I was, and I saw the disgust that flicked across his face.

Milton and Dovegni argued back and forth for a few minutes, each presenting the virtues of their candidate as the rest of the council looked ready to dose off. Until, finally, Boccius sat forward.

'Terame is a completely inappropriate candidate. He is a known gambler with creditors spotted all over the kingdom. I'll not be surprised if he bankrupts his territory in his lifetime. He is the last man anyone would want involved with managing a coffer. Welkin shall have the position.' He sat back and crossed his arms, nodding at Dovegni.

Milton wore a scowl that seemed to drag the rest of his face into it, but he said nothing as he studied Boccius. He commanded more loyalty on the council than Dovegni, but he couldn't win a majority with Boccius and his supporters throwing in their lot against him. And on a matter of such small importance, all were likely to vote with an eye on nurturing alliances. The vote was cast, and Lord Terame lost.

'Very well. I will notify Lord Welkin at once. Thank you for you counsel, gentlemen.' I rose from my seat, and the council rose with me. They began milling about and tittering amongst themselves as I withdrew from the table, and luck would have it that Dovegni moved towards Boccius and engaged him in low conversation. I watched Milton watch them, and when I caught his glance he gave me the slightest nod, which I answered with a slow smile, before leaving the room.

In the end, I didn't even need Gwinellyn to cast a vote. Once Milton's vote was secured, all it took was a discreet gift of funds to the guild's scholarship program to win Dovegni's. After all, there was no alliance between Boccius and Dovegni. The rest of the council wouldn't vote against the two most powerful players and risk being seen as subversive, and I was named regent within the fortnight. Boccius, the buffoon, never stood a chance.

CHAPTER
TWENTY-FOUR

I began my reign saddled with a treacherous council and a step-daughter who spent even more time in the infirmary than she had before her father's death. I visited her frequently, but she spoke only on trivial things, such as the progress of the beech trees that had been planted in an avenue through the Summer Garden, or the state of the little herb patch she had established and tended herself. Her sleeplessness was written in the dark circles beneath her eyes, making her beauty seem more fragile and ethereal than ever.

Council and stepdaughter aside, the court itself was a source of irritation. The courtiers I had seen so often hanging from Linus now pestered me even more for favours, and their words were as sweet as honey in my presence but as sharp as knives as soon as my back was turned. Leela was as unflinching and honest as ever in her reports to me, never sparing me from the harshest gossip, knowing as I did how it was more important for me to know the real feelings of the court rather than to flatter my pride with a softer version.

They called me the Whore Queen.

Those who thought the sudden death of the king so soon after our wedding too suspicious even called me the Evil Queen.

But they could call me whatever they wanted. I was still queen.

And I lived as though no one could touch me. I rose late every morning and took to breakfasting in my bedroom, rarely emerging before midday to attend to the business of the day. I refused to engage in the myriad of ceremonies and rituals that had always attended Linus's morning routine, insisting on only Leela serving and dressing me before noon. This offended a mass of noblemen and the daughters and wives they had hoped to foster on me, so I soothed tempers by assigning a host of new roles to the more public parts of my day. Even the cupbearer had an assistant by the time I was through. Those arrangements meant I spent the first few weeks of my reign with a permanent headache, but it was worth it to have those few quiet hours of peace in the mornings.

I was highly protective of that peace, so when Draven swept into my room one day with no warning, no knock, no announcement from the guards stationed at the entrance to my apartments, my first reaction was anger. I hadn't finished my breakfast and my sanctuary was already being invaded. The identity of the invader hardly mattered.

'What have you done with my guards?'

He arched an eyebrow. 'I've not touched them. They are right where you left them.'

'Then how did you get into my private apartment unannounced? They wouldn't have just let you in. They're under strict instructions to bar entry to almost everyone.' My irritation did me the favour of hiding my shock. My heartbeat felt heavy and unsteady as I took him in, his dark hair dishevelled, his posture casual as he leaned against the doorframe with his arms folded, and I considered firing my entire retinue of personal guards. 'Did you scale the wall and climb in through a window?'

He didn't reply, only watched me with that unflinching gaze. Well, if he had a purpose for being here, I certainly wasn't going to wring it out of him. I slowly continued to eat, keeping my expression mild. I paid careful attention to my plate as I selected my next bite, my fork hovering in the air before finally skewering a mushroom and popping it into my mouth. The flavour really was sensational, buttery with just a hint of lemon, and I chewed slowly, savouring every moment as the tension in the room steadily rose.

'If you've quite finished your breakfast—' Draven began, his voice quiet but taut as a bowstring ready to snap.

'I haven't,' I interrupted. 'Perhaps you'd care to wait outside until I'm done?'

He paced towards me and leaned over the table, placing his hands either side of my plate. 'I would not care to wait outside.'

I shrugged and turned my eyes back to my plate. 'Suit yourself.'

His fingers began to drum a steady beat on the tabletop as I picked up a piece of bread and smothered it with raspberry jam, acting for all the world like the brute wasn't looming over me.

'While I'm pleased you are enjoying your stint ruling the kingdom,' he said slowly, 'I hope you have not forgotten that our bargain remains unfulfilled. There is still one more apple.'

I took a small bite, chewed leisurely, then swallowed and looked up at him. I could see the anger lapping at the corners of his expression, no matter how hard he was trying to remain composed.

'You must think me a bumbling idiot if you expect that I could have forgotten a single facet of our wretched deal.'

He straightened and regarded me. 'I'm glad it hasn't fled your mind. Because now that your *husband*,' he paused and curled his lip as though the word left a bad taste in his mouth 'is out of the way, there is nothing keeping us from our final purpose.' He strolled to my bed and ran his hand down the heavy curtain, then trailed his fingers across my covers. I continued to eat my bread, trying not to be irritated by the fact that he had moved to my bedside table and begun picking up each object on it, studying it for a moment before placing it back down.

'Interesting that you say *our* purpose, when you've never actually told me what you hope to get out of this scheme of yours,' I said between bites.

'What, you haven't worked it out yet?' He picked up the hem of the nightdress flung across the bed and rubbed the fabric between his fingertips. The action—and the accompanying thought that the material he was so interested in had been against my bare skin not so long ago—momentarily distracted me, releasing memories I had locked up the moment he stepped foot in the room. They ran rampant through my mind, through my body. His hand sliding up my dress, his mouth in my hair, the smoke and clay smell of him, his fingernails against the soft skin of my thigh. I blinked myself back into the room and hoped he hadn't noticed the heat in my cheeks, the parting of my lips. Fortunately, he was still facing the bed.

He dropped the nightdress and turned back to face me, his eyes fixing on the bread in my hand. 'What in all the Shadow Realm are you doing?'

I paused my chewing. 'What?'

He nodded at the bread. 'What have you done to it?'

Raising my eyebrows in surprise, I looked at the bread, which I had been taking tiny bites at the edges of, slowly working my way towards the centre in a spiral. 'I'm eating it.'

He shook his head in disbelief, but was that the hint of a smile I saw at the edge of his mouth? 'Please stop. It's distracting.'

I rolled my eyes and dropped the last few bites to my plate. 'Fine. I'm listening. What exactly do you want me to do now?'

He pulled an apple out of his pocket and tossed it from one hand to the next for a moment, before placing it on the table before me. The sight of it made bile rise in the back of my throat.

'And who is this foul thing for?' I asked, the near humour of a moment ago draining from the air.

'The young princess.' He circled behind me and stood right by my shoulder. I didn't move as he picked at a lock of my hair and rearranged it, always seeming determined to touch things he should keep his hands off. My chest suddenly felt tight, my breathing constricted, like I was being buried, his every word another shovelful of dirt being heaped on my cold corpse.

'What will it do to her?' I asked, not wanting to know, but needing to know.

'That really depends. My original intention was simply to marry her and become king, in which case the apple would have her fall in love with me much like Linus fell for you.'

Now he was jumping on that dirt he'd already heaped on me, packing it down, filling my nose and mouth with it, crushing me with it. 'Why don't you just give it to her yourself?' There was barely any sound to my voice.

'She's never seen me before in her life. I doubt she'd trust me. Not true of you, however. She seems to like you, doesn't she? Poor little motherless child.' He paused as though studying my response, but I remained as still as stone, masking the battle going on within me at the thought of this dark, cruel man married to the beautiful Gwinellyn. Jealousy snarled through me as I thought of him with his hands on her, kissing her like he'd kissed me, touching her like he'd touched me, and I couldn't stand it. But piled on top of that steaming mess of feelings was the cold weight of dread at the thought of how vulnerable sweet little Gwin would be to someone like Draven.

'So that's it, then? You helped me become queen only to cast me aside?' I finally looked up at him, studying his face, trying to see the depths of his character there. What was the worst of him? Had I already seen it? Was there even more? What would he do to Gwin as her husband? What would he do to Brimordia as its king?

What had I unleashed?

He rested his hand lightly on the exposed skin of my shoulder and I hated the longing that coiled low in my abdomen at the touch. 'I have been contemplating an alternative to marrying the girl. This is where you have a choice to make.'

A choice. Most assuredly a choice of how much rope I would like to hang myself with. 'Come out with it.'

'Marry me yourself.' He said it so simply, like it was nothing, like this was merely a casual breakfast chat. 'There are others of the Rauzac line in Yaakendale who might contest your claim once you are queen in your own right, but I'm willing to take the risk and deal with such threats when they come.'

There was something in his voice just beneath the studied indifference. He wanted me to pick this option. To *marry him*. The idea was a dangerous one, a frightening one. I could barely hold my own against him now, how would I do so if he was in my bed?

'And Gwinellyn?' I asked, pushing the thought of marriage and all that it would mean to the side for a moment. It was too big and too heady a concept for me to grapple with right now.

'You'd have to kill her, of course,' he said matter-of-factly, like the stink of treason, of murder, wasn't suddenly making me feel like throwing up everything I had just eaten. 'No one would support your claim over hers.'

A heavy beat of silence echoed through the room. He brushed his thumb back and forth over the skin of my shoulder. Back and forth, back and forth, like he was wearing away at me, grinding me down until I would be left defenceless. 'Wouldn't you like to be married to me, Vixen?' he purred.

I shrugged his hand off and rose from my seat, putting some distance between us. I was beginning to see that he used our physical proximity as a way to unbalance me. 'I don't want to hurt Gwinellyn.'

He cocked his head. 'So, you pick option one?'

'No,' I snapped. 'Maybe I pick neither.'

He smiled coldly. 'That won't end well for you. You made me a promise and I made you a queen, remember?'

'Exactly. I am a queen,' I said, drawing myself up and glaring at him. 'Maybe I choose to throw you into the dungeons and let you rot down there.'

He sighed. 'I had hoped I wouldn't have to threaten you but suspected you might make it necessary. Let me explain something to you. Your position is a precarious one.' He tugged one of the camellias from the vase by my breakfast tray and twirled it in his fingers. 'Your advisors and lords already mistrust you. If you broke our deal and lost your glamour now, how long do you think it would be before they cried profane magic use?' He began to pluck the petals from the flower. They dropped to the tabletop one by one, scattering across the wood like little pink slivers of flesh. 'What a perfect villain you'd make. The wicked whore who poisoned the king, first with love and then with death.' He stared at the centre of the camellia, now bereft of petals, before letting it fall.

'What makes you think I wouldn't drag you down with me?' I said, though I knew he would be too slippery to hang on to. I'd rather go down standing tall and owning my actions than howling about the man who made me do it to people who wouldn't believe me.

'Come, Rhiandra, you are smarter than that. A wicked queen casting a spell on the king is a much better story than one where you are just a puppet. Imagine how the Grand Paptich will fawn over the chance to make an example of you, to hold you up as the embodiment of the evil nature of women.' He approached me and I didn't back away, staring him down as he took my limp hand in his. 'Marry me,' he murmured as he raised my hand to his mouth, 'and rule Brimordia by my side.'

'A sham marriage,' I said, snatching my hand back. 'And a sham position for me. A queen only has power alone. I'd be a figurehead with you as king.'

He laughed, the sound dark and rumbling from deep in his chest. 'No sham, my dear. I might rule the country,' he sank to one knee slowly, his eyes still fixed on mine, which were wide with shock at the sight of him kneeling on the floor, 'but you'll rule me. Marry me and I will be a husband to you in every sense of the word.'

Kneeling may have been a sign of surrender, but he looked anything but conquered as he took my hand again. This was no declaration of love.

I could tell my mouth had fallen open, but I couldn't seem to shut it. 'I... I have to think about this,' I stammered finally, backing away until I felt the bed behind me and sat down heavily. Not a good choice of places to go. All being on the bed did was bring his words into hyper focus. *I will be a husband to you in every sense of the word.*

He smirked as he rose to his feet, straightened his clothes, and pushed his dark hair from his face. If my response had humbled him, he didn't show it. 'You do that,' he said, turning to leave. 'I'll give you three days to make your decision.'

And just like that, he was gone again. The only sign he'd been there at all was the crumpled nightgown, the rearrangement of my side table, the scattering of petals over my breakfast.

CHAPTER
TWENTY-FIVE

S herman scurried after me, bending and scraping as he tried to match my stride. 'Your Royal Highness, it would be for the best if you allowed your generals to take care of matters regarding the protection of the borders. They have a wealth of experience and are really best placed to make such decisions.'

I stopped suddenly, causing him to run into one of my attendants. I eyed him as he cursed at the woman and fluffed about straightening his clothes, distaste creasing the skin of my nose. 'Sherman,' I barked, and he snapped to attention. 'Is the patronising tone a deliberate affectation, or do you lack the self-awareness to notice it?'

He spluttered, his face turning red. 'I am merely pointing out to Your Royal Highness—' he began, but I cut him off.

'That I am not competent in making military decisions and should leave it to the men, yes, I know. But if they were as good as you say they are, the attacks would have stopped, and we wouldn't be having this conversation.'

He opened and closed his mouth a few times, looking like he was casting about for a reply—or perhaps he was just trying to catch an insect for his lunch—but I had spotted Gwinellyn walking a path on the other side of the fountain with someone dressed in black. I started towards them, my pace quickly picking up, my heart beginning to pound. The sound of her laugher drifted to me on the breeze, a tinkling harmony against the falling water.

The sound of half a dozen attendants rushing to catch up with me forced me to stop and spin on my heel. 'You're dismissed,' I said curtly. 'All of you.' I looked pointedly at Sherman. 'I wish to walk alone.'

Gwinellyn's face was glowing with pleasure, which was not a common sight these days. She paused as she caught sight of me, and my eyes zeroed in on the way her hand reached out and touched her companion's forearm to halt him, so casually, almost instinctive.

'Let me introduce you to my stepmother,' the girl gushed, turning to me with a grin. 'Have you met Lord Martalos?'

Draven bowed low, keeping his grey eyes fixed on me as he did, a mocking smile curling at the edges of his mouth. 'Your Royal Highness.'

'Why are you unchaperoned?' I snapped, and the smile slipped from Gwin's face.

'I thought—'

'And you should be at your lessons. If you're going to be queen, start acting like one.' She flinched a little as my words cut into her and her eyes grew glassy, but she kept her head high as she mumbled 'As you please, Your Royal Highness,' and she took off across the lawns without another word.

'By the sky, Rhiandra, you're going to make this too easy,' Draven drawled.

'Stay away from her.'

He laughed as though he didn't notice I was trying to fry his innards with my glare alone. 'If you keep talking to her like that, she'll come straight to me.'

I balled my fists in my skirt, glancing around to make sure no one was within earshot. My attendants had done as I commanded and left me alone, and while there were others out promenading around the gardens, they were nowhere near us. 'She is going to be married to the Oceatold prince. You can't just pluck her for yourself.'

He shrugged. 'A political match won't trump love for a six-teen-year-old, particularly if she is enchanted. We can elope to avoid any objections and then return to take the throne.' He squinted at the palace, shielding his eyes against the sun. 'I think I'll rather enjoy living here.'

'You said you'd give me time to decide,' I hissed, moving closer to him.

He tapped a finger against his wrist. 'Tick tock, Vixen, before I make the decision for you.'

The flutter of voices caught my attention, and I glanced around to see a pair of courtiers drawing closer to us, the lady twirling her parasol and gripping the elbow of her gentleman.

'You need to leave the palace grounds before someone catches you,' I urged, hoping that would be enough to move him on and give me time to think, but he didn't look even slightly concerned.

'As charmed as I am by your concern for my welfare, you needn't worry I thought it pertinent to secure a legitimate reason for being here. The late Lord Martalos was well known at court in his heyday, but his son,' he flicked out his arms and dropped a quick bow, 'has spent his young life sequestered away with his ailing mother.'

'You're... staying?'

'This will be my court soon. I ought to know it. And it ought to know me.' He cocked his head as he watched me grapple with the implications of this news. 'Why the scowl, Rhiandra? You'll make me think you don't want me around. That's no way to begin a marriage.'

'I haven't agreed that we will be married!'

'And I don't doubt that you're trying to find a way to slither out of keeping your deal with me, but there isn't one. Not if you wish to retain any of the power you've worked so hard for. Think of all you've done to get here.'

The two courtiers drew within earshot of us, and we both watched them approach as they whispered to one another and shot us speculative glances.

'I want the whole three days to make my decision,' I said, keeping my voice low.

'Why delay the inevitable? You already know what your choice will be.'

'And that means,' I continued, as though he didn't speak, 'you don't follow me around trying to bully me into making it sooner. You said I could have time, so give it to me. Unless you aren't as confident in the outcome as you pretend to be.' I cast him a sidelong glance.

The young woman smiled nervously at us, and her suitor tugged her lightly to steer her in our direction. By the blood of Madeia, if they were about to start petitioning me for favour I would scream.

'Have your time. I'll leave you be,' Draven said, turning back to me, a soft breeze stirring the dark hair on his forehead as he held my gaze. 'But come midnight on day three, I'll want your answer. I'm most *eager* for it.'

I was the first to look away, a slight warmth to my cheeks, much to my chagrin. As the young couple reached us, I gave Draven a curt nod and strode away, leaving them looking deflated and a little offended. I would not glance back, even though I could feel his gaze sliding over me as I walked away, making me feel unsteady and conscious of my every step.

It was a relief to retreat into the stone embrace of the palace, even though my personal mob waited for me there, shifting and tittering and no doubt whispering cutting remarks to one another in retribution for my abrupt dismissal. I eyed the handful of women for a moment, then scowled when I heard Sherman wheezing his way towards me.

'Paper and pen,' I barked at my nearest attendant, who was barely more than a girl and had been foisted on me by her ambitious father. She jumped with fright and hurried quickly away as I stalked back into the depths of the palace, my pace relentless as I tried to keep far enough ahead of Sherman that I could pretend I couldn't hear his efforts to call out to me. When the girl caught up with me, I paused to snatch the items from her and drew a few murmurs of shock from my attendants when I slapped the paper against a wall, scribbled a few lines and folded it haphazardly.

The sight of their wide-eyed faces sent my breath huffing through my nose. 'Why are you all here after I dismissed you? Anyone still within my line-of-sight next time I glance behind me will lose their position at court.'

The sounds of footsteps hurrying in the opposite direction to me as I continued on was immensely satisfying.

Leela had been lying on a chaise lounge by the window flipping through a pamphlet on dress design when I barged through the door of my apartment. She jumped to attention at the sight of me and I waved the folded paper at her.

'Deliver this to the address at the top,' I said as I pulled my fingers from the lace gloves I was wearing and flung them on a settee. 'And don't send anyone else. I want you to go yourself.'

She peeled open the paper and raised her eyebrows as she scanned the words, but one pointed look from me staunched whatever she had been about to say.

'As you wish, ma'am,' she said, inclining her head.

'Oh, and send word to Mrs Corkill that I want to throw a big celebration for Aetherdi. I know it's short notice, but I want to invite the whole council and she'll have to throw an elaborate dinner for them.'

Leela gave me a hard look. 'Is there any reason you've decided such a thing?'

I waved her off. 'To charm them all, why else?'

She didn't look convinced, but she bobbed a curtsey and left without another question. When she was gone, I strode to the cupboard skulking in the corner of my bedchamber. The thing looked monstrously elaborate even in a royal apartment. I opened the doors and paused to pour myself a glass from one of the crystal decanters before continuing. My hands were trembling.

Sipping from the glass, I slowly lifted the false backing, revealing my reflection a hairsbreadth at a time. Impressive cleavage, slender neck, pointed chin... and twisted, shiny skin, a sea of white crests and vulnerable pink troughs. I studied myself, nursing my drink, noting the new hollows around my eyes, the line between my brows, neither of which were usually visible. My mind raced along well-worn paths, weighing actions and consequences, predicting and plotting and worrying over everything I didn't know, constantly asking *what if, what if, what if.*

What if I gave Gwinellyn the apple?

I'd be done with the deal. I'd keep the glamour and fade into obscurity as the woman who *used to* be queen. I'd be relegated to a footnote in history. An amusing little anecdote about the maisera who managed to bag herself a king and wore a crown for a few mad months until the world righted itself again.

What if I refused the choices Draven offered?

I'd lose the face I'd come to believe was mine, the face that had won me a life that was beyond anything I could ever have thought possible. I had power, influence, I made decisions that mattered, and a host of people waited on my every whim. I was no longer the little bastard girl whose mother forgot to feed her. When I entered a room, all eyes turned to me. No one ever forgot I was around. The thought of giving all that up was insufferable.

Draven's words whispered through my mind. *What a perfect villain you'd make.*

I could never explain away the transformation from my glamoured face to my real one. And it would take anyone with half a brain only a few moments to begin connecting dots that would lead from an enchanted face to a dead king.

Then what if I killed Gwinellyn?

I drained the glass, the heat burning down my throat and settling in my stomach with a friendly warmth that thawed the frosty edge of my troubled thoughts. After eyeing the bottle for a moment, I poured myself another.

I could do it. The timid creature barely lived anyway. Tortured little princess, demeaned and ignored, and all tied up believing in her own worthlessness. It would almost be a kindness.

I drew the cover back over the mirror and closed the cabinet as I nursed my glass. Drinking in the middle of the day. I was turning into my mother. Padding over to one of the windows, I stared out over the gardens to where they fell down the hillside, giving way to the sprawling city beyond. Even on a day so full of sunlight, the mountains in the far distance were hazy, ghosts haunting the horizon. I thought of the fall spawn creature in Dovegni's dungeon. Were there more like her out there in the Yawn?

Scanning the grounds, I gave each person I picked out a once over, not moving on until I was satisfied that they weren't a man in black. There was too much I didn't know about Draven, about his intentions, about how he might respond in different situations. About how I would survive being married to him. Any choice felt like a gamble on long odds.

An attempt to deceive him felt like the longest odds of all.

What if, what if, what if.

CHAPTER TWENTY-SIX

I fluffed at my skirts, rearranging them over and over as I awaited my guest. I was seated in my private drawing room, not wanting to overwhelm him with a reception in the state rooms, and I picked at a spread of cakes and sandwiches as I waited. His arrival at the palace had just been announced, and I wondered what was going through his head as he was led through the lobby and up the winding staircase. My note gave no clues about why he had been summoned to the palace; he must be having a nervous breakdown as he considered possible explanations. Maybe he thought the queen would want to reprimand him herself for his illegal trade in plants with magical and hallucinogenic properties.

I smiled in amusement at the thought, imagining how he would be ringing his hands in a panic, and considered pretending that was indeed why he was here. But I had a favour to ask, and playing a prank wasn't likely the best way to begin asking it—especially when I would already have a whole lot of explaining to do.

'Cotus Yvenou to see you, Your Royal Highness,' a footman announced.

'Good. Send him in,' I replied as I straightened up and folded my hands in my lap.

Cotus entered the room with his shoulders stooped, head down, and a cap clutched in his big hands. He bobbed a bow, then another two for good measure, and cast a covert glance up at me.

The glance caught and held. His eyes bulged. His gaze roamed over my face as he straightened up slightly, blinking as though to clear his eyes. 'Rhiandra?' The question was hushed, like he barely dared to ask it.

'Yes,' I said, smiling. 'It's me.'

His mouth fell open slightly. 'But... your face... what happened to you?' He shook his head, like he was shaking water from his ears, then glanced around the room. 'What are you doing in the palace?'

'It's a long story. Let's go for a walk.' I moved closer to him and lowered my voice. 'The walls have ears here.'

As we made our way to the gardens, I waved off my attendants, bidding they go and do something useful. Cotus watched me like someone had smacked him over the head and he was still seeing stars as I ordered people around and swept through the hallways with the confidence of someone who knows exactly where they are going, but he refrained from asking any more questions until we were safely outside and walking through the thick, golden light of the late afternoon.

'Where should I start?' I asked.

'Last time I saw you, you were covered in burns.'

I resisted the urge to sigh. Of course, his most pressing concern would be with my appearance. Never mind that I was a queen. 'I was healed with druthi magic.'

'But you look... I've never heard... how could...' Each attempted question trailed off unfinished and he glanced at the ground, rubbing his neck.

'I am well known to the Grand Weaver,' I said with an air of finality. It wasn't an answer to any of his unasked questions, but I hoped it would hint at just enough to satisfy him, or at the very least that he would be too uncomfortable to press further. Dovegni and his guild were shrouded in enough mystery that maybe, just maybe, Cotus might believe him capable of magic far more powerful than the average druthi.

'And now... I'd heard rumours about the new queen, but I never thought...' He fell silent again, and I could feel him gaping at me, but I stared straight ahead to better hide my irritation. If only he could just spit out what he wanted to say and stop stumbling over himself.

'I came to the palace as a maisera, and King Linus fell in love with me.' My words were blunt and matter-of-fact. 'It was quite the whirlwind romance,' I added, reminding myself that I needed to sell him a story, and it would be far more convenient for him to believe that I had been swept away by a fierce love, and not that my path to queen had been carefully planned and deliberately tread.

'Of course. It must have been. I'm... sorry for your loss, your husband... may his flight be swift.'

I watched a small bird flit across the lawn before us, proudly puffing out his red chest, his tail flicking back and forth behind his head. He caught sight of us and turned a small, black eye on me. 'And now I must rule until his daughter comes of age,' I said. 'Which brings us to why I asked you here.' I stopped and glanced around. I chose this spot because there were no trees or hedges within earshot, nowhere someone could eavesdrop. 'I need your help, Cotus. You're the only person I can trust.'

'You know I'd do anything for you,' he said, his face earnest, and I smiled. Perhaps it was wrong to leverage his feelings for me, but I needed someone whose loyalty I could be sure of.

'Princess Gwinellyn is in danger from the same enemy who poisoned her father.' It wasn't a lie, I thought grimly. 'I don't know who is an enemy and who is a friend to her, so I need her to leave the palace. I need her taken somewhere safe.'

He nodded, a solemn frown turning at his mouth. 'You need me to escort her?'

I drew in a deep breath. So far so good, but here was the important part. 'I need more than that from you. I need the enemy to think she isn't coming back.' I held his gaze, searching his pale blue eyes for any sign of resistance. This was a huge risk. If he turned on me, I was done for. Milton would cackle with glee as he sentenced me to burn. I shook off the shudder at the thought of being at the mercy of fire again and focused on Cotus, on his kind and devoted face. 'I need you to take her into the Yawn. I need you to pretend to try to kill her. And I need you to make her believe I ordered you to do so.'

He stared at me with wide, troubled eyes. 'If she thinks you are trying to kill her... if she thinks I am... we will both lose our heads for it. It's a dangerous plan.'

I was expecting this exact objection and I had a plan. I cradled my face in my hands, blinking hard until my eyes were glassy. 'You're right,' I cried, my shoulders slumping. 'It is a terrible plan. I'm sorry I asked it of you, I just didn't know what else to do.' I reached out and laid my hand lightly on his forearm. 'I'm scared, Cotus. I'm so glad you're here, even if you won't help me. You know you've always made me feel safe.'

His chest puffed up, his shoulders rolling back, and he patted my hand with his own. 'I didn't say I wouldn't help you. Just that it's dangerous plan,' he said.

I nodded, my eyelashes fluttering against my cheeks as I glanced down. 'I just wish I could think of another option. But I'm sure you'll think of something, won't you?' Smiling at him hopefully, I saw his brows pull together, his lips pressing into a tight line as he tried to come up with some idea that would validate my faith in him.

'Couldn't you inform the Captain of the Guard and order round the clock protection?' was what he eventually settled on, because he clearly hadn't listened to a word I'd said.

I sighed, trying to keep it pretty and sad instead of irritated. 'I wish I could, but I don't know who to trust. I fear a greater plot to overthrow the Crown, and there could be any number of people in on the scheme.' Then I widened my eyes for added drama and glanced at him with a tiny gasp. 'There was a guard lurking around the night Linus was killed. And following me around the next morning. You don't think... no, he must have been there for my protection. But just suppose...' I let the thought trail away, enticing his imagination to fill in the blanks.

'Maybe you shouldn't stay here either, Rhiandra. It might not be safe.'

His concern was touching, but inconvenient. 'If I were to leave, who would discover the plot against Gwinellyn? The risk to me is not so great, really, since I'm only regent. The princess is the one in real danger. We have to protect her. Please, tell me you'll help me protect her.'

He frowned down at my beseeching face for a few moments, clearly torn.

'I just need her to be somewhere safe until I can figure out what is going on,' I pressed.

'How will she survive in the Yawn?'

I almost had him, I could see it. He just needed to swallow this one last piece of the story. 'Baba Yaga will help her.'

'Baba Yaga? The witch?' He ran a hand through his hair, leaving a dishevelled mess behind. 'Why would she help? She'd probably eat her.'

'You know she's helped girls at the Winking Nymph with women problems.' I almost rolled my eyes at the light blush that coloured his cheeks. 'In any case, leave that part to me. Please, Cotus? Will you do as I ask?'

He seemed to be literally chewing over my question, his jaw working away like he had a wad of tobacco in his mouth. 'If there's nothing else—' he began, his words hoarse.

'There isn't.' I took his hands in mine and held his gaze. 'Please. There is no one else I know who is so clever that they could brave the Yawn. You're my only hope.' I touched his cheek lightly, laying it on just a little too thick, but he didn't seem to mind. 'Let's just agree to this so we can talk of other things. I've thought of you so often in the past months. I want to know all about what you've been doing. In fact, once Gwinellyn is safe, wouldn't you like to come and work for me here at the palace? Having you close at hand would give me so much comfort.'

And little by little, I ground him down. I sold him gilded promises of a life as a member of my personal guard, implying just enough of a relationship that could extend beyond the professional to keep his colour high and his gaze shifting. By the time I was done with him, my favour was so tangled up in this new dream he'd never thought to reach for that he was no longer sure of what exactly he was agreeing to. Was it bribery? Of course it was, but a greedy man wouldn't label it that way. No need for such a blight on his conscience.

And it was bribery for a good cause, after all.

He agreed to return with the morning with his belongings in tow. He had wanted to give Madame Luzel his notice so she would have time to hire on someone new, but I wanted him to disappear in the night. There was enough risk already in me making this connection with my old life. Not everyone would be so easily fooled as Cotus.

All that was left for me to do was to invite Gwinellyn for dinner.

The way Gwinellyn twisted her napkin was driving me to distraction. The girl was the heir to a kingdom, and she looked as though she would bow down to a rabbit, all knotted up with anxiety as she was. I drummed my fingers on the tabletop as I watched her smile at the footman who served her meal, unaccountably irritated. She wasn't cut out to rule. Surely, I was doing both her and Brimordia a favour by getting her out of the way.

'It looks so different in here,' she said quietly. Twist, twist, twist.

'Would you have preferred I live in a shrine?' I snapped.

'No, I didn't mean that at all.' She blinked at me in wide-eyed confusion and I gritted my teeth against a tirade of angry words that wanted to pour from me. Words of irritation. Resentment. Guilt.

I stood up and sauntered over to the side table to pour myself a glass of wine, which I swallowed in a few gulps before pouring myself another.

'Is anything the matter?' Gwin's voice was small, apologetic. 'Have I done something wrong?'

I turned and leaned against the side table, my lips pinched tightly as I studied her. 'Do you know what I think you need?' I asked. 'I think you need to have a little fun. A little adventure. You always look so sad.'

She ducked her head. 'I know I'm nothing like you. You're so brave and strong.'

'You don't need to be anything like me,' I muttered to myself, before crossing the room and pulling a chair close to her. 'Everything has been so dour and gloomy around here, with us all dressed in black and the court in mourning. I'm tired of it.' I produced a tiny snuff box from within my skirts and shook it in the air. 'I have an idea for a way to spice things up a little around here.'

To her credit, she wasn't just a guileless lamb being led to the slaughter. She frowned. 'What's that?'

I opened the lid and sat the box before her. The bluish powder within glistened. 'Have you ever tried swoon?'

'I've never heard of it.'

Of course she hadn't, being locked away behind the palace walls. She hadn't seen the hovels full of hollow-eyed addicts in the Trough, their skin tight against their bones. The drug was wonderful; it made people bright-eyed and healthy and euphoric, and if they had enough, it gifted visions and scraps of magic. I'd seen someone on swoon shatter a glass with only their mind. But it was easy to get hooked on. And once someone was hooked, they had to keep taking it, or it sucked the life out of them. Magic was corrosive.

But I was only going to give her a little.

'It's an adventure in a box. Wouldn't you like to escape all that grief and doubt you carry around with you all the time?'

'I don't know,' she said slowly. 'The physicians have always told me I have to be careful with what I put in my body.'

'And yet they have you on that foul-smelling tincture that makes you drowsy and stupid. You need to stop letting your fits define you, Gwinellyn, or you will always be the timid, fragile creature everyone tells you that you are.' I licked my finger and dipped it in the swoon. It sent up a little puff of dust that smelt like sage and jasmine. She chewed on a fingernail as I withdrew my powder-coated finger and held it out to her.

'What do I do with it?' Her tone was hesitant, but there was a flicker of curiosity in her eyes, which surprised me. I thought it would take a whole lot more pushing to get her to agree. I lifted my finger to my mouth and rubbed the bitter-tasting powder into my gums, bracing myself for the heady rush of euphoria that swept through me, the energy that suddenly crackled through my body.

I blinked slowly and let out a soft, smiling sigh. 'Your turn.'

She mimicked me exactly, licking her finger and dipping it into the box. She wavered for only a moment once she withdrew it, but took a deep breath, met my eyes, and stuck her finger in her mouth. Her eyes widened, her pupils dilated, and colour flushed her cheeks.

'Oh,' she breathed.

'It's good, isn't it?' I purred. 'Have some more.'

By the time she'd dipped her finger in the powder three or four times more, she was limp with ecstasy and her pupils had almost completely swallowed her irises as her gaze roamed the room, finding delight in the fringe of a curtain or a swirl of mortar. She didn't seem to notice I'd taken no more after that initial dip, and the small dose of the drug left me with a lurching stomach and a pounding headache as it wore off.

As the moon rose, I hauled Gwinellyn up from where she was kneeling over a fruit bowl, running her fingers over apples and oranges and persimmons as though they were made of precious stones.

'Come on,' I said as I hauled her to her feet. 'It's time to go.'

'Oh no,' she cried, slumping back down to the ground. 'No, I can't. Have you seen this one?' She held up a persimmon with a brown blotch marring its waxy skin. 'It's all wrong. No one will eat it. It will be all alone if I leave it.'

'For fall's sake, bring it with you then,' I snapped, slinging her arm around my shoulders and dragging her back to her feet. I dragged, cajoled, and ordered her through the apartments into the bedchamber, finding the door behind a curtain in the wardrobe that led down the narrow staircase. She asked where we were going once or twice, but she was easily distracted by the way the light glinted on a window or a puff of dust curling in the air. When we emerged at the bottom of the staircase, the room beyond was dark and still. The portraits I had hated still hung on the walls, their gazes disapproving as we moved through the antechamber with only slivers of moonlight to guide us.

Dust sheets covered the furniture, and the bed was stripped of its covers to stand bare and strangely vulnerable. For a moment, as I stood in this apartment clutching a drugged princess by the hand, I suddenly felt the desperate wish that I could turn back time, go back to these rooms and make different choices, choices that wouldn't have ended in this night.

But I couldn't go back. And I had to get Gwinellyn out of the palace.

She was growing increasingly drowsy. Her head lolled to the side, and she sagged against me, causing me to struggle under her weight, but I managed to get her out the doors of my old apartment and into the gardens where Cotus was waiting in the dark.

'She's completely dipped. How much did you give her?' he asked as he took Gwinellyn's other arm.

'Enough that you won't have to dose her again before you get out of Lee Helse. Did you manage to find what I asked for?'

'Yeah. Don't know how she's supposed to believe you want her dead if you're packing her supplies.'

'You don't tell her they are for her. Just stock your cabin and leave her nearby. We can't leave her out there with nothing.' I could see the silhouette of a horse snorting and pawing at the ground ahead, jostling the small wagon latched behind it.

'It's going to take more than some food and cold weather gear to help her survive the Yawn,' he said as we drew closer.

The horse danced away from us, shaking its head and snorting at the puffing figures hobbling towards it in the dark. Cotus dropped Gwinellyn to catch the horse's reins, and I stumbled against her sudden weight. 'Remember, stop for some swoon blooms once you're in the Yawn and make sure she knows what you're doing. I'm willing to bet that she'll go looking for them now that she's had a taste of it.'

'Though how that'll—'

'Cotus,' I snapped. 'You're questioning me *now*? Don't you think we are a little too far into this plan for you to begin doubting me?' By the fall, I could practically smell his fear. He was hesitating to take Gwinellyn from me now, to lift her into the wagon and ride away with her, and the longer we were stuck waiting here, the higher the likelihood we would be caught. 'Remember why we are doing this,' I urged. 'We are trying to keep her safe. Follow the plan, and when you come back, you'll have your new position here at the palace to return to and I'll send you back into the Yawn to check up on her in a few weeks. Now, *hurry*.'

He finally thawed and took the limp Gwinellyn from my arms. With some manoeuvring, we managed to settle her in the wagon beneath a rug, and she stirred enough to mindlessly stroke the fabric and begin babbling about how bright the stars were before she settled and seemed to slip back into a stupor. We shuffled sacks of grain and flour around until she was hidden from sight. Cotus had driven through the gates under the pretence of an extra delivery of food for the Aetherdi feast, and with the token I had given him to demonstrate his legitimacy, he'd sneak right back out without anyone giving him a second glance.

'Right. I'll be getting on,' he rumbled, looking down at me hopefully. I took a step away, but even in the dark I could see he was disappointed when I did, so I blew him a kiss. Best to keep him buttered up as much as possible.

'Ride fast. Don't get caught. And hurry back,' I said as he climbed onto the wagon. He flicked the reins and the nervous horse lurched forward to trot down the winding road that would take them back through the palace grounds and out the gates into the city. I watched until they turned a corner and dropped out of sight, whispering 'be safe' and sending up a silent prayer to Aether and Medeia.

As I snuck back through the doors of my old rooms, I heard the bells of Taveum's spire chiming the hour, marking the end of my three days grace. Closing the doors, the hairs on the back of my neck prickled with premonition.

CHAPTER
TWENTY-SEVEN

L eela was waiting to ready me for bed when I returned to my
suite. If she wondered where I had been, she didn't ask. Once
she left, I didn't sleep. I couldn't settle. I read for a while, but my
mind slipped off the pages like they were greased with butter, and
I ended up pacing the room, my fingers fidgeting with my silk robe
and my stomach full of jitters. The fire died down to embers. I
checked my appearance in the mirror on the dressing table, fussing with my hair and considering changing my robe and dabbing
rouge on my cheeks, before moving to stand by the window with
my arms hugged around me. I stared out at the flickering torches
in the gardens below, guttering points of yellow in the black of
the night, and an awareness slipped over me. I knew he was in
the room, even though the latch had not clicked, even though he
hadn't made a sound. The air stirred with the smell of smoke.

'How does your magic work?' I asked without turning away from the window. 'Do you step through the world from one shadow to another? Do you travel through the dark realm?'

He chuckled quietly, the sound closer than I had expected it to be as it curled across my skin. 'Nothing as dramatic as that.'

'Then what?'

A beat of silence. 'What would you do with such a secret if I gave it to you?'

What would I do? Use it to fill in a tiny piece of the gaping abyss of what I knew about him, this dark man, my partner in murder and treason, who I was so entangled with that I couldn't get free of him without cutting him out. I turned and picked out the shape of him in the gloom, the glint of firelight in his eyes. 'If we are to marry, I think I deserve to know more about you.'

There was always something catlike in the way he moved, and never more so than when he approached me now, his steps deliberate and smooth. Being within an arm's reach of him colonised my skin with goosebumps. 'Does this mean you've made your decision?'

I took a deep breath, dwelling in the pause, wondering yet again whether I would come to regret what I was going to do next, whether I'd look back to this moment and rail against my stupidity. 'Princess Gwinellyn is dead.'

His gaze was unwavering as he studied me. 'Already? I haven't given you the apple.'

'I wanted it done. So, I paid someone to do it.'

'A loose end,' he said. 'What if this someone decides to turn on you?'

'You never specified how she should wind up dead,' I replied, hoping the flash of irritation would hide the lie. 'Let me worry about loose ends. I'd have hoped you'd know by now that I can handle myself. You may have given me the tools to get myself here, but I wielded them.'

He ran his fingertips, feather-light, up the bare skin of my arms. 'I've noticed.'

'Why do you want to be king so badly?' I asked, trying to ignore the fluttering of my heart.

'You're full of questions tonight.' His pewter eyes looked black in the dim light, like gaping pits I would tumble into, ever falling into bottomless dark.

I drew away from him, moving to sit in an armchair. I crossed my legs, folded my arms, and pinned him with a stare. 'I know next to nothing about you. You need to answer my questions if you expect me to make you king.'

A flicker of amusement crossed his face. 'Trying to add conditions to a deal we've already agreed on is cheating.'

I didn't respond, letting the silence stretch taut between us.

He smiled as he prowled towards me. 'What's wrong, Rhiandra? It almost seems like you still don't trust me.'

'That's because I still don't,' I said immediately.

'After all we've been through together? Why, that hurts my feelings.'

'I'm almost certain you don't *have* feelings.'

Cocking his head, he sank down into a crouch by my chair, brushing his hand across my knee in a gesture that seemed so casual but that sent a shiver through me, raising the hairs on my arms and pinching my nipples into hard peaks. He held my gaze. 'What do you know about feelings?'

'Why do you want to be king, Draven?' I repeated. He took my hand.

'I know men have hurt you,' he purred, pressing his lips to my fingers. 'But I won't be like your last husband, or those who paid to take their pleasure with you.'

'Why should you be any different?' I swallowed at the sudden need clawing at my throat as he brushed his lips back and forth across the top of my hand. I was losing the thread of my resolve and felt it unspooling to lay limp and forgotten around me.

He lifted his gaze, searching my face for a response, and what he saw there seemed to please him. 'What are you fishing for? Aren't you brave enough to take what you want?'

My breath trembled. His hand moved slowly up my arm, coming to rest on my elbow. 'This is not a good idea,' I said, more to myself than to him.

He didn't acknowledge my words. He stayed poised before me, studying me like a snake about to strike. Then he burst the distance by leaning in and taking my lips with his. If there had ever been a question in his words, there was none in his kiss as he slipped his hand to the back of my neck and held me in place, his fingers tangling in my hair. I didn't need to be held in place, though; it was like something that had been straining to escape my skin was suddenly released and I kissed him back with reckless abandon, not thinking about everything he hadn't said, about the way he was manoeuvring me like a piece on a game board. All I cared about in that moment was the earthy smell of him, the way his arm was curling around my waist to drag me closer, the texture of his shirt beneath my fingers as I ran my hands over him, seeking. Something hot and brilliant thrilled along my nerves when I found bare skin, smooth and warm and rippling, and he broke the kiss to press his mouth to my neck.

'Stop,' I gasped, suddenly pushing at him, and for a moment his grip on me tightened, but he slowly released me. When he met my gaze, his eyes were vicious.

'Why?'

'If we are to marry, I think it should be celibate.' The words came out in a rush, a last, desperate grasp at handling a situation that was rapidly whirling beyond my control.

His mouth twitched. 'No.'

'Are you in love with me then?' I was aiming for flippant, for mocking, but the words came out high-pitched and unnatural. Oh, please let it just be that he's in love with me. I knew what to do with that.

He pinched my chin between his thumb and forefinger. 'What a dirty word to hear coming from your mouth. I know better than to leave you with an *unconsummated* marriage as an escape route, my dear. But just because this is a business transaction doesn't mean it can't be *fun*.'

If my stomach dropped with disappointment, I wouldn't let him know it. The idea that he could equate any of this with *fun* when all I could find between us was torment and this damned, ceaseless yearning, should have been enough to make me put a stop to the whole thing. I could have pushed the issue, could have insisted, but I had seen something in that moment that drew my curiosity. There it was in his eyes. Something coming undone, the smooth composure slipping to reveal something ravenous lurking beneath. And whatever had spurned me to push him away shrivelled up and died. 'You're a scoundrel,' I hissed.

'And you're a coward.' He pulled me to him again and his hands roved over me, overwhelming whatever defences were left, claiming territory, pushing my robe from me and finding the laces of my shift, slipping the fabric down my arms, exposing skin that he met with his lips. I closed my eyes and wound my hands into his hair. My skin thrummed, tracking the movement of his lips as my shift slithered over my chest and pooled around my waist.

I opened my eyes and stared at the ceiling without seeing as his tongue traced teasing spirals over my breast, and when he took my aching nipple in his mouth, I bit my lip to keep from crying out. I was too hot, as though I would erupt if he didn't touch me where I needed him. And I was trembling like a naïve little maiden.

'This isn't natural. It's not normal to feel like this.' My words collapsed into a moan when a hand skated between my legs.

He slid lower, kissing his way down my stomach, pushing my knees apart to nip at the sensitive skin of my inner thigh. 'My dear, this is how it *should* feel.'

I couldn't bear the sight of him between my legs, couldn't untangle the feelings attached to it, the longing and thrill and naked vulnerability, so I closed my eyes again, dropping my head against the back of the chair as I lost myself in the prickle of stubble, the gush of breath, the brush of lips as he moved closer to where I was wet and wanting.

His hands tightened on my hips as he ran his tongue over my clit, and I was liquid. I was heat. I was thoughtless flesh and need, and I pressed him to me and trembled and tried to keep from begging. It took only a few moments of his mouth on me before I was curled with tension, desperate for release. But he pulled away and I cried out in wordless protest, my eyes scraping open to find him watching me with a cunning look on his face.

'Marry me, Rhiandra,' he crooned as he danced his hand up and down my leg.

A necessary, blessed burst of anger rocked me. He thought he could manipulate me like this? I was the fucking queen of Brimordia. I was the one who seduced my way to the top.

'I'll not be some obedient wife,' I said, my voice unsteady despite the force of my words. 'I want the power you promised me.'

'I know.'

My hands in his hair tightened. 'You think you do, but you don't. Not yet.' I dragged him to me, found his lip with my teeth and bit down until he flinched, but it only seemed to rouse him. He pulled me roughly from the chair onto his lap, and I kissed him like a savage, slipping my hand down between us to find the waistband of his trousers, exhilarated to find him hard. I slid the length of him free and stroked him slowly, attuned to the way his breath stuttered, breaking the kiss to watch his face, relishing in the parted lips, the mussed hair, the flush of colour, the hooded eyes.

But he had other ideas than to let me own his pleasure. He stilled my hand with his and twisted us around in a startling rush of movement until my back was against the stone floor. He hovered over me, still in his shirt, the neck open to reveal the smooth expanse of his chest, a slight dusting of curling hair, a silvery scar cutting perpendicular to his collar bone. Dark sleeves billowed around me as he slowly pinned my captured hand above my head. 'Is that a yes, Vixen?'

He ground his hips against me and I squirmed, almost mad with wanting it over, wanting to be done with the heinous ache that was consuming me, wanting him to just *fuck* me. I'd worry at the consequences later.

I yanked at his shirt with my free hand, because if I was going to sell myself to some beast of the shadow realm then at least I should know what he looked like, but he dropped his head and nuzzled at my neck with a dark laugh. 'I'm waiting.'

'Fine,' I gasped.

He shifted slightly, and in the space of a moment he was slipping into me, hot and hard and filling me until there was no space for thought or breath or fear.

'Yes?'

He moved slowly, unbearably so, and it was all I could do to surrender, to hiss 'yes', one rush of fevered breath into the night, and let him consume me. His pace quickened without hesitation, as though he had been barely holding back. He took my mouth with his, kissing me wildly, his tongue slipping into my mouth as he swallowed my cries. He released my hand to grasp at my hips, pulling me tightly to him with greedy, wanting fingers, crushing me against the floor, his body demanding and unrelenting as he thrust into me. Pleasure wrapped around me, winding tighter and tighter, bars on a dazzling prison, until the tension snapped, burning through me, warping me, sending me thoughtlessly raking my nails across his skin and crying out, barely biting back the words that wanted to burst from me. *I surrender, I surrender, I surrender.*

I looked up at him in all his fierce, terrifying beauty, and there was no restraint, no calculation. Just need. Just a low, guttural groan, a shudder, a sinking of teeth in my shoulder, a final, powerful thrust into me, and we collapsed in a heap, still entwined, a medley of damp skin and short, shallow breathing

A moment passed. Then another.

And as a few of my senses returned to me, I wondered what I'd done.

Draven turned his head, and I could feel his smile of triumph against my temple. 'Deal.'

Thank you for reading Her Dark Reflection! I hope you enjoyed the book. Book two in the series, Her Blind Deception, will release in June 2023 and you can preorder it here

Her Blind Deception

Winning power is easy, but keeping it is a whole new game.
After being tricked into marriage at the height of her victory, Rhiandra finds herself tied to the dark and devious Draven. But he's manipulated her for the last time. As she struggles to maintain control of her crown and gain control of her new husband, she's determined to evade his influence and outwit her own heart. After all, how can she trust him when she's hiding a secret that could unravel them both?

Meanwhile, the crown princess is in hiding, enchanted by a new world free of the restraints of her old life, and content to stay far away from her stepmother. But a dead princess is no small thing to forget, especially when she is very much alive. The question is, how long before she's found?

Her Blind Deception is the second book in the Dark Reflection series. Blood will be spilled, magic will change

hands, and war will raise its hackles as a game of love and betrayal stakes entire kingdoms on the outcome.

Because when you're the villain in the story, how far will you go for revenge on those who hurt you? How far will you go for revenge on those you've loved?

If you'd like to be kept up to date on new releases, as well as enjoy access to freebies and other goodies, you can sign up to my newsletter hereor by scanning the QR code below. You can also follow me on Instagram here or join my Facebook reader group here

Hailey Jade has tried to quit writing, but the characters who live in her head will not stop yammering. She's hoping that building them ink-and-paper homes will make them pipe down long enough for her to get some sleep. She likes creating fantasy worlds populated by complicated, morally-grey characters who try to resist their attraction to other complicated, morally-grey characters, but who inevitably fall in love, because everyone needs a Happily Ever After.

Hailey has completed a Bachelor of Arts and a Master of Teaching at Flinders University, and spends her daylight hours trying to convince reluctant teenagers to love books. She lives in regional South Australia with her partner, bouncy baby boy, and feline overlord.

Also by Hailey Jade – When Day Breaks: a Swan Lake Retelling

'You're acting like this is the cruellest punishment I could devise. Believe me when I say it's not.'

Odette is content with the path her life is taking. Promised in marriage to the prince of a neighbouring kingdom, she awaits the day she will become queen and finally have some power to make her own choices. So when a violated treaty ends in a curse that steals her away, she pours her energy into breaking it. But the sorcerer who has cursed her is not open to negotiations.

Alexey Rothbart is brooding, sarcastic and bad tempered and he has no interest in returning Odette to her life and her prince. But he also didn't count on having to subdue a will as strong as his own.

Their collision will shatter their worlds and when they are left standing in the wreckage, they have a choice to make. What do they want? And are they brave enough to take it?

More Books by Midnight Tide Publishing

Life for Eden is simple, until she's given to the Nightmare King.

Wishing for more adventure in her life, Eden, a fae of the sun, accepts an invitation to a ball in another king's court. Despite her over-protective mother's ire, they travel away from home for the first time and into the middle realm.

Draven, known as the Nightmare King and ruler of the dark realm, desires only to remain in his kingdom to maintain control and order over his ravenous creatures. However, he finds himself drawn away by the mysterious summons of his brother, who desperately needs his aid.

In one evening, thrust unwittingly together, Eden and Draven find themselves beguiled, betrayed, and betrothed. Neither are prepared for what it means for them, or for the immortal realms.

As politics and death intertwine, can two entirely different fae learn to rely on one another? Or will the chaos of the dark realm bleed into the other courts, destroying every last hint of light, including Eden.

Seeds of Sorrow is a romantic retelling of Hades & Persephone with a fae spin on it! If you love immersing yourself in dark, descriptive worlds, political intrigue and romance, you'll love this.

Printed in Great Britain
by Amazon

18225617R00200